Eben Beukes

Winter's Day

1

CHAPTER

I t was still bitterly cold when I parked the rental Malibu at the gates of Santa Fe's ancient Rosario cemetery and pulled my hopelessly inadequate windcheater tighter and zipped it all the way up to the neck. At nine in the morning the subzero temperature of the desert night had only started lifting and by noon would transform itself to the baking dry heat the place was known for. Jamming down the wide brimmed Stetson I had bought the day before in San Antonio in an attempt to shield my face and ears against the bite of the early morning breeze I locked the car and stood for a moment casting an eye over the rough cast stone walls of the chapel where the whitewash had faded to a not unpleasant kaleidoscope of nature's preferred colours.

In that dusty corner of New Mexico it meant shades of brown and tan.

The ancient wrought iron gate creaked and swung at an angle as I pushed it open and stepped onto the cobblestones lining the small courtyard. There was a musty smell about the place which I put down to piles of dead leaves from the still bare cottonwood trees piling up against the wall where the wind had blown them. The building, my pocket sized guide book had it down as the historic Rosario Chapel, looked new by centuries old Santa Fe standards and, unlike the rest of the town, was not in the adobe style. Stepping up to the imposing wooden door set beneath a stone arch bearing an inscription in the weathered stone I could not make out, I pushed to find it locked.

There was a cast iron knocker which I used but no-one came and after a while I thought of studying the small plaque denoting opening hours to find myself out of luck. Today was not my day and to-morrow did not look good either. But should I care to return Saturday between twelve and three the building would be open to the public. There followed instructions and contact information regarding funerals which I read halfway through while considering my next step.

After a while I exited the courtyard, closing the rickety gate behind, and took a stroll amongst the somewhat random scattering of the graves. The dead had been buried here since the town was founded in 1610 --- the oldest continuous municipality in the USA --- and I reckoned there would be hundreds, possibly thousands, under that hard sunbaked soil. Some with headstones, others marked simply by a rough hewn stone slab sunk into the ground, some with nothing at all.

The main town plaza where I had left the hotel twenty minutes earlier was already bustling with tourists and stony faced Navajo Indians setting up their sidewalk stands but here, in this shaded corner guarded by Chinese elms and cottonwood trees, it was only the crows and me. There were two of them, sitting close together on a low branch and watching me with interest, one deciding I had nothing to offer and going back to preening its wing feathers. Its companion watched my every move with some intent, its head cocked at an angle as it followed my progress with quick eyes that seemed as black as its feathers. There was something eerie about that crow, that silent watcher over the dead and I shrugged off the feeling and glanced around.

The place was vast, it seemed to stretch for hundreds of yards in all directions, the main entrance on Rodeo Road a distant source of traffic hum and the shudder of exhaust brakes as the eighteen wheelers rolled up to the traffic lights.

Walking to a small clearing near the centre of the graveyard I did a slow three sixty looking for I knew not what. Well, I knew what I was after, of course, but where to start?

Which was when I spotted him. He was sitting on a low parapet surrounding a gravesite and glanced up as I strolled over. Coming closer I could see he was at least in his seventies with an unruly mop of very white hair and a three day stubble to give it balance. Watery blue eyes looked me over from a deeply tanned face that cracked into a thousand wrinkles when he smiled.

'A good day for it, mister,' he said in a smoker's voice waving a hand in the general direction of the graves all around as he struggled to his feet.

'A good day for what?' I asked as we shook hands.

'To visit the dead,' he said, introducing himself as Samuel Rico Pickens. Adding, after a moment's thought, 'the Second.'

'Family?' I asked, nodding at the gravestone he had been viewing.

'Mah pappy,' he said, 'Samuel Pickens. His friends called him Slippery Sam, dunno why. He passed on this day, goin' on forty nine years now.' A small posy of wild flowers lay on the chipped stone covering the grave and after a moment's silence Pickens lifted his gaze to meet mine and asked whose grave I had come to see.

'I'm a writer,' I said, 'working on a book about the lives of the lawmen of the Old West. This town was on the old Santa Fe trail down to Mexico and many a desperado came through here. Many lawmen too. I was wondering if any lie buried here, a name or two I can look up and perhaps find a story there?'

Standing with the breeze flapping his too short trouser legs around scrawny ankles, the emaciated waistline bunched up under his belt like a drawn back curtain he looked more like a scarecrow than ever as he scratched his head, seemingly considering this startling bit of information. 'I dunno,' he began slowly, 'There be many a graveyard about this town, each of them religions burying their own away from the others.' This strange phenomenon merited a moment's reflective silence culminating in a shake of the head as the thought was dismissed. 'Ole; Sam, he was Catholic,' he said, stating the somewhat obvious.

'What about strangers?' I asked as I glanced wistfully around while wondering if I would be better served searching the archives of the local newspaper.

Sam Pickens the Second shrugged, 'Goin' on more'n hunnert years now they buried some, them bad ones – those they hanged or shot – on Bucket Hill other side of town. Reckoned they didn't deserve being buried here, next to decent folk. Could be a place to look. Of course,' he added with a frown, 'there'd be some sheriffs lying right here, deputies too, I guess.'

I nodded, things weren't looking promising. 'Anyone here tend to this place, a caretaker maybe?' I glanced around as I spoke seeing no sign of life over at the chapel or any other visitors. This made him think again as he licked his lips and squinted at the sun that was climbing fast in a clear blue sky. 'The council sends in a gardener now and then don't they? Ole Jerry Jace, works down at Lucky's Bottle Shop most days. You musta seen him, short fella with big droopy whiskers?'

He looked disappointed when I said no, shrugged and brightened up as an idea came to him. 'Ole Sheriff Joe Don Earl done buried here, over in that next row.' I followed as he led the way in a shuffling step that raised small puffs of dust around his scuffed boots.

The headstone, in the half shade of an old Ponderosa Pine, was well kept. The inscription in the granite informed the reader that Sheriff Joe Don Earl was born on February 2, 1885 and died in Santa Fe on April 22, 1945. The stone was erected in loving memory by wife Mavis and sons, Joel and Ed. Below, in cursive script, it said: *Died in the line of fire protecting his country and nation in its hour of greatest danger.*

His guns are silent now but his voice rings in our hearts forever and his smile in our mind's eye until the day we shall all meet again.

'How did he die?' I asked, producing my pocketbook to take notes.

'It's a long story.'

'I'd like to hear it.'

Leading the way deeper into the shade of the tree Sam Pickens found an old iron bench and sat down, shifting to make space for me. He stared into the middle distance for a moment as if to gather his thoughts and began. 'There was a lot going on up on that hill over in Los Alamos in that year. It was when they first tested that atom bomb, the one that blew up them Japs. I wasn't born then but my pappy tole me the story. It was all very secret until that day thirty or forty of them guvvermen G men rode into town and caused a mighty rumpus. Blockin' off roads and hassling people. A right ready mess it was and then, just as suddenly, they were gone! That was when they done brought them three dead bodies back from Raton up the railway line, two of them buried right o'er there.' He pointed to the end of the nearest row of sites.

'A third man was badly burnt, we heard, was taken up to The Hill and we never saw him. Some say he was radioactive and was buried in a special place.'

'How does Sheriff Earl fit into all this?' I asked.

'He tried to stop 'em, did'n' he? When they had done stole the thing and were hoofing it. Down Albuquerque way.'

'What thing?'

'The secret thing they were building at The Hill, of course.' He stared at me with a look suggesting I might be a bit slow on the uptake and I decided to change tack.

'And they shot him?' I prompted, scribbling furiously.

'Sure did. See that stone over there, second from the left?' I nodded, 'That be the man who shot him. They found the gun on him that matched the bullet.'

Fascinated I walked over to the headstone which was white marble and with the light sharp off the shiny surface I had to don my sunglasses in order to read the inscription:

Werner Jaeger

Died April 22, 1945

Here rests a soldier and a brother
For he who spills his blood with me shall be my brother
Ruhe in Frieden, Standartenführer
Das Volk Entspringt!

Stunned I read it through twice before becoming aware of Pickens' searching eyes studying me with new interest. I must have read the last few lines out loud for he asked whether I spoke German.

'A little,' I admitted, then turned to ask him who had erected the stone.

'I was here wasn't I?' he said with a cackle of glee, 'just goin' on thirteen years old I was, back in 1960, when the two strangers came to see Mama. She still had the ole hotel downtown then and this was just after ole Sam had passed. I remember them saying how sorry they were not comin' in time to see him.' His voice softened as the memories flooded back. 'Nice enough couple they was, the woman, now she was real pretty while the man had this speech thing, you know?'

'An accent?' I offered.

'Yep. German someone said but what do I know? Anyways they were kind to me and while they were here this stone was made and we all came here on the day it was set in the ground. The man, I think Winter was his name, took out a book and read something from it and then ---' he shook his head in wonder.

'What?' I prompted.

'Well, he took a step back, clicked his heels and saluted but different, you know?'

'You mean not like we do, the American Army?'

'Yep, Like this.' He showed me, a salute with the palm of the hand facing forward.

'Wehrmacht,' I said, shaking my head to discourage any questions.

A sudden clattering sound had me glance up sharply to see the two crows rising from where they had been sitting on the branch

6

to lazily flap their way to where a man and women with two small kids in tow had just pushed open the chapel gate to enter, the kids chattering excitedly and wielding what looked like packets of crisps. Hovering close the crows were making their own noise as they watched the kids for any sign of a stray morsel.

When I turned back to face Pickens I found myself staring at a small object suspended around his neck on a strand of rawhide which he now held out for me to see while glittering eyes studied me looking for a reaction. 'My pappy done gave me this, just before he passed. It was sewn into the lining of the jacket this one,' he pointed at Jaeger's grave, 'was wearing and a friend of Sam's found it when laying out the body. Ole Sam bought it off him and always kept it close.'

Stretching out a lightly trembling hand I touched the silver medal with its central Teutonic cross before running my fingers lightly over the oak leaves and crossed swords as shivers went down my spine. It was the *eisernkraus*, the Knights Cross of the Iron Cross, with oak leaves and swords, World War II Germany's highest award for a serving soldier.

Turning to Sam I said, 'Thirsty? Feel like a beer?' I certainly was.

He nodded eagerly, 'Sure do!'

'Then come, I reckon we have a lot more to talk about.'

In the end it took more than nine months of the kind of research and countless interviews that took me from the high desert of Los Alamos to the corridors of the National Archives in Washington DC. And, ultimately, all the way to the war records housed in the Bundesarchiv in Koblenz, Germany, to put the story together of what had happened that fateful April in New Mexico as Germany lay dying and the USA came very close to facing Hitler's final revenge.

Some facts will probably never come to light but I think it happened something like this.

2

CHAPTER

New York, April 9, 1945

'Korsika.'

She pronounced it slowly and clearly, carefully forming each syllable. At the same time turning over the domino piece, willing him to look at it. Two single black dots against the white ivory background.

Snake Eyes.

Max Winter was motionless, eyes staring fixedly at the object on the small table between them. Then, in a voice so soft she had to strain to pick out the sound he said it again, 'Ivan...'

With a barely audible sigh Esther Stern leaned back in her chair. For a moment she took in the quiet in the room, the only sound the traffic on West 75th Street five storeys below and, somewhere down a corridor, the staccato bursts of a typewriter. Idly twirling a pencil she went over the previous ten minutes in her mind, all the while keeping her gaze fixed on the man reclining on the couch, eyes unfocused and seemingly oblivious of his surroundings.

"Ivan..." What was this? In all those months, years, she had been his analyst, he had never uttered that word. More importantly, had never shown any signs of resistance, not when under deep hypnosis such as now.

And to happen now, at this crucial moment when the instructions had come to activate Elektron. A disaster!

Summoning her powers of concentration and speaking in the low sonorous voice she used for these sessions she tried once more, reciting the lines from Goethe's epic poem, the German rolling fluently over her lips all the while keeping her eyes fixed on those of the man as she held up the domino piece, slowly moving it to and fro, willing him to follow the motion.

'Ivan...'

She was suddenly afraid, a new chill in the room having her huddle her shoulders, the hand holding the pencil trembling and causing her to drop it. He was blocking! Instead of the programmed "Siegfried" there was this, this *Ivan?!* God in heaven what was she going to do?! Her masters in Berlin would not believe this, the consequences would be terrible!

Forcing herself to calm down, steady her own breathing while intensely aware of the cold sweat on her palms and down her back, she went over the whole session in her mind once more. It had started as always, the scientist from Los Alamos known to his colleagues as Anton Berkowitz, had telephoned the day before informing her he was in New York for his regular three monthly appointment with his cardiologist. As always she arranged to see him the next morning while cautioning him to ensure he wasn't followed.

As was her standard practice over the past five years she had given her secretary the day off, cancelling appointments and arranging a time when she knew the building would be at its quietest. As always he was punctual to the minute which, she mused wryly, was to be expected from a German. The next ten minutes was spent on a step by step update of progress on the Manhattan project and the planned Trinity experiment, a source of growing excitement at the Los Alamos nuclear facility. She had asked about the device, how far it was from being ready and he had asked for a pen and paper, spending the next twenty minutes in silence as he scribbled down the calculations that would later that day be radioed to the Nazi Underground in Mexico and from there to Germany in the diplomatic pouch of the Spanish Embassy.

As he worked, recalling the figures effortlessly from memory, she glanced over his shoulder at what to her was nothing but hieroglyphics but to the waiting nuclear physicists in Germany would provide invaluable information in the race to build the bomb.

Finishing he had wordlessly handed the pages to her before moving to the chaise longue she used as her patient's recliner to lay back, eyes closed and hands folded over his chest. As always it took merely seconds to place him under hypnosis and the analysis to begin.

At the age of fifty six Esther Stern had been a Freudian psychiatrist for more than twenty years. Following training in her native Vienna she had moved to New York initially working as a staff psychiatrist at Mount Sinai Hospital before setting up private practice in Manhattan. Most of her patients were wealthy women, many Jewish like herself and with the usual array of trivial neuroses that needed little more than someone to listen to.

Esther Stern had always been a good listener. And a good judge of the human species. And so it was that on that day in January 1939 when the tall middle aged gentleman with the faint but unmistakeable Latin American accent had come to see her, she knew within a matter of minutes that this was no ordinary consultation. Wearing a beautifully tailored cashmere coat which he carefully draped over the back of a chair, he had placed hat and gloves on the polished surface of the desk before straightening his cuffs and fixing her with a broad smile displaying evenly matched teeth beneath a neatly clipped greying moustache.

Introducing himself as Ferdinand Feldman, an Argentinean businessman, he had come straight to the point. He was there on behalf of a German client who had a somewhat unusual request. There was a young physicist, a German like herself, who was working on a government project. It was a secret project and something the German government was eager to learn more about. The young scientist would provide that information. But, alas, there was a problem.

Growing increasingly alarmed Esther, who had never knowingly met a Nazi and was now almost certainly in the presence of one, asked what problem?

The man was having dreams, apparently. Nightmares to be more precise. As part of his preparation for taking on this role so vital to his country, a certain degree of conditioning had to be undertaken. The word "conditioning" was uttered without the slightest trace of irony although both parties knew what was being implied.

'Nightmares?' she had asked, striving to keep the panic out of her voice while wondering whether she could telephone for help before this dangerous man did something dreadful to her.

Nothing serious Feldman had assured her with a supplicating motion of spread hands, all the while smiling. Things going back to his childhood, sometimes featuring his twin brother, sometimes fantasy things that we suspect is just anxiety neurosis. You know.

'I am afraid I cannot help you, Mr Feldman,' she had finally said, mustering all her nerve while rising to show him the door. The visitor said nothing, made no effort to move. Never losing the smile he reached for something in an inside pocket of his pinstriped jacket before laying it on the desk. It was a black and white photograph, professional quality, of an elderly woman glancing somewhat anxiously at the lens from the confines of an armchair. Directly behind her, a patronising hand resting on her shoulder, stood a stranger wearing a black leather raincoat over a white shirt and tie. The whole topped off by a black fedora hat.

'My mother...' Esther said at length, a clammy feeling tightening in her chest.

'And living peacefully in her home in Dresden where the local officials have been instructed to ensure that no harm befalls her.'

Picking up the photo to study it closely before returning it to a pocket Feldman shook his head in mild amusement, 'What is it with the Gestapo and those leather raincoats? So dramatic, don't you think?

Holding up a hand to stifle her rising protest he went on, 'You are no doubt well aware that the Führer had ordered all Germans home, Frau Stern? Failure to do so is seen as treason with consequences for any family members in Germany. Unless, of course, there are special circumstances...'

Shocked, she couldn't decide what was the most chilling, the beautifully modulated public school English in which the message was imparted or the all too explicit nature of what could happen. He did not even have to conjure up the image of the precarious status of those Jews still living in Germany.

Banning the images from her mind with some effort she turned her attention back to the patient as she once again gently encouraged him to relive the latest nightmares focusing on the role the mysterious twin brother could be playing. In the past the dreams had been little more than manifestations of anxiety, neurosis induced by the time of his initial conditioning, starting years earlier when still a child. Then gradually there had been increasing references to his brother and, more recently, the frequent headaches.

She had tried in vain to learn more about the kind of mind control that had taken place but any attempt at gleaning information from Feldman at subsequent meetings had been quickly squelched, usually with a smile and another photograph of her mother.

The patient's steady narrative a distant drone she thought back of the time, at a convention, when she had discreetly asked a colleague, a distinguished parapsychologist, about the status of mind control experiments. Only to be informed by the professor, a man considered by his peers to be eccentric beyond redemption, that outside of the limited field of hypnotherapy, there was a small subset of humans where mental telepathy was real. Twins, for instance, especially if identical, developing from the same ovum. He had cited some examples but admitted that hard scientific proof was still elusive.

The brother. This Alex. Could it be? Could this brother hold the key to unblocking "Ivan?"

Glancing down at Berkowitz, real name Max Winter, she knew it was the only hope.

Fifty five minutes later, at eleven twenty on the morning of April 9th 1945, Esther Stern met with Feldman on the third floor of a rooming house in a downtrodden area of the Bronx. To minimize the risk of the radio message to follow being traced the meeting place was always changing but she had the vague feeling she had been in that building before. Still somewhat breathless from climbing the rickety stairs she handed the envelope containing the scientist's scribbled notes to Feldman who pocketed them without as much as a glance. His manner that morning was brisk and, could it be, mildly anxious? Gone was the smile and the usual smooth demeanour as he came straight to the point. 'Elektron. Did you activate?'

Feeling for the back of a kitchen chair, other than a bed and a cupboard the only furniture in the room, Esther sat down. Slowly raising her eyes to meet the quizzical stare of the man looming over her she said in a shaky voice, 'We have a problem ---'

3

CHAPTER

Berlin, April 9, 1945

There was complete silence in the room as Adolf Hitler read the decoded signal eight hours later. The hand that held the paper shook slightly but not as much as the other hand the man, abandoning all attempts at control, now kept perpetually tucked behind his back. Those assembled watched as silent words trickled over his lips while stealing anxious furtive glances at one another.

Himmler was there, ominous in his gleaming black SS uniform, as was Goebbels, for once managing to control his volatility. And Fegelein, quiet and watching, his dark gaze flitting from face to face before settling back on the bowed form of the Führer. Standing to one side, nearest to the door, was Bormann. The Reichsleiter was as impassive as always, never smiling, seldom speaking but always watching. The hour was late and earlier, following the evening debriefing, the usual fantasy circus of moving non-existing or decimated army units around a map between curses and rants, Hitler had dismissed his commanders declaring himself tired and retiring to his private quarters.

Hours earlier, as the others filed out he had drawn Bormann aside to enquire about Elektron, to be reassured that the signal to activate had been sent as ordered, a reply expected at any second.

And now it was here and the core group, the selected few who were in the know, had been summoned. Still silent they watched as he slowly lowered the flimsy and screwed it into a ball, knuckles white as the only sign of a building inner rage. Thirty feet above the ground shook in a dull rumble as the Russian artillery opened up again, a sound all those in the bunker had grown used to over the past forty eight hours. According to the latest reports the Russians were still several miles away but all of Berlin was now within easy reach of the 6 inch heavy guns. As a thin film of dust drifted down no-one lifted their gaze, with ten feet of solid concrete between them and the hell that was now loosed upon the citizens of the city, they were still safe.

At least for the moment.

The Führer was shaking now as he slowly straightened up, still clutching the scrunched up leaf of paper. As he slammed his fist down on the table his face, now mottled and distorted in fury as he struggled for words, nobody moved. For they had seen this all before, become used to it as one disaster followed on the heels of the previous.

'Idiots!' he screamed, 'traitors all around us! Nobody follows my orders. I will...we...' Words failed him as he shakily reached for a glass of water.

'May I?' Goebbels asked gently taking the flimsy from Hitler's quivering hand without waiting for an answer. Hitler was sitting now, staring at the scattered maps on the table as if seeing them for the first time, a hand waving Goebbels away. There was a lull in the shelling outside and the only background sound in the room was the dull hum of the generators down the corridor. All listened as Goebbels read the message out loud, his face showing no emotion as he finished.

It was Himmler, his tone as unperturbed as always, who broke the silence. 'It seems, *mein Führer*, that there might still be a way to activate our plan. Perhaps this twin brother is the key to activate Elektron ---'

'How?!' a clearly agitated Goebbels snapped, waving the signal in a gesture of hopelessness. 'How do we find this, this brother? Is he even alive?' He glanced over at the seated form of Hitler who had his head supported on a trembling hand as he gazed down while shaking his head.

'Years ago, when we first started the project I visited the Winter family and after being familiarised with the work of Professor Schmidt with the twins, realised that they were close in ways we perhaps do not always fully understand. It was then I decided to ensure the one that wasn't selected, Alex, should be carefully watched and kept out of harm's way, at least as far as possible.' Himmler paused to bestow a wintry smile on the Führer who had now lifted his head off his hands and was studying him with renewed interest.

'You mean you can find him? Put him in contact with his brother? Perhaps activate...' Fegelein asked, his features animated as he stepped forward excitedly allowing Himmler to smell the alcohol on his breath.

Cutting short his customary sighing chuckle Himmler nodded, 'but of course, dear Fegelein! Major Alex Winter of the Pioneer Unit attached to General Heinricki's Army Group Vistula is at this moment constructing pontoon bridges for our victorious forces to cross the Oder River and engage the Russians.' He did not find it necessary to, in the presence of Hitler who still believed the war could be won, add that the bombed out bridges were being hastily repaired to enable the fleeing German forces to retreat rather than attack.

Nobody in the room was surprised at Himmler's revelation, the man was a constant source of conspiracy and backroom manoeuvres, always one step ahead like the evil genius he was.

All heads swivelled as Hitler finally spoke, all signs of the rage of minutes earlier now gone. 'Bring him here, Heinrich,' he said softly. 'I want to speak to him.'

'At your command, *mein Führer!*' Himmler said with a slight bow before clicking his heels and leaving the room.

* * *

They met in the small room in the forward section of the bunker where Himmler had set up a temporary office. Himmler had dismissed the clerk who had been retrieving stationary from a steel cupboard and as they waited for the corporal to wheel out his trolley and close the door behind him, he studied the man now slumped on the only other chair in the room.

SS Standartenführer Jaeger was thirty six years old but that night he looked fifty. His normally full features were deeply lined and above the grime stained cheeks red rimmed eyes stared bleakly back at the man who had recalled him from his position at the Cottbus highway two hours earlier. Himmler took in the dust stained and crumpled black tunic, torn sleeve and a streak of dried blood just showing at one wrist. Finally his gaze settled on the Knight's Cross and he smiled.

'How goes the battle for the IIIrd Panzer Army?' he asked in his soft, toneless voice.

Jaeger shrugged, 'I lost my last tank at dusk and my unit is down to 40 percent strength. If we don't fall back and regroup...'

Himmler shook his head, 'There is to be no retreat. The Führer is clear on that.'

Jaeger let his hands fall helplessly to his sides and fought the urge to light a cigarette. The Reichsführer did not approve of smoking, didn't really drink either, for that matter.

'Come *Standartenführer!* Why so gloomy? I have had my eye on you ever since we gave you the oak leaves to the Knight's Cross a few weeks back, after that magnificent tank action at Remagen...'

'You do recall that we lost that battle,' Jaeger offered wearily.

Himmler dismissed the observation with an impatient wave of a hand. 'Once you've had the chance to refresh while my aide attends to your rather battered uniform – very nice by the way,

Hugo Boss perhaps? --I have a special mission for a man of your talents and, may I add, loyalty to the Fatherland. I have a Junkers 55s aircraft standing by at Gatow airport. You are to go directly there and fly to a Luftwaffe airfield at the Seelow Heights. The pilot has his instructions and has prepared a flight plan. From there you will proceed to General Heinricki's headquarters and be directed to where this man is. You will bring him back here immediately.'

With a barely supressed sigh Jaeger leaned over to take the slim manila folder Himmler was holding out. There was a few minutes silence as Jaeger studied the details of the man in the photograph.

'Out loud, please,' Himmler said.

'Major Alex Winter, born 7 December 1910 in Charlottenburg, Berlin. Parents Baron Dr Heinrich Winter, industrialist, and Magda Winter. Identical twin brother Max. Trained as civil engineer at the Massachusetts Institute of Technology, Christchurch, USA 1928 to 1933. Brother Max Winter studied physics at MIT at that same time. Returned to Germany 1934, Max returning a year later. Started work as engineer in his father's factory, Krause-Winter Metallwerkte GmbH, leaving two years later to take up a position with a rival firm, Brede Bayerische Stahl, in Munich.' Here Jaeger paused, a frown creasing his forehead, 'Why?' he said, 'why did he leave? He was set to take over a multimillion dollar business from the old man, yet he left to work for some minor competitor?'

'Political differences,' Himmler said with a sigh, 'Dr Heinrich Winter was a founder member of our glorious Nazi party whereas his son sadly is not. Very much against our ideals I'm sad to say.'

'What about the brother?'

'The brother is the reason you are here. Max Winter did join the party shortly after his return to the Fatherland. Back home he worked with Professor Heisenberg, whom you might know is in charge of our nuclear weapons project. As most of our top nuclear physicists, traitors all, fled to America when our Führer began clamping down on the Jews, it was decided to insert him into that circle to keep us informed of their progress towards building a nuclear weapon.'

'A spy...' Jaeger said, subconsciously removing a cigarette from a silver case drawn from his tunic pocket. Seeing Himmler's frown he put it back reluctantly.

'Assuming the identity of a certain Jewish physicist who had been a professor at our Heidelberg University where he had been a pioneer in nuclear physics, Winter was inserted into what the Americans have codenamed The Manhattan Project.'

'Presumably he must have been known, have met at least, some of the scientists on that project? How did he manage to ---'

'A degree of plastic surgery was necessary,' Himmler said with just a hint of impatience as he indicated Jaeger should read the rest of the file. 'Also an extended period of debriefing of Professor Anton Berkowitz. The deception has worked remarkably well, Winter able to feed us a steady stream of invaluable information.'

Suppressing with an inner shudder the image of what the "debriefing" of the Jewish scientist would have entailed as well as the man's ultimate fate, Jaeger said, 'I thought after the destruction of the heavy water plant at Norsk Hydro our own nuclear project had been stalled?'

Himmler nodded, 'The reason why Max Winter's work in America became all the more important. Knowing Alex Winter's opposition to our ideology we staged a fake boating accident and subsequent disappearance at sea, where Max was thought to have drowned, the body never recovered. This was of course the time he left for America. At the time the brothers had not spoken to each other for more than a year, nor seen each other.'

Jaeger read on: 'When the war started Alex Winter was drafted into the engineering corps, the Pioneers, and his unit attached to the General Paulus' 6th Army. He was at the battle of Stalingrad where he was awarded the Iron Cross, Second and First Class, for several acts of bravery on the Volga River. Wounded during the last phases of the battle he was evacuated to Berlin spending several weeks in hospital before being returned to active duty. By that time the 6th Army had surrendered to the Russians and Alex Winter was re-assigned to the 9th Army.'

Jaeger looked up, 'Here the report ends apart from a list of details regarding specific actions the major was involved in and details of how his decorations were awarded. None of this explains why it is so important to find this Major Alex Winter,' he concluded, tossing the file back on the table.

'A small project codenamed Elektron,' Himmler said with a soft chuckle.

'I don't understand,' Jaeger said.

'Then let me explain, my dear *Standartenführer.*'

4

CHAPTER

lex Winter cursed as the shackle anchoring the last of the pontoons sheared, the flow of the river instantly slewing the platform sideways sending two of his men tumbling into the river.

'Quick Heinz, drive the boat up against the side! Leave the men, they can swim out!' Balancing on the rocking pontoon closest to the gap he was gesturing wildly as men rushed up on the other side to aid those desperately hauling on the stay ropes. In the distance he could hear the sounds of battle as heavy guns duelled across their heads, clouds of billowing smoke on the horizon marking where buildings and equipment was burning. A straggly stream of Wehrmacht infantry was steadily making its way to where the bridge was hastily being constructed a short distance upstream from where the railway bridge had been destroyed by RAF Lancaster bombers two days earlier.

The River Oder, border between Poland and Germany and a place he had visited with his parents as a child, picnicked at and swam in. Now a battle front with the flood plain on the Seelow Heights side re-flooded barely ten days ago by his own Pioneer unit blowing up the upstream reservoir and drainage ducts to create a marsh and slow down the advancing enemy. Where wild ducks had called out to one another before the air was now filled with the incessant chatter of machine gun fire and the piercing shrieks of Katyusha rockets screaming across.

It seemed a good idea at the time, flooding the plain, he had even agreed with his commanding officer for a change and carried out the work with his usual efficiency. That was of course before they knew the remnants of a desperately retreating field hospital unit had been cut off from their planned route of evacuation, in fact being abandoned by the SS Panzergrenadier regiment they were attached to. And now it was up to him and his men, all of them exhausted beyond the level of mere human endurance, to rescue the situation, get the poor bastards out that were now wearily limbering up to where he would hopefully have the last pontoon in place. If Sergeant Schreiber could just get that damn coupling to slot home.

Lifting his gaze he studied the group now steadily growing at the far side of the river. They were what he expected, harried looking doctors and medics with bloodstained white smocks, field nurses in curiously old fashioned wear, orderlies helping along the wounded, some on crutches, others on stretchers.

All of it in deathly silence. That, he decided, was the eerie part. These survivors, many fresh from battle judging from the state of their uniforms were too shell shocked, too war numbed, to utter even a single protest. Or maybe it was the fear the Russians would hear them, hone in once more with the mortar fire that had destroyed the last of their ambulances and trucks several miles back?

The last pontoon in place and the men quickly shoving the covering metal tracks in position, he strode across and gave the order to let them through. As the first bodies stumbled by, the bridge now swaying slightly at the unsteady transfer of their mass, he studied the faces. Saw nothing, unseeing eyes averted from his, expressionless faces coming in and out of his focus, one or two of the nurses glancing uncertainly his way as they struggled under the weight of the wounded men they were supporting.

A doctor came up to Winter, a colonel of indeterminate age whose stained and crumpled white overcoat struggled to cover the expanse of his barrel chest and gut. Pausing to catch his breath he offered Winter a cigarette from a crumpled near empty packet. They lit up and after recovering from a fruity cough the colonel said, 'Thank you, Major, for saving our backsides to-day. The Russians would have had us by now if we hadn't managed to get through to HQ at Seelow and have them send you down here.'

There are trucks waiting a mile up the road,' Winter said, pointing in the direction of a distant farm building rising above a stand of willows.

Turning to where the last of the column was now coming across he decided to go and check on the MG 34 machine gun platoon guarding their retreat and prepare to place the charges that would blow up the bridge he had just built. There would be no time now, the Russians that close, to dismantle it again. Only the motorboat they used would go back on the trailer.

As he reached the bank on the far side he saw the group of men standing next to where the boat was tied up. SS Einsatzgruppen judging by their uniforms. Winter felt his stomach tighten, he knew well enough what that meant. The einsatzgruppen – special units – were created by Himmler to carry out much of the dirty work of the SS. Often made up of Ukrainians, freed jailbirds and court martialled Waffen-SS soldiers they were responsible for many atrocities and were despised by the regular Waffen-SS.

Their presence could only mean trouble.

As he came up their leader, a sturmbannführer, stepped forward. 'I have orders to confiscate this motorboat, Herr Major,' he said in his bad German as his men made an attempt to untie the craft.

'Really?' Winter said coldly, 'whose orders?'

'Mine!' the man whose name ribbon identified him as Olesnicky, said to the laughter of his men, all who were heavily armed, some raising their machine pistols in a show of menace.

'May I ask to what purpose?' Winter asked icily, aware of the eyes of his own men, who had now laid down tools, staring at him apprehensively.

'We need it to transport ammunition,' came the glib answer.

'Or is it perhaps to make your escape down the river to the Baltic?' A cold rage was building and twisting his insides, his voice tight.

The Ukrainian said something but all attention had shifted to the bridge and Winter turned to follow the gaze of the others. A man was approaching, walking purposefully, a Waffen-SS Panzer sergeant at his side hefting a Schmeisser machine pistol. Winter took in the tall man's matt black uniform with the SS runes and the gleaming silver death's head badge on the peaked cap. Even at a distance he could make out the standartenführer epaulettes – Waffen SS, equivalent of a Wehrmacht colonel – also, the Knight's Cross.

Then he was there, a slight smile lightening the pale features as he studied the frozen tableau with interest tapping a cigarette on a beautifully engraved silver case before accepting a light from his sergeant. 'It is customary to salute a senior officer, *Sturmbannführer* he said to Olesnicky without looking at the man who was now clearly uneasy.

'*Zu befehl, Herr Standartenführer!*' the Ukrainian stammered managing what Winter thought could be a salute of sorts.

Nodding the colonel turned his attention to Winter, 'Pioneer Major Alex Winter, I presume?'

'*Jawohl, Herr Standartenführer,*' Winter replied, wearily stiffening to a salute while wondering what fresh horror the glorious Reich was about to visit on them. 'I am in charge of the operations at the bridge and these men --'

Jaeger held up a hand, 'No need to explain,' he said softly as he picked at a fleck of tobacco on his lips, 'I think I understand the situation all too well.' Was it Winter's imagination or had a distinct hint of coldness crept into the man's voice? By the shuffling of the feet of those assembled he sensed others had noticed too.

'I think this is a matter that can be resolved to our mutual satisfaction if you two gentlemen would care to accompany me over there,' he indicated a dense clump of bushes close by, 'where we can have a more private discussion?'

Olesnicky and Winter glanced at each other, shrugged and followed Jaeger who led the way at a leisurely pace. He still had his back turned when the two joined him at the far side of the bushes and as he turned there was a Walther P38 in his hand. Before anyone could react he fired twice, the impact of the bullets flinging Olesnicky into the thick foliage of the bush where he hung suspended like a discarded scarecrow.

'Shall we rejoin the others?' Jaeger asked, calmly unscrewing a bulbous silencer before leading the way back without waiting for an answer from a stunned Winter. Back at the boat there was a commotion amongst the einzatsgruppen members as they glanced wildly about while shouting at each other in their language.

'Men,' Jaeger said holding up a hand for quiet. 'There has been an accident, I'm afraid the *Sturmbannführer* has been wounded. Our medics will attend at once.' As he spoke he paused next to the team manning the MG 34 light machine gun. It took but a moment for an experienced eye to confirm the weapon was readied, a loaded feeding belt snaking into a metal ammunition box.

Moving with effortless ease Jaeger swung the machine gun around on the tripod, cocking it in one fluid motion followed by an ear splitting staccato of death as he mowed down the rest of the SS platoon before they could as much as raise a weapon. Next to him and off to one side his sergeant, teeth bared in a snarl, finished off the job with a few well directed bursts from his machine pistol.

'Filthy scum!' Jaeger said as he calmly ground out his cigarette under a jackbooted heel. 'A disgrace to the name of the SS.'

Recoiling in horror from what they had just witnessed the two man machine gun team stared in stunned silence at the menacing figure of a black clad angel of death, their gaze flickering uncertainly between Winter and the SS stranger. Then one, a boy of no more than sixteen, started sobbing softly.

'Very impressive, *Herr Standartenführer,*' Winter said between clenched teeth as the shock slowly drained from his body. Another lasting nightmare image for these young faces now staring up at him to revisit one future day. If they made it to a future. He did not say it, just strode across and laid a reassuring hand on the heaving shoulders of the young soldier. 'It's alright, Weber. Go over to the proviand cart and drink some coffee with sugar. Go now!'

Turning to face the others he found Jaeger staring at him with a wolfish smile, 'Surely we are not going soft, Major Winter? Not with a war going on?' Laughing softly he made a motion in the direction of the pioneer team who, a tableau frozen in time, was staring at him, uncertain what to do, indicating they should carry on before taking Winter by the arm and leading him back to the bridge. 'My name is Jaeger, lately from the IIIrd Panzer. I am here to escort you back to Berlin at the orders of *Reichsführer* Himmler.' With this he handed Winter a letter taken from an inside pocket. It took Winter several seconds to read it down to the signature, his incredulity growing with every sentence.'

'I don't understand,' he said handing the letter back to Jaeger who folded it carefully before restoring it to his pocket.

'Then I will explain as we cross over to the other side where I have a field car waiting that will take us to the Seelow airfield. For a brief moment Winter thought of protesting, a notion quickly dismissed as he realised the hopelessness of his position. This hard man would take him away using whatever force of persuasion required and, witnessing the scene of a minute ago, undue concerns regarding military protocol or due process did not feature strongly. With a suppressed sigh he nodded, mumbling something about needing a minute to speak to his squad.

Enjoying a fresh cigarette, Jaeger waited as Winter paused to hand instructions to his crew, placing Sergeant Meier in charge. Then they were walking briskly, following the muddy path across the swamp in the wake of the field ambulance stragglers.

'You have a brother ---' Jaeger began.

'My brother is dead' Winter said automatically.

'Max Winter is alive and well and living in the USA under an assumed name. He is an undercover agent for the Reich at present involved in the final stages of a vital operation that could change the course of the war.'

'…he died in an accident at sea…' Winter protested lamely as his brain struggled to digest this stunning revelation.

'A staged incident to let the world believe he was dead and enable him to take on another's identity. Things are coming to a head but Max is severely stressed and has been calling for your help. The *Reichsführer* has decided to send you on this mission, leaving for America immediately. Full details will be provided when he meets with you later to-day.'

'Madness,' Winter heard himself say, 'even if what you say is true it is still madness! The war is over! Can't you see that? Just look around you!'

'Whose uniform is that you are wearing, Major?'

'*Wehrmacht*. It is a *Wehrmacht* uniform…'

'Is that the same *Wehrmacht* you, as an officer, swore an oath of allegiance to?'

'Yes,' Winter said dully, his mind striving to conjure up a picture of his brother when last they had seen each other, all those years ago. Then, of course, he would only have to look into a mirror.

'Then it is agreed,' Jaeger said pleasantly, 'we go to America!'

At the far side Winter paused to look back on the river, to where his men were back at work, placing the explosive charges, one or two stealing glances in his direction. The barrage had shifted to their west and he could make out billowing clouds of thick smoke beyond a far bend of the river. The river … How quietly flows the Oder, he mused. Will I ever again get to picnic on your flowering banks, river? Splash in your cool softly eddying waters? My brother and I?

With a sigh he turned to follow Jaeger to where a mud smeared Kubelwagen was parked at the side of a road.

5

CHAPTER

'Thirty minutes,' Jaeger said as he leaned back against the rear seat rest of the open field car, 'then I expect to see you back here.' The unspoken message was clear, don't make me come looking for you. In the driver's seat the sergeant grinned as he twisted to present a light to the Standartenführer's cigarette.

Pausing on the pavement Winter glanced around, taking in the devastation that was evident all around, obscuring and obliterating a neighbourhood that was once so familiar. Whole houses were destroyed, the rubble spilling out onto streets that were themselves scarred with deep craters where the bombs from the never ending air raids had left their mark of indiscriminate destruction. Turning into the street they had passed the wreckage of several burned out cars and at one point had to stop while the driver dragged a fallen tree branch out of the way. Few pedestrians were about, mainly women and mostly thickly wrapped in overcoats and hats despite the heat of a perfect spring day. As if they anticipate the prospect of being homeless come nightfall, Winter thought, sleeping rough and clutching one another for warmth while ignoring the pangs of hunger that was now surely a daily reality.

Shaking off the thought he stepped up to the gate of the old house which, at least from the outside, seemed largely intact and miraculously untouched by the bomb that had all but destroyed the home of the Schumachers next door.

The porch was covered in dust and there was no sign of the potted ferns that had once adorned a small display stand in a corner. The doormat with its message of welcome looked vaguely familiar as he rang the doorbell, a faint tinkling sound somewhere inside just audible. Somewhere at back a dog barked and for a moment he wondered if it could be little Fritzi before deciding the dachshund, a childhood pet, would be long gone.

There were shuffling footsteps in the hall and then the front door creaked open and the face of an old lady peered around it.

'Hello Lottie,' Winter said as the old servant gasped in shock, taking a step back as he made to enter.

'*Gott in Himmel!* Master Alex! It *is* you!'

She hadn't aged he decided, taking in the stooped frame, the winkled knobbly hands and the lined cheeks supporting a set of watery pale green eyes, the whole capped by wispy strands of silvery hair creeping out from beneath starched white maid's cap. She appeared to be exactly the same as when he had last seen her, what? Five years ago?

Patently there was a point in a long life when further aging became irrelevant really and the process stalled, much like a T34 Russian tank, he thought, that second after the Panzerfaust slammed home before the tank erupted in a cauldron of smoke and fire and death.

Striding down the dimly lit corridor where the portraits of his ancestors stared disapprovingly down from the walls he entered the large high ceilinged drawing room where he knew she would be. His mother.

And she was just the way he had left her all those many summers ago, sitting in the same wingback chair, an embroidered rug spread across her legs, slender very white fingers folded neatly across her lap and resting on a leather bound volume she had been reading. A black shawl nestled around her slender shoulders, a large hand painted brooch securing the lace at her neck.

As always the hair was carefully brushed out and a golden blonde – she had dyed it for as long as he could remember. Glittering ice blue eyes stared at him over the rims of half moon reading glasses.

'Alexander,' she said without the slightest hint of surprise or, for that matter, joy. 'How nice of you to visit.'

Crossing the floor, the thick pile Persian rugs soft under his footsteps he took the outstretched hand bending down at the waist to lightly kiss the slender fingers. As expected the touch was icy cold, almost as icy as the enormous solitaire diamond that graced a finger, next to a very slim gold wedding band.

'Baroness,' he acknowledged taking the chintz visitor's chair she waved him to. He had long ago realised his mother detested the more traditional "mutti" preferring, in fact insisting, on being addressed by her title.

For a moment they sat in silence as the servant was instructed to bring refreshments before being waved away. It gave Winter time to look over the room, deciding it was pretty much like stepping into a time warp of the past. Everything was familiar, from the furniture to the paintings to the fine drapery on the walls and, fronting the windows, heavy scarlet curtains. He wondered if that was still the case with the bedroom upstairs he had shared with his brother.

But something *was* different and in an instant he saw it, the large glass fronted veranda doors leading out to the rear garden were boarded up, the wooden planks only half hidden by curtains lopsidedly hanging from a sagging rail. How well he remembered those doors and how they would be left wide open during summer with light streaming in and on those many occasions when his parents entertained the glitterati of old Berlin. It all seemed so far away now.

His gaze settled on the large ornately carved sideboard, like most of the furnishings something that had been in the Winter family for centuries, and the collection of silver framed portraits displayed there. Even from twenty paces away he could make out the profile of his late father, Baron Doctor Heinrich Winter, wealthy industrialist and doyen of Berlin high society.

Arch Nazi.

'How is everyone?' he asked for something to say while struggling to ask what he had really come for.

'We manage,' Magda Winter said evenly, 'Lottie and I. Gunther has been called up to serve in the *Volksturm,* to defend our city against the barbarians that want to destroy us.'

Gunther. The old manservant. God, he must be more than seventy years old! Was that what it had come to now, old men and boys manning the barricades?!

'I am proud that you are doing your duty, Alexander. Your father would be proud. You are the bearer of the Winter name, the baron of this house and I hope that one day you will decide to honour that commitment.'

He knew what she meant, didn't have to think back to that last acrimonious family meeting when he had stormed out of this house swearing never to set foot there again, the old man cursing the day he was born.

'It is not safe here, mother,' he said, ignoring the look he received for the tone of familiarity. 'The war is lost. Half of the neighbourhood is in ruins. It is a miracle this house is still standing but the Russians will be here any day now. I want you to pack some personal items and go to the house in Innsbruck where you will be safe. I can arrange for transport ---'

'The Baroness will not be leaving,' she said firmly and Winter knew instinctively there would be no point in pursuing the matter. She would be here when the enemy came and, he thought wryly, God help those Russians.

Glancing at his watch he realised time was running out. Time to get to the purpose of his visit. 'Max...' he started hesitantly, leaning forward to take her hand in his, 'Max is alive, mother. He did not die in an accident as we were told.'

'I know,' she said calmly, withdrawing her hand.. 'He is in America, in the service of the Reich.'

'What?! You knew?!!'

The Baroness Winter shrugged, indicating to Lottie who had silently entered with a tray to set it down on a side table. 'Of course, I knew, Alexander. We all knew. It was thought at the time to keep his mission from you, all part of the tight security and the importance of the mission.'

Too stunned for words he drew back to watch the old servant pour the tea before accepting a cup from a shaking hand. After Lottie had left he asked his mother what it was all about and between frequent sips of her tea and long pauses as she searched her memory she told him the story. 'The Baron, your father, was a founder member of the Party. They all visited here in those early days, Himmler, Goebbels, Hess and, of course, the Führer. You and your brother were still very young, only ten years old at the time. Your father, being a man of great learning, had many friends who were scientists and medical doctors. One of them was Professor Dr Hans Schmidt, a distinguished psychiatrist and neurologist. In long discussions with your father they discovered a shared interest, that of mental telepathy and hypnosis. Dr Schmidt had a theory that identical twins, like Maximilian and you, share a special gift of extrasensory perception. Your father was eager to pursue this and so the experiment started.'

She paused as a coughing fit interrupted the narrative and he watched in silence as Lottie entered with several tablets on a platter and a glass of water. 'My heart,' his mother explained as she dutifully took the medicine.

The experiment... My own father allowed some mad scientist to experiment on us? How come I don't recall any of this?!

Sensing his impatience his mother continued. 'Your brother was more susceptible to the hypnosis, Dr Schmidt always found you an unsatisfactory subject. Frequent sessions happened right here in this room and it was then that another scientist, a young Dr Mengele, started coming to the house. A medical doctor, he had a special interest in twins and at that stage they also started trying some medications.'

'They drugged us?'

'Oh Alexander, don't be so dramatic! It was just some harmless potions that enhanced extrasensory perception, that's all.' She dismissed it with a wave and continued. 'By this stage the Party had come to power and our Führer foresaw the possibility of a future war, to restore our Fatherland to her rightful borders. Return to us the *lebensraum* that had been forcefully taken from us by our enemies. He rightfully identified America as a future enemy and it was at this time, you were in your final year at school, when it was decided to groom a scientist to work amongst the Americans. This was the time that there was much talk about a very powerful new weapon, an atomic bomb they called it, being a possibility. Another visitor, a Professor Heisenberg who would go on to win a Nobel prize for physics, felt that the Americans, with their huge resources, might be leaders in this race.'

She paused for a sip of water and Alex struggled to control his impatience. 'Was this the time Max got sick?' he asked. 'The time he was taken to a sanatorium in Munich for treatment, staying there for more than three months?'

The Baroness nodded. 'That was what we told you, on the advice of Professor Schmidt. By then he had decided you were not suitable, "resistant" he called it and that it was better to concentrate on your brother. He then underwent highly specialised, still experimental, therapy to prepare him for his mission.'

His mission...

The voice droned on, faltering between coughing fits, but he was only half listening for he knew the rest of the story. His brother had returned, on the surface back to normal after a debilitating illness never quite clarified and by the following year, 1934, they went off to the Massachusetts Institute of Technology in the USA. Alex to study mechanical engineering, his brother to study nuclear physics. As students their paths largely diverted as they developed separate interests, separate groups of friends. They no longer shared a room, in fact were in separate residences.

As far as he knew his brother never showed any interest in politics and certainly never indicated any inclination of following in the footsteps of their Nazi father. How well the puppet masters had covered their tracks!

'... in 1939 he was finally sent back to America and now...'

August 1939. He remembered it like yesterday. The day his brother was said to have disappeared at sea. A brother he had not had any contact with for going on a year as they went their separate ways, Alex walking out of the life of his father with a deepening sense of disgust.

Spreading his hands to halt her narrative he asked when last she had heard from Max. 'Never,' she said, 'that would have been too dangerous. You see, he is no longer known as Maximilian Winter but as someone else, a Jew of all things! At least that is what Heinrich told me. He hears from him often, all secret of course, and keeps me informed. I am so proud.'

'Heinrich?' he asked with a frown.

'The *Reichsführer*, of course. Your father's old friend, Himmler. He was here only yesterday, to tell my you were coming and would be sent to contact your brother.'

Himmler... Why did that not surprise him.

With a sigh he glanced at his watch. The half hour was up. Rising he asked whether there was anything she could tell him about the relationship between him and his brother, when they were boys. Anything he might not know.

She laughed, a strange tinkling sound in that large old room where the only other sound was that of the ancient standing clock in the hallway as it struck the hour. 'You were strange children, especially when still small. Always together, even sharing your own strange language. No wonder the doctors saw the potential for an unusual bond between you.' She chuckled, shook her head. 'It was strange! Max would hurt his arm and you, somewhere else in the house at the time, would run to me complaining of a pain in your arm. Without knowing about what had happened!'

He nodded, 'I remember that.'

'You both loved to read. All kinds of books. As you will recall your father kept a large library. You had your favourites and used to quote to one another from it. Very strange I always thought.'

It was time to go. Leaning over he kissed her on both cheeks and was it his imagination or was there just the hint of moisture on those waxen cheeks. 'I love you, mother,' he said and, without looking back, made for the door. Something told him he would never see her again.

'*Tschüss...*'

The emotionless farewell from the woman in the chair stirred something deep, long forgotten now, and for a fleeting moment a sad smile.

No *auf wiedersehen* for him.

A sound from the room had him break his stride. It was his mother's voice, so soft he almost missed it. *'Ich liebe dich, Alex,'*

In the hallway he paused, his father's library was directly across, the door askance. On impulse he pushed it open and entered. It was the way he remembered it, book lined walls all the way to the ceiling with a large writing desk in a corner and two red leather club chairs facing. The large fireplace was empty and cold and he had a sudden flashback of the Baron holding court at that fireplace as visitors of importance were entertained over cognac and fine cigars. Lifting his gaze he could just make out the shape of the snooker table at the far end of the large room, its green baize hidden under the folds of a dust cover.

The old study... How often had he and his brother sneaked in there to purloin leather bounds volumes from the fine collection that still rested on those same shelves! They were all there, Goethe, Nietzsche, Heidegger and Schiller. Herman Hesse and Thomas Mann. And, surprisingly, William Shakespeare and Joseph Conrad and volumes of English poetry. His gaze settled on another old favourite, Sir Walter Scott, the complete collection. How he had devoured those stories! He remembered clearly how he and Max had stolen upstairs to their bedroom to read those great adventures in the dead of night when the old house was quiet and, for once, empty of guests.

There had been a comfort in those stories of gallantry and high adventure. On impulse he reached for a volume glancing down fondly at the picture engraved on the leather cover. It had been their very favourite and its very touch felt so right he pocketed it without further thought.

A soft cough behind him had him turn to find Lottie standing there holding out a small parcel. 'For you, Master Alex. For the journey. Looking past her towards the end of the corridor he noticed for the first time a full length curtain shrouding the distant corridor and as a sudden premonition filled him he strode past the retreating Lottie and yanked the curtain aside. Behind the curtain, where the kitchen used to be, was now a huge gaping hole and a pile of rubble and timber. Beyond it, where the gazebo had been, was a crater with whorls of blue smoke slowly wafting up from it.

'The bombers?' he said softly.

She nodded mutely, still holding the parcel.

'How do you prepare the meals?' he asked, fighting the rising sickness in his stomach.

'We manage,' she said with a shrug, thrusting the package upon him. The *Reichsführer* brought some food...' As she saw his expression of incredulity she added quickly, 'The Baroness does not know, Master Alex. Please, she has not been well for some time now. Her mind, it sometimes ---' Old hands dropped lamely by her sides as he took the parcel.

'God bless you, Lottie,' Alex Winter said softly as he kissed her gently on the forehead. Then, almost as an afterthought, he added, 'God help us all.'

As he exited the front door, cradling the small parcel Lottie had thrust upon him *(knackwurst* at a guess. From people who had almost no food in the house) the sergeant turned to Jaeger who was surveying the scene with a sardonic smile. 'A touching family scene, *Herr Standartenführer*,' he said. 'Do you have any family to visit?'

'The Reich is my family, Willi,' Jaeger said as he watched Winter turn to take one last look at his childhood home. 'You should know that!' But there was something in his eyes that said different.

6

CHAPTER

It was a few minutes past ten on the morning of 11 April 1945 when the M8 armoured car pulled up near the gates of Buchenwald Labour Camp. Up in the turret Captain Frederick Keffer of the 6th Armoured division of the US 3rd Army surveyed the scene through slowly traversing field glasses. What he saw was a white flag slowly stirring at a flagpole in the slight morning breeze. Men were everywhere, most in striped prisoner's wear, a handful in what looked like olive fatigues. No sign of field grey clad German soldiers.

The gates stood wide open but there was no sign of anyone leaving.

Giving the order to advance to his driver the captain made way for his gunner to man the 33mm M6 turret canon as the car lurched forward over uneven ground.

Reaching the town of Weimar the day before, the colonel had received word of a large concentration camp being nearby. Of the Wehrmacht there had been no sign for several days now, the Germans having withdrawn to regroup after being driven back from the Rhine crossings. Not expecting any resistance he had dispatched Keffer with a three man crew to reconnoitre the area where the camp was thought to be.

Approaching the gates the crew of the M8 were greeted by a rousing cheer as the vehicle was identified as being American. Men were pouring out of wooden barracks everywhere, some running up to wildly wave their arms as they shouted with excitement and joy. Further back others, seemingly too weak to walk, were being supported by fellow prisoners and even those were unable to hide their unbridled joy at finally being liberated.

Surrounded by a jubilant crowd the armoured car was forced to a halt, Keffer climbing onto the hood to survey the sea of faces. Everyone was shouting, mostly in German but there were a handful of Russians amongst them, those were the ones he had spotted earlier wearing the remnants of military uniforms.

Raising his arms in an attempt to restore calm he asked if anyone spoke English. Several men stepped forward, one a distinguished looking elderly man whom Keffer asked what had happened to the guards. It seemed they had abandoned their prisoners the previous day, most fleeing into the nearby woods when news reached that Allied units were approaching. Excited chatter and gesticulations from several of the Russians had the English speaker hastily add that the Russians had also staged a revolt, capturing and killing several of the guards.

Nodding the captain slowly rotated to survey the scene. Only now was he becoming aware of the emaciated state of the men thronging all around him. Walking skeletons most of them, the shapeless pyjama like striped clothing hanging off them like so many items of washing on a clothes line. A thousand eyes stared up at him, eyes huge in wasted faces where it seemed nothing but skin covered the bones beneath. Raising his gaze he could make out an unfamiliar pile a short distance away on the side of what appeared to be a parade ground of sorts. It took him a full five seconds to finally realise what he was looking at – a mound of rotting corpses piled on high.

Which went some way in explaining that unfamiliar stench that had been assailing his nostrils ever since driving through the gates.

Fighting to control the nausea rising at the back of his throat he reached for the radio handset his sergeant was holding out,

Company HQ on the ether. 'Get me the Colonel,' he said hoarsely, 'I've just seen what hell looks like.'

It was five hours later that the prisoner who had been urgently asking to see the officer in charge, finally got to sit down opposite the team seated behind the trestle tables hastily erected to process the camp's inmates. The major conducting the interviews had already listened to more than a hundred tales of unfathomable deprivation and horror that day and as he wearily dragged on a cigarette he motioned for the new face to proceed. Next to him a uniformed clerk slotted a fresh page into his typewriter and reached for a drink from his canteen.

'My name is Dr Barry Sibul,' the old man said in a surprisingly firm voice and in excellent English. 'I am -- was – professor of physics at Leiden University. I was sent here in June 1943 together with several others from the university...'

'All Jews,' the major said unnecessarily, a comment that raised an eyebrow from the other man who continued, '... Most of them dead now. I believe I am only still alive as the Nazis thought I might be of future help in their project.'

'What project?' a man who had hitherto been sitting quietly in a corner of the tent, asked. The old man glanced at him, taking in the uniform that was devoid of all insignia yet belonging to a man of definite authority.

'The bomb,' Professor Sibul said, 'the nuclear bomb the Nazis are working on. You see, nuclear physics was my field and that is the reason I needed to speak to you so urgently.'

Interested now, the man from the Office of Strategic Services leaned forward. 'Go on,' he said.

'Professor Anton Berkowitz is a fake...' he began, 'I knew him well and the man who now uses that name is not him. He is a spy and I suspect right now in the United States of America.'

Glancing at the OSS man the major shrugged, 'Must be dozens of them,' he said. 'With the war about to end does it matter?'

'This man, whatever his real identity, is a nuclear scientist involved in the field of atomic weapons research. In late 1939 I was brought in to provide technical briefing on aspects of such a bomb while still working in Leiden. I heard Berkowitz, whom I knew well, was in the building and went to find him. Purely by chance a small party of senior SS men passed by in a corridor. I overheard them addressing the stranger I had been ordered to provide a briefing to earlier as "Professor Berkowitz," at which there was general laughter. I tried to contact my friend in the days and weeks that followed only to discover he had disappeared, never to be seen again.'

The OSS man nodded thoughtfully, 'And you think he might have been inserted into whatever nuclear program the USA might have?'

'Yes.'

'Thank you, Dr Sibul,' he said, 'we will look into this, I promise.'

They watched in silence as the old man shuffled out, squinting uncertainly as the bright sunlight outside touched his silvery hair turning it to hues of white and light blue.

'We'll take a short break,' the major said, beckoning a hovering serviceman to bring over some fresh coffee. Turning to the OSS man he asked what he thought.

'I don't know. Like you said, the war is all but over, hard to think how relevant this is, even if true.'

'Is there a project back home to build such a bomb? A thing that can destroy a city I think someone said?'

Getting to his feet the OSS man smiled down at the major, 'If I told you I'd have to kill you,' he said and headed for the exit.

With the direct telecommunications links between mainland Europe and the UK still not restored the more urgent OSS signals were radioed to US Military Intelligence HQ, London, for analysis and processing. The field radio available at Buchenwald was a standard SCR 300 and on the day the operator experienced significant static as the message was first relayed to US 3rd Army HQ and from there across the English Channel. Hence it was no surprise really when "Berkowitz" morphed to "Burkelitz" and eventually, somewhat bizzarely, to "Benkenlitz."

CHAPTER 7

FBI Special Agent Hank Brewster grunted as he leaned back in his swivel chair, the worn leather warm and sticky against his sweat soaked shirt. It was hot in the office, the desk fan not quite doing it, an unusually sunny spring day out there on the streets of New York City. In the outside office he could hear the rhythmic rat-a-tat as his secretary worked the typewriter, a bit like the stutter of his old Ford straight eight when he started it up in the mornings.

The sun was streaming straight through the open venetian blinds now, drawing a step ladder pattern on the paperwork strewn across his desk, blinding him when he stared down at the sea of white. 'Zelda!' he shouted towards the open door, 'bring me another Coke, will you? And shut these goddamn blinds when you're at it.'

Satisfied that the pause in the typing signified his request being attended to he turned to the report still grasped in a ham like fist. He had to push the chair back, out of the harsh light, to read it once more. So there was a spy out there somewhere, a nuclear scientist and probably sneaking around either Hanford, Oak Ridge or possibly the top secret site at Los Alamos.

Another fucking one. Christ! Wasn't the war over? Reaching for a panatela slim cigarillo from the selection he kept in a shirt pocket he lit it absently from a Zippo on his desk, leaning back at a precarious angle to blow a slow satisfying stream of blue smoke at where the ceiling fan was listlessly pretending to work.

Since the uncovering of the Duquesne German spy ring back in 1941 the New York Field Office at 26 Federal Plaza in Lower Manhattan had been tasked with all military espionage matters in the USA. Brewster had been involved from day one and, frankly speaking, was getting just a bit tired of the bullshit. A saving mercy had been the sheer incompetence of the spies, something he ascribed to a cultural barrier, the culprits so often sticking out like balls on a dog.

Pathetic really.

Now, of course, the focus was shifting to the Russians, the Director in Washington reckoning the war being all but over the next threat would be coming from the communists. God knows, with thirty years service behind him and the scars to prove it, he didn't know if he had the stomach to go down that road once more. How he missed the good old days when organised crime was run by tough men who, for all their sins, were red blooded Americans to the core.

With a sigh he turned to the document resisting the impulse to scrunch it up and toss it into the out tray, knowing how much Zelda hated that. Well, we know about Fuchs, of course, have a couple of men down at Santa Fe keeping an eye on him and whatever other commies might be hunting around Los Alamos. But until now there had been no real concern, no threat to whatever they were working on down there. Why would this one, this Benkenlitz, be a threat? Was he even in the country?

It wasn't like he didn't have enough bloody work as it was, what with OSS in Washington clamouring for experienced investigators to be seconded to Germany to help with the processing of the suspected war criminals they were bringing in. Not to mention the latest reports regarding a major drug smuggling operation the military had gotten wind of, some bastards stealing army medical supplies, morphine and penicillin, to sell on the black market. Military fucking Intelligence (was there even such a thing?) screaming for FBI help.

What did they think? Agents grew on his hairy back or something?!

In his mounting agitation he had bitten through the end of his cigar and with a grimace of distaste he ground it out against the side of the waste basket, the desk ashtray a bridge too far. What was it someone had told him when he complained the other day about the pathetic instructions that came with a new vacuum cleaner he was trying to assemble for the wife? The three page instruction pamphlet a garbled mess of nonsensical gibberish drawn up by some illiterate moron that should not be allowed to change a light bulb let alone be entrusted near anything that required an intellect greater than that of a six year old.

What do you do, Hank, his friend had said, when you're the foreman in charge of a factory floor producing a new product for which there is a huge order and the manager comes up to you, says you gotta draw up an instruction sheet to go with it? Easy, he said, your harried foreman looks around at his workforce, all of them busy as hell getting the product made, none of which he can spare. Then he spots that one useless no-hoper lurking somewhere at the back, trying to look like he knows what he's doing. The one guy he can spare without jeopardizing the production line. Problem solved, except of course the idiot doesn't understand the product so he writes the kind of crap no sane person can follow. But who cares? The work gets done, the product gets delivered. On schedule.

The recollection made him smile as Zelda placed the chilled drink on his desk and moved across to the window to close the blinds. 'Of all the men we currently have hanging around waiting for an assignment, who do you think is the one we can spare the most?'

He wanted to say "most useless" but checked himself, that would be bad for morale.

His secretary frowned as she scanned the busy desk for any paperwork he had finished with and could be filed. 'I dunno, we're pretty thin at the moment, I guess there's that new kid that was sent down from Quantico just the other day.'

'The redhead?'

'Rusty Miller. He's from Louisiana, worked as a sheriff's deputy until he joined the Bureau.'

'Rusty a nickname, him being a redhead?'

Zelda shook her head, 'Nope, apparently he was christened that.' She had found what she was searching for, holding up a sheaf of papers for him to look at. 'Have you finished with this? Head Office wants feedback on it so you'd better dictate something.'

But Brewster's thoughts were elsewhere, 'Funny people, the hillbillies,' he said chuckling. 'Rusty. Why not? The whole thing is probably a wild goose chase anyway.'

Zelda glanced at her boss askance; if he thought hillbillies came from Mississippi rather than the Appalachians, why should she care?

Regaining his desk with some effort Brewster told her to find Miller, send him in.

Zelda did not move, instead she studied her nails, arms outstretched and hand dorsiflexed to get that wide angle view. Looking good she decided with a slight nod of the head, yeah this colour was a keeper. Offhandedly, without looking at Brewster she said, 'This spy, he's a scientist right? Working and probably living inside a military controlled area?' Not waiting for a reply from the puzzled looking agent she added, 'and as you know our boys are not allowed inside any of those military facilities, that being the private dung heap of the army's rooster boys.'

'What are you saying?' he asked looking at her askance, deciding he liked it when she talked dirty.

'Seems little point in sending another FBI man when he can't get inside. Would be so much better if it was someone from, say the War Office, or perhaps some audit office, know what I mean?'

She had finished studying her nails and was heading for the door. Pausing she turned, 'If you look at the back of the file you'll see a few phone numbers I dotted down, should you want to consider that angle.'

As he watched her retreating form Brewster shook his head, a wry smile followed by a soft chuckle. 'You're something else, Zelda, something else.' With a grunt he reached for a desk phone and opened the file.

8

CHAPTER

Los Alamos, New Mexico, April, 1945

Max Winter lay quite still as his eyes grew accustomed to the dark. It took him several seconds to familiarise himself with his surroundings as the objects around the room slowly took on shape. It took him an extra second to remember who he was, where he was.

By the time he rolled out of bed he was Anton Berkowitz, Jewish nuclear scientist. German spy. As usual he had slept badly, a nagging hangover from the party at Oppenheimer's house the previous evening no doubt contributing. But it was the dream that was haunting him, steadily weakening him, drawing him closer and closer to, what? It was always the same, the man and the horse, wildly galloping into the night, the boy helpless in his tightly clutching arms, the nameless terror closing in, the urgent whispering growing in intensity. *Erlkönig...* What did it *mean*?! This children's verse from a long forgotten childhood?

Sometimes he saw the terror, a dragon with a long and curling tail. A tail he was reaching for even as the dragon glared at him, eyes of fire burning brightly, pale blue smoke slowly escaping from its gaping mouth. And as his terror grew he reached for the hand that was always there, the voice whispering in the darkness, Ivan... Ivan will come and he will slay the dragon...

But that was the part of the dream that had now turned to sheer terror. For the reaching hand was no longer there, the calming voice silent.

Splashing cold water on his face he looked at himself in the mirror, trying and failing to remember what Max Winter had looked like. Were the scars of the surgery becoming more visible, in tandem with the scars inside his mind? Did the plastic face age in the same way its nurturing soul did?

He had no way of knowing.

Glancing down his gaze settled on the four inch line of scar tissue on his right thigh. It had been throbbing lately, the tissue raised, an angry red. The scar that had been there ever since he could remember. An identical mark on the thigh of his brother, except Alex's was on the opposite hip.

It was something his parents had never raised, any questions by the young boys always brusquely fobbed of with stern reminders that their bodies should be kept pure and dedicated to the cause of the glorious new Germany that would soon rise from the ashes of the old.

But they were not fooled for long. Young inquisitive minds quickly discovered the entity of the birth mark, except in their case it was equally apparent that theirs were not mere blemishes of the skin, a sometimes cruel quirk of nature. Their mark was man made, a surgical scar. The later accidental discovery – an overheard conversation – that they had been born by caesarean section, had put the final pieces of the puzzle together.

The brothers had been joined at the hip at birth. Most likely little more than a bridge of skin. But the stigma of such an aberration was unthinkable for both parents. This, this *thing*, was not possible for the House of Winter. A surgical separation of the twins was quickly, and secretly, arranged and the whole matter was never to be raised again.

It never happened.

It was snowing when he left his quarters to head for the Technical Area at the opposite side of a partially frozen over Ashley Pond where, only a few years earlier, boys from the Ranch School had played pond ice hockey before the government had taken over the place. Turning up his collar against the soft feathery flakes drifting down like so many falling petals from a strange white flower to settle like icy fingers on his cheeks and down his neck where the heavy jacket did not quite close, he started trudging aware that already his hands had lost all sensation.

Snow in April, was it an omen he wondered? This monster they were about to unleash, would it set the very atmosphere on fire as some predicted, cause a nuclear winter? He paused to glance around, rubbing his hands together briskly to restore circulation as his breath came and went in puffs of condensation. No, he reasoned, the scientific evidence for such a catastrophe was not there. The hill on which Los Alamos was constructed was 7,400 feet above sea level, significantly higher than the surrounding desert of New Mexico and snowfall, even in spring, was not all that unusual.

Nobody was about but plenty of vehicle tracks in the snow pointed to others having passed earlier. Most likely the security detail he decided, perhaps some of the party Oppenheimer had assembled to head for the remote Trinity site where they would test the bomb as soon as they could figure out a better way of holding the enclosing explosives jacket together around the plutonium core than with duct tape and chewing gum.

The core... That enigmatic billiard ball sized sphere of nickel encased solid plutonium 239 that had arrived only days earlier from its Oak Ridge Laboratories birthplace in the centre of a heavily armed convoy. The heavy metal ball that was now resting in its small carry box on an ordinary deal wood table in an ordinary room in that oblong building near the edge of the ravine he was now approaching.

Others would be there already he knew instinctively. Otto Frisch, brilliant somnambulist who seemed to speak in mathematical riddles only occasionally intelligible to surrounding mortals, young Richard Feynman, eager as a Cocker Spaniel puppy and, of course, the omnipresent Enrico Fermi whose natural curiosity would lure him away from his own nearby laboratory in Los Alamos' remote Omega Canyon.

'Can I give you a ride, Dr Berkowitz? I presume you're heading down the canyon, for the experiment?' It was Sergeant Johnson, one of the local security detail, his face pinched and blue-white despite the heavy greatcoat and army issue muffler.

"The Experiment," Max thought wryly as he climbed into the passenger side of the open Jeep, instinctively reaching for something to hold onto as the sergeant rammed the vehicle into gear to send them spinning and bouncing down the winding dirt track. Lady Godiva, he seemed to recall its initial title. (God alone knew where they had got that from, probably one of Feynman's jokes) Now referred to as the Dragon Experiment. Better still, "Tickling the tail of the Dragon."

Minutes later he was there, the sudden stillness in the large room a welcome relief from the bitterly cold wind outside. The team was already assembled, the stack of uranium hydride blocks steadily building as two technicians carefully positioned them around the middle section of the ten foot high aluminium structure known as "the guillotine." Frisch, Feynman and a young female mathematician who was newly arrived on the Hill and whose name was not yet known to Max, were clustered around the deal table in a corner studying a large diagram spread open. Max's entrance was greeted with the usual detached indifference theoretical scientists seemed to reserve for their peers. As usual the only warmth in the room would come from the dragon when the core was dropped.

Crossing over to where the monitoring equipment was assembled he quickly set to work checking the connections to the neutron scanners positioned at different levels on the pyramid-like structure. The steady rhythmic flashing of the tiny red lights indicated that the power supply was steady and a quick mental calculation had him decide that the intervals were in keeping with the amount of uranium stacked so far.

As a theoretician on the team his function was to double check Otto Frisch's calculations, make sure runaway enthusiasm did not lead to a runaway critical reaction that would send them all to a place from which there was no comeback. Another task was the analysis of the collected data afterwards and he presumed that was why a mathematician was also present.

Or, perhaps it was to share the blame should the experiment go wrong and Frisch accidentally trigger a brief incident of supercriticality as had happened a few weeks earlier when he had leaned too close to a stacked assembly of uranium blocks. The hydrogen in his own body had reflected enough neutrons back to the core to very nearly irradiate them all. Only the man's quick reaction in knocking the assembly over had saved them that day.

He watched as the technicians passed the core up the outside of the guillotine to be carefully fitted into the small basket where it hung suspended over the central shaft of the structure. This was always a tense moment, the personnel all too eager to get out of there before the ball dropped. The central idea was to monitor the rise in core activity as the released ball dropped by gravity through the surrounding segment of uranium blocks for a split second reaching the condition for an atomic explosion – the closest they could go to starting such an event without blowing themselves up.

The whole setup in an effort to calculate exactly how much uranium was needed to build the bomb.

'Last blocks going into place now, Doctor!' the technician called over his shoulder. Seated in front of the monitoring screen Max noted the anticipated slight rise in neutron activity, duly recording it in the ledger open on his lap. The steady flicker of the assembled red lights had increased but was still safely below a critical reading.

'Stand by, thirty seconds!' Frisch said as he moved closer to stare up at the suspended core. There was silence in the room now as the technicians joined the rest of the team who had retreated to the far corner of the room.

'Ready,' Max answered as he reached for the release lever.

Glancing around to see if everyone was at their appointed stations, Frisch joined Max and gave the order to release the core. It seemed to hang suspended for a second before starting its descent into freefall, speeding up to a blur before shooting through the stacked core to land in the padded receptacle bucket a fraction of a second later.

In the instant it took to traverse the outer casing the red monitor lights went berserk as all flickering moulded into continuous light and the dragon stirred.

There was a moment's stunned silence then everyone seemed to explode in a burst of relieved laughter and clapping. 'That was a close one!' Feynman exclaimed with a laugh as the excited chatter died down. 'I think we're about as close as we can go now. I suggest we all go into town and have ourselves a few drinks at the La Fonda! Who's with me?!'

A general cheer settled the matter and, Max mused, why not? It was a Friday and Oppenheimer was away, meeting with General Groves in Washington. Nobody did much work on The Hill over weekends as it was, their boss having gone as far as declaring Sundays a day of rest for all.

As the others filed out, a technician stayed behind to return the core to its shoe box size transport container. The rectangular receptacle was studded with rubber tipped outer prongs to presumably protect against an accidental blow and Max could never quite fathom why such a bump would pose a threat to a solid chunk of hard metal with a density close to that of lead. Acting on an impulse he decided to check on the explosive casing he was working on, before following the others.

The Technical Area consisted of twenty six regulation Army barrack style bungalows labelled A to Z on makeshift placards mounted at their entrances and placed at seemingly haphazard angles to one another yet close together. His lab, as he liked to think of it, was housed at the far end of the Technical Area and it took him five minutes of brisk walking to reach it, long enough to leave him shivering, his breath escaping in puffs of condensation from lips gone numb with cold. Once inside he discarded his coat and hat and exchanged good mornings with two technicians who were having a coffee break, gratefully accepting a steaming cup of the warming liquid one held out. As he paused to pat his pockets and glance around for his notebook and pen a voice behind his back had him stiffen.

'Dr Berkowitz?'

If there was such a thing as one's body freezing into a state of immobility Max Winter felt that now. *The voice! Could it be?!*

Struggling for a moment to control his jumble of thoughts, he hesitated.

'Dr Berkowitz?' Louder now, the figure closer, the voice tailing off as its owner hesitated.

Turning slowly he worked at keeping his face expressionless, that of a scientist meeting a new colleague for the first time. *It was her!! Gott in Himmel! How?! Why?!*

With great effort and putting on his broadest Bavarian accent he replied to the affirmative, holding out a hand that was suddenly cold and clammy.

'Dr Eva Molnar,' she said as they shook hands, 'the new mathematician. Newly arrived from Berkeley.'

Mistaking his no doubt shocked expression for one of bewilderment she hastened to explain. 'I've been recruited to help with the complex calculations regarding the explosive force needed to...' she hesitated, smiling uncertainly, 'to...you know.'

'The device,' he heard himself say, 'we call it the device...'

She was as beautiful as he remembered her. Almost ten years ago, at MIT. The rich auburn hair perhaps worn a trifle shorter, a few tiny wrinkles at the corners of the eyes when she smiled, like now. A bulky sweater over a man's shirt with dark brown corduroy pants shoved into knee high cowboy boots – nothing like the frilly summer's dress he had last seen her in that day his brother left for Germany and she was too late to stop him. The day she told him, Max Winter, through tears of rage how much she hated and despised him and his lies. How she hoped he died of shame and how she never wanted to see him again.

And here they were again, after all those years. Surrounded by more lies, better and bigger lies. Lies that would shake the world and she did not recognise him! The realisation brought a strange mix of fear and excitement and, yes, just a pang of long forgotten longing,

It was the eyes that had it. Those dark brown pools of wonder that seemed to look into a man's forever leaving him feeling slightly uneasy. The same eyes that was staring back at him with a faintly quizzical expression.

The name was different now, she had been Eva Buirski then, a bubbly laugh-a-minute co-ed from some small town in Maine. She shared some classes with Alex and himself and the way he remembered it, his brother was quite taken with her.

He was about to mumble some or other excuse to escape, get away and marshal his thoughts but realised she had followed him down the corridor and they were now in the room where he worked on the design of the explosive casing.

'Is that, is that what I think it is?' she asked, pointing at the convex structure sitting on a sturdy workbench in the centre of the room. It was multifaceted with myriad looped wires trailing from each of the components to a small black fuse box clamped to one side. Several hexagonal segments measuring a few inches in diameter lay scattered around the table and she could see the perfectly machined cavities on the inside surface where the explosive would go.

Sensing his sudden hesitation she hurried to add, 'It's OK, Dr, I have been given full security clearance by Dr Oppenheimer himself as well as a briefing by Dr Fermi as to the structure of the bomb.'

'The device,' he said mechanically as he watched her gingerly touch the metallic surfaces, the yellow light from the naked overhead bulbs glinting dully off the very red nail polish she wore. 'This is part of the final assembly, a section of the lenses. The final device is large enough to fill the centre of the room and made up of several of these segments.'

'It is not charged, is it? I mean, the explosive charges ---'

'Are kept locked away in Building S which is down a nearby canyon. Oppy will not let us keep explosives on The Hill.'

She nodded, glanced around taking in the room with its scattered tools, discarded pieces of wiring and a dozen different electronic gadgets interspersed with several notepads and thick technical manuals. Even a large cylindrical coffee urn on a desk. There was something unusual about it and reflexively she touched its cold steel surface noticing that it was heavy with no sign of an electric cord or a nearby wall socket.

Noticing her puzzled frown Berkowitz hastened to explain it was broken and he planned to fix it, as soon as he found the time. Meanwhile, he shrugged apologetically, they were reliant on ersatz army issue coffee from the canteen. He indicated a wastebasket overflowed with discarded carton coffee cups and Eva smiled wryly as he gaze shifted to the rest of the room taking in the motley assembly of coaster chairs that looked as if they had been scavenged from a factory fire sale.

'A boys' room,' she nodded as she surveyed the posters on the walls. Scantily clad female forms in sultry poses courtesy of motor product companies with one or two screen goddesses thrown in. 'It could do with a woman's touch. I think I'll start by having someone sweep it out, a bit of dusting won't hurt either.' Turning to face Max who had difficulty meeting her gaze, she asked to be shown his calculations. Apparently there was no time to be lost in getting up to speed with how far the project had progressed.

Max had lost the last bit of her request, a blinding headache coming, as it always did, from seemingly nowhere and with it the nausea and the blurred vision. Mumbling an excuse he fled the room, a lasting image the faintly puzzled expression as she watched him go.

9

CHAPTER

The Fieseler Storch levelled out at ten thousand feet, the sunlight bright off the massed clouds below. They had taken off from Berlin's East-West Axis, the road to Gatow Airport overrun by the advancing Russians and Tempelhof a smoking crater riddled ruin from where the Lancasters had left their mark two days earlier. Leaning back against the hard backrest and jostling Jaeger next to him in the cramped confines of the little plane's cabin, Winter lit a cigarette and let his thoughts drift back to the day's events.

The news of the encircling enemy did not seem to perturb Himmler in any way Winter could discern, the mask beneath the black death's head cap as inscrutable as ever. As usual the Reichsführer had a plan in place for just such an eventuality, one of many such Winter thought grimly. It proved to be a small plane parked in a garage close to the Brandenburger Tor.

Jaeger's sergeant had the field car ready when they reached the exit ramp to the bunker at Hermann-Goeringstrasse, Winter's last vision of Himmler a face enshrouded in black and slowly receding into the background shadows of that rat's trap they were hoping to escape from.

Like a bat from hell, he thought grimly, about to return to its master who, in the world Winter found himself in now, could well be Satan himself. As the car wove its way between the mounds of rubble and bomb craters that were now the streets of Berlin the sergeant glanced over his shoulder at Winter to ask, with a grin, how he was enjoying his day that far.

Winter had thought that over, instinctively raising a shielding arm as the cratered wall of a nearby apartment block came crashing down in a rumble of dust and the warning shouts of men. Just what kind of a day *was* he having? Eventful, he decided at length. Yes, that was it, eventful. It had started off doing what he does, building a bridge, then quickly progressed to being a witness to a squad of renegade soldiers being ruthlessly executed by the other man in the passenger seat now studying him with a bemused grin. Then it was off to good old mother and more family secrets that he really did not want to know. Top it off with a visit to whatever the scene in that bunker represented and now, apparently, if they could escape the boiling kettle of a doomed Berlin, further adventures on foreign soil.

Just living the dream, he thought bitterly. Or was it the Chinese curse of living in interesting times?

'I saw dead people,' he said, more to himself than the company.

'There are dead people on every street corner now, Major,' Jaeger said shaking his head, 'nothing strange there.' A Schmeisser machine pistol rested on his lap and he raised it now as several running figures emerged from the ruins of a cellar, lowering the weapon as they were recognised as civilians.

'I saw dead people back there in that bunker. They were moving around and talking and some were even laughing. But they were dead, they just didn't know it yet.'

There seemed to be no answer to that and they drove the final few blocks in silence, the only sounds that of distant gunfire and the sudden roar of a low flying fighter aircraft as it swooped in search of a target.

The Fieseler Storch was where Himmler had said it would be, fuelled up with the pilot standing by. Luftwaffe flight lieutenant Hans Schiffer saluted as Jaeger stepped up and handed him his orders in a sealed envelope. As Winter waited for the man to do his pre-flight checks he noticed a second plane parked further towards the back of the garage. This one was an Arado trainer and he could not help wondering whether that would be part of Himmler's own exit strategy.

With the pilot at the controls the three of them pushed the plane out of the hangar positioning it so that the nose pointed down the road towards the distant Victory Column, a structure Winter was amazed to find seemed untouched by the carnage all around.

A little more than three hundred yards ahead the road was blocked by a bombed out military truck, the space around just wide enough for a car to pass. No way the plane's wings could navigate that gap. Jaeger pointed that out and was about to send Willi in search of some soldiers to clear the wreckage, when the pilot assured him in an unnaturally calm voice that the Storch would be well airborne before reaching that spot.

With a grim smile Jaeger led the way aboard and to Winter's surprise motioned for him to move further back to make space for the sergeant who was coming as well. Winter was about to point out that the Fieseler was a three seater and then there was the matter of the shortened runway but any protest was drowned in the roar of the engine and then they were off, the machine slewing alarmingly from side to side as the pilot worked the pedals before, seemingly at the last moment, pulling back on the stick with the little plane rising into the air with a protesting creaking that seemed to be all around them.

It was ten minutes after takeoff, Schiffer setting a course that had them heading towards where the setting sun was colouring the horizon in shades of orange and vanilla, that Winter realized he did not know their destination. He asked Jaeger, raising his voice to be heard over the noise of the engine and the rush of wind past the ill fitting Perspex windows of the aircraft.

'Wilhemshaven,' came the answer, 'it is still in German hands and our transport waits in the docks area.'

Willi grinned and nudged him, 'Don't worry, Herr Major! The *Standartenführer* always has a plan ready. You'll see!'

Winter was about to reply when there was a sudden whooshing noise, a great gust of wind that rocked the little plane, sending it banking sharply left and into a steep dive.

'Enemy fighter!' their pilot shouted as he fought the controls at the same time glancing sharply over his shoulder and skywards. Looking out the starboard window Winter saw s line of jagged holes in the wing, strips of metal flapping wildly in the slipstream.

From the corner of his eye he could see the face of the sergeant which had taken on an instant hue of white, teeth bared in a snarl like that of a cornered wolf. Jaeger, however, seemed as unperturbed as ever, his features not showing the slightest sign of alarm.

'Hold tight!' the pilot shouted as he righted the Storch, sending it into a steep dive for the cloud cover beckoning below. Already a mile ahead they could see the fighter, Winter made it an American P51 Mustang, banking and climbing, the rays of the setting sun flashing off the silvery fuselage. 'He's coming back!' Willi shouted, his voice harsh with fear. 'This time he'll finish us for sure!!'

'Look!' their pilot shouted pointing to something on their port side. All heads swivelled and it took Winter a moment or two to make out what he was indicating. It was still only a speck on the horizon but growing larger at an incredible rate and heading straight for them. Levelling out to head back to his helpless target the pilot of the Mustang saw it too, instantly breaking off his attacking run to desperately climb in an effort to escape.

Time seemed to freeze as all stared in fascination and then the Messerschmitt ME 262 flashed past at well over 600 miles per hour, streaks of vapour trailing from the twin jet engines, the high pitched scream of the turbines only reaching their ears a second later followed by the dull thud-thud as its nose cannons opened up.

Half a mile ahead the Mustang pilot tried desperately to evade the lightning death coming his way at the speed of sound, throwing his craft into a backwards flip followed by a spinning leaf fall earthwards but all to no avail.

As the occupants of the Storch watched in morbid fascination the American plane exploded in a bright orange ball of flame, debris spiralling down and disappearing into the cloud blanket below.

There was a moment's silence and then Jaeger said it for all of them, 'Poor bastard, never had a chance.'

There seemed no answer to that and they flew in silence for what seemed like minutes as their pilot resumed their course westwards. A quick check had confirmed that the machine gun bullets had miraculously avoided any major damage, only a slight correction on the controls required to keep them flying.

It was their pilot who finally broke the silence, 'If only we had more of those in the air a year or two earlier, what a difference that would have made!' he said, wistfully, shaking his head.

It was Winter who saw it first, the mottled camouflaged shape creeping up on their starboard side as the Messerschmitt crept into view less than fifty yards away, the pilot a grinning face high up in his bubble cockpit as he raised a thumb. The voice that came over the radio as clear as if in the same room. 'Good evening, *kameraden*!'

'You're late,' Jaeger said impassively, 'you were supposed to pick us up twenty minutes ago.'

'My apologies, *Herr Standartenführer*. There was a refuelling problem and I had to evade some enemy fighters.'

Jaeger nodded glumly as Winter stared at him with a look of incredulity. 'You, you *arranged* for this escort? My God, I...' Words failed him as, perhaps for the first time, the apparent importance of their mission struck him. What was really going on?!

'Compliments of *Reichsmarshall Göring*,' the voice on the radio said in apparent answer to Winter's question. 'I'll be watching over you from here on in. Good flying!' And with that the Messerschmitt peeled off and disappeared into the sun, climbing at a rate Winter would not have thought possible to, within seconds, disappear from view.

10

C H A P T E R

A pall of thick smoke hung over the harbour district of Wilhelmshaven as they broke through the cloud cover, the city in darkness with only the occasional glimmer of light visible in the blackness of the night. In the distance, near the water, large oil dumps were on fire, flames leaping fifty, sixty, feet into the air and sending thick black clouds into the sky. They were flying at near stalling speed now, the pilot hunched forward over the dim lights of the control panel as he searched for a sign of the city's airfield.

'The city is in total blackout,' he said, anxiety turning his voice into a low murmur. 'They have been hit by Lancaster bombers four nights in a row. And those bastards are dropping ten ton bombs. *Mein Gott,* ten ton! Imagine that thing dropping on you!'

'The smoke curtain over the airport was so thick Schiffer could not see the runway although his altimeter read a matter of only feet now. 'Brace yourselves!' he shouted as he pulled back the throttle and then they were down and with such force Winter thought the wings were about to snap off. Peering past the heads of Jaeger and the pilot he could make out a series of dim lights dead ahead and seconds later they pulled up next to a staff car parked at the edge of the runway, its lights on and engine running.

Jaeger was the first out and returning the salute of a young SS officer who studied the papers handed to him before handing them back with a crisp salute. *'Heil Hitler!'*

'Heil Hitler,' Jaeger acknowledged wearily as he motioned the rest of the party who had by now disembarked towards the waiting car. 'You come too, Lieutenant,' he said to the pilot, who hesitated then, deciding his craft was in no fit state to take off without some repairs, shrugged and followed. 'Just look at those craters on the runway,' he said, pointing at the sector of the tarmac lit up by the car's beams, 'How the hell did we manage to miss them?!'

'The devil looks after his own!' Willi said with a laugh of relief and, for once, Winter could only agree with him.

Twenty minutes later they reached the waterfront where one of the Kriegsmarine's latest long range submarines lay at berth, a single shielded arc light casting a dim yellow light onto the gangplank and for'ard deck. A small party of workers were loading supplies from a truck parked nearby and by the feverish pace of their labours Winter could tell they were anxious to finish and get away from there.

'Hear that dull rumble in the distance?' Jaeger said, 'it's the Lancasters, over water you can hear them from miles away. I reckon we have ten minutes before the first bombs fall.' There was not a trace of worry in his voice or, for that matter, his demeanor. Just another day at the office in the life of a stone killer, Winter thought and immediately felt guilty. He had no right to brand the Standartenführer like that, he decided. It was war and war was hell.

He watched as Jaeger climbed up to the conning tower to confer with the captain, an Oberleutnant Dietrich, who looked no older than about eighteen, who studied the document handed to him before returning it with what Winter could only assume to be some sort of a salute.

'The last supplies are being loaded now,' he said as the first of the air raid sirens started up, the new sound causing the workers to go faster if that was even possible. Excusing himself he shouted some orders down to an unseen figure in the gloom of the foredeck as Jaeger came back down the gangplank. For the first time Winter noticed a small leather satchel the man was carrying and which he now handed to his sergeant. 'You will take this to Lisbon, Willi, as I explained to you earlier. At the airport there you will be met by a Herr Müller, from the embassy and you will go with him and hand him this.'

'The *Kamaradenwerk*, it begins?'

Jaeger nodded. He turned to Schiffer, 'You will fly Sergeant Meier there.'

'My orders are to return to Berlin.'

'Here is your new orders,' Jaeger said softly and something Schiffer saw in his eyes made the other man take a pace back, a protesting hand dropping lamely by his side. Winter could not be sure but thought it was the menacing tone or perhaps the Walther P38 that had appeared in Jaeger's hand. 'You will go with the sergeant to where a Junkers 88 aircraft is waiting at a hangar at a small airfield on the outskirts of the city.' He inclined his head in the direction of the SS lieutenant waiting by the car, 'The *Obersturmführer* will take you there in the field car.'

'*Zu befehl!*' Schiffer said crisply, his eyes on the pistol.

Turning to Willi Jaeger held out his hand, 'It has been an honour serving with you, *Oberscharführer*,' he said, 'go now.'

Winter watched as the small party departed, Willi glancing back at Jaeger one last time, a strange look in his eyes.

The bombers were overhead now, the first of the bombs crashing down, a huge fountain of water erupting near the harbour inlet. 'Leaving now!' the captain shouted as the last of the loading crew scrambled down the gangplank and into the truck that already had its engine running.

'Coming?' Jaeger asked with a sardonic grin, 'or are you waiting for a formal invitation, Major Winter?'

CHAPTER 11

Esther Stern stared down at the open drawer of the steel filing cabinet in dumbstruck disbelief, as a sudden icy fear gripped her insides, had her gasp in shock. The Berkowitz File was gone! Stepping back she mechanically felt for a chair and sank into it. Good God! How...?

A sudden thought had her glance wildly in the direction of the door leading to the small waiting room and secretary's post. Could Betty have taken it? Or, perhaps she herself had been busy with it, making some notes, forgotten to replace it?

No, she decided firmly, the secretary would never remove a file without strict instructions to do so and she herself would never leave a patient's file lying around on her desk.

Especially not *that* file...

Leaping to her feet she quickly rifled through all the hanging files – perhaps she had simply misfiled it – but that hope was soon dashed. A check of the other drawers drew a similar blank as did a general search of both rooms. Finally sinking into her desk chair she forced herself to accept the unthinkable, someone had taken the file. Someone had been in that office earlier and for no other reason than to remove that one file. Who could it be?!!

Feldman? Betty, perhaps bribed by someone but, again, who? And why? There were no signs of a break in, she had checked for signs of that, so either someone had a key or the thief was particularly skilful.

A sudden thought had her blood run cold. The FBI! The government would have those skills and the daily papers were full of spies being caught by the FBI. And what was Feldman, and by proxy herself, other than a spy.

Forcing herself to be calm, think rationally, she thought it over for several minutes before deciding there was only one thing to do. One chance to save herself. She would have to talk to the Bureau, come clean so to speak but, of course, with just enough spin to distance herself from the others. Yes, she decided with firming resolution, that was the thing to do. Hesitant no longer, she crossed the room to take down a beautifully framed picture that took pride of place on an opposite wall. It was a Van Gogh, a print of A Wheatfield with Cypresses, circa 1889. Painted while an inmate at San Remy asylum for the mentally insane. As a psychiatrist it, all of Van Gogh's later works, held a special meaning for her.

Working quickly she took a letter opener from the desk and slit the brown paper backing to, with some effort extract, the slim manila folder she had secreted there shortly after first being drawn into what she now thought of as the last gamble of a madman. It was her insurance policy detailing everything she knew about The Spear of Wotan as the mission was known then. The file was slim but stiff and a quick calculation had her realise it would not fit into the small clutch bag she had brought with her that morning. Scanning the outer office she found what she had been looking for, a fair sized brown leather bag she sometimes used when planning to do some light shopping on her way home.

Mondays were Betty's day off it being the day Esther normally ran a clinic at nearby Mount Sinai Hospital as well as catching up with academic meetings and also attending to any outstanding practice matters. Subsequently there were no patients scheduled, nothing to stop her from dealing with the issue right away. A search of the phone book had her dialling a downtown number and talking to a friendly sounding female who, after a brief discussion, put her through to Special Agent Brewster's office. Five minutes later Brewster's secretary walked into his office and pointed at his desk phone, 'Why aren't you answering that, once again?'

Putting his paper down with a sigh the G-man scowled up at the infuriating woman now towering over him, arms akimbo and wearing that schoolmistress look he had come to hate. And fear.

'How many times have I told you I don't want to be disturbed when I'm having my morning coffee?'

'Oh for heaven's sake!' she snapped back, 'you're for ever on a coffee break. This call might just be important.' Reaching she snatched up the phone, pressed a button and handed it to him firmly.

'What is it?' he asked not bothering to hide the irritation in his voice, clamping a hand over the mouthpiece, 'not another one of those fruitcakes wanting to warn us about a suspicious foreign looking man in a raincoat who was overheard speaking German in a bar?'

'This one is a local psychiatrist, a lady doctor, and she has a rather interesting story. I suggest you listen to her.' And with that she turned on her heels and strode out, collecting an overflowing ashtray in the process and closing the door behind her. Stupid idiots! If only they had women running the place things would go so much smoother.

Back behind her own desk she dialled a number from memory and found herself speaking to Agent Rusty Miller who had been at work at his desk one floor down. 'Come upstairs,' she said while studying her nails, deciding a fresh coat of that nice new red she had picked up at Macy's earlier might be in order, 'He'll be calling for you in about ten minutes.'

'How can you be so sure?' Rusty laughed as he reached for his jacket draped over the back of a chair. He liked Zelda although she was probably too old for him. Had been thinking about her lately.

'It's hardly rocket science,' she sighed hanging up.

Ten minutes later he found himself sitting across the desk from a weary looking Brewster who asked how far he had gotten with the Berko... Berko... The atomic spy case.

'Benkenlitz,' Miller said helpfully, shifting uncomfortably in his chair under the baleful eye of the chief. 'So far nothing definite, sir. I have checked out Hanford and have almost finished going through the list at Oak Ridge. So far nobody with that name or anything like it. Also no reports from our men on the ground at those facilities of anything suspicious.'

Seeing the look of displeasure on the chief's face he hastened to add, 'There was one incident in the last few days, sir. One of the couriers from Hanford was confronted by a man who wanted to snatch the bag he was carrying down to Los Alamos. The local police thought it was just a ---'

'What the hell are you talking about, Miller. What couriers?'

'An army lieutenant, sir. Blocks of uranium are transported from Hanford down to Los Alamos in satchels attached to the wrist of these officers who are armed and travel by train down to New Mexico.'

He was about to explain further but Brewster was fast losing interest, wearily dismissing the issue with a wave of a hand.

'This just came in,' he said, tossing a scribbled note across the desk. 'A lady, a shrink by the name of Esther Stern, phoned to say she has vital information about a security risk at one of our top secret nuclear weapon facilities. Someone she had been treating is working there as a spy. She wouldn't give a name but wants to meet in person.'

'This could be the break we need, chief,' Miller said excitedly as he scanned the note. 'Central Park?' he frowned, 'she wants to meet in the park, who not here?'

'She's afraid of being followed, reckons her own life could be in danger if she's spotted talking to us. She's got some papers that'll help us.'

Miller nodded, this was exciting stuff. The reason he had joined the Bureau! 'Eleven o'clock,' he said, 'she'll be waiting at the carousel off Fifth Avenue.' Glancing at his watch he pocketed the note and reached for his hat. 'I'd better hurry.'

Watching him go, the tall loose limbed figure momentarily darkening the doorway, Brewster sighed. Like a bloody puppy, he thought. A big goofy Spaniel puppy. All eagerness and boundless energy. Had there ever been a time when he had been like that? The thought brought a wry smile to his lips. Yeah, he'd been there, guess they all had. A long time ago, before you realised most cases just turned out to be the kind of bullshit the local cops could have handled if they hadn't been so riddled with corruption or sheer incompetence.

Still, it was good to see these young guys get up and go like that, all the while knowing that sooner or later that fire will burn itself out, just like it always did.

At the secretary's desk Zelda smiled up at Miller while informing him that, unfortunately, there wasn't a car available right away but that she had called for a cab which would be waiting outside. As usual she had been listening in on the conversation. 'Things are looking up,' Miller said returning the smile while nodding in the direction of the office he had just left. 'For once he's not calling the lady a broad or a frail.'

'Classy. She must have made an impression on the old goat,' she sighed. 'Now hurry along, you have less than ten minutes to get to your date.'

'Maybe it's time you and I have *our* hot date?' Miller said over his shoulder and, for once, this unexpected toss away left Zelda speechless.

12

C H A P T E R

'She's leaving now,' the person in the phone booth said as Esther Stern left her office building to, ignoring a roving cab, start walking briskly down the street.

'Stay with her until she's entered the hospital grounds,' the voice at the other end of the line said.

'I don't think she's going to the hospital.'

'Why?' Feldman enquired, 'what makes you think that?'

'She's just turned down a cab and now she's heading down West 75th Street, heading in the direction of the Park.'

'Stay with her,' came the order after a moment's hesitation. 'Is she carrying anything with her?'

'Only a handbag, a big flat one.'

Feldman's mind raced. A big bag. Big enough to conceal a file? Could it be? 'I'm coming right away,' he said urgently, in his excitement momentarily breaking into rapid German. 'I'll wait at the boat pond next to the Metropolitan Museum, at that phone booth we've used before. Call me in fifteen minutes.'

A sudden rain shower had Esther fumble for her umbrella as she waited to cross Sixth Avenue, the traffic slowly picking up as lunch hour drew near. While she waited she scanned the passers by, the usual mix of tradesmen, office girls and off duty servicemen, the sailors especially rowdy with no skirt going unnoticed or unrated. The occasional mother out for a stroll and pushing a pram.

Usual stuff. Finally she was able to reach the sidewalk bordering the west border of Central Park, turning right to head in the direction of the carousel. Dismissing a lewd pass from a drunken sailor with a withering look she turned down one of the walks leading through the park and soon she could hear the music from the ride and the excited chatter and laughing of the children.

Burger watched her go, watched her head for a seat on a park bench close to the steps leading up to the street immediately across from where the lights of the carousel were flashing brightly in the rain puddles, watched as she carefully wiped the wooden bench with a scarf before sitting down and looking around. There was a phone booth fifty yards away and Burger reached it slightly out of breath from the brisk trot. Feldman answered at the first ring.

'She's taken a seat near the carousel at the top end of the Park. It looks like she's waiting for someone.'

'I'm coming,' Feldman said as he left at a brisk walk, turning his coat collar up against the rain that was still sifting and dripping down the brim of his fedora.

At that moment Rusty Miller was stuck in traffic half a mile away and cursing the cabbie under his breath. Christ! New York cab drivers were known for two things, a foul mouth and no respect for traffic rules and he had to find the one that refused to cut a few corners, mount a pavement or two, even when assured his passenger was a government agent and on an urgent mission. So he leaned back against the seat and lit another Lucky Strike and thought about what he was about to discover. Could this just be the lead he knew had to be out there somewhere? The one that would earn him his spurs at Head Office?

It was Burger who saw Feldman approaching first. While standing in the shade of a large oak a short distance behind and to the side of the woman, for all appearances reading a newspaper. Raising a waving arm to alert the fast approaching Feldman Burger pointed towards the seated Stern who was studying a small wristwatch, a frown creasing her brow. Pulling down his hat to shield his face Feldman slowed to a walk and turned away from the path that would shortly have led him into the woman's line of view.

'You got the file I retrieved from the woman's office?' Burger asked when Feldman reached her side.

Out of breath from the fast walk across from the Met Feldman nodded while staring hard at the figure of the woman seated twenty yards away, her back to them. 'Yes. You made sure of not being seen when you broke into her office?'

Not waiting for an answer he wondered out loud what the person of interest could be carrying in the bag she was clutching to her side and why she kept glancing at her watch while anxiously scanning the passers by. 'She's waiting for someone,' Burger stated the obvious, methodically checking the surroundings.

Feldman knew what he had to do, yet he hesitated. During their long partnership, as he liked to think of it, he had grown quite fond of Esther Stern, even fantasized about her while knowing their relationship would always have to be that of puppet and puppet master. Some things in life were *verboten*, She *was* Jewish, after all.

Let Burger do it? For perhaps five seconds he toyed with the idea before deciding no, although well aware of his partner's reputation as an artist with a stiletto, this called for something a trifle more delicate. Bloodwork with a knife tended to be messy and that wouldn't do, not here, not in Central Park with people everywhere. With a sigh he reached into an inside pocket of his raincoat to withdraw a silencer which he proceeded to screw onto the barrel of a small automatic pistol. It was a .22 calibre, an assassin's weapon, and more than adequate for the task in hand.

Standing close to a large rhododendron bush, his back to the stream of pedestrians, his actions went unnoticed as Burger kept watch. A few whispered words of instruction, a minute's pause as they waited for the right moment when the crowd had thinned optimally and with a nod from Feldman they moved out of the shadows and approached the figure on the bench. Burger took up position a few feet behind the bench while Feldman, the automatic hidden under the folds of his raincoat now draped over an arm, strode up to face the woman who was about to die.

'Hello, Esther,' he said softly and as her eyes widened in sudden fright he moved in and squeezed the trigger twice in quick succession. The first missile penetrated the heart, the second, a split second later, slashing through Stern's right shoulder as she jerked violently to one side. Burger, moving with languid ease, leaned over from behind, cheek close to the woman's as if whispering a discreet message in her ear. In reality it was to hide a hand that was ready to clamp around her mouth should there be a cry of alarm.

As Feldman stooped to retrieve the bag he found himself looking into the eyes of Esther Stern even as the light flickered and faltered deep insides those pools of liquid brown. With a shudder he strode quickly away, Burger heading the opposite way while scanning the faces in the crowd, deciding no-one had noticed a thing.

Rusty Miller arrived two minutes later, quickly spotting the woman he was about to meet where she was sitting on a park bench, wearing the hat she had described. Walking quickly over, thankful for the warm scarf he had purchased only that morning, the wind now icy and picking up, he suddenly checked his stride. Something was wrong, a quick survey of the surroundings had him decide it was the figure on the bench that was wrong. The way it sat unnaturally still, leaning slightly to one side, chin lowered onto breast and with a hand resting to one side, palm turned upwards. It had started raining again, the wind driving the heavy drops sideways and in his face and yet, as people all around scurried for cover, umbrellas blossoming like so many brightly coloured poppies in a field, the woman never moved.

Running now, people hurriedly making way, looks of alarm on their faces, he reached the bench a shout dying on his lips as he saw the widely staring sightless eyes and, as he knelt down to fumble for a pulse, the very red blood now seeping through the front of her coat and running down the outstretched arm, a small pool forming. Glancing wildly around for any sign of an assailant Miller realised with a sickening certainty that the case had suddenly gone from rookie routine to red hot to ice cold.

He was about to straighten up, call for help, when he noticed something on the surface of the bench. It was next to the index finger of the bloodied hand, a sign of sorts. Squinting to get a better look as the rain proceeded to wash the blood away, he realised it was writing. The dead woman had tried to write a message in her own blood. There was what looked like an "a" and an "l" and possibly another "a" and, could it be, yes! A definite "m" followed by a half circle ending at the tip of a finger from which life had ebbed away.

"Alamo?" Was that it? Clearly it was a desperate message but of what? The name of the killer, perhaps a half completed name? Other possibilities came to him as he carefully undid the front of her coat to stare at the two closely grouped wounds, both quite small and either a stiletto or a small calibre bullet. The Alamo, could that be it? No, meaningless, dismiss. And then it struck him just as the first bystander, by now there were half a dozen gathered to stare in stark horror, began shouting loudly and waving at a police cruiser going by.

Los Alamos. The secret nuclear facility at Los Alamos, New Mexico. That was what she was trying to tell him.

13

CHAPTER

'Force six,' Oberleutnant Dietrich shouted, 'hardly a storm, *Herr Standartenführer!*' They were running on the surface, heading into the teeth of the northwesterly, the apparent wind effect enough to drop a man's core body temperature down to dangerous levels within a matter of minutes where they were huddled together on the exposed bridge of the U boat.

'How long before we're there?' Jaeger asked, shouting as his voice was snatched away by the gale.

'All depends on how much surface running we can safely do,' the captain shouted, 'This is a new Type XXI boat, almost twice as long as the older U boats and, with its streamlined hull, twice as fast underwater at more than sixteen knots. Surfaced and in calm seas we can do twenty five knots.' Adding, with a bitter laugh, 'Almost as fast as a destroyer! But that is also if a patrolling Catalina doesn't spot us first!'

Doing the mental calculation Winter, who was by now, after seventy two hours at sea about as miserable as could be, concluded there was up to another week to go. The thought left him feeling more nauseous than ever.

Anxiously scanning the ominous grey skies, now shrouded in a sea mist, while straining for even the slightest sound of an approaching aero engine, the men on the conning tower chewed over this less than savoury possibility, collectively deciding that in the scope of things, it wasn't worth worrying about.

Wrapped in a bulky seaman's coat over a thick sweater, both borrowed from a crewman, Alex Winter had by now lost all sensation in his feet, his hands painful cramping blocks of ice as his breath came in puffs of vapour instantly blown away by the freshening breeze.

At least it was better than down in the depths of the submarine from where they had emerged minutes earlier. After moving out of Wilhelmshaven in the middle of heavy bombardment from seemingly endless rows of Lancasters, some of the explosions raising huge waterspouts within yards of the boat, they had quickly submerged to only many hours later, surface. Winter, who since childhood had never shared his brother's love of the sea and sailing, became aware of an old familiar tingling in his stomach. As the nausea of seasickness rose once more at the back of his throat he swallowed hard and forced himself to lift his gaze to the distant horizon in an effort to overcome the wild rocking motion as they rolled and battered their way through the heavy swells.

As bad as it was up there on that conning tower, icy spray from flying wave crests streaming down his face and stinging his eyes, it was better than down there. Down there they had been running shallow, the big diesels breathing through the snorkel that now towered above their heads. The captain afraid of being spotted by a night fighter preying in the skies above while they were close inshore. Apart from the unbearable stench inside that narrow steel coffin the worst was whenever the snorkel dipped beneath a wave, instantly shutting with the diesels drawing air from inside the confines of the hull, the effect on the human ear excruciating as the pressure dropped.

A pale moon was slowly creeping out between patches of streaky cloud cover bathing the ocean in eerie hues of silver, the flying crests off the tops of the Atlantic rollers vaguely reminding Winter of the flowing manes of galloping horses. It was crowded up in that narrow space, each man only allowed a few minutes of fresh air with a steady stream of crewmen lining up at the ladder as they impatiently awaited their turn. At a signal from the captain Winter followed Jaeger down the ladder and through a narrow passage to a small lounge where a warm cup of tea could be had.

It was hot down there and he pulled off the coat and gloves tossing it to one side as numb hands eagerly clasped around a mug of the steaming drink. Raising his eyes over the cup to meet those of Jaeger he wondered for the umpteenth time what it was that made that owner of the sardonic smile tick.

'Judging by the slightly greenish tinge on those fine aristocratic features I gather we are not feeling altogether well, Major?'

Could that be it? Winter wondered. A deep seated resentment of the privileged classes? Was that why this intelligent man had become a Nazi? In that case, what had driven his own father down that path? Dismissing the thought with a weary shake of the head, he settled back against the soft cushions of the bunk as his mind drifted back to the events from that, now seemingly distant, morning when he had been ushered into the Führer's bunker.

Heavily laden with crates of assorted ammunition loaded at Seelow the Junkers landed fast and hard on an airstrip hastily prepared on a public street near the centre of Berlin. Slewing violently to a halt mere yards from the wrecked remains of a tank panic driven soldiers were desperately trying to haul away, Jaeger and Winter were the first off the plane followed by two senior Wehrmacht officers that had been summoned to whatever remained of army headquarters.

Thankful to stretch out after the cramped ride Winter accepted a cigarette from Jaeger, turning slowly to survey their surroundings as he drew in the nicotine. It was foul Russian tobacco and after a coughing fit he ground it underfoot. What he saw was utter devastation, a once proud city fast being reduced to a smouldering heap of rubble. A few blocks away he could make out the shell of the Reichstag, a building he had visited on a long ago trip with his father and now little more than a defiant symbol of a defeated nation awaiting its fate.

A car was waiting and as they weaved their way through the rubble strewn streets scattered groups of civilians and soldiers were seemingly aimlessly picking their way through the ruins. There was a lull in the shelling and in the uneasy silence he could hear people calling out to one another as a dog barked somewhere close by. A pall of smoke and fine dust hung over the city quickly settling on his clothing and coating his dry lips as he wondered when last he had eaten, deciding he wasn't hungry anyway.

Turning into Vosstrasse and approaching the bunker near the Reichstag there were more soldiers about, many wearing the SS runes and several military police, the silver gorget plates on their breasts gleaming in the pale afternoon sun. After a brief challenge from the guards they drove down the ramp to the basement parking and seconds later were whisked into the maze of corridors and rooms that was the front bunker. Soldiers were squatting everywhere, many sleeping, the few lacklustre eyes that were raised to study the newcomers reddened with fatigue. The place was damp, moisture on the walls in places and there was a smell Winter found hard to place. The smell of fear, perhaps?

At the entrance to the afterbunker, a few steps down, to Winter's mind allowing for even more concrete between the hierarchy and whatever ordnance the enemy could come up with next, they were met by Major General Mohnke, head of the Führer's bodyguard section who personally vetted all new arrivals to the Reich's inner sanctum. The tiny sparsely furnished room was crammed with SS officers and all looked up as Mohnke rose from behind his desk when the guard at the door announced the arrival of the small party. Scowling, he held out a hand to scrutinise Jaeger's orders when a soft voice at the door had everyone lapse into instant silence.

'No need to trouble yourself, my dear Mohnke. I have been expecting the *Standartenführer* and the Major. This way please, gentlemen.' The order – *Reichsführer* Heinrich Himmler was unfamiliar with the concept of requests – was punctuated with the soft apologetic chuckle Winter remembered with icy clarity from a childhood that now seemed a lifetime away. The effect on the room was electrifying, instantly gone was any sign of weariness amongst those gathered there as the general mumbled an apology of sorts, largely ignored as Himmler was already leading the way down the corridor at a brisk pace.

As they wove their way past a series of offices with uniformed female secretaries scurrying about amidst the sounds of a generator somewhere mixing with the aromas from a hidden kitchen, Winter marvelled at how little the man in the gleaming black uniform had changed. The war that had aged them all beyond their years seemed to have left no mark on the Reichsführer, the full features as youthful as ever, the spring in his step even more energetic if that had been possible.

Here, Winter mused, if ever there was such a thing, was a true war lover. The thought made him shudder.

Only vaguely aware of the eyes on them as they passed through a larger meeting room of sorts, the place crammed with enough brass to command several armies if only such armies still existed anywhere except in the crazed mind of a madman, Winter found their party halted at a steel door by a tall SS captain who, after a brief discussion with Himmler, opened the door to usher them through.

'Heil Hitler!' someone barked and instinctively Winter found himself saluting, one man amidst a sea of outstretched arms and snapping heels. The reception room doubled as a small lounge and they were all there, Bormann, Goebbels, Goering, Fegelein and several others with familiar faces but names that had already slipped his mind. Yesterday's men, already dead but not knowing it. Or did they? All smiling and studying the newcomers with interest. All except Martin Bormann, the Führer's secretary, who was studying Winter with hooded eyes, a slight frown creasing his forehead.

At first Winter did not notice the figure seated behind the desk, his attention drawn by the German Shepherd that rose from the carpet and came over to greet him, tail wagging. Instinctively he stretched out a hand to pat the animal, the most normal creature he had seen all day.

'Blondi likes you,' a voice said as all conversation instantly died down, 'She's a very good judge of character.'

It had been more than ten years since Winter had last met Adolf Hitler, at that time an occasional visitor to the family home. The man who rose unsteadily to move around the desk had aged beyond imagination. Bowed and moving with difficulty the uniform seemed a size too big, especially around the collar. The now familiar haircut was there as was the clipped bottle brush moustache and not a gray hair in sight but the dark eyes were lustreless, the voice hinting at a deep seated weariness. Winter could not help noticing how, surrounded by a sea of decorous uniforms decorated with myriad insignia of rank and medals, the Führer's own uniform was almost Spartan. Light brown jacket worn over a neatly pressed white shirt and dark necktie, the solitary military emblem an Iron Cross worn outside the left breast pocket.

There was no doubt however as to who was in charge in that little room which, to Winter's admittedly tired mind, resembled more and more a crowded stage scene from a Wagnerian opera. The Ring des Nibelungen perhaps.

Crazy Horse he thought, the Indian warrior chief who espoused the elaborate bonnets worn by others, never had more than a feather or two in his hair. Didn't have to prove anything. With an effort he shook off the image and took the hand offered to him, working a smile into the effort. The flesh was soft and cold and Winter was aware of the slight tremor, wondered about the other hand kept tucked behind the man's back.

'An honour, *mein Führer!*' he heard himself say, bowing slightly at the waist as he had seen the others do.

'Excellent! Your mother, things are well, I trust?'

Casting his mind back to the demoralising visit to the family home (was it only an hour ago?) Winter strove to project a positive note, 'Very well. Thank you, *mein Führer*'

'Good, good.' Momentarily lost in thought, Hitler raised his gaze to look at Winter again, the voice suddenly stronger, focused. 'You have been chosen to go on a vitally important mission for Germany. A mission that will take you into the midst of the American enemy and will place us in a strong position to face the great challenge now upon us.'

Uncertain if this stunning statement required a response Winter searched for words and was rescued by a woman who unexpectedly entered the room through a door he presumed led to the Führer's private quarters. Eva Braun took scant notice of all eyes now turned on her, a fleeting look of puzzlement crossing her youthful features as she noticed Jaeger and Winter whose somewhat battle scarred uniforms stood out from the pristine refinement surrounding. Dismissing the thought with a shrug she held out what looked like a treat for the dog and all watched as Blondi dutifully followed her into the other room before the door was shut.

There was a moment's uncomfortable silence then Hitler turned to Himmler, 'Perhaps you had better explain, Heinrich,' he said as he sank back into the padded chair behind the desk, swivelling to stare at a landscape portrait on a wall. It was of an idyllic alpine landscape, Bechtesgaden Winter thought. Memories of happier times.

Turning to focus on Himmler he strove to marshal his thoughts. Fatigue was fast setting in now and he had to force himself to concentrate, the man's soft voice not easy to follow as it was. Standing beside him he was aware of Jaeger's gaze on him, a question behind those hard to fathom eyes. Concentrate!

'... Norsk Hydro's destruction three years ago set back our own nuclear weapons program due to the shortage of heavy water for the reactor. You brother's mission has become even more important now, more than just passing on information regarding the progress of the Americans on their Manhattan Project. It has become clear that they are about to test the first such bomb and this, we believe, is our chance to capture that weapon. In our hands it would provide a powerful bargaining tool when it comes to negotiating terms with the Americans.'

As always Himmler was careful not to suggest any consideration of a "surrender," that would be sure to send the Führer into another of his rages. "Negotiating terms" sounded so much better.

Winter's head was spinning and as he took an involuntary step back in the vain hope of finding a chair he felt Jaeger's steadying hand in the small of his back. Jesus Christ! Was he hearing right?! Did these madmen really believe they still had anything left to bargain with, that there was anything more to do than wait for the Horsemen of the Apocalypse to gallop in and end it all?

'Your brother has taken ill from the strain of the massive responsibility and has asked for you ---'

Involuntarily Winter shook his head, only to instantly freeze as he noticed the look in Himmler's eyes. If ever there was a window into hell that was it. *Zu befehl, Herr Reichsführer!*' he managed hoarsely, snapping his heels together like the good soldier he was.

'Good,' Hitler said as he turned back to face the gathering, a lopsided attempted smile sending shivers down Winter's spine. 'Excellent! I know you will not fail Germany!' He had risen from behind the desk again and this time Winter noticed the uncontrollable tremor of the hand held hidden, noticed the fingers twisted in a claw like grip that left them white and bloodless. Turning his head slightly he noted the averted gaze of all present. Some things were better not to notice.

Turning to a hovering aide Hitler motioned the officer to open a flat leather case the colonel had been holding. At a signal from a grinning Himmler for Winter to take a step forward, the Führer took a small gleaming ornament from its resting place on a cushion of blue velvet. It was the Knight's Cross and as the medal was draped over his neck Winter stood frozen in helpless stupor. 'For services to the Reich,' Hitler said as he patted Winter's arm with a shaking hand before slowly sinking back into his chair.

At some unseen signal there was a sudden burst of conversation in the room as those present crowded around to shake Winter's hand. Then he was led out into a large common room where a party seemed to be gathering steam, champagne flowing freely as platters of food was carried in by kitchen staff. In a corner a few couples were dancing to distinctly American sounding music on a gramophone and Winter noticed quite a few of the officers, female secretaries and uniformed clerks were now quite drunk. At irregular intervals they would become aware of muffled explosions from somewhere above, an occasional shell sending a soft spray of dust sifting down to settle on the milling crowd who would quickly resume festivities as if the approaching Armageddon above was little more than a minor distraction.

As he sipped the champagne and exchanged inanities with a floating parade of faces Winter found himself feeling increasingly alienated. Essentially a loner, he had never felt less alone than when alone and it was a relief when a grimly smiling Jaeger rescued him, indicating it was time for them to leave. The Standartenführer had spent ten minutes alone with Hitler and the man's inner circle while Winter was being entertained outside and now clutched a brown briefcase that would appear to bear meaning to whatever their mission was.

Pausing at the top of the steps leading to the higher level front bunker Winter turned to look back at the scene he was leaving behind. So this is how it all ends, he thought with a strange sense of detachment. The glorious dream of the Third Reich, a proud German nation risen from the ashes like the Phoenix, now reduced to a drunken pathetic orgy of doddering old fools and lost souls shouting at the devil as they waited for the final curtain to come down.

'What are you thinking?' Heinrich Himmler asked Martin Bormann where they were standing alone at a far corner of the room while surveying the scene where all semblance of discipline had by now taken flight.

Inscrutable as always Bormann shrugged, 'The Führer always maintained that you cannot understand National Socialism if you don't understand Wagner.'

Himmler nodded sagely, 'And which work exactly did you have in mind?'

'*Götterdammerung*,' Bormann said softly, 'The Twilight of the Gods...'

$$14$$

CHAPTER

It was twenty minutes past two, the afternoon sun pleasantly warm on the back of his neck, when Rusty Miller stepped off the train at Lamy Station. A dozen or so uniformed soldiers disembarked, mainly enlisted men, a sergeant shepherding them towards a waiting army bus. Most of them were pretty young, teenagers really and they were noisily chatting away and Miller had them down as returning from leave. Other passengers numbered several Mexicans including a couple travelling with a small girl in a brightly coloured party dress. The couple were elderly and Rusty thought the girl would be a grandchild. They headed for a battered pickup truck where a man dressed like an extra from a John Wayne western helped the woman and child aboard, tossing their luggage on the back as the old man laboriously climbed onto the loading tray, closing the tailgate behind him. Minutes later the army bus rolled off in a cloud of dust closely followed by the pickup truck and Miller found himself alone on the platform.

A cough made him turn to see the conductor studying him with a bored look as he surveyed the scene for any sign of potential customers. Deciding the man on the platform was a stayer and with no-one else in sight he climbed back on board and, leaning out at arm's length, waved a flag which was a signal for the engineer to get moving. The expression on his age worn features said I hope someone's coming for you, buddy. It's a long walk to town.

Setting down the battered suitcase to ease off his jacket Miller looked the place over. Little more than a siding with a single platform and token attempt at a covered shelter of sorts it was for some unfathomable reason the main station for those travelling to and from Santa Fe, twenty miles away. A short distance away were a few scattered dwellings and a canteen which had smoke drifting from a stovepipe chimney but he had eaten a sandwich bought through the train window at one of the many stops and the hip flask in his pocket still had some rye. Running a hand through his hair and replacing his hat after dusting it off he surveyed the surrounding landscape.

The New Mexico desert stretched out all around him for as far as the eye could see. Flat as a biscuit with rolling hills on the horizon and an endless sea of yucca bush and small piñon pines scattered in between. At that hour the air was still, allowing sounds to travel far, and he heard the car approaching long before it pulled up, the driver leaning out the window as he worked the horn.

Miller glanced around, seeing no-one else decided it had to be for his attention. Shrugging he hefted his suitcase and strolled over.

'Meester Miller?' the driver, by appearances an Indian with possibly Mexican mixed in, enquired, pointing a finger at Miller to avoid any misunderstanding as to whom he was addressing.

'Let me guess,' Miller said wearily as he pulled open a rear door of the ageing Buick to toss in his suitcase, 'you're the taxi I asked for.'

'*Señor?*'

'Never mind. Yes, I am Miller. I'm going to the La Fonda Hotel, Santa Fe. Know where it is?'

'*Si*, on the plaza. I take you.'

There was a meshing of gears and with a lurch they set off, the ancient suspension groaning as they negotiated the rough track that served as the main road into Santa Fe. Along the way they passed a small party of Indians squatting next to the road seemingly in the middle of nowhere but apparently known to the driver as a desultory wave was exchanged. The men looked like ranch hands with their cowboy shirts and broad rimmed hats while the women were in rawhide with colourful Indian blankets wrapped around. Thick black hair was worn plaited and turquoise and silver jewellery showed in places. One, an old woman, had painted markings on her forehead and cheeks. Joe, Miller had since learned his name, did not deem it necessary to slow down, leaving the party motionless as clouds of fine dust billowed around them.

Like a tableau, Miller thought, a still portrait of a world most Americans probably likened to the Wild West and long gone.

The small plaza was deserted as they pulled up outside the adobe entrance to the hotel, most onlookers having retreated to the shadows of the surrounding shaded shopfronts to escape from the baking heat of the day. Heat waves were shimmering off the metalwork of parked cars and from somewhere inside the building came the sounds of music and laughter. Surveying his surroundings as Joe retrieved his luggage Miller decided he could be on a film set, what with the Indians squatting in the deep shadows of an oblong building's long veranda, backs against the wall and trinkets for sale displayed on blankets at their feet, uncurious eyes settling for a moment on the lanky newcomer before fading back into unfocused ennui. Indian blankets, pottery and trinkets displayed everywhere with no buyers in sight. A mangy dog with its ribs showing looking him over before it too flopped down in the shade and dozed off.

Noticing Miller's interest in the scene Joe explained, 'Every morning many Indian come to sell, too many for places by the wall. They draw tickets and the ones with a number get spot on wall. Others go home, sometimes many miles. You lucky to have ticket you sit all day, no lose spot.'

'What building is that?'

'Is Governor's Palace. Long time ago my people get angry and attack building, kill all inside.' He shrugged, 'then soldiers come and take back, kill many Indian.'

'Your people, Navajo?'

Joe nodded somewhat glumly, 'White man has been sneaking up on us long time now.'

There seemed nothing to say to that and, paying off the taxi driver, Miller went inside and, pausing for a moment to adjust his sight to the cool darkness, located the small reception desk behind which a middle aged woman was watching him.

'Afternoon, I'm Rusty Miller. I trust you have a room booked for me?' Raising his hat he placed it on the counter as she studied the book before reaching a key off a board behind the desk. It seemed to be the only key there.

'Sign here,' she said listlessly, shoving the register across. 'A week's rent has been payed in advance.' She droned on about the place's facilities and house rules but Miller's attention had been drawn by the smiling man in the light grey suit who had sidled up and was extending a hand.

'Hank Meads. Head Office has asked me to show you around, make sure you have everything you need.'

Thanking the receptionist for the room key and clutching a copy of the local newspaper he retrieved from a nearby lounge chair Miller asked Meads to give him five minutes while he dropped his suitcase in his room and he would be right back to join him for a much needed drink.

The room on the second floor was small but comfortable and looked out on a steeple roofed church across a small parking lot. Noticing his interest the bellhop explained that it was the Loretto Chapel that housed the miraculous staircase, a tourist attraction. The look of gleeful anticipation on the youngster's clean features prompted Miller to ask the obvious as he handed over a few dollars, 'Miraculous staircase?'

'The completed building was not large enough for the usual staircase to the gallery. Then along comes this visitor, a carpenter, and builds a spiral staircase!'

'Truly a miracle,' Miller agreed working at keeping the irony out of his tone while wondering how many more "miracles" he was doomed to encounter in what was hopefully going to be a short stay.

After splashing water in his face and using a toothbrush he took the creaking elevator down and followed Meads to a secluded corner of a small lounge where a hovering waiter was sent off with an order for two beers. After a satisfactory glance at each other's IDs, standard Bureau practice when out in the field, Meads proceeded to bring Miller up to speed. 'There's normally two of us in town, the other guy, Jackson, is currently up in Virginia briefing the bigwigs at HQ. You'll be the third and hopefully we can keep you under cover so to speak while you're here.'

'Under cover? You mean it's known about town that the two of you are FBI?'

Meads' reply was lost as they were interrupted by the arrival of their drinks and Meads smiled up at the Indian waiter as he set the beers down. There were no accompanying glasses and Rusty had been around the south long enough to know none were needed. 'Thanks, Juan. Bring us some refills in about twenty minutes, will ya?'

Turning back to Miller he raised his beer in salute and took a long deep pull before setting it down with a sigh of satisfaction. 'Mother's milk. Here's the picture, Jacko and I have been stationed here now going on six months. Initially we passed as tourists but after about three weeks and a few sessions of questioning the locals the penny sort of dropped. No, I think the town pretty much has us pat. Which may explain why the boss sent you down. Would have been nice to let us know exactly what you're doing here, though.'

'Your brief is to monitor any suspected spies, right?' Miller said, ignoring the question for the moment.

'Yep. Fuchs mainly. One of the scientists up on The Hill. A known Commie and someone we suspect is passing secrets on to the Russians. The project chief, Oppenheimer himself, is under suspicion but no proof as yet on either of them. So we watch and we wait for any sign of a leak.' Patting his pockets for a cigarette Meads lit up and leaned back in the easy chair, blowing a series of smoke rings at the ceiling. 'Problem is we aren't allowed on The Hill. That's where they all live, the scientists. Security there is provided by the military and we have no jurisdiction. So we hang around town and watch them when they come into town which is mainly weekends and often to this hotel. They have Sundays off, something to do with Oppenheimer's religion I suspect – he's a weird one, Hindu or Buddhist some say – and that's when this place gets really busy.'

'How many people are living up on this Hill?' Miller asked, pushing an ashtray across the scarred top of the coffee table.

'About four thousand, including the military security detail, the scientists and technicians as well as secretaries and WACS. Quite a few of the scientists have their wives living up there as well, even kids. When the project first started, back in 1943, there were only a handful of them up there, living in dormitories that formed part of an old ranch school that was situated up there. Since then the military have built a whole town, I believe, but apart from a movie theatre there's still no real entertainment on site and hence they flow into town whenever they get the chance. Same applies to the soldiers.'

'Hmm. What about their mail? Do you monitor it?'

'Some. The private stuff. Anything remotely to do with the project gets censored by the military who get to see all outgoing mail before we do. Different story with incoming stuff though. Whoever is spying up there isn't getting it out by mail or phone. We have a tap on the lines.'

Miller nodded knowingly, normally a phone tap would take an order from a federal judge but the FBI was a law onto itself and with a war on they got cut plenty of slack.

'What about the townspeople, do they know what's happening up there?'

Meads shook his head, 'Uh uh, don't think so. Lots of speculation, of course, but the prevailing thought is that new technology is being developed and tested, perhaps something like the V2 rocket that has been falling on London or more powerful explosives for use by the bombers who use a large part of the desert further south as a bombing range.'

'How close to The Hill can outsiders get?'

'Los Alamos is on top of a large mesa, flat topped hill in Mexican, and about two hour's drive from here. Lots of canyons leading off the mound, some ending blindly, many used for testing of explosives. A lousy unsealed and winding road with lots of trucks, not the kind you want to travel at night. You can get right up to the gates, a patrolled security fence surrounding the place. I'm told there's a second, inner fence around the so-called Technical Area where the actual project is happening.

They paused as the waiter arrived with their next round. The beers were icy cold and dripping moisture and Miller found himself slowly relaxing as the golden liquid found its way down to where he was feeling the first stirrings of hunger. 'What about these scientists?' he asked, reaching for a handful of peanuts the waiter had brought in a small bowl.

'Foreigners almost to a man. Germans, Poles, English, Danish, you name it. Even some Russians, believe it or not. Many of them Jewish refugees. A handful of female scientists too but, apart from the wives, they're mostly American.'

'Sounds like the Tower of Babel.'

Meads laughed, 'You could say that. I'll point them out to you when they come in here. Most of them do, I think it's the wives mainly who want to come to town. Some of them have been living up there since the start of the project and I reckon they're getting sick of it.'

The Project, Miller thought. Never a word about the bomb and definitely never a word like "atom" or "nuclear." But somehow he thought the locals knew a lot more about what went on up on that mysterious Hill than what he had been told. On his way down he had wracked his brain as to what would be the best way to approach this. What did he have to go on? A mysterious scientist by the name of Benkenlitz who nobody had ever heard of. A word scribbled in the blood of a dying woman on a park bench and rapidly washed away by the rain. Alamos, at least that was what he thought it was.

The woman a New York psychiatrist who never got around to disclosing how she knew this. A subsequent search of her downtown office revealing signs of an earlier break in according to forensics who had examined both the door locks as well as the filing cabinets. No clue though as to any patient files being removed, the backroom boys still painstakingly going through those files with others doing discreet enquiries as to the patients listed there.

'Mr Miller? Mr Rusty Miller?' The young man, a uniformed Army captain pronounced the "Rusty" hesitantly, unsure if this was a term of familiarity or really the man's name. He was paused ten feet away and had been scanning the room where two other groups of men had since taken seats, finally settling on Miller as the most likely person of interest.

'That's me,' Miller replied rising to hold out a hand.

'Captain Mike Fiorentino, from Los Alamos. I'm your liaison up at The Hill.'

'Pleased to meet you,' Miller said with a smile, turning to introduce Meads who was now studying him with an ill concealed look of incredulity.

'If it's OK I'd like to take a trip up to The Hill now, Lieutenant. I take it you have a car outside?

'Yessir. Parked in front of the hotel.'

'Excellent. I just need to make a quick pit stop,' he nodded in the direction of the front desk, 'something to clear with the management. I'll join you outside in five minutes.'

As they watched the retreating back of Fiorentino Meads raised his hands in a gesture of exasperation, 'What the hell?!'

Miller laughed, 'Meet the man from the Fissionable Materials Branch of the Federal Internal Auditor's Office. I'm here to audit the books, make sure all nuclear materials produced up north and transported down here have been properly accounted for.

Regardless of how top secret this might all be, there still has to be proper accounting, especially in wartime.'

'Well blow me down with a ... Brewster arranged this?'

'Sure did. Reckoned sending another FBI agent wasn't going to hack it. Which means you and I have just met over a beer and, at best know each other from some distant meeting, I think it was at a ball game in L.A.'

'I've never been to L.A.'

'Neither have I. Perfect.'

And with that he strolled out, pausing at the desk to pick up a tourist's brochure, before stepping into the bright sunlight where Fiorentino was waiting behind the wheel of an olive military pool Ford.

Sinking back into the easy chair and calling for another beer Meads shook his head and allowed himself a small smile. 'Bloody Federal Internal Audits Office! Was there even such a thing? Still, he had to admire the guile of the devious old bastard in that dusty little office in New York. It was worthy of a toast.

15

CHAPTER

Ultra XB 1879/Dolphin 8. The duty officer, a naval commander, read the transcription through twice while savouring a biscuit dunked in a cup of tea. Decoded barely twenty minutes ago the intercepted Enigma signal was sent from U2512 and monitored by both US and British Intelligence operated radio stations – collectively known as "Y Service" -- before being relayed to the Government Code and Cipher School where it had taken the cipher clerks less than half an hour to decode. The deciphered transcript was immediately sent by teleprinter to the Submarine Tracking Room located deep underground in the British Admiralty's London "Citadel."

Under the top secret Ultra directive, in the attempt to keep from the Germans the knowledge that their highly sophisticated code had been broken, all intercepted Enigma naval signals were decoded only at the somewhat unimposing Hut 8 at Bletchley Park, deep in the English countryside.

Simultaneously received by several listening stations in Britain, France and the US Atlantic seaboard and utilising aspects of frequency strength and, to a lesser extent radio direction finding methods, the source was determined to be from somewhere in the Caribbean, close to the northern Mexican coastline.

Directed to the German High Command Headquarters, Berlin, It read simply: *Der Elektron ist gelandet.* Elektron has landed.

Reading the short sentence a second time, a look of puzzlement on his features, the commander took his feet off the desk and, calling over a young cipher clerk, asked to be put through to a certain Mr Winn at the Admiralty and in charge of Project Fred, the code name for the Ultra Project. After a short discussion it was decided the intercepted signal merited action and that it be forwarded to the US Naval Intelligence HQ at the State, War and Navy Building on 17th Street NW, a few blocks away from the White House in Washington DC.

Despite the late hour --- 04h00 to be precise – the Vice Admiral in charge of Naval Intelligence was in his office tersely awaiting news of an anticipated Japanese aerial attack on a convoy steaming off the Philippines. Studying the flimsy he reached for a desk telephone and minutes later was speaking to a ranking subordinate who, rudely awakened from a deep sleep, struggled to sound alert and on top of things.

'Sir?!'

'Sorry to wake you, my boy,' the admiral chuckled, 'but something's just come in that puzzles me.'

Instantly awake now the officer's first reaction was news from the Pacific, he asked as much.

'No, this is about an interception by Ultra, a U boat has landed something or someone in the region of the Texas or possibly Mexican coast. Codename "Elektron." U2512. Seems to ring a bell, wasn't that the one that a few nights ago was spotted by a trawler who were surprised that the Nazi boat didn't stop to finish them off with its cannon as they have been wont to do?'

'Yessir. Some three hundred miles off Cape Hatteras. The trawler skipper reported that he only had a brief glimpse in the fog and that the U boat was going at full speed, heading south by southwest, and that despite the fact the Coast Guard had two cutters out there looking for survivors of that tanker that had the fire.'

'Hmm. You don't think this U boat had anything to do with that?'

'Doubt it sir, the tanker did not report a torpedo hit, rather a fire in the engine room. There is something else though ---'

'Oh?'

'Twelve hours earlier one of our long range aerial patrols had spotted a U boat running on the surface heading due south and towards the area where it was spotted by the trawler. It was near dawn, already light, a time when U boats would normally be underwater. It dived the moment it saw the plane and, unfortunately our aircraft was at the end of its patrol and short of fuel. It dropped a few depth charges but was not able to hang around. No debris was spotted.'

There was a few moment's silence as the admiral mulled this over. 'Sounds like a man in a hurry, this U boat captain. A man on a mission of utmost importance.'

'Did you say U2512, Sir?' The officer had been scanning a folder containing recently recorded U boat movements handed to him by a secretary together with a steaming mug of coffee. Not waiting for an answer he went on, a note of excitement creeping into his voice. 'Something interesting here, Sir. We received information from a source in Wilhemshaven, Germany, that this vessel departed that harbour on the evening of April 9th. The source was a dockworker loading the boat and he reckons there's gold bullion on board. Not just that but also the presence of two men, not crew members, both in military uniform. He also mentioned that this boat was bigger than any he had seen before, a new type. We suspect it to be the new prototype XXI, built in Hamburg, with unknown capabilities.'

'Which leaves us with the question, Jack, is this just Nazis leaving a sinking ship, taking their loot with them, or is it a mission against the American people?'

'The war is all but over, Sir. What would the point of such a mission be now?'

There was an audible sigh over the line and the sound of a new voice in the background. 'God alone knows, Jack. Time will tell, I suppose. Better pass on the information to Coast Guard HQ at Maryland, ask them to send a plane out that way, maybe a cutter too. It worries me that this U boat captain is in such a hurry. Doesn't sound like just a getaway run to me. I'll let you get on with it, boy, news from the Pacific coming in now. I'll see you at the morning briefing. And with that the line went dead.

* * *

Two hours earlier, almost two thousand miles southwest, Alex Winter had touched earth for the first time in eight days.

The coarse sand sank away under his feet and for a moment he threatened to fall backwards into the cold Gulf water they had left seconds earlier. Regaining his balance with an effort Winter prepared to follow the dimly outlined form of Jaeger up the steep incline of the beach but he was too late, a rushing wave clawing around his ankles and up to his knees. Cursing softly he clutched the suitcase and tried again, this time gaining the dry higher reaches to join Jaeger who was now scanning the tree line looming against the darkened horizon.

Turning to look back at the sea Winter thought he could just make out the small rubber inflatable where it rose over a white cresting wave, the two crewmen crouched low, the soft hum of the muffled outboard engine coming in snatches as the swells rolled and receded. Of the U boat there was no sign although he knew it was there, waiting to retrieve the dingy and its crew before slipping under the surface on its journey to... where?

Not that it mattered he concluded. Where were any of them headed now that the war was lost, the country in ruins? What was the old saying, for the man who is going nowhere any road will take him there?

Suddenly cold he clutched the thin jacket tightly around his shoulders then set about wiping the sticky sand off his feet and ankles before laboriously struggling to don the socks and shoes he had been carrying and rolling the trouser legs down.

The suit that had been in the small suitcase lying next to him was old and a size too big but whoever had packed it most likely only had a rough idea of the future wearer's measurements. Provided by the Abwehr he thought, or perhaps the Gestapo, it nevertheless had American labels and cut. The nondescript grey felt hat, somewhat battered by a rough passage, was a better fit.

Patting an inside pocket to ensure his falsified documents were still in place he turned to face Jaeger who had produced a pair of binoculars. 'There!' he exclaimed in German before checking himself and changing to English. 'The signal. They are waiting up near that rocky outcrop over on the right. Come!' Acknowledging with three brief flashes of a torch Jaeger reached for his suitcase and led the way.

The going over the sand was hard and both men were panting slightly by the time they reached a firmer rock strewn section and then the first of the undergrowth. A voice was calling softly and minutes later they had gained a small clearing where three men were waiting. They were Mexicans, the leader introducing himself as Ramon without bothering to introduce his two compatriots who stood around scowling, one carrying what looked like a lever action rifle. Winter guessed Ramon at about fifty, the others younger and possibly sons.

'Welcome!' Ramon repeated relieving Jaeger of his suitcase while one of the others took Winter's as the party started up the hillside following an uneven footpath. At the top they rested for a moment and Winter took the opportunity to study the surrounding landscape. It was wild low lying country with here and there a patch cleared for likely farming. Not a light in sight and no sign of others about. The drop off was just south of the Mexican border with Texas and the plan was to trek inland parallel to the Rio Grande border and cross into New Mexico at El Paso, a day's journey by car according to Jaeger's calculation. From there it would be a few hundred miles of all but deserted roads to their destination at Santa Fe.

'Where's the car?' Jaeger asked, glancing around.

Turning Ramon waved and in answer a set of headlights fifty yards away and partially hidden in the shadow of a tree flashed briefly. Peering into the gloom Winter could make out the form of another man in the driver's seat.

Strolling over to the car Jaeger looked it over. It was a battered looking pre-war De Soto, the driver's door creaking audibly as he got out to join the party.

'Seems we have a slight problem here,' he said evenly. 'There's room for maybe five in that car and there's six of us.' With this he turned to face Ramon who was smiling as he held out a hand.

'Not everyone will be leaving, *Señor*. Let's have the money now.' He indicated the leather sling bag dangling from Jaeger's shoulder, adding, 'Please, no monkey business, *Señor*.' What little moonlight there was glinted on something metallic in his hand and Winter decided the odds were in favour of a gun.

No surprise there.

'The agreement was two thousand dollars American,' Jaeger said as he removed the bag, moving slowly while keeping his eyes on the Mexican. 'I have it right here.'

'I think we will just take it all, *Señor,*' Ramon said with an apologetic gesture of the hands, the gun moving in a lazy arc but still covering the two newcomers. To the side someone laughed softly to be silenced instantly by a look from Ramon.

'You are making a mistake,' Jaeger said, his voice soft and steady with something there Winter had last heard at the bridge at Seelow. 'There will be consequences ---'

'You mean trouble from Germany? The war she is over, *Señor*. Sadly you lost.' He raised the gun and pointed at the bag, 'The money.'

Without a word Jaeger held out the leather bag, Ramon taking it. As Jaeger stepped back to rejoin Winter, standing close with his back to him he whispered, *'In my belt, against my back. Take it, now!'*

As Ramon fiddled with the clasps of the pouch, pocketing his gun in the process, Winter's fingers brushed against the cold steel of an automatic nestling in the small of Jaeger's back. Easing it out he wondered if it was chambered, ready to fire and in answer to his thought the other man hissed between clenched teeth, *'Just cock and fire. Now be ready!'*

'What?!'

'Do as I say!'

All eyes were on Ramon now, the young man with the rifle lowering it as they willed the thing to open and spill its riches. With a last effort Ramon yanked it open before staggering back, a cry dying on his lips as he stared at a wildly shaking and clattering insect-like creature emitting a high pitched metallic sound and spilling onto the ground where it raced around on spidery legs.

A split second's stunned silence was shattered as Jaeger, gun in hand, fired rapidly, Ramon and one of the men dropping, the second man's scream ending in a spray of frothy pink bubbles as a bullet ripped through his neck.

'Shoot!' Jaeger shouted as he swivelled to draw a bead on the driver who had spun and was running for the car. Still too dazed to move Winter saw from the corner of his eye the young boy with the rifle bring it up and acting purely on instinct he raised his own gun and fired.

It was a big gun, American Colt automatic he thought, and the impact of the heavy missile spun the young man away into the night like little more than a prize target at a funfair shoot. Still moving in seemingly slow motion Winter traversed to see the driver slump forward and crash into the hood of the car as Jaeger shot him in the back twice in quick succession.

As suddenly as the tranquility of the night had been shattered, as quickly the eerie silence returned. There was the smell of cordite in the still air and a loud singing in Winter's ears as he stared numbly down at the heavy gun in his hand.

He had just shot a man! Killed a young boy!

Sweating freely he stared numbly down at the ground suddenly so close now as he retched again and again until there was nothing left in his stomach. With great effort he climbed back on his feet, the nausea of a moment earlier replaced by a dizziness and a buzzing in his ears.

After a moment's disorientation he became aware of a hand on his shoulder, 'Good work,' Jaeger said as he retrieved the Colt from Winter's unresisting hand. During the encounter Jaeger had reverted to speaking German and surveying the carnage surrounding them Winter for just a moment thought he was back on the Eastern Front with men dying like flies on a desolate godforsaken landscape. He watched in silence as the other man checked the Colt before returning it to the back of his belt, the other handgun already nestling in its shoulder holster. Then Jaeger stooped and picked up the object that had jumped from the bag and Winter saw that it was a mechanical toy, a wind up brightly coloured beetle.

'*Kleine Hansie,*' Jaeger said noticing his companion's flabbergasted stare as he rewound the key on the toy before carefully restoring it to the bag. 'A good luck charm,' he added, 'from my wife. I carry it always.'

Not so lucky for the Mexicans Winter thought numbly, a distant part of his brain registering that this was the first time Jaeger had mentioned a wife.

Still kneeling Jaeger said over his shoulder, 'You look a bit shaken there, *Herr* Winter. I would have thought a man who earned the Iron Cross at Stalingrad would have seen killing before?'

'It wasn't like this ---'

Rising Jaeger nodded, 'I know. Still, it's good to know the Wehrmacht at least taught you to shoot straight. Come.' And with that he led the way to the car, motioning Winter to bring along his suitcase.

Passing by Ramon they hesitated as the wounded man stirred and raised himself on an elbow to squint up at them. He was mumbling something and blood was around his lips and streaming down the corner of his mouth. Without ceremony Jaeger rolled him onto his back to rifle through his pockets. A variety of items were glanced at and tossed aside before he rose to look at Winter, shaking his head. 'Just checking to make sure he doesn't carry any papers about tonight's rendezvous, anything to hint at our presence. Nothing.'

'Then how do you explain the dead bodies and the missing car?'

'It's just Mexico,' Jaeger said with a shrug as he hefted his suitcase, 'Nobody cares.'

'Pliss, *Señor...* Water...' Ramon had rolled back to face them, a pleading look in his eyes, the voice barely audible. Without looking at the man sprawled at his feet Jaeger sighed and produced the Walther, shooting him once between the eyes. Then, with a silent gesture, he led the way to the car, dragging the lifeless form of the driver off from where it was draped against the hood, the body sagging to the ground like just another bag of potatoes.

The car started first go and then they were bumping along a winding road leading down to the valley and to where the lights of a small village could now be seen.

They rode in silence and after a while Jaeger, who was driving, said, 'It upsets you, what happened back there. The killing thing?' He was speaking softly, his features lined by the dashboard lights.

Winter thought it over before replying, 'Yeah, it bothers me. The killing thing.'

For once Jaeger's tone was sober, even reflective, as he replied, 'When I was very young we didn't have much. I watched my father work himself to death in a job he hated, listened to his bitter complaints how all his hopes and dreams turned to nothing. Watched my mother grow weary and old as she lived with a man that had stopped living years before, caring for an only child that was somehow different from other children. A child with perhaps potential but a child who would never be given the chances in life others would have. So I grew up with little expectations for a life other than my father's but, even at a young age, I promised to myself that if ever I found that one talent that sets me apart from the crowd, I would be true to that talent.'

Winter knew what he meant, knew what he would say next, asked nevertheless. 'Then you discovered that talent,' he said softly as he searched for his cigarettes, lighting one from the car's dashboard lighter.

'When the Party came to power and *Reichsführer* Himmler formed the *Waffen SS* I knew I had found my calling. I have been true to my talent.'

Leaning back against the seat Winter smoked and thought about it, decided that in his own dark way this enigmatic man was right, killing was a talent and he was in the company of a very talented man indeed.

'You have a gift too, Major Winter,' Jaeger said conversationally as he skilfully negotiated a sharp bend that sent the big car skidding sideways before being wrestled back onto the narrow track.

Winter said nothing.

'I read your file. You earned the Iron Cross at Stalingrad, crossing the Volga at night, alone on a small motor boat to rescue several soldiers trapped on the other side. In the exchange of fire you were severely wounded yet you managed to bring five men back to the German lines. Men who would otherwise have ended up being prisoners or even shot. One thing the file doesn't say is why? Why you felt you had to do it. Why you insisted on going alone when you knew the risks.' He looked at Winter, the now familiar sardonic smile back in place.

'Why, Major Winter?'

Winter shrugged, shivered. It was suddenly cold in the car and the heater did not seem to work. 'They were my men,' he said at length. 'We had been together for two years and they trusted me and I trusted them. The mission was to try and bring a line across the fast flowing river to enable a landing party to cross over quickly for a planned flanking operation. I was on the German side supervising when the Russians discovered the party and all hell broke loose. They were my men. I had to go.'

After a while he added, 'It got me out of the *kessel* of Stalingrad when I was flown out to a hospital in Krakow. Less than two weeks later the 6th Army was encircled and all those men, the ones still alive, are now Russian prisoners. God help them ---'

'And there we have your gift,' Jaeger said, his eyes back on the road where an intersection was heralded by a truck rolling past, its dim headlights lighting up trees on the far side.

'My gift,' Winter said laughing bitterly, 'what is that my dear Jaeger, staying alive?'

'Loyalty. The simple loyalty of a brave man. That is your gift.'

16

CHAPTER

It was nearing midday when they were ready. The corporal in charge of the platoon ensuring no unauthorized personnel were on site and everyone accounted for gave the all clear. Satisfied that his recording instruments were activated and reading Berkowitz signalled that he was set. All eyes turned to the assembled explosive device where it rested on a sturdy trestle one hundred and fifty yards away, an assortment of cables trailing off to various monitors ensconced behind solid cement blocks surrounding the device.

They were in a small closed canyon off the back of the mesa at a point furthest away from the west gate entrance to The Hill. Earlier that morning the explosive lenses had been carefully packed at the S Block facility before being transported down the canyon to be assembled around the cavity where the plutonium core would sit come the Trinity test. That cavity was now packed with sensors connected to the recording devices on the outside. The whole contraption measured six feet in diameter and, as usual, the "jacket" containing the explosive lenses was held in place by seemingly haphazardly applied strips of adhesive tape.

The overhead sun was baking now, the chilling effect of the morning fog long gone and Berkowitz cursed himself for leaving his hat in the car. Absently he accepted a mug of tea one of the physicists had poured from a thermos flask. It was treacly sweet and hot and paradoxically came with a cooling effect. The warm sensation in his stomach reminded him that he had skipped breakfast that morning, the encounter of the previous day with Eva Buirski-Molnar having left him feeling faintly nauseous.

He had realised it for what it was, the taste of fear. Why?! He thought for the hundredth time, what was the odds? Why did she have to turn up here when he was so close!

'... Dr Berkowitz...?'

'What?' Shaken from his reverie he realised the others were looking at him questioningly.

'Ready,' he said quickly, forcing his mind back to the control panel in front of him.

'Fire!' Joe Jaworski shouted, simultaneously depressing a button switch on a separate control board. One hundred and fifty yards away there was a muffled explosion that sent the remnants of the device ballooning outwards before settling into the raised dust like so many feathers from a shotgun blasted turkey.

'Looking good!' Jaworski shouted as he prepared to lead the way forwards at a brisk pace. The physicist was the only one amongst them with experience of high explosive use in the combat arena and as always Berkowitz found the man's unbound enthusiasm vaguely discomforting. Seated next to Berkowitz the explosives physicist Ted Hall was about to rise and follow when a voice behind them said, 'Mind if I come along? Perhaps you can explain to me what it meant by these "lenses" you guys are forever talking about?'

Not daring to turn around and face the instantly familiar Berkowitz busied himself with taking readings from his monitor while next to him a smiling Hall proceeded to explain how lenses was simply a term borrowed from optics where the explosive charges where shaped and placed in such a way as to focus all their force on a central core much like an optic lens would direct a beam of light. The man not altogether comfortable in the company of ladies he gushed and from the corner of an eye Berkowitz thought he detected a spreading blush.

'How clever,' Eva replied as she stepped up to join the physicist who was leading the way over the uneven terrain. In the passing she flashed a smile and hello to a still seated Berkowitz who, keeping his head down, muttered a reply.

Once they were a safe distance away he raised his gaze to study the retreating form of a woman he once knew, albeit a long time ago in a different world and as another man. She was as beautiful as he remembered her, the long auburn hair, worn loose in their student days and now tied in a bun under the broad rimmed straw hat. The same lithe figure and suppleness of movement that had stirred a strange mix of desire and jealousy inside him all those years ago.

A lifetime ago.

She was wearing a pair of loose fitting corduroy pants tucked into tan leather riding boots and the chequered man's shirt showed off her small firm breasts to good effect. A red bandanna around the neck lent colour and the midday heat had brought a faint sheen to her skin that almost glowed.

Looking down he noticed that his hands were shaking and he quickly placed them on the small field table and reached for his notebook, shoving it into the briefcase by his side. Did she recognise him? He didn't think so, not yet. But he had seen the puzzled look in her face the day before and it was only a matter of time.

He knew that with the level of paranoia now sweeping The Hill, the FBI lurking off site and Captain Fiorentino's suspicious eye forever on all of them, all it would take to unmask him would be for her to enquire about him, hint in a puzzled way that she had seen him before somewhere.

Hastily scooping up his belongings he headed back to his car parked nearby. Time was running out! He would head back to S Block and complete his calculations and then, in the seclusion of his small office, work on the final design for his own gadget, the coffee urn as he liked to think of it all but ready. Did he have enough high explosive? A quick mental calculation had him decide he had stashed away enough baratol but still needed another two sticks of composition B, the faster expanding explosive needed to properly shape the explosive wave.

It had taken him all of eight months to secrete away enough of the substance from the workshop without raising suspicion but now he would have to take risks. For time was running out.

From now on he would be careful, avoid the parties Oppenheimer was forever throwing or the variety shows and movies staged at the entertainment hall. Soon it would be all over, he would have completed his mission and then his handler would arrive to safely get him back to the Fatherland. To a hero's welcome from a nation that had so viciously been targeted by the agents of Bolshevism and moral decay. Yes, a few more days and he would be ready to send the pre-arranged signal, always in the form of the letter to his analyst in New York, who would forward the hidden message to the Argentinean he knew simply as Rex but whom he suspected went by another name.

As always the letter would be censored by whoever read his outgoing mail on The Hill, he suspected the omnipresent Captain Fiorentino, with the incoming mail no doubt passing through the scrutiny of the FBI in Santa Fe.

Aware of the now wearily familiar dull headache building and with it the vague nausea his mind drifted back to that first time he had gone to Oppenheimer telling him about the increasing anxiety that was clouding his mind. Ever intruding thoughts about the fate of his family in some Nazi concentration camp, wondering if his wife, Elsa, was even still alive. How all this was leading to severe depression and how he wished to be allowed to see his analyst in New York, the person who had treated him before he was recruited into the project. And all the while struggling to hide his contempt for this nation of weaklings who did not understand that strength and personal growth came from subjection to a great cause as a people strove towards their rightful destiny as the *herrenvolk*, the undisputed chosen ones.

Oppenheimer sympathetic as always and arranging things with security allowing him to travel to New York for those special sessions.

Leaning back in his chair he closed his eyes, willing the nausea to pass. The pain was more intense now and shrouded in the darkness of his inner eye, far away and growing, he could see the dragon. It was looking at him with its red eyes. Nothing more, just looking.

And waiting.

17
CHAPTER

It was just before dawn of what promised to be another day of suffocating heat when they drove into the border town of Juarez with only the bridge across the Rio Grande between them and El Paso, Texas. Winter was driving, Jaeger dozing in the passenger seat. They had taken turns during the course of the previous day and late the night before had pulled over to snatch a few hours troubled sleep, both by now too exhausted to concentrate for what passed as country roads in Mexico. Along the way they had to refuel twice and if the locals did not quite believe their story of being *turistas,* they certainly believed their American dollars. At the last stop they had managed to locate a small tavern where a hot meal of chilli beans and tacos was to be had, while a mechanic fixed a puncture and managed to procure them an extra spare for an a price just this side of an arm and a leg. Too tired to haggle Jaeger shrugged and paid the man who was kind enough to throw a ragged road map into the bargain.

They had been keen to put as many miles as possible between them and where the dead bodies were by now likely to have been found and the old car was starting to show the strain of being driven hard and fast. It threatened to overheat whenever the winding road forced them to slow down and Jaeger reckoned it was nearing the end of its usefulness. The original plan had been for the Mexicans to deliver them to a point where another party would take over and get them safely across the border while providing transport for the journey to Santa Fe.

That deal was now patently lost and Jaeger admitted he had no idea where the rendezvous was to take place. In fact, word of the shootout might by now have reached the others leading to a hot reception. Then again, as Winter had pointed out, the plan might always have been to kill them on that beach with no further processing planned.

It did not warrant too much thought.

Driving through the still sleeping town they found a truck stop with an all night diner and soon were sitting down to a breakfast of grits and eggs with freshly baked bread and surprisingly good coffee. Discreet enquiries from a group of Mexicans at the next table had confirmed that a bus service was running up to Albuquerque, a sleepy looking waitress obliging with directions as well as times of departure. No need to hurry, they still had plenty of time to catch the nine o' clock bus so how about some tortillas or American pancakes to round off the meal?

An hour later, having confirmed the location of the bus depot, they found what they were looking for. A few street blocks away several small shops fronted on a small plaza and parking lot. At that early hour business was already brisk, several customers heading for parked pickup trucks laden with groceries and fresh produce, the parking lot a busy place with spaces being filled as quickly as they became vacant.

It was the ideal place to lose a car and, with a bit of luck, nobody would investigate for a day or two. All the time they needed. While sitting in the parked car Jaeger took the cash out of the leather pouch and, handing half to Winter, instructed him to deposit it in more than one pocket, to not arouse undue suspicion if they were patted down at the bridge. Who knew what the American practices were in wartime?

At the border post two bored looking US customs officials boarded the bus to check passports. Apart from a few Indians and a small group of rugged looking cowboys who by their loud conversation had been having themselves a time down in Juarez, Jaeger and Winter were the only non-Mexicans on board and this warranted slightly more interest from the border guard. Jaeger had little fear that their fake American passports, courtesy of an expert forger sitting in a small office in Berlin's Abwehr headquarters, would stand up to scrutiny. The real test would be to pass for American citizens. Jaeger's English being limited not to mention heavily accented, it had been that Winter would do the talking.

'You two travelling together?' the fat officer asked as he slapped at a mosquito settling on the back of his neck. He was as wide as he was tall and waddled visibly as he progressed down the aisle. His wheezy voice was disinterested but Winter knew better than to underestimate the man whose small green eyes seemed to miss little.

'Yes, officer. Mr Jaeger and I are holidaying together, we're both from Florida, Fort Lauderdale.' After a moment's hesitation he added, 'Our car broke down in Juarez and it will take a week to fix, a part has to be sent for. So we thought we'd spend the time taking a look at Albuquerque.'

'And Texas,' he added, noticing the frown on the man's broad forehead. He had the distinct impression that no-one went to Albuquerque.

'And Texas, of course,' Winter confirmed.

'What about him,' the man said, nodding at Jaeger, 'lost your voice mister?'

'A cold,' Jaeger replied in a hoarse whisper, 'Sore throat.'

'Hummpf!' He eyed Jaeger for what seemed like an eternity before, with visible reluctance, turning his attention back on Winter who was doing his best to project his law abiding citizen's expression.

'You'll need a rental,' the man said, his eyes narrowing, speculative. 'Ask for Bill Dyson when you get to Albuquerque. Runs Dyson's Garage in the centre of town. He'll fix you up. Tell him Little Joe sent you.'

Jaeger raised his eyebrows, *'Little* Joe?' he whispered.

Winter raised a hand to suppress a cough, discreetly pumping Jaeger in the ribs. His eyes said what the hell are you doing?

'What?' the fat man said, hitching his belt.

'Nothing,' Jaeger said, 'just checking I've got the name right,' adding, after a moment's pause, 'Officer.'

Little Joe grunted and tossed back their passports, Winter managing to rescue them before the items hit the ground. They sat still as the big man slowly traversed his gaze over the rest of the motley crew, the Mexican peasants studiously keeping their collective gaze downcast.

'Hmmph!' Little Joe finally wheezed, turning on his heels to waddle back to the front of the bus where his partner was waiting, a broad smile on his face. As he approached he made a limp wristed signal with a pudgy hand, nodding in the direction of Winter and Jaeger. This evoked a guffaw from his companion who shook his head as he led the way off the bus.

Then, with a grinding mesh of gears and clouds of black smoke, they were on their way, the highway stretching out ahead like a long flat black ribbon. 'I think he takes us for homosexuals,' Jaeger said at length, lighting a cigarette.

'You think?' Winter said wearily, 'two respectably dressed white men travelling together on a long road trip? Now what about that would possibly be suspicious?'

Jaeger snorted and stared down a grinning Mexican across the aisle who quickly looked away. 'Damn *untermenschen!*' he hissed under his breath but Winter had already nodded off.

18

CHAPTER

'I've managed to get you a car,' Fiorentino said, as he placed a steaming mug of coffee on the desk at Miller's elbow. 'One of our pool cars. You'll have to update the log book as you go along, I'm afraid. There's a stack of petrol coupons in the glove box.'

Miller grunted a thank you and absently reached for the coffee. They were seated in the captain's office, a small cramped clapboard box with barely enough space for two desks, a couple of army issue office chairs and a three tier filing cabinet. A small table in a corner housed a pile of military manuals and some loose stationary items. A thin layer of fine dust covered it all and the pages of a file ruffled rhythmically as the languidly revolving blades of the overhead ceiling fan sailed past.

Although the door was shut the sounds of a typewriter in the adjoining secretary's office was clearly audible.

'If you tell me what you're looking for, maybe I could help?' Fiorentino said after studying Miller's silent form for a while.

'How many people are on The Hill now?'

Fiorentino shrugged, 'About four thousand, including the military.'

'How many work directly on the project? I mean scientists, people who would have either intimate knowledge of what is being done, or who would have full access to that information?' He wanted to add, *by the way, just what exactly is the Project?* Deciding that Fiorentino wouldn't tell him even if he knew.

'One hundred and twenty top level scientists, the numbers have grown quite a bit in recent months. Then about the same number of technicians and, of course, a few hundred secretaries and clerks.'

'You do security checks on them all, the scientists?'

'Of course but more than half of the top scientists are foreigners, Germans and Eastern Europeans not to mention a large number of British. There's little doubt that quite a few would be communists, especially the Brits but Oppy argues they're indispensable to the work and with the war costing the lives of God knows how many thousands of our boys every day out there, he doesn't care if they're Martians. As long as he meets his deadline.'

'Which is?'

'Classified.'

'Where is the big man, by the way? It looks like I'll have to meet up with him to get some background on these people.'

There was a knock on the door and at Fiorentino's command a secretary in WACS uniform entered carrying a piled on stack of personnel files. 'Where shall I put these, Captain?'

Fiorentino gestured towards the corner table and asked her to get an orderly to bring in a folding trestle table, space for more files. 'Oh, and get us some more coffee, will you?' Waiting for her to leave and close the door he picked up a pen and sat back idly doodling on a foil of A4 paper. 'You're not really from the Audit Department of the Fissionable Materials Office, are you?'

Well, Miller decided, how long was he hoping to keep up the charade anyway? Main thing was it got him inside, for the moment at least. 'What makes you think that?'

'Well, for starters, you haven't shown the slightest interest in looking at any records of such materials, secondly you ---'

He was halted in midsentence as the other man, smiling, held up his hands in a gesture of surrender. 'OK, okay! I don't need you to be a believer, never thought I'd fool you for long anyway.'

'You're looking for someone,' Fiorentino said, 'a spy perhaps, someone posing a clear risk to what we are doing here.'

Clasping his locked fingers behind his neck and arching his tightening back Miller shrugged, 'Maybe you're right. I am from the government though and I would appreciate if you'd keep your suspicions to yourself. I won't be here much longer.'

Coaxing a reluctant nod of agreement out of the other man Miller asked again about the whereabouts of the Manhattan Project Manager.

'He's over at the Trinity test site, about four hours drive from here, in the desert. He's been there since yesterday and might only be back by to-morrow.'

'Big test coming up, of this "Gadget?"'

Fiorentino nodded carefully, 'You could say so.' Adding, 'I don't know where or how you heard about Manhattan but it's ---'

'I know,' Miller said, 'classified. What about the General, Groves?'

'He's away most of the time, in Washington and the Pentagon. I think a lot of the time is about securing more finance for this place.'

They sat in silence as two fresh mugs of canteen coffee were deposited on the desk, then Miller pulled across another of the personnel files and started reading. Most of the data was technical, the subject's academic qualifications, career and scientific contributions. Shorter notes on personal life and family. Of the dozens of files he had read so far two were Nobel Prize winners and half a dozen others reputations as world leading nuclear scientists preceded them. Three were Jewish refugees, all from Germany and one was Polish. Amongst them were also chemists, mathematicians and an electronics engineer. Most, however, were nuclear physicists and that number included Oppenheimer, a theoretical physicist. There could be little doubt what the Gadget was about.

After a while Fiorentino excused himself to attend to an unrelated security matter leaving Miller alone with his stacked files. Leaning over Miller retrieved the sheaf of paper Fiorentino had scribbled on. He smiled as he looked at the little sketch, a circle with a roughly drawn shield at its centre and the semicircular words Department of Justice in the top half and Federal Bureau of Investigation in the bottom half. Pretty smart guy, Fiorentino. As he tore the page into shreds, tossing it in the wastebasket, he decided he liked the man.

Lighting a cigarette he swivelled his chair to gaze out the solitary window. From where he was he had a view of the inner fence encircling the Technical Area and the access gate guarded by an armed soldier who checked the IDs of those passing through. Glancing down at his own ID card dangling around his neck from a lanyard Miller afforded himself a wry smile. Black on white it recorded a large letter D followed by a three digit number as well as six other smaller digits in a bottom corner. No names on The Hill, at least not for the scientists who all probably knew each other from before anyway. Or visitors, such as himself. Presumably to confound any outside spies who could deduce something from the names living on that mesa.

Should he visit the Technical Area, get the captain to give him a guided tour? But what did he expect to learn over there?

Benkenlitz. Was there even such a name? Working from a list provided he had so far concentrated on those scientists whose names started with a B, prioritising the ones with non English sounding surnames. Even then the list was sizeable and he was beginning to get the impression that the files were not going to give him the answer. The closest he had got so far was a Dr Berkowitz, a chemical physicist and a German Jew. The man, who was married but with the wife back in Germany, had fled Nazi Germany in 1939 to join the physics department at Berkeley where he was later recruited by Oppenheimer himself to Los Alamos. No details regarding the fate of the wife. All in all a record not much different from several of the others he had been through. He marked that one as a possible while he wracked his brains at how to take that further.

Another thought, what if the spy was not a scientist but, say, one of the technicians? Working in the Technical Area they would have access to a lot of information. If indeed there was this spy, how would he, or she, get the information out? Logic told him most likely by a rendezvous with someone outside, in Santa Fe. All outgoing mail was censored by the military with incoming mail read by the FBI. Phone calls, although not forbidden, would run the risk of being monitored by army signallers on The Hill; too risky.

Collecting his hat and telling the secretary he would be over at the canteen if Captain Fiorentino was looking for him, he stepped outside in the bright sunlight. What a strange place, he thought as he paused for a moment to adjust his eyes to the glare. High above the surrounding desert with unseasonal snow one day and eighty degrees heat the next. And through it all the air as clear and crisp as only a desert can be first thing in the morning. And to think that where this bustling pop up community now bustled and hummed all around him a mere three years ago there was nothing except an elite ranch school where the rich would send their sons to be toughened up. He could only speculate at how many millions, make that billions, Uncle Sam was forking out to make all this happen.

Big money, could that be the motive for a spy? No, he decided, this was not about money. This was about something far more intangible, ideology.

Tilting his hat at a smiling young woman who was shepherding two small kids across the street, he set off for the canteen and an early lunch.

19

CHAPTER

It was early afternoon when Feldman and Burger drove into Santa Fe. On the long trip down from New York City they had plenty of time to fine tune a plan to activate what Feldman called his sleeping beauty, a term that always brought a smile to his companion's face. Of course, it all depended on the men on their way from Berlin making it safely to Santa Fe.

His last communiqué with Berlin, two days earlier, had assured him that was the case. The way he saw it Berkowitz had by now assembled the ingredients for the bomb as instructed under the impression it was to be used as an instrument of blackmail, to negotiate a favourable deal for the Fatherland. The new plan, of course, was something different altogether, an alternative endgame that had been programmed into the young scientist's mind years ago in Germany. "Korsika," together with the domino, were supposed to set it in motion.

But something had gone wrong, something to do with his twin brother. A problem that could hopefully be resolved by bringing them together. What was it Esther Stern had said, something about a mental block, a way of shutting out bad thoughts, that she had never been able to elucidate from her sessions with Berkowitz? But there had been clues, like "Ivan." What did it mean? In her analysis during that last discussion she and Feldman had she suggested a possible pact between the two brothers.

'A *pact?*' he had asked.

'When they were very young. From what Professor Schmidt told me the two had always shared a room and the other one, Alex, had developed a way of calming young Max – our Berkowitz – by which means we're not sure. However, on the occasions when he had woken screaming in terror from some nightmare and the mother had gone to check, she had found him already calmed with the brother reading to him. She always found it most odd.'

'At the time Schmidt, in the process of shaping their subject's subconscious, had tried to find out more about this mysterious reading but could not extract that from Max and the mother didn't know. It was thought risky to interrogate Alex who had on earlier assessment been found to be an unsuitable subject and hence a risk to the whole project.'

Thinking back of Esther now, the psychiatrist warming to the subject, the mystery of the Corsican Twins as she called them, he had felt a slight pang of regret. What an interesting woman she had been, such a pity she had to die. But the instructions from Berlin had been clear, all traces of Berkowitz and his contact with the woman had to be erased, now that the plan was coming to a head. Still, a pity. Having never felt much attracted to women Feldman had been slightly disturbed by this strange feeling of remorse and it was with some effort that he banned it from his mind.

An earlier trip to Santa Fe, a practice run for the mission at hand, had revealed that most of the bigger hotels in Santa Fe were permanently full, a spin off from the activity on The Hill. In a way it suited his purposes and after a search he had found a small hotel in a quieter part of town less frequented by the tourists. He had made an effort to befriend the desk clerk, an elderly sad faced Mexican who might not necessarily have believed Feldman's story but had no hesitation in accepting a one hundred dollar retainer, there being the promise of more to come should there be a future phone call, an urgent message for Mr Feldman.

As usual he had booked two rooms and it was settled that he and Burger would explore the town separately and liaise at pre-arranged times and venues. An hour later, having deposited their luggage in their rooms, he dropped Burger off in the centre of town then drove on to the local post office.

Earlier, while refuelling the car at a service station, he had bought a small paperback guide book of Santa Fe. At the post office he now bought postage stamps and a manila envelope large enough to accommodate the booklet. Then took it over to a secluded corner of the shop and produced the item from a jacket pocket and leafed through it until he found the right page. It was of the historic bridge over the Rio Grande at Otowi Crossing and included a colour photograph. On the main road connecting Los Alamos and Santa Fe it was a few miles from the town centre and quite secluded, the only building close by a small house where visitors sometimes stopped for tea and refreshments.

Satisfied that the area was open enough yet with enough cover for an observer to survey the surroundings before approaching the rendezvous he carefully folded the corner of the page and inserted the book into the envelope. He then addressed it to Dr A Berkowitz, PO Box 1663, Santa Fe. This being the address for all mail to Los Alamos.

There was a post box at the door and on the way out he deposited the package. He knew it would be opened and checked by the local FBI who, puzzled by this unusual way of getting a locally purchased item, might want to question Berkowitz regarding that. Having no access to The Hill however posed a real problem and, should the situation arise the subject had been briefed in the past, just a matter of the eccentricity of your average dotty scientist. For some weeks now Berkowitz would have been expecting the arrival of the booklet denoting the place of rendezvous, the time always ten a.m. or, failing that, eleven p.m.

The stage was set. Now it was just a matter of killing time.

Pausing at a small sidewalk cafe to enjoy a coffee and a donut he noticed the headlines of the local newspaper discarded on a nearby table. Going over to retrieve The Santa Fe New Mexican he read the article that had caught his eye. It seemed there had been a shooting on the Mexican side of the border on the Gulf. No less than three dead men but one, a seventeen year old had survived and was receiving treatment at a nearby hospital. The Mexican Federal Police have reported that the party had been at the beach to pick up two white men who had landed by boat, possibly a submarine. The arrangement had been to take them across the US border, their ultimate destination unknown.

For undisclosed reasons there was a shootout and the two strangers took off in the party's car. So far no sign of the car had been reported. The Mexican authorities have notified the US customs who would be on the lookout for any suspicious activity. The article went on to speculate as to the nature of the mission these, no doubt very dangerous, men were on, raising the possibility of spies or perhaps smugglers.

The news was bad enough for Feldman to lose interest in his donut, the coffee growing cold as he pondered this startling new development. There was little doubt the two men in question was Jaeger and Winter. On the positive side they had got away and hopefully were uninjured. They would be making their way to New Mexico but he had no details of their planned route or where they would be now.

He also had no way of contacting Jaeger prior to his arrival in Santa Fe which, if all went to schedule, should be to-morrow.

Telling himself that Berlin would not have entrusted the mission to someone who was not very skilled at this kind of thing, he forced himself to relax, enjoy his coffee. Things were coming to a head and fast. Time to start thinking of an alternative plan should the mysterious brother not make it.

20
C H A P T E R

Jaeger's back was killing him by the time the bus pulled over at the small town or Las Lunas and he was glad to get off and stretch his legs. Several Mexicans disembarked and were met by a squat middle aged local wearing a singlet that might once have been white and struggled to cover an impressive beer gut. Shifting a frayed at the edges straw hat to the back of his scalp he scowled at the new arrivals who greeted him with equal lack of enthusiasm. Jaeger took them for relatives or at least close acquaintances and once again marvelled at the distinct lack of bonhomie that seemed to inhabit the local peoples.

Something to do with the climate he decided as he spotted a small cantina next to the bus stop, a dishevelled looking Winter having joined him by now. 'Time for a quick beer?' he asked the bus driver who shrugged, replying there would be a twenty minute stop while a mechanic adjusted something to the engine. Turning Jaeger could see the hood of the ancient vehicle now raised with the torso of a grease stained overall clad form buried in its depths and apparently unperturbed by billows of steam rising from inside.

Inside the cool dark interior of the bar they ordered two cold beers from a grossly overweight Mexican barkeep with a tired scowl and a Zapata moustache luxuriant enough to hide any smile should that alien thought ever arise. Drawing up barstools at the scarred wooden counter Jaeger paid the man who grunted and shoved the money down the front of his apron. No change was offered.

The bottled beer was refreshingly cold and no glasses appeared to be necessary. There was however a slice of lemon peel wedged in the neck of the bottle which presumably acted as a filter of sorts. It was not what the two newcomers were accustomed to but then, Winter reflected, there was no sign of a buxom flaxen haired waitress either or, for that matter, an oompah brass band.

Turning on his stool to survey the room Winter thought he could make out a few deal tables with an assorted mix of rickety chairs, the solitary window hung with a heavy blanket that sagged in the centre and served as a curtain. A stray ray of sunlight struggled through a gap in the curtain highlighting the small puff of dust raised by the entrance of the two men. The walls were rough cast and bare save for a solitary sombrero hanging from a nail, possibly left there by a customer. Turning back to the bar counter he noticed an old man on a stool near at the far end who seemed to be studying them with interest.

'You gennulmen from the guverrmen?' he asked in a reedy voice that ended in a fruity cough.

'What makes you think that?' Winter asked.

The old man pointed with a hand clutching his beer, 'Why them fancy suits, I figure. Folks down here don't go for them suits much.'

Winter glanced down at a by now decidedly grubby and rumpled suit and shrugged, 'No, just tourists. What about you, you from here?'

Ignoring the question the old man called for another beer and when it was slid across the bar counter to be expertly fielded he abandoned his stool to take up one next to Winter. 'Mother's milk,' he said after a long satisfying tug at the bottle, smacking his lips in appreciation.

Winter studied the wiry frame topped by a wild mop of gray locks and a tobacco streaked full beard and reckoned him for somewhere in his seventies. The lined skin was deeply tanned which made the gaze from the startlingly blue eyes seem even more intense.

'Sam Pickens,' he chuckled, holding out a hand which Winter shook. 'People call me Slippery Sam, beats me why.' He inclined his head towards the packet of cigarettes Jaeger had placed on the table and the latter shoved it across without comment. They watched as Slippery Sam carefully extracted one from the packet appreciatively smelling it before placing it in his lips and staring at Winter in an expectant way. After a second Winter realised the man was after a light as well and with a suppressed sigh lit it for him.

'I just thought, what with them state police out there,' he nodded his head in the direction in which Albuquerque presumably lay, 'you gents might be some of those G men we see about.'

'What state police?' Jaeger asked, suddenly interested.

'That road block on the other side of town, they're stoppin' and searchin' everyone now, just checkin' the folks in the cars and trucks. Something to do with a shooting across the border. You'll see 'em soon enough when you get back on the bus.'

'You've just come that way?' Jaeger asked, his voice calm, neutral.

Slippery Sam nodded, 'Sure did. That's my truck outside there. Yessiree!'

'*Señor* Sam iss pilot,' the bartender offered as he collected the empties and ran a wet cloth over the bar surface, 'he stay at airport. Live there.'

'Sam Pickens' Aviation Services,' Slippery Sam said proudly, indicating a faded logo on the breast of what now, at closer inspection, looked like a one piece flying suit. Or, judging by the oil stains and grease marks, possibly an air mechanic's overalls.

'What airport?' Winter asked as he exchanged glances with Jaeger.

'On the edge of town, you passed it comin' in.'

'I see,' Winter, who had noticed nothing even vaguely resembling an airport in their passing, said. 'And you are heading there now?'

'Yep. That's where Miss Rosie and I live!'

'Miss Rosie being your wife, I presume?'

Slippery Sam laughed spraying flecks of beer foam as he thumped the bar in glee. 'Nooo! She be my ol' plane, she be. Miss Rosie and I we done crop spraying all over this here county, yessirree!'

'Sam,' Jaeger said, rising and motioning over the bartender, 'Let me buy you beer while I have a quick chat with my friend. 'Another round!' he said to the bartender sliding over some notes and joining Winter who was already heading for the bus. No words were spoken between them as they instructed the bemused driver to retrieve their suitcases from the roof of the bus as they would be spending the night in Los Lunas.

'But there's nothing here, *Señor!*' the man protested, raising his hands in a gesture of puzzlement.

'It's the waters,' Winter, who was suddenly feeling strangely lightheaded, offered. The absurdity of the whole situation starting to get to him.

'What waters?' the driver asked as he glanced from gringo to gringo, now deciding they were clearly crazy.

'The healing waters of Los Lunas.'

'There are no healing waters in Los Lunas,' the man countered, desperately glancing around for someone to support this statement.

Winter shrugged as he retrieved his suitcase and handed the man a handsome tip. 'Perhaps I was misinformed but we'll check it out anyway.'

Pausing at the cantina's entrance Winter said, 'How much time you think we have?'

'Not long. Let's get the pilot to take us back to his plane and get us out of here.'

Back inside they took up position on each side of Slippery Sam who was by now well into his third beer and softly whistling a tune that sounded vaguely familiar.

'Mr Pickens,' Jaeger said with a smile, 'we have a little proposition for you...'

21

CHAPTER

Twenty minutes later the old Ford pickup screeched to a halt in a cloud of dust, the journey to the other end of town having taken no more than five minutes of as terrifying a driving experience as Winter ever hoped to have. Not that the dog sleeping on the tray at back seemed perturbed enough to bother waking up during the trip, presumably used to the experience as pretty much everyday.

'This, I presume, is the place?' Jaeger said as he dusted his pants and sleeves with the brim of his hat while surveying the barn and taking in the faded yellow biplane parked next to it. a limp windsock to one side suggesting the presence of an airfield although it was hard to see evidence of one.

'Sure is!' cackled Slippery Sam who had insisted on another beer for the trip and was in the process of downing its dregs.

'Why does it say Rodriguez Aviation up there?'

Sam let out a bellow of glee slapping his thighs, Winter thought the dog, which had joined them by now, was having fun too, at least judging by its wagging tail. 'That's ole Pedro, he used to be here. Haven't got round to changin' the sign yet.'

'How long have you been the boss?' Winter asked as he stepped through the open hangar doors looking for signs of another plane.

'Seven years!' Slippery Sam said proudly, 'and that's Miss Rosie over there.'

Jaeger and Winter stared at the crop sprayer, a tail dragger biplane that looked like a survivor from the First World War and likely some death defying barnstorming since. The fuselage sported two open seats and Winter thought he could make out strips of duct tape patching here and there. Whatever identification signage had been painted on the fuselage had long ago faded into oblivion.

Exchanging glances they took in the surrounding barren countryside finally settling on the highway half a mile away where there seemed more traffic now than was the case earlier.

There was nothing for it. 'Can you fit both of us in that?' Jaeger asked.

'No problem!' Sam exclaimed taking the suitcases and shoving it into a compartment behind the rearmost seat. They watched in silence as he picked up a crooked stick, seemingly at random from the rubble strewn yard, and proceeded to check the level of fuel in a fuselage mounted tank.

Winter thought he could make out some glistening at the end of the withdrawn stick but Sam declared himself satisfied and indicated they should climb into the rear seat. 'You first,' Winter said to Jaeger who, being the larger man would presumably be better able to support the weight of the other sitting on his lap.

If Jaeger shared Winter's soft chuckle of amusement he did not show it.

'Contact!' Slippery Sam shouted as he spun the prop and seconds later the ancient radial engine sputtered into life belching thick clouds of blue smoke that brought the taste of bile to Winter's throat. Then they were away, Slippery Sam yanking the chocks from under the wheels and swinging into his pilot's seat in one single fluid move. There did not seem to be a need for pre-flight checks or passenger instructions and then they were taxiing down a roughly scraped section of earth that finally identified itself as Los Lunas' airfield. It took no further than a hundred and fifty yards for the machine to obtain lift off and all down that bumpy run they were chased by the dog wagging its tail and barking insanely.

'She normally comes with,' Slippery Sam shouted, 'you're sittin' in her seat!'

Then they were banking steeply, the town falling away to their left, the plane heading straight for a stand of blue gum trees before gaining height at seemingly the last moment to hop over the topmost branches much like a grasshopper would over a tree stump. Holding on tightly to the metal edges of the cockpit, his fingers fast going numb from the cooling effect of the headwind, Winter gritted his teeth and tried to think of a childhood prayer, realising there had not been any. Not in the Winter household where National Socialism was the only religion.

Glancing over the side he saw desert as far as the eye could see, interspersed with scattered high rising mesas and, in the distance, the snow capped Sangrĕ de Cristo mountain range. It was bitterly cold now, his light clothing offered little protection and the buffeting from the onrushing air thundered in his ears and made all conversation impossible. There was nothing for it but to hunker down and ride it out as he quietly resented Jaeger who, sitting lower and shielded by the body on his lap, was no doubt having a much easier time of it.

Their pilot had stated that the trip to Santa Fe, sixty miles away, would take "no time at all" and that he would put them down at Boyd Field, what used to be the old airstrip, before business moved to the new airfield further out of town. Something in his tone had suggested his presence at the more controlled environment of the town's new airport might not be all that welcome but the two men were in no position to pursue that any further. Perhaps, was the conclusion, the stated proximity of a friendly little tavern quite close to Boyd Field explained things.

Time would tell.

Until then they had to survive the trip and it did not help that Slippery Sam appeared to have an insatiable curiosity about the landscape they were flying over, keeping low and seemingly following the contours of the mesas and canyons passing under their wings. Sometimes, without warning, he would swerve to swoop low over a section of the yucca scrub covered desert to excitedly point at some unseen object before turning them back on course again. On one occasion it was a small party of Indians, the children excitedly waving back.

In the heat of the day, the baking sun now directly overhead in a cloudless sky, air pockets had developed and increasingly as they struck these and the little biplane dipped sharply before wearily struggling for altitude again, the airframe would creak and groan and vibrate with enough force to be audible and palpable to its two increasingly worried passengers.

More ominous was how the engine would splutter briefly before resuming its already erratic beat. The image of the wet spot on the end of the fuel measuring stick foremost in Winter's mind as he wondered whether to tap Slippery Sam on the shoulder, ask him to put them down somewhere, anywhere, before they ran out of goddamn gas and crash. But then these things can glide, can't they? And there seemed plenty of flat hard desert around to land should they have to.

With a silent vow never to complain about the comfort and level of commercial air services again, he forced himself to calm down and sit it out.

Twenty long minutes later the small town of Santa Fe came up on their starboard side, Slippery Sam's waving arm directing their attention to it. As low as they were already flying Miss Rosie now showed definite signs of wanting to land, the plane's wheels seeming to tickle the treetops as the pilot brought her in. From what Winter could make out the airfield was not much of an improvement on the one they had taken off from but here and there was a building with a few trucks and cars parked about and a half dozen aircraft of different sizes parked outside hangars near one end.

Then they were down, the landing surprisingly soft as the propeller immediately raised clouds of dust that had them cough but quickly subsided as Sam throttled the engine down to an idle.

Taxiing slowly in the general direction of what was possibly a small airport lounge and office area, they suddenly veered sharp left passing close to the building and heading for a small parking lot now empty of any vehicles.

Logically this would be where they got off but it seemed their pilot was not much for conventional behaviour as he now pointed Miss Rosie's nose towards what could only be described as a road. Plainly the airfield was not fenced off and they were now on their way into town.

Admittedly the immediate surroundings were flat and clear of impediments but Winter thought it prudent to undo his seatbelt and lean over to tap Sam on the shoulder. 'Where are we going?' he shouted as the man turned an ear, pulling off his leather flying cap.

'What?!'

'Where are we going?!' Winter repeated, anxiously eyeing a pickup truck coming their way, the driver pulling off to the side and cheerily waving as they trundled past.

'Mama's Place!'

'I see,' Winter shouted back, not really seeing at all.

'The bar, Mama Teresa's place,' Sam shouted, deciding some sort of explanation was indicated.

An intersection was coming up and to Winter's relief no traffic was approaching. A road sign flashed by, "Rodeo Drive." and the first of the scattered houses with the occasional car parked outside. Slumping back Winter gave up passing along information to Jaeger who, trapped by the weight on his lap, had by now realised he was at the mercy of a madman. Possibly two mad men.

Just when Winter, spotting a sharp corner coming up and Slippery Sam slowing down, was readying himself to climb onto a wing and make a jump for it, they screeched to a halt in the courtyard of Mama Teresa's famed establishment.

'Yippee!' Slippery Sam yelled as he cut the engine and jumped down, moments later joined by his two passengers who were stomping their feet and blowing on frozen hands as they surveyed their new surroundings.

A sprawling flat roofed adobe construction it featured a wing off to one side with several doors opening to a small paved area adorned with palms in earthenware pots. Two sedans were parked in front of what was likely a motel. The main building had louvered swing doors below a somewhat gaudy painted sign reading Mama Teresa's Lounge and Cocktail Bar (ambience selecto) and, in smaller writing below, meals and rooms to let. The dirt parking lot led straight up to the front entrance and thousands of feet had worn a broad furrow to its inviting interior from where Latino music was wafting.

An assortment of kitchen chairs were lined up against the whitewashed wall facing the parking lot, a few small tables scattered here and there. A dog of uncertain lineage soaking up the sun against the wall raised its head to study them with little interest before dozing off again.

The reflected sharp sunlight was blinding and it took a moment for Winter to spot the woman as she rose from a chair to stride over.

'It's you,' she said in a sharp heavily accented voice, confronting Slippery Sam, arms akimbo. 'And drunk as *everytime!* Why I not surprised?'

Slippery Sam shuffled his feet and looked embarrassed. 'Aw, Mama ---' he began only to be cut short as the tiny Mexican woman, Winter judged her no more than about five feet tall and somewhere in her fifties, shifted her attention to the two strangers.

'And who you have here? They escape from prison?'

'No! No,' it came in unison, the men glancing at each other and shaking their heads in denial. 'These are tourists, Mama. Their car broke down and I gave them a lift,' Sam said, spreading his hands in a pleading fashion.

'Ha!' Mama Teresa said, eyeing the two strangers with suspicion. Running a hand over his two day stubble while stealing a glance at an equally dishevelled Jaeger, Winter decided her sceptical stance was entirely understandable.

'You have money?' she asked and when Jaeger patted the leather satchel suspended under his coat she nodded, satisfied. Turning to an increasingly fidgety Sam she said, 'How is dog? You be here, who feed dog?'

'She's all good, Mama. Missing you.' Sensing more was needed he hastened to add, 'Luis, my mechanic, look after her. No worries.'

To this she snorted then, to the surprise of the two strangers she put her arms around Slippery Sam and gave him a hug. 'Bad man, you,' she said. 'You promise never fly drunk no more!'

Sam started to say something then dropped his arms to his sides in a gesture of defeat.

'You stay?' Mama Teresa said, eyeing Winter and Jaeger. 'I have place,' she inclined her head towards the line of doors to the side, 'Good, clean. Have shower and toilet.'

They were only too glad to accept and moments later found themselves inside the cool interior of the bar where the Indian barman had Slippery Sam's beer ready even before he crossed the doorstep. The room was large and surprisingly tastefully decorated with one wall covered with old framed photographs of bullfighters and people and buildings, none of which was familiar to the men. A scattering of Indian tapestries and pottery adorned the other walls while the polished wood bar counter, running the length of the room, had a mirror behind it fronted by a kaleidoscope of liquor bottles of every description. Several brand logos were on display as was a wall mounted old long barrelled Henry rifle offset next to an Apache war bonnet and a set of tomahawks.

Several men, mostly Mexican and Indian, but also a few whites, were seated on barstools and studying the newcomers in the mirror.

'You thirsty?' Mama Teresa asked, adding, 'Not Mr Sam, he *always* thirsty!'

Taking the men's momentary silence as a yes she shouted to the barman to bring over two beers and a wine for herself. And for Jose' to go and fetch the guest's luggage from the airplane.

Not even the mention of a plane parked outside merited any attention from those at the bar and Winter decided he liked this place, even though he suspected he was inside a dream of sorts.

'You want eat?' Mama Teresa said as the beers arrive. 'I have tortillas and beans. Also, you want, I make hamburger.'

After she left to give instructions to the chef, Slippery Sam pulled up a chair and sat down. 'She's a tough ol' biddy,' he said, shaking his head with a wry smile. 'I've been trying to make an honest woman of her goin' on ten years now but no dice. This comes between us,' he added wistfully taking a deep and satisfying tug at his beer.

'How far are we from the centre of town?' Jaeger asked.

'Straight down this road. It'll take you to the central plaza, maybe two miles. Town's spread out and it can get hot out there. There's a bus but it's better to have a car ---'

If Winter and Jaeger thought the three hundred dollars they had already paid Slippery Sam allowed a little leverage they kept it to themselves. 'How much?' Winter asked with a sigh.

'I reckon a fifty would do it. Man builds up a mighty thirst in this place.'

Winter watched in silence as Jaeger handed over a few notes.

'Mama has an ole Dodge parked at back. I'll put in a word, reckon she'd let you borrow it for a few bucks.'

Glancing out the bar's front facing window Winter saw Jose' retrieve their bags from the plane's luggage compartment then, after glancing furtively around, reach further into the cavity to extract a canvas holdall. It was stuffed to the limit but appeared not to weigh much at all. He watched as the Indian hefted the holdall over a shoulder before picking up their bags to take it inside.

'What do you reckon is inside that canvas bag?' he asked Jaeger who had also been watching. Jaeger didn't answer, turned to Sam instead. 'Do you make these trips often?' he asked, 'bringing in those bags, I mean?'

Slippery Sam glanced around before moving closer and dropping his voice. 'People have *needs*, you get? If I don't bring in the weed someone else would have to do it.'

'Just what we thought,' Winter said with a smile, 'the man's all heart.'

22
CHAPTER

'There's a Detective Sergeant Kelly on the line for you,' Zelda said as Brewster finally picked up. 'Says it's to do with the Stern case.'

Brewster grunted, it was late afternoon and he was trying to work up the energy to take on the rush hour traffic. The last thing he needed now was for some cop to come up with a long boring report back on a case that looked like it was going nowhere as it was.

'Put him through,' he sighed, digging in his pocket for a fresh cigar.

The detective, who sounded every bit as world weary as Brewster felt, came straight to the point. 'Got something here that might interest you, Chief. We've been chatting to the receptionist of the shrink that got killed, the Stern dame. She's been through all the late doc's files and there's only one missing. A certain Doctor Berkowitz. And, get a load of this, the man visits two or three times a year, all the way from a place called,' there was a pause and a rustle of paper before the voice came on again, 'Los Alamos. Some secret government place near Santa Fe.'

'I know where it is,' Brewster growled.

'Better still, there would sometimes be another man present during these sessions. A Mister Kruger, although the receptionist thinks it might be a fake name. He's not a patient, no file and he's only there when this Berkowitz comes.'

'Would she recognise either of them?' Brewster asked as he wrote down "Kruger" next to "Berkowitz."

'She reckons yes, says he is of foreign appearance and speaks with a slight accent. Eastern European she thinks, or maybe German.'

'Get an artist to draw up a picture.'

'There's one more thing,' Kelly said. 'The shrink used to dictate notes after consultations and Mrs Morello, that's the receptionist, would type them up before filing. But in this case she never did dictate, the only notes in the file handwritten ones and apparently not very much either. She reckons there might have been a second file, one the doc kept in secret but she's never seen it.'

'Hmm. OK, Kelly, thanks for the call. And, Kelly?'

'Yes?'

'Don't call me Chief.'

He killed the line and leaned back in his chair, the cigar forgotten between his fingers. Why break in to steal a file that has nothing in it, together with the appointment books?'

There was only one logical answer. He pressed the button to Zelda's line and when she answered asked her to get Miller on the line. Knowing she had probably been listening in anyway he didn't bother to explain.

23
CHAPTER

'I'll finish loading the lenses,' Berkowitz said from where he was studying the assembled test device. 'You go over to the monitor site and check the connection to the diaphragm microphones, last time our calibration was out and skewed the readings.' The technician gave an affirmative reply and headed back to where the rest of the party were by now assembled, calling to an assistant to bring along a large tool chest mounted on a trolley.

It was hot down in the canyon, one of those early summer mornings when the last of the snow had melted to sludge and the smell of the earth was fresh in his nostrils. Seemingly impervious to the humidity that had others remove their jackets and roll up sleeves, Berkowitz had kept his on and buttoned.

There was a reason for this. Hidden in an inside pocket was a thick wad of window putty, an item he had purchased from a hardware store in Santa Fe a few days earlier. Similar in colour to the sticks of Composition B he had been packing into the metal casing of the lenses it would suffice to fool anyone but the closest observer. All the lenses bar two had by now been carefully fitted into the frame and it took only a few seconds to swap the two sticks of the explosive for the putty which he carefully moulded to the shape of the lens cavities before fitting the last piece of what the team called "the jigsaw puzzle."

Then, the two sticks of Composition B nestling snugly against his chest in an inside pocket, he rose to his full height and stretched his by now aching back. From a corner of his eye he could see the technician strolling backwards towards him rolling out from a small drum the cord leading to the detonator.

'All loaded?' the young man asked, his open schoolboy's face flushed and sweat glistening between the strands of his brush cut.

'Loaded,' Berkowitz confirmed, 'I'll leave the arming to you.' With that he strolled back to where the rest were by now sharing the contents of a large Thermos flask containing tea. It was a drink he at best tolerated but with so many British on the project, it had seemingly become omnipresent. Glancing back he could see the technician connecting the detonators and for a moment he was worried the man might smell the putty, the only physical aspect that would be discernible other than a chemical analysis. No, he decided firmly, the young man would be in a hurry to get away from the bomb he had just armed, he would dismiss any unusual smell as coming from the surrounding piñon pines and desert flowers still showing signs of the previous night's thunderstorm.

The walk to where the others were waiting was uphill and left him sweating and slightly out of breath by the time he joined them at the control point. Declining an offer of "a cuppa" from a toothy Englishman whose name he had forgotten if ever he knew it he mumbled something about a headache and went over to the car that had brought them down from The Hill for a bottle of water from a cooler in the trunk.

Back at the table where the monitors were set up he sank into a chair and studied the dials. For this experiment they had also assembled a modified seismograph, Feinberg suggesting that reading might help gauge the effect of the blast although most of the others assembled were sceptical. He knew that they had it almost right now, that the time for finally testing The Gadget was fast approaching. He also knew his own, miniaturized, version would be ready even earlier.

The previous evening, at the usual weekly colloquial Oppenheimer insisted on hosting for the scientists, the man had once again impressed on all the deadline they were now working against. General Groves increasingly anxious they have something to tell the president before the man discovers the true cost of the project, Project Y to all concerned, which was now approaching two billion dollars. No less than six Nobel laureates had been present at that meeting, the mood strangely subdued as the enormity of what they were about to create, began to wear on their collective conscience. Oppenheimer once again reminding them of the terrible cost to human lives the war in the Pacific was exacting, reminding all that they held the key to ultimately saving countless lives.

Oppenheimer himself was present now, having arrived minutes earlier accompanied by Fermi who seemed constantly at his side these days. Berkowitz, who had known him since the project started, noted how gaunt and harassed looking the scientist had become, the culmination of months of mounting stress now showing clear signs of taking its toll. He was smoking a cigarette and seemed ill at ease, sneaking frequent glances at his watch while following their activities with that keen sense of observation he always seemed to have.

'Ready?!' Feynman called, glancing around to check all were in position, all monitoring devices in record mode. The army corporal in charge of the explosives had declared the range clear and given Feynman the OK signal.

Joe Jaworski at the detonator control panel raised a hand in affirmation, 'Ready!'

'Fire!'

There was a muffled boom, the noise of the explosion bouncing off the surrounding hills in a series of receding echoes to be followed by a moment's stunned silence as men glanced at their screens before exchanging puzzled glances. No-one ventured to meet the gaze of the tall man who now stepped forward to confront a clearly perturbed Feynman who was tracing the recorded pattern on the printer with a finger that shook slightly.

'Problem?' Oppenheimer asked in the soft voice he used when struggling to control a rising agitation.

Feynman nodded numbly, 'Section eleven and twelve didn't detonate properly. I just cannot ---'

'It's the faulty lenses,' Berkowitz interrupted, rising from his canvas chair and tossing a pen in a show of disgust. 'The latest batch from the metallurgy section have tiny cavities and cracks dissipating the force of the explosion.'

Oppenheimer looked quizzically at Feynman who nodded, 'Yes,' he said lamely, 'we have been dealing with it, the technicians are trying to get them perfect but it takes time ---'

'How long?'

'One more week. I promise, we'll be ready.'

The rest of the team had gathered and there was a general consensus that it was a minor fault, something that would be solved in time for the planned testing of The Gadget which was, under pressure from Groves, fast approaching. They were working on the implosion bomb and all present knew the timing of the explosion in each of the lenses would have to be exact within one hundredth of a second while the explosive yield of each charge would have to be exactly equal for the device to work. Even a slight irregularity could cause a failure to obtain a uniform compression of the plutonium core to the point of becoming critical fast enough to trigger a nuclear explosion and not a fizzing meltdown which would be a disaster.

Twenty minutes later Berkowitz was back in his workshop on The Hill. Ensuring he was alone he took the two sticks of Composition B from his inside coat pocket and placed it in the bottom drawer of the steel filing cabinet, carefully locking it and pocketing the key. Later, after dark when the place was deserted save for the odd light in one or two of the technical block windows where some scientists were working late, he would return to work on his own Gadget.

Aware of the first pangs of hunger, he had skipped breakfast that morning as the anxiety of the planned switch of the explosive had gnawed at his insides, he started for the canteen.

Stepping outside into the brilliant light the headache was suddenly there again. More intense now and with it the blurring of vision and the dreaded nausea. Stumbling, slightly dizzy, he stood for a moment, forcing down his breathing and willing himself to focus, overcome the feeling of impending doom that seemed to close in from all sides. After a while he willed himself to continue but now changing direction to head for his quarters.

Rest. He needed rest. And time to think. For something was wrong, something was coming for him and then suddenly he knew what it was. What it had always been. Alex. Alex was coming. Yes, that was it he decided while subconsciously running his fingers over the scar that had been throbbing lately.

Alex was coming, like he always knew he would. Like he did during those long dark nights when they were children and he woke up screaming, the Erlkönig coming for him...

'Ivan ---' he was now intensely aware of the voice inside his head. His brother's voice, soothing and soft as things in the dark receded and their saviour appeared and drove off the demon king of the elves. "Ivan," It bothered him that he could not recall the rest of Alex's words. It bothered him that Korsika was there, all the time now, yet without any meaning. Korsika and two small dots staring at him, boring into his mind,

The headache suddenly overpowering he stumbled into the room and barely reached the bed before collapsing across it as the first wave of a convulsion ravaged his body and the blackness engulfed him.

va studied the bracelet, slowly turning it as the light
teased the opal to exquisite shades of blue while the
beaten silver was heavy and somehow cold to the touch.
It was beautiful, a one-off piece amongst a sea of Indian
jewellery, several others now displayed on the counter in front
of her.

'How much?' she asked at length, reluctant to remove the
bracelet from her wrist.

'Two hundred dollars,' the saleslady replied, adding quickly, 'the
madam can pay it off, of course.'

Eva smiled wanly as she slowly slid it from her arm. She could
afford it, even though it was outrageously expensive. But it would
be indulgent and somehow wrong when she was widowed and still
grieving and not really looking for the good time the young women
from The Hill seemed so intent on having.

Shaking her head she handed it back to the Mexican woman,
selecting a smaller piece instead, a necklace and paying for it. She
allowed the item to be placed around her neck, barely hearing
the woman's cooing about how it became her, highlighted the
darkness of her hair. Her thoughts were suddenly far away, her
mother drawing her future husband aside to tell him in hushed
tones to watch out for Eva wasting her money on buying scarves

whenever she was stressed. She could still see Larry roll his eyes and wink at her.

When did her mother know anything about her, she thought, suddenly angry at the recollection. Had she ever had to give up the only man she ever really loved? Seen him walk out of her life after a single misunderstanding, a moment of madness to destroy a universe of happiness? Only to have a second chance at love and lose that too in a world gone totally mad?

Mumbling a thanks and pocketing the receipt she hurried from the shop, the atmosphere in that tiny overstocked environment suddenly overpowering to the point where she couldn't breathe.

Outside it was late afternoon, the cool breeze coming in from the distant mountains refreshing after the heat of the day. The sidewalks surrounding the plaza were crowded with late afternoon shoppers and people out for a leisurely stroll. There were families with children, the smaller ones riotous and loud as they raced between the sidewalk display stands, avoiding seemingly unavoidable collisions with the effortless agility and confidence of the very young.

Sounds were everywhere as the shouts of the children mixed with that of the traffic which had now picked up as businesses started shutting and people headed home. Narrowly dodging a small boy on a tricycle she took a seat at one of the sidewalk cafe's and ordered a beer. It was a taste she had acquired when she had first started seeing Larry and what better than a cold one in a climate such as this.

Larry. Good old reliable Larry with his boyish smile and goofy manners and all the innocence in the world. Larry, who was going to take her to Coney Island but somehow never found the time as the war caught up with them. Larry, the starry eyed young man who went to war because it was the right thing to do, leaving behind a young bride with a cheery I'll be back before you know it, pumpkin! This lot'll be over by Christmas, you'll see!

The coldness of the beer was refreshing and she could feel a pleasant buzz coming on, slowing her down, easing the gnawing anxiety that had been building since that chance meeting on her first day on The Hill. Calling over a hovering waiter and ordering another drink she eased back in the chair and let her mind drift back over the events of that day.

Could it be possible?!! Could this Dr Berkowitz be Max? Surely not! But the resemblance was uncanny, especially the voice. Oh, there were differences for sure, but it had been what, eight years? A lot can change in eight years. But, if it was him, and increasingly she was becoming more convinced, why the deception? There was so much secrecy surrounding Project Y as she had been instructed to call what they were doing on The Hill that it was just possible Max, if it was him, was working undercover for the government in some nebulous role or other.

There were whisperings of spies all over the place and thinking back of her own rigorous security checks still brought a chill if not a hint of a blush to her cheeks. (Did they really find it necessary to delve into her personal life like that? Did old lovers really have to come into it?)

Old lovers. Accepting the fresh beer from the smiling waiter she let her mind wander down the path of distant memories. All the way back to Boston and when they had all been together at MIT. Alex and her. How well she remembered the day they met, on the steps of the physics building; she sunning herself, arms clasped around her knees while lost in thought. And suddenly he was there, sitting down beside her as if they had always known each other, and coming up with that corny opening line about Heisenberg's Uncertainty Principle being wrong, how her presence next to him proved that.

Startled she had asked why, suddenly feeling like a schoolgirl wondering whether she was blushing. He was so handsome and talking to her! Oh she had noticed him before, all the girls had and she was aware, even now, of jealous eyes watching them.

'Oh it's simple,' he said as those deep blue eyes smiled at her, small wrinkles at the corners belonging to a man who smiled often. 'The great Professor Heisenberg states that the position and intention of an object cannot be known at the same time.'

She looked at him in puzzlement, unnerved by his closeness and vaguely aware that her heart was about to jump through her throat. 'I thought it said the position and velocity of a particle cannot be measured exactly at the same time, not even in theory?'

Leaning back on outstretched arms he cocked his head the mocking smile now more pronounced as he shook his head. 'And here I thought you were a romantic.' Suddenly serious he glanced around before leaning closer to whisper in her ear. 'Heisenberg was wrong for the simple reason that here we are, me sitting close to you while at the same time knowing that you are the most beautiful girl I've ever seen. No uncertainty there.'

And with that he had brushed his lips across the back of her hand, the touch sending electric shocks all the way down her spine. 'I...I don't know what to say ---' she stammered.

'Then say yes,' Alex Winter said as he glanced at his watch, suddenly businesslike as he realised a lecture was about to start and he would have to run to make it. 'I'll pick you up at seven! We can go dancing down at the Odeon!'

He was halfway down the steps when she realised he had not asked for her address. 'You don't know where I live!' she called after him only to have him shout back that he'd find her.

And that's how it started, she thought wistfully, the love of her life. One glorious summer, even as the clouds of war started gathering on that distant horizon, until, in a moment of madness, she destroyed it all.

If only she could turn back time, have the moment over, explain to him how it was all a misunderstanding! Something that happened because she loved him so much that... the beer suddenly bitter and way too cold she pushed it away while thinking of what Einstein had once said, '*...the arrow of time is nothing but an illusion, however persistent that illusion might be...*'

If only that was true! Then she thought of F Scott Fitzgerald, a writer both she and Alex had read, and his stated view that there were no second acts in American lives and the sadness deep inside her was suddenly too much to bear.

A breeze had sprung up from nowhere and made her shiver as she glanced around, noticing that the crowd had thinned, the plaza fast emptying as people headed home and the shops closed. With a sigh she rose and located her bag, deciding after a moment's hesitation to go in search of the group of girls she had come into town with. They had agreed earlier to meet for cocktails at the La Fonda before heading back to The Hill.

Walking across the uneven paving, careful not to twist an ankle, she thought back of that last day and how she had been too late to catch him at the train before he left for Germany. How, realising the horror of her mistake, she had rushed down to the station in a blind panic and all in vain. Then the months of unanswered letters and the growing despair as war came and with it the realisation that, at least for her, the man she loved was dead.

And now, back on her narrow horizon, was the face of the man she hated more than she ever felt possible. The man who had caused her so much pain, the one mistake she could never correct.

Yes, she knew now with deadly certainty, it *was* him.

What was she going to do?

CHAPTER 25

It was after ten when Winter opened his eyes. Sunlight was streaming through the window where the curtains had been drawn aside and it took him a second or two to focus on the form standing next to his bed and eyeing him with an expression of disfavour.

'Iss time get up!' Teresa said in a voice that invited no contradiction. 'You lazy man! Just like my husban' was.'

Resisting the inclination to enquire about the fate of the missing husband Winter swung his legs over the side of the bed to instantly become aware of a splitting headache. Sitting quite still for a minute he fixed the woman with a bleary eye. 'What time is it?'

It had taken him a moment to realise where he was but the time and indeed, the day and date still eluded him. Not waiting for a reply he asked for some aspirin and then, as an afterthought, enquired about the whereabouts of his compatriot.

'He go town early,' came the reply as Teresa impatiently gestured for Winter to vacate the bed so she could make it. 'He say you stay here, wait for him come back.' She was bustling about the room now, casting a disapproving eye at his clothing discarded on and around the room's solo chair. If she was in the least disturbed by her guest's near nudity it did not show.

'Go take wash,' she said, adding that the bathroom was down the corridor, 'you smell bad like old fool next room. He still drunk, too much tequila!' From this Winter gathered she was referring to Slippery Sam and a glance out the window confirmed that the biplane was still in the parking lot. Tossing him a towel she declared her intention to wash his clothes while Raul, in the kitchen, would fix him some breakfast. She would bring him some aspirin as soon as she found time. She was a busy woman and everyone wanted something from her *all* the time. Shaking her head at this injustice she shooed him out the door.

A hearty breakfast omelette washed down with plenty of coffee as well as the headache pills Winter found himself with time on his hands. Until now it had been an insane whirl of events in which he was little more than an unwilling spectator, dragged along ever closer to the dark heart of the whirlpool. And now there was this sudden hiatus, this oasis of calm, even – could it be – normality?

Suddenly the war seemed so far away and he found himself struggling to recall the faces of the men he had fought alongside, so many dead now. What was happening to those he had left behind on the banks of that river, were they still alive? Russian prisoners perhaps?

And his brother? What was he going to face when they finally met, would they still have anything at all in common? The headache was fading as the aspirin kicked in but he knew it was more than just fatigue that had brought it on. Knew instinctively it had something to do with Max just like it always had in the past.

That and the increasing throbbing in his thigh.

Dismissing the thoughts with an angry shake of the head he retrieved from a pocket the slim leather bound volume he had taken that day from his father's library, turning to where he had last read a section during their ocean voyage.

--- The eyes of the Templar flashed fire ... 'Hearken,' he said, 'Rebecca; I have hitherto spoken mildly to thee, but now my language shall be that of a conqueror ---'

As the lines of Sir Walter Scott's great novel came back to him he felt a sudden stab of pain as memories, long suppressed flooded back. Trapped in the past now he read on, the words of the fair Rebecca ringing in his soul.

--- *'My strength thou mayst indeed overpower, for God made women weak, and trusted their defence to man's generosity. But I will proclaim thy villainy, Templar, from one end of Europe to the other --- '*

Rebecca ... Eva... The pain was real now, as real as the knowledge that it would always be with him. How ironic, he thought bitterly, that it was Ivanhoe who came to the rescue of the fair Jewess, defeated the Templar and wasn't that the same Ivanhoe he and Max turned to in those dark hours, alone in their room?

His brother the Templar, who betrayed him that terrible day in Boston. And turned away the one love of his life.

As the painkillers took effect he found himself growing sleepy and, pocketing the volume, he went out into the rear garden and found a secluded spot in the shade of a large oak tree. Settling down in the padded leather of an old car seat that served as a couch he was soon asleep.

He was still relaxing under the welcoming shade of the old oak in the small courtyard when Jaeger appeared. Once again Winter was surprised to see how well rested and full of energy his enigmatic fellow traveller looked. And what a contrast that made to his own washed out appearance in the bathroom mirror earlier. The man seemed to thrive on lack of sleep and, neatly shaven and dressed in freshly ironed white shirt under his lightweight suit, he looked like just another Texan on his way to a lucrative business deal.

The grey fedora had been replaced by a black Stetson and Winter thought the slim black necktie with its silver clasp was a nice touch. All the man needed to complete the image was a pair of hand tooled boots and a beaten silver belt buckle. And a gun on his belt instead of where it now rested under his coat.

A gunfighter comes to town, he thought to himself. Somehow the image fitted.

He was about to ask Jaeger where he had been when he became aware of a second person in the doorway. The man standing quite still while surveying the scene, a slim cigarillo between slender fingers.

'Meet Mr Feldman,' Jaeger said, 'I caught up with him in town as previously arranged. He's our contact.'

Another surprise Winter thought but then nothing really surprised him any more. Slowly climbing to his feet, his bone weary body fighting him all the way, he studied the newcomer as he approached. Tall and thin the man moved like a ballet dancer and there was something about his clothing that suggested European or possibly South American origins. 'Pleased to meet you, Mr Winter,' Feldman said in a softly modulated voice with just a hint of a hard to place accent.

The offered hand was limp and as cold as the man's black eyes. The thin lips beneath the pencil line moustache curled in a lazy smile and Winter thought he detected the hint of a perfume.

'Mr Feldman,' he acknowledged with a slight bow, 'perhaps the two of you can let me in on our little game now? For instance when am I to meet my brother and what exactly I'm supposed to do then?'

God he was getting tired of all this!

'Oh I don't think we have long to wait, Mr Winter. The signal has been sent and the meeting set up. To-morrow, I think, we shall be able to conclude our business.'

'Let's go and find a table in the bar,' Jaeger said, inclining his head in the direction of the back door, 'it's time we go over the details.'

Their progress was halted by the decidedly shabby form of Slippery Sam Pickens propping up the doorframe while blinking uncertainly in the sharp light before fixing them with bloodshot eyes and rubbing a hand over his stubbled jowls. 'Ah, there you are,' he said gazing at his new found friends with undisguised pleasure.

'A man can die of thirst in this place. Come, come inside and Teresa, grand ol' lady that she is, will bring us some beers!'

And with that he turned unsteadily to lead the way back inside, Jaeger with a sigh observing that by all appearances the man had already had a few.

26

CHAPTER

It was going on lunchtime when Miller finally got to see Oppenheimer. They met in his cramped office in the Technical Area and when she ushered him in the secretary gave him ten minutes, "no more, he's scheduled to meet the General at half past and the poor man's dead on his feet as it is."

She was right about that, the man who rose from behind the desk to meet him, hand outstretched, was pale and visibly tired, red rimmed eyes evidence of a frantic schedule that left little time for undisturbed sleep.

The handshake was limp but the smile, if weary, was real. 'Mr Miller, nice to finally meet with you. I knew you were coming, of course, if somewhat puzzled as to the exact nature of your presence here on The Hill.' Removing a pile of paperwork from a chair he motioned Miller to take a seat while calling for some tea and pulling up the other visitor's chair.

The secretary put her head around the door to ask what he would like, Mr Oppenheimer usually had tea, adding with a stern look that being when she could persuade him to have anything at all.

Miller said tea was fine and turned to face the scientist who was studying him with a quizzical half smile. 'You look tired, Mr Miller. Sleeping OK?'

'Now that you mention it,' Miller said rubbing the back of his neck, 'I wake up with shortness of breath and a dried up nose, not to mention a bloody headache.'

The other man laughed softly, 'It's something we all experienced when first arriving. It's the height above sea level, almost seven thousand five hundred feet up here, takes time to get used to it. Now, what can I help you with?'

'As you know I'm from the office of the Fissionable Materials Board, the matter being one of auditing the use and disposal of such materials. As we speak our facilities at Oak Ridge and Hanford are in full production of enriched uranium as well as plutonium, virtually all of which is then sent here for use on the project you are overseeing. I do not have the clearance to know the exact nature of the project but common sense suggests it is regarding some new development on the military front.' As the words rolled over his tongue Miller thought he sounded like a politician tiptoeing his way around a tricky issue, while hoping he had correctly pronounced the technical bits, sounded like someone who knew what the hell he was talking about.

'We keep meticulous records, Mr Miller, I can assure you all fissionable material is fully accounted for.' Oppenheimer glanced around at the pile of scattered papers and files on his desk then stood up abruptly to go over to a bookcase where he, after a brief search, extracted a file from amongst a stack of others, handing it to Rusty. 'This should be up to date.'

He remained standing, stealing a glance at his wristwatch and blushing slightly as he realised this could be seen as being rude. The moment was rescued by the secretary entering bearing a tray with a pot of tea, cups and a small plate of cookies. Once again Miller was reminded that Dr Oppenheimer was due to meet the General in less than ten minutes and that the man in question did not like being kept waiting.

'There is another matter ---' Miller said as he accepted a cup of tea, lumping in some sugar before settling back in his chair.

'Oh?' Oppenheimer had sunk back in his chair and was staring down at a cookie in his hand, apparently puzzled at how it had got there. Miller realised the man was dead tired and struggling to keep up with events as the project, by all accounts, was racing to its culmination. He decided to be succinct.

'We have been contacted by the FBI regarding new information of a spy being present on The Hill. Information I am not at liberty of divulging, except to say it raises the risk of sabotage and with large quantities of fissionable material present, as well as our records showing quite a lot of conventional explosives, this is a matter of real concern.'

Oppenheimer sighed visibly, raising his arms before dropping them lamely to his sides, the forgotten cookie a casualty in the process. 'Please, Mr Miller! This spy thing has been with us since the start! There has never been any suggestion of ---'

'Dr Berkowitz,' Miller said, cutting the scientist short, 'what can you tell me about him.'

Momentarily stunned, Oppenheimer glanced helplessly around before fixing his visitor with a now piercing gaze. 'Berkowitz? Why him?' Sighing again he held up a hand in a motion of surrender, 'Never mind. What can I tell you? I've known the man for at least three years, ever since he came over from the Rutherford Lab in the UK to Berkeley and from there to work on the Project. A refugee German Jew he is an explosives expert and vital to the work we do. I don't know much about his personal life, he tends to keep to himself, but his bona fides have been fully checked by security which I would think included the FBI and ---'

'Our records show that on no less than six occasions, roughly at six monthly intervals, you gave permission for Dr Berkowitz to take leave of absence in order to seek medical attention. During which he travelled to New York where he consulted a psychiatrist, a Dr Stern. Were you aware of that aspect?'

Another sigh. 'Dr Berkowitz suffered from a condition of anxiety depression, something related to his time as a prisoner of the Nazis when I believe he was tortured. At times, when the workload became excessive, his condition deteriorated to the point where he would need treatment, I would agree and sign the necessary papers. There being no psychiatrist resident in Santa Fe he would make the journey to New York. He would always be back within three days at most.'

Something he saw in Miller's expression had him hasten to add, 'Although a key person in our Project, Dr Berkowitz, does not have overall knowledge of the exact technical aspects of the design of The Device. He is involved with only a part of it.'

How coy these scientists could be with terms like "The Project" and "The Device," Miller mused, when any idiot knew they were building a bloody big bomb and not just some or other rocket that seemed to be the prevailing theory circulating amongst the good folk of Santa Fe. 'I would like to ask him some questions,' he said, this time joining Oppenheimer as the other man stood.

'They were testing down in the valley this morning but should be back on The Hill by now,' Oppenheimer said as he held out a hand indicating the end of the meeting. 'I have to run but my secretary will arrange for someone to take you over to Dr Berkowitz's workshop.' At the door he hesitated, broad rimmed hat in hand, 'Take it easy on him, will you? The man is stressed out as it is, we all are.'

Miller was about to follow him out the door when the secretary reminded him of the audit file still lying on the big man's desk. Something in her look told him the lady wasn't one little bit fooled by his bona fides even if her boss was.

At that moment Berkowitz was sitting on his bed paging through the Santa Fe Guide he had received in the morning's post. The headache from earlier that day had largely gone leaving him with a slight fuzziness of thought and still the growing feeling of impending doom. He found what he was looking for on page thirteen. So it was to be the bridge at Otowi Crossing. In their screening of the package someone had smoothed out the folded back page corner but the indentation was still there to see.

A glance at his watch confirmed he was too late for any meeting to-day, it would have to be that night or, better still, to-morrow. Rising unsteadily to his feet, the sudden motion left him dizzy and holding onto the bedpost until his vision cleared. There was something wrong with him, he knew that with increasing certainty, but what to do? All he really wanted was to sleep now and escape all these thoughts milling through his brain, driving him steadily insane.

To-morrow. To-morrow he would get his final instructions. He would arrange to hand over the thing he had been secretly building for so long now, the thing that in the hands of the Reich would provide the ultimate bargaining tool ensuring the survival of their glorious dream.

Come to-morrow.

There was a stranger in his workshop when he walked in a short while later. Spotting his boss, Ben, his senior technician, inclined his head towards where the man was examining something on a workbench, simultaneously rolling his eyes. 'Gestapo,' he whispered solemnly. It was a private joke between them, a tacit acknowledgement to the good doctor's well known rough passage in the hands of the Nazis before his escape and now the term for any government security officer snooping around.

'He says he's from something called the Fissionable Materials Branch of the Federal Internal Auditor's Office,' Ben added, coming closer and dropping his voice even more. 'I reckon the Federal bit is about right but I sure smell a cop.'

As Berkowitz came up to the bench Miller turned to extend a hand with a smile, introducing himself along the lines the technician had just mentioned.

'What can I do for you, Mr Miller. As you can see we're pretty busy here.'

The man had been examining the coffee urn!! *Gott in Himmel!* Why had nobody stopped him?! They all knew it was just a useless piece of junk he was set on repairing, a hobby of sorts for a well known eccentric. In their busy working day no-one ever paid it the scantest attention where it was stashed in a corner. Suddenly cold and sweating he moved away to the far end of the room where his writing desk was, willing the red haired stranger to follow. Gaining his chair with some effort he sat down quickly bidding the visitor to a vacant lab stool.

'I have a few personal questions, Dr Berkowitz. If it's awkward here we can go somewhere else, the canteen perhaps?'

'Fine,' Berkowitz managed with a croak, clearing his throat before adding, 'Here is fine.'

Miller nodded and opened a thin manila folder. 'It's about these trips you did to New York, the last very recently. Where you went to see a certain Dr Esther Stern, I believe? Kindly tell me about the nature of your visits if you don't mind.' The toothy smile and the schoolboy open looks did not belie the fact this was expressed as something more than a request for a friendly chat.

Fighting for time, a few moments to gather his panicky thoughts, Berkowitz said something about not hearing from her recently and how was the doctor?

'That's the problem,' Rusty Miller replied, 'she's dead.'

27
C H A P T E R

ittle Joe Kowalski shifted his ample butt to a more comfortable position on the barstool and ordered another beer. Thumping his belly with a ham like fist he belched and lowered the level of the beer by a third with a long satisfying pull at the longneck. The drive down from El Paso had been hot and thirsty work and the burger and fries he had wolfed down earlier at a roadhouse did nothing for his indigestion. The dishwater coffee didn't help either.

'Tell me again about the two *gringos* who came in here earlier,' he growled reaching for a bowl of peanuts the barman slid across.

Shrugging, a long face seemingly sagging under the weight of a magnificent droopy moustache, the Mexican resumed polishing the scarred counter. 'I already tole you, *Señor*. They get off the bus then have drink with *Señor* Sam. The bus go they no get on, leave with Sam.' An expressive gesture of the hands indicated there was nothing more.

'This Sam character have a surname?'

'He be Meester Pickens. He fly airplane.' A swooping motion of a hand served to illustrate the latter revelation should the fat gringo be slow on the take up.

'And that's the airfield down the road?'

'*Si.*'

'I just drove past there, there's no plane. Where does this Sam fly to?'

Again an expansive shrug as the man's eyes shifted to a new customer in the doorway. 'Sometime he spray the fields, down by the river. But not now. Sometime he fly people to look at river and sometime he go to Juarez, or Albuquerque, maybe Santa Fe.'

The latter pricked Little Joe's interest enough to lower his beer. 'Santa Fe? Why?' he asked while glaring at the newcomers, two Mexican peasants, who wisely opted for a table at the far side of the room.

Deftly opening two beers behind against the side of the counter – clearly the newcomers were regulars – the barman leaned closer and lowered his voice. '*Señor* Sam go see special lady —'

'Who is the woman? You have a name, address?'

Scratching the back of his head as he stared at the ceiling fan the man hesitated, make a show of thinking. Leaning over the bar Little Joe grabbed him by the shirtfront, pulling him up close without any sign of effort. 'The name,' he repeated, softer this time, he always found that to be more intimidating.

'*Señora* Teresa! She be at Mama Teresa's Bar.' Sensing something in the big man's face he hastened to add, 'Sam funny man, always park airplane in front of Mama's place. Everybody knows!' With that bit of startling information he freed himself from Little Joe's grip and went over to the two men who accepted the beers without a word being spoken. Both men making a show of not looking at the big Americano.

Nursing the last of his beer, the first tinge of a pleasant little buzz coming on, Little Joe mulled that one over. Could be was the conclusion. With knowledge of a police road block ahead and several dead bodies in your wake, that would be a neat way of jumping the closing net, hitching a ride on a plane to Santa Fe. After all, wasn't that one of the places the two had mentioned when he saw them on the bus at the border post? The more he thought about it, the more he liked it.

Throwing some money on the counter he called for another cold one, for the road, and thought about the ten bucks he had given the barman at the start, just like he'd seen Humphrey Bogart do in The Maltese Falcon. Shit, the man had hardly given him a nickel's worth for his money! For a moment he thought of taking five bucks change, be nothing to wring it out of the scrawny wetback, then decided against it.

Bogey would never do that. Nope, Little Joe, he said to himself as he eased his weight off the stool, you're about to move up to the big time now, get some class. You have to act the part.

Cradling the beer he walked out, pausing in the doorway to give his eyes chance to adjust to the glare. Heck it must be all of ninety degrees out there he reckoned, easing off his sweat soaked jacket and tossing it onto the back seat of the car together with the necktie. If any of the handful of people about noticed the gun in the shoulder holster they kept it to themselves. Back in the car he dug a roadmap out of the glove box and, after a minute's study, eased the car back onto the highway and distant Santa Fe.

It was baking in the car and a toss up whether it was cooler with the windows down or up and with the fan going. After a minute's fiddling with the knobs he gave up on trying to find a radio station and settled down to his thoughts. It had been a downer when he and Lew, his partner, discovered the two whites they'd let through at El Paso were suspects for a killing across the border, something they had decided to keep to themselves.

But, wait a minute, Little Joe had thought, this could be the chance he had been waiting for. His chance to make a splash, get accepted into the State Troopers or even the Marshalls, a long time dream hitherto unrealised. Imagine bringing in those two, just him alone, all nice an cool like, handing them over to the law with a smile and a bit of advice to watch the big one, the man a bit of a handful but nothing Little Joe couldn't handle.

The thought made him smile. Yeah, that would do it. As it was he had some leave due and here he was, on the road and in a suit just like he'd seen Bogey wear and wasn't the big Colt .45 just like the one the man packed?

So far the trail had been pretty easy now that he thought of it. Following the route of the bus and then finding out from the State Troopers at the road block that there had been no-one but Mexicans and Indians on the bus that had passed earlier on route to Albuquerque. No-one answering to the description of the two men travelling either way all day. So he had backtracked to the last bus stop and struck gold. A sudden thought had him hesitate. What if the men – they must know by now they were being hunted – were hiding out in the little town he'd just left, that barn at the airstrip perhaps? Taking another pull at the beer nestling between his legs he shrugged it off. Nah, he reckoned them for men on a mission.

Santa Fe it was.

It was late afternoon, the distant mountains glowing in the dying rays of the day, when he found the place. He had checked into a motel near the centre of town an hour earlier and enquiries had directed him to Mama Teresa's together with a discreetly delivered suggestion that it might not be quite the place a gentleman of his ilk would necessarily want to frequent. Apparently the clientele was known to be not quite selective. There was a band over at the La Fonda if that was the kind of thing he was after. The latter was delivered by an old coot with the scrawny neck behind the reception desk with a kind of dead pan look that vaguely reminded Little Joe of a preacher in the small town he'd grown up in.

He said he'd make a note.

Then he was parked outside the place and looking at the plane. A piece of junk he'd say, wondering what kind of a nut would go up in that. But, he guessed if a man was desperate enough he'd try anything. The car was pointed at the front entrance and he could hear music coming through windows opening onto the veranda. The parking lot was full, mostly pickup trucks and old tired looking sedans. He sat for a minute, suddenly uncertain of what his next step should be, acutely aware that if these guys were the killers they'd be packing and decidedly dangerous. He had thought about going to the local cops but then what? They would take over, probably exclude him altogether and where would the reward in that be?

No, he decided with a set of his jaw, Bogey wouldn't go to the cops. No sirree! He would walk in there and take charge and if the boys wanted to play rough, well he, Little Joe Kowalski, was ready for that too. Tucking the Colt into his belt at back he got out of the car and slipped on his jacket. After a moment's hesitation he reached for his hat, a wide brimmed Texan number in white with alligator skin headband adorned with beaten silver decorative plates. Most of the Mexicans and Indians wore beaten down straw hats so he'd stick out but he reckoned the hat would provide a degree of camouflage, prevent the perps – he'd come to think of his quarry as "perpetrators" – from spotting him straight up.

Then, hitching his pants, he strode through the front door and into the cool dimly lit interior of Mama Teresa's.

Giving his eyes a moment to adjust to the gloom before settling on the bar counter at the far end he took in the situation. Two men propping it up, both with their backs to him but studying him in the mirror while nursing their beers. Neither of them looking anything like his quarries but looking guilty all the same. A third man at the other end of the long counter, American businessman judging by his suit and hat and reading the paper.

Two Indians in workmen's clothes playing pool under a flickering overhead light while another pair looked on, neither exhibiting signs of having anything riding on the game. Their necks swivelled around as he entered, liquid black eyes studying him with nothing more than mild interest. Dismissing them he shifted his gaze to the corner where four men were seated around a deal table, none looking his way. He recognised the two smartarses straight away, the big one facing his way. The old coot he had figured for the pilot but the fourth man was the odd one out. Smartly dressed in a city slicker's suit complete with necktie and a red bandanna tucked into a breast pocket, a homburg hat resting on the table at his side and next to a silver and ebony walking stick.

The sight of this stranger – it had to be a European – took him momentarily aback, long enough to realise that conversation in the room had stopped, everyone studying the newcomer with curious interest. Christ! Smooth, be cool! Striding over to the bar he picked a stool where he could see the four at the table in the mirror and ordered a beer, give himself time to think over his next move. Gradually the conversation around him picked up again and there was still no sign he had been made.

But he had. Seating himself so he could watch the parking lot Jaeger had seen Little Joe pull up, had watched as the man pondered his next move for several minutes before getting out of the car. Had seen the automatic being tucked into the man's belt. From that position he could even make out the Texas plates, final confirmation that it was indeed one of the border guards that had questioned them on the bus. But what was a border guard doing here? Ruling out co-incidence and not knowing enough about the internal machinations of the US law enforcement setup he had to assume the man had been tracking them. Perhaps that was what border guards did.

He couldn't take any chances, not at this stage of the game when they were so close. Still watching the man crossing the parking lot Jaeger asked Winter to take up Slippery Sam's kind offer to drive him to town in Mama's old Dodge while he and Mr Feldman would stay for another drink as they had some business to conclude. They would all meet up later for drinks at the La Fonda, Jaeger's treat. If Sam was a bit perplexed at this unexpected generous offer it did not take him long to down his beer and start the laborious and somewhat hazardous process of getting to his feet.

Winter had caught Jaeger's eye directing him towards the parking lot and with an almost imperceptible nod he reached for the keys the other man slid across the table. A glance at Sam had him suggest it would be safer if he drove.

An astute Feldman had taken in the whole situation without a word being spoken, having earlier been briefed by Jaeger as to the details of their journey that far. Clearly something dangerous was coming, most likely belonging to the footfalls of whoever had just entered the room. As always the threat of imminent danger filled him with a sense of deep calm, almost a feeling of anticipation, a tingling sensation of being alive. He sat quite still, eyes on Jaeger, whom he realised was clearing the decks for action, waiting for the man's next move.

Over at the bar Little Joe loosened his necktie and, still keeping his back to them, studied the tableau in the mirror. The big man worried him, the man with one hand out of sight under the table. Sweating now he decided to wait for them to get up, move towards him, give him a chance to see their hands nice and clear, not clamped around a piece of hardware.

The thought of backup crossed his mind again, to be instantly dismissed. He could handle this. But, wait a minute! The blonde one was getting up, reaching a hand to steady the old coot who was well into the bag and grinning like the idiot he was. Then they were heading for the door leading to the back section of the place and most likely for a toilet.

Glancing across at the two at the table the big man still had his hand under the table and was now looking straight at him! It was a casual glance over, or was there a hint of growing puzzlement?

Still hesitant he nodded as the Mexican behind the bar suggested another drink, turned to see a faded grey sedan slowly back out from around the side of the building before heading down the road, a cloud of blue smoke in its wake. The driver was the blonde one with the drunk sitting in the passenger seat. So they had fooled him but maybe it was for the better, take them one at a time. He was pretty confident now that he hadn't been recognised and now things were looking even better. For the other two were rising and heading for the door.

Tossing money on the counter he was about to follow when a loud voice from somewhere over his left shoulder demanded to know from the two men where the hell they thought they were going, now that lunch was ready and what was the idea of giving

Sam Pickens all that liquor, didn't they know the man was a drunk and a bum?

The woman – he reckoned her for a breed, half Mexican – stood five foot nothing but had the voice of a two hundred pound truck driver. Arms akimbo and clearly angry it was a safe bet he was looking at Mother Teresa, the owner of the joint. Swivelling his gaze back to the front entrance he cursed softly for the two men had disappeared. Moving quickly to follow he was confronted by the woman stepping into his space and fixing him with blazing eyes. 'What you looking at? You wanna eat? Good food. You like chilli beans, very ---'

Roughly shoving her aside he made for the door in time to see the two get into a car and pull out. Cursing, louder now, still forcing himself to be calm he walked quickly to where his own car was parked and seconds later swung into pursuit.

28

CHAPTER

Driving slowly, giving the man time to keep up, Jaeger brought Feldman up to speed. They were heading into town as Jaeger searched his mind for the best spot to take the man down. The fact that he was following them was confirmation that they were being hunted. The question was whether the chaser was acting alone or had backup. A scan in the rear view mirror showed no sign of a radio aerial so most likely he couldn't call in help that way.

They would have to neutralize him and fast.

'The Basilica of St Francis, a street block away from the central plaza,' Feldman said in his usual calm beautifully modulated voice while studying his carefully manicured fingernails. 'I visited it yesterday, looking for a spot to set up the meeting with Berkowitz. The parking lot is secluded and at this hour there should be few tourists about. Keep on this road, I'll give you directions.'

Still puzzling over who the stranger in the car with the perp was, Little Joe kept the other car in view but keeping well back. Traffic was light, even approaching the centre of town and few pedestrians were about. Lunch time followed by siesta time, it was that kind of town.

Minutes later they drove past the central plaza with the La Fonda Hotel on the corner and, turning right went down a narrow one way street that fifty yards on intersected with the imposing front facade of the centuries old church. Driving around the back of the building they entered a small parking area with plenty of shaded cover from planted trees. A few cars were randomly parked as well as what looked like a school bus. Cruising slowly past Little Joe saw the two men get out and stroll across to what looked like the back entrance to the building, disappearing into the darkness inside.

Picking a spot under a shade tree he parked and, hitching the Colt on his hip, followed. It was cool inside and following a hubbub of voices he entered a large pew filled area which was clearly where the sermons were held. Staying back in the shadows he spotted his quarry across the room where the man had seemingly joined a group of tourists who were studying a stained glass window, what looked like a guide conducting a walking tour. But where was the stranger? There was no sign of the man but the front entrance to the place was wide open, sunlight streaming through the doors. Could it be he went outside, for a smoke maybe? Or taking a leak in the washroom?

Edging closer, inside the room now and pretending to study the carvings on the pulpit, he watched the scenario from the corner of his eye. Patience, his chance would come to put the bite on the big guy, just wait for him to move away from the group which included small kids. Couldn't take a chance though, the guy might want to play it rough, nothing he, or Bogey, couldn't handle.

More people entering now, twos and threes, a family with a baby in a pram for Chrissake!

Glancing at his watch he figured they had been standing around there for going on fifteen minutes now and still no sign of the other man. Dismissing it with a shrug he stiffened for his man was walking his way but still chatting to the group who appeared to be heading for the back exit.

Tilting his hat low over his brow and eyes he stood aside for the group to pass and by the time they got outside his man was already in his car and pulling out. Deciding he had been made Little Joe ran for his own vehicle reaching it in seconds and slamming the door as he reached for the keys and fumbled for the ignition. He never saw the dark shape rising from the floor behind his seat until the piano wire slid across his head to instantly tighten around his neck cutting off any attempt to call out. The pain was excruciating, blackness building on the periphery of his vision while there was a loud rushing sound in his ears as blood and oxygen was cut off.

Arms desperately flailing as he tried to pull free from the hands only to encounter a strength greater than his own he had a fleeting glimpse in the rear view mirror of the stranger's face. It was entirely expressionless, no sign of effort, dark eyes quietly studying him with a sense of emotionless curiosity.

A killer, wearing the mask of death.

The man was so close he could hear his heavy breathing, smell his perfume even as the darkness closed in. Desperate hands smashed against the steering wheel which emitted a sharp series of blasts from the car's horn, enough to have the tourists glance over, a mother remarking that it was rude of the man to be so impatient, honking for his passengers to come back to the car.

Little Joe's last conscious thought was of the smiling face of a little girl in party dress waving to him as she was ushered into the tour bus.

Five minutes later Feldman joined Jaeger where he was parked in front of the church. Without exchanging words he handed over the contents of Little Joe's pockets as well as the gun. A cursory glance at an ID badge confirmed it was indeed the border guard and not a cop, not someone who would be quickly missed.

'The body?' Jaeger asked as he eased the car back into the light traffic.

'I left it behind the wheel. Arranged him so it looks like he's taking a nap. Too many people about to shift him to the trunk.' Feldman's tone was matter of fact, the man discussing little more than a routine administrative matter that had been satisfactorily cleared up. There was a time when all this would have upset Jaeger, shocked him even. But that was a long time ago. Nodding he drove off, thinking maybe they'd go back after dark and dispose of the body before the cops found it.

After they had left Mama Teresa's the man who had been sitting alone at the end of the bar reading the morning paper cleared space for the bowl of steaming chilli he had ordered and called for another beer. As he dug in the slight frown of puzzlement that had appeared earlier deepened. Dropping in for a spot of lunch and a drink on his return from a surveillance spot on one of the scientist's from The Hill he suspected of being a spy, he had been quietly minding his own business while listening and watching the scenario around him in that barroom. What had just happened?

He wasn't sure but five years as a G man and ten years a cop prior to that had gifted him a fine sense of what his late mother called an atmosphere in a room. Something had gone down there, right in front of his eyes. But what? Who were the people at that corner table and the guy in the white Stetson who appeared to be tailing them?

Finishing the bowl of chilli he pushed it away and called over the woman known as Teresa who was stacking glasses behind the bar. 'The men who were sitting at that table, are they staying here?' he asked, inclining his head in the direction of the corner table.

Instantly suspicious, wondering what Slippery Sam had been up to this time, she nodded carefully, '*Si*, all except the tall thin one with the fancy clothes.' She wanted to ask why but clammed up when she found herself staring at an ID card that had FBI printed on it next to a photograph of the man she was facing.

'Why don't we go and take a look at your guest register, shall we?' Special Agent Meads said with a smile, indicating she should lead the way.

29

CHAPTER

It was raining on the Kaiserdamm Strasse when Himmler's black Mercedes limousine drew up at the junction to Heer Strasse. They were still several hundred yards away from the shore of Berlin's Schwanenwerder Lake, their progress halted by a large crater where a Lancaster's bomb had left its mark the night before, the still burning wreck of a Wehrmacht truck blocking the rest of the road.

Having gone over to inspect the obstacle his driver returned with the news there was no way he could manoeuvre the big car past. A sudden series of loud explosions somewhere close by had the corporal instinctively duck before sheepishly straightening up to meet Himmler's gaze. As always the Reichsführer SS remained impassive, cold eyes behind round rimless lenses slowly taking stock of their surroundings.

To his left was the expanse of the Grünewald, many of the park's trees now showing signs of the bombing raids while to his right, faintly visible through a haze of smoke, was the outline of the Reichssport Field Stadium, now the headquarters of the remnants of a tank battalion. Lingering his gaze for a moment he reflected how it seemed like only yesterday he had attended the glorious Olympics at the side of the Führer right there.

Still smarting from days before being relieved of his command of Army Group Vistula, defending the Eastern Front from the advancing Russian forces, he was determined to win his way back into the favour of the Führer. The successful outcome of Elektron would ensure that, give their glorious Reich its long overdue moment in the sun. Despite the atmosphere of doom and defeatism in the bunker below the Reich Chancellory he for one did not believe the war would be over in two weeks as so many of the generals, cowards and traitors all, were whispering. No, Wenck and his army would break through soon enough and with summer coming they would be ready for that final devastating counter attack that would see the Russians pushed all the way back to Moscow. He was ready!

Never one for sentiment he turned his attention to his aide, a young SS Lieutenant, who informed him that he had commandeered a passing Kubelwagen on the other side and if the Reichsführer wouldn't mind stepping this way they could be at the lake's edge in minutes.

Not bothering to answer Himmler got out of the car to follow the man and a short while later they reached the spot where a small barge was moored next to the bombed out remains of a bridge. Turning up the collar of his leather coat against the sifting rain he climbed down and following the directions of a saluting Waffen SS Hauptsturmführer went aboard and, ducking his head, entered the vessel's small cabin.

Apart from an elderly man in civilian's clothing who rose to his feet with some effort, the only other occupant was a boatswain who saluted and followed the officer out onto the deck leaving Himmler alone with the man who seemed strangely calm, a man resigned to his fate.

'Guten morgen, Herr Professor Doctor Schmidt!' Himmler said in his soft high pitched voice as he peeled off his gloves, tossing them onto a bunk together with his cap that was dripping water.

Returning the greeting the doctor lapsed into silence, knowing why he had been brought there he waited to hear what this menacing creature wanted of him. Himmler did not waste time with small talk, was not interested in the man's journey from Munich which included a crash landing at Gatow Airport from which he was lucky to walk away from and, with that airport now definitely in Russian hands, no clear pathway of how he was going to leave Berlin.

'Korsika,' Himmler said, sitting down next to Schmidt and occupying what the old man would normally have considered his own personal space. 'I trust you have been informed that Elektron have shown signs of regressing, refusing to follow instructions?'

'Yes. I have been told.'

'Good! Good.' Schmidt could not be sure whether the man was rubbing his hands together as a sign of being pleased or simply to warm them. Behind the glasses the eyes remained expressionless.

'You will then also know that his twin brother is now in place and about to meet with Elektron, the reason being to re-activate his programming. This rendezvous was arranged, with some difficulty, at your suggestion when it became clear there was a problem. There being no time to lose we dispatched this other Winter but now I need to know what exactly is supposed to happen.'

Until now the Reichsführer had been staring into space, seemingly lost in thought, now he turned his full attention on the other man who seemed to squirm under the scrutiny.

'I... I... well, it's a long story,' Schmidt began waveringly as he searched for the correct opening.

'Take your time,' Himmler said softly, adding with a soft chuckle, 'we have plenty of time.' The last bit was drowned out by what sounded like heavy machine gun fire in the distance. Dear God, what was this madman talking about?! According to the SS officer who had brought him the Russians where in some areas no further than eight hundred yards away from the city centre, only a lack of fuel preventing the tanks from penetrating deeper while they waited for supplies to come up.

Steeling himself he strove to banish the rising panic from his voice, 'In the early stage of the experiment we worked on the two boys together, making it out to be a game, the idea to make them cleverer so they could trump the other children at school.

Always under the benevolent supervision of the parents who were there as a calming influence during the more stressful parts of the psychotherapy. Then, gradually, we began to notice rising resistance from the older brother, Alex. He had managed to erect a wall, a mental block, against the programming which was then already at an advanced stage. More worrying was that he was striving to desensitize his younger brother when they were alone in their room at night.'

'Which was when you separated them, took Elektron away for final programming,' Himmler said stating a fact, willing the scientist to pick up the pace.

'Yes. This was also when we performed the operation.'

'Ah, yes. The operation. Tell me about that.'

Schmidt licked his lips, he was so thirsty but dared not antagonise the man now by asking for a break and something to drink. Forcing himself to think he went on, 'At that stage Moniz, a Portuguese neurologist, was doing work on pre-frontal lobotomies. He had found that by surgically isolating certain areas of the brain he could alter behaviour. This was mainly aimed at obtaining a calming effect on neurotic patients. We saw other possibilities using this technique, the chance to program a subject to carry out certain actions even if this would previously have been against their nature. Moniz developed a far less invasive surgical technique which avoided some of the complications of the more radical leucotomy.'

'Complications?'

Schmidt grimaced, a pained expression replacing his normally serene countenance to be quickly banished. 'We did not appreciate these unfortunate side effects at the time. Many are now only ---'

'Be specific, Professor!'

'Ah, yes... Well, in some there would be loss of intellect, in others personality changes. It is a matter of the inhibiting function of the neo-cortex being lifted, the patient becomes like a small child again.' He sighed, 'using our highly specific minimalist technique we have managed to obtain, I believe, an excellent balance. Max

Winter retained all his considerable intellectual powers, the man is after all a scientist of some prowess. The operation made him that much more susceptible to our hypnosis induced psychotherapy, removing as it were his inhibitive blocking pathways.'

'A man with no inhibitions,' Himmler said wonderingly and without a hint of irony. 'No moral inhibitions. Sounds like a psychopath to me.'

Schmidt said nothing.

At a signal from Himmler an aide who had been hovering just outside the cabin door approached and was despatched to find some water. Turning his attention back to Schmidt he continued. 'What do you expect will happen when the two brothers meet?'

'We discovered that a particular poem, Erlkönig by Goethe, which we used during the early programming stages, had an unsettling effect on young Max, invoking a profound state of anxiety with nightmares and flashbacks. His brother then found a way of calming him down and bringing him back to reality. This was at the time we separated them and unfortunately we never found out what the technique was. I thought that if we invoke the poem when they are together and combine it with our trigger of Korsika and the dominoes, we could snap him back.'

'This you conveyed to our agent in America?'

'*Jawohl, mein Reichsführer!*' he said quickly, a note of anxiety now clearly audible in his voice.

A solitary ray of sunlight had managed to penetrate the gloom outside and traversing the dirty and cracked cabin window of the barge lit up the myriad dust particles circulating inside the confined space. It reflected off the man in black's curiously flat rimless lenses in sudden flashes and if anything made him appear even more menacing. Forcibly suppressing a rising feeling of impending doom Schmidt forced himself to meet the man's gaze while aware that his fidgeting hands betrayed his inner tension.

'Something that puzzles me,' Himmler said softly, 'is why this "Korsika" trigger was necessary. That and the domino?'

It was a question the professor knew was forthcoming and for which he had formulated the reply that was least likely to antagonise the man now sitting across from him. Only to, with the fear threatening to overcome his senses, strike a mental blank. 'I...er...'

'Go on,' Himmler prodded with a half smile that, if possible, made him look more reptilian than ever, leaning closer to study the other man's features with cold interest.

'Elektron's humanity ---' came the helpless answer. 'Despite all our programming he persisted in showing signs of a moral compass, I...we, thought it too risky to install the final act which was against his inner nature. The risk was that it could work its way through his programmed psyche and undo the rest of what we had installed. There was also the chance Korsika would never be needed. In the end it is a sleeper mechanism, deeply buried using drug induced hypnosis.'

'Humanity,' Himmler said softly, 'a moral compass?' Shaking his head at this alien concept he was silent for a while then finally nodded. 'One last thing. This psychotherapy went on for quite a while for both brothers. What could happen in the case of Alex Winter when all this happens? Could he unexpectedly regress?'

Reaching for the offered water bottle and greedily swallowing the refreshingly cold water, Professor Schmidt wiped his lips with the back of a sleeve before answering. 'It is possible,' he admitted, 'we just don't know.'

Rising and reaching for his gloves and cap, Himmler had one last question. 'How many others did you program using this technique?'

'Just two,' Schmidt said lamely, 'a boy and a girl.'

'And?'

'The boy developed an insanity neurosis, we sadly could not use him. The girl did retain good cognitive function and could be successfully programmed. Also psychopathic, she had one unfortunate side effect. However we were able to place her, not being her controller I'm not sure of what happened to her but I do believe she is in America.'

'Hmm. This skill, this "side effect." What is it?'

'She likes to kill people,' Schmidt said simply, not quite managing to hide the revulsion in his voice.

Himmler, who did know what had happened to the woman he knew as Heidi, nodded his approval.

Pulling on his gloves and settling his officer's cap at the correct angle he called out to his aide that they were leaving.

'What happens to me?' Schmidt asked, a plaintive tone creeping into his voice.

Turning to bestow a reassuring smile Himmler said, 'This boat will take you back to the Wannsee point of the lake. There you would be close to the Potsdam road where lots of refugees are now making their way. You should be able to find a ride to safety.'

'You mean I will be left all alone?' came the incredulous cry.

'Aren't we all, my dear Professor. Aren't we all?'

Striding back to the waiting Kubelwagen accompanied by the SS Hauptsturmführer from the boat, Himmler gave instructions that the professor's body be dumped overboard after he was shot, then to bring the launch back ashore. They might need it later.

There would be no loose ends. He alone now controlled Korsika.

'How much is missing?' Miller asked tossing another personal file across the desk to join a growing pile and leaning back, hands clasped behind his head, stretching his aching back.

'I'm not entirely sure,' Captain Fiorentino admitted glumly, 'the records are at best incomplete but my best guess is about twenty pounds in total.' Seeing the look of incredulity on the other man's face he hastened to add, 'You know what these scientists are like, it's crazy to leave them in charge of explosives.'

'And this is both Baratol and Compound P?'

'Yes.'

There was a moment's silence as the two men mulled this over. They were sitting in the security man's office, a bottle of Jack Daniel's open on the desk between them, two half drained glasses momentarily forgotten, dying light from the day's last rays turning the liquid to a golden hue.

'Would you say enough to detonate a device, a small one?'

'What do you mean?'

'Oh come on!'

Fiorentino sighed, 'I ran it past one of the physicists earlier, he wasn't sure but reckoned it could be. In the hands of an expert. The problem is nobody knows, at least not until they test this Device which in coming up soon.'

'Shit!' Miller said at length.

'Double shit,' Fiorentino echoed, reaching for his glass and draining half its contents in a gulp. Grimacing as the alcohol hit the spot he asked about Berkowitz. 'You reckon he's your man?'

Miller shrugged, 'Could be. I've sent off a request to headquarters for an in depth check of the man's background but that could take days, even weeks. We don't have that kind of time. Not with things coming to a head and especially not with a load of explosives missing.'

'And Berkowitz one of a group who has access to the explosives,' a frowning Fiorentino added, pouring himself another small one. 'What's your next move?'

'I'm going to search his room, that's where I'll need your help. Then I'm going over the lab where he works.' Rising from his chair he reached for his jacket. 'Let's go for a bite, I'm starving. Then I'll get you to corner the good Dr Berkowitz into a friendly chat regarding the protocols for safekeeping of the explosives, giving me the chance to visit his room.'

If The Hill had one thing going for it the food was always good. They both had steak with fries, lots of gravy and pancakes and syrup to settle things down. The whole washed down with a few cold ones.

It being a Friday evening the place was quieter than usual, several buses having taken people down to the town where there would be some live music and dancing. Some planning a trip to the cinema. Of course there was always the music evenings regularly organised by Kitty, Oppenheimer's wife, for those more culturally inclined. It was over at the Fuller House main admin building and the first strands of the string instruments warming up was faintly audible through the open windows of the canteen.

Throughout the meal the two men had been on the lookout for Berkowitz, to the point of discreetly enquiring whether anyone had spotted the good doctor, always under the pretext of settling a dispute between them regarding the town of Munich they knew he hailed from.

By eight it was clear he wasn't coming, the kitchen about to close and few people about. Fiorentino suggested they swing by the Technical area and see if he was perhaps there, many a scientist known to keep erratic hours which the captain put down to the questionable mental stability of the group as a whole.

The guard at the security gate checked their IDs and not knowing what Berkowitz looked like, was of no help in answering their query regarding the man's movements. Waving them through with a shrug he stated that perhaps half a dozen or so people were still inside the complex which explained why the lights were on in several of the huts.

Passing by the area housing the gas stocks they heard voices approaching and withdrew into the shadows. It was two technicians, heading for the gate and chatting about a baseball game, their voices fading quickly as they rounded a corner. Hut E was in darkness save for the light over the small porch. Doors to the Technical Area were never locked, in fact notable was the absence of any lock. Once inside Fiorentino switched on the lights figuring that no outside observer would find that unusual.

They started with the outer office but a quick search revealed little of note other than endless paperwork consisting mainly of numbers entered next to dates, the odd diagram equally unintelligible to anyone other than a nuclear physicist. Quickly bypassing two smaller rooms that held little promise they found themselves in the main workshop where Miller had hours earlier met Berkowitz. On that occasion the man had feigned a severe migraine headache excusing himself with the promise to answer any further questions later. A chat with the two technicians present at the time had yielded little other than a jargon of technical data with the lingering vague suspicion they were having him on, taking the interfering ignoramus for a ride.

The room was unchanged from earlier, a veritable scrap yard of tools and devices scattered about various workbenches in seemingly haphazard fashion, a large desk in a corner littered with paperwork. A stack of hardcover files arranged alphabetically on a steel bookcase. An assortment of mugs next to a small washbasin next to a wall mounted hot water geyser, red light above the tap indicating it was switched on. Jars containing ground coffee and sugar nestling against the back wall.

A second, free standing, coffee urn on a workbench an oddly out of place item amongst the array of monitors and gauges scattered about. Shrugging it off he located what he was searching for in a far corner. A row of personal lockers, each identified with the owner's name on a card in a door mounted slot. The lockers were ancient, the metal dented in places with beige paint flaking off.

Berkowitz's was the third from the far end. It was locked, the flimsy obstacle posing no problem for Miller who had it open in a matter of seconds with the application of two picks and a deft twist that had Fiorentino wonder just where the man had acquired that particular skill.

Swinging the door open it took him a matter of seconds to decide there was nothing of interest there. No purloined state secrets, no diary documenting dark deeds, above all no stashed explosives. Just an old sweater, a baseball cap and some small change. The only item of the slightest interest a pocket sized travel guide to Santa Fe and surrounding districts, a quick scan failing to reveal any scribbling, anything at all. On impulse he shoved it in a pocket. Striving to hide his disappointment he shut and locked the door motioning Fiorentino that it was time to leave, see if they could check out the man's private quarters.

'What makes you so sure Berkowitz is a spy?' Fiorentino asked as they made their way outside.

The question had been at the back of Miller's mind and he shrugged it off. The connection with the murdered Esther Stern? The fact that the man's file was missing from the analyst's office? He had no other suspects and no other leads, it had to be! Everything pointed to this being his man. But he had to have proof!

'I just know,' he said simply leading the way through the gate and across the main street to the single men's quarters at a pace.

Minutes later they were inside the long dormitory building and, Fiorentino having checked earlier, headed for Berkowitz's room which was at the far end of a dimly lit corridor. The place was largely deserted, the evening still young and the men out enjoying themselves. Here and there a light shone under a door, music coming from somewhere but uncertain as to which room. There was no light under the door of Number 14, Berkowitz's room and after listening with an ear to the door Miller whispered that he was going in and for Fiorentino to keep a lookout. 'Go to the entrance hall and if you spot him coming ring his phone from the front desk and I'll get out.'

Fiorentino nodded and headed down the corridor, an uneasy feeling at the pit of his stomach. Jeez! What if Miller was wrong? Breaking into the private quarters of a top scientist like that, Oppy would have his balls!

Once more Miller's pick did its work and seconds later he was inside, carefully shutting the door behind. This time he did not risk the room light, switching on a small electric torch he had brought along. The next ten minutes was spent carefully going over the room, once again coming away disappointed. The man lived like a Spartan, was the conclusion. Almost nothing personal, it could have been a bloody hotel room, the only thing missing an ashtray with the place's logo, or a Gideon's bible. No photographs, didn't everyone have family photos? Moving over to a small bookcase he bumped his shin painfully on an unseen coffee table eliciting a muffled curse as the table overturned with a loud crash. Standing quite still for several seconds he listened for any outside sounds before righting the table and resuming his search.

A handful of well thumbed books on the shelves, mostly technical but a few in German and what appeared to be novels, or possibly works of philosophy or even religion. Not knowing any German he couldn't tell. Upending each book by its back binding he checked for any loose objects and found none. Likewise no scribbled messages or highlighted printing. An odd one out a tourist booklet much like the one nestling in his pocket, this one for New York City. Frowning he sat down in the only chair and quickly paged through it, finally settling on a page detailing upcoming social events for December, the year before. There had been a show on Broadway and the opening night, a Friday, was underlined in faint but still clearly visible ink. Sitting back he searched his mind, was that one of the times Berkowitz had been in New York? He couldn't be sure, something he would check.

The rest of the room and small en-suite bathroom, a rare luxury in that building, revealed nothing of any interest. No hidden explosives, no mysterious code books, no shortwave radio, no false moustache or fake spectacles. Nothing. Glancing at his watch he realised he had been there for more than twenty minutes. Hastily checking that he had left no trace of his search he switched off the flashlight and opened the door to the corridor, carefully peering down both ways before stepping out and shutting the door behind him.

Twenty yards away and hidden in the shadows Berkowitz was watching, shockwaves reverberating through his body upon recognising Miller as the man who had been questioning him earlier. *Mein Gott!* They were after him! Any moment now he could be arrested, exposed. Clutching the basket containing his washing he waited with bated breath for Miller to round the distant corner before quickly heading for his room. He had been doing his washing in the communal laundry when, returning to his room, he heard a crash followed by someone cursing inside, the sound instantly freezing mind and body. Someone was inside his room! The room he had locked as he always did, someone was prowling about, someone who wanted to remain undetected to the point of not switching the light on.

Anxiously glancing around to confirm no-one else was about he had retreated to the laundry room and taken up position where he could see the intruder when the man came out.

Inside his room he hesitated. Should he switch on the light? No! They might be watching and come back for him. Sitting down on the bed to think he waited for his pulse rate to come down, for his breathing to return to normal. Gone was the headache of earlier to be replaced by a sudden cold clarity. The time was now! This was after all what he had been preparing for so long, he would contact Feldman who would get him out. To-night! Forcing himself to think clearly he thought through the details of the escape plan they had drawn up during that last visit to Dr Stern. First the phone call, then he would get in his car and meet Feldman whom he knew was waiting for him in Santa Fe right now.

Then, with a hand that shook only slightly, he reached for the phone and dialled a number from memory.

* * *

Having dropped off Jaeger earlier at Mama Teresa's, Feldman got back to his own lodgings shortly after sunset. Parking the car he spent a leisurely few minutes gazing over the surroundings, enjoying the sounds and smells of a country town settling down for an evening of relaxation and perhaps indulgence. In the distance he could see the dying rays of the day just touching the tops of the Sangre de Cristo mountain range, reflections hinting at remnants of snowdrifts in the cool embrace of deep ravines. All around were the sounds of birds flying to and fro in a frenzy of activity and cacophony of excited chatter.

People's voices were drifting on the still heavy air and there was the first stirrings of a welcome breeze coming down from the mountains. Here and there people coming out of their homes to sit on the porches, watch life go by.

A beautiful evening that, just for a fleeting moment, took him back to an earlier life, now long buried, in old Buenos Aires. A city he would soon be returning to as the long planned comrades network became operational with the resettling of countless Nazi luminaries as well as tonnes of gold and more stolen money than a mere mortal could comprehend. A wealth he was due to share in most handsomely. He wondered idly whether Jaeger knew that the submarine that had landed Winter and himself on that Mexican beach had a further mission, to deliver another shipment of gold to Argentina before returning to the Fatherland.

Shaking off the thought that had brought a wry smile to his lips, he stubbed out his cigarette and went inside. At the desk Alvarez slid across his room key together with a scribbled message which a frowning Feldman read through twice before shoving it in his pocket.

'What time did this *gringo* phone?'

'One hour ago, *Señor*. I put time on back of paper,' Alvarez said with an expansive shrug quickly followed by an ingratiating smile. 'This is one you wait for, no?'

Momentarily lost in thought Feldman nodded absently as he tossed a few dollars on the counter, quickly snatched up by the Mexican. 'You've done well. OK if I use the telephone in your office?'

There was no phone in his room, something he had not needed until now. Seconds later he was seated behind the desk, the door of the small cubicle pointedly closed, the Mexican's broad back visible through the glass where he was leaning over the counter, reading a newspaper. Producing the slip of paper he dialled the number and, after a short delay caused by a busy switchboard, was put through to the room of Dr Berkowitz.

The conversation that followed was short and agitated, Feldman reminding the man they were on an unsecured line and that his mental health issues was private business and that, as his psychiatrist, he would of course see him at the earlier time arranged. With that the man who had identified himself as "Dr Frank" terminated the call.

Sitting back for a moment Feldman wiped his brow with a colourful handkerchief and felt a sudden urge for a drink. Something had happened, that was clear. Or was it perhaps simply that their man was breaking under the pressure? Either way the meeting was going to be tonight, things were moving into the final phase. Reaching for his hat he rose and, with a backwards glance at the smouldering remains of the note in the ashtray, he made for the door. First he had to collect Jaeger, then head for where Winter was hopefully still at the La Fonda.

At least Burger was out there keeping an eye on him, the one man who held the key to the whole mission.

31

CHAPTER

appy hour was long gone but the scene was still bustling in the lounge of the La Fonda, the dinner crowd having wandered in with tourists milling about, mothers helplessly trying to herd kids who were racing about in that hyperactive stage before succumbing to terminal sleepiness, salesmen slowly getting stoned at the corner bar. The room was hazy with cigarette smoke and the laughter of the crowd mingled with the screams of kids and the noise of traffic on the plaza.

It was a beautiful evening, the cold weather finally giving way to a late spring with perfume in the air and a pleasant warmth inside the packed room. The Hill dwellers were down in force, it being a Friday night, the women in their pretty floral dresses and precious black market nylon stockings, the men mostly semi-formal with some of the older scientists in suits and ties. A scattering of men in uniform were gathered around a group of excitedly chattering girls who had come down from The Hill for the evening in the army bus.

A three piece combo had been busy on a small stage near the entrance, playing lots of Glen Miller and some wartime songs from artists Winter did not recognise. He was sitting at the bar alone, enjoying a beer, Jaeger and Feldman yet to show up.

Letting his thoughts drift over the earlier events at Mama's he decided, yes, the stranger in the big hat *had* been the border cop and the look in Jaeger's eyes was a clear sign he had made him too. Was that the reason Jaeger had sent him off to the La Fonda? Get him out of the way so he could take care of business? Winter decided he would rather not know what the latter entailed and wondered about their next move. Jaeger had earlier dismissed any suggestion of enquiring about Berkowitz and hinted at an alternative plan should they not meet up.

Banning these thoughts from his mind he called for another beer and swivelled to survey the room where the crowd was steadily building, marvelling at the strange fact that here he was, the enemy in their midst and no-one knew. Was he even really there?

Or was it just all the product of an over tired mind?

Truth be told, he *was* tired. The long journey and all that had happened along the way was finally getting to him. That pervading sense of the unreal, of some twilight world he had somehow fallen into, was growing by the hour. A sudden thought had him smile grimly, could it be that he was actually dead? Died in that action on the Seelow River, or perhaps incinerated in the bombing raid at Wilhelmshaven?

He shook his head to clear the nebulous thoughts, taking another sip of the refreshingly cold beer. No, this was real. His brother – his nemesis – was near. The dull throbbing of the scar on his thigh told him that. That and the slow gnawing empty sensation deep in his innermost being that once again, just like always, his brother would find a way to bring destruction upon the life he had so carefully tried to rebuild all those years ago.

Suddenly utterly alone he rose and walked unsteadily over to where the band was taking a smoke break, chatting and laughing amongst themselves as a waiter brought around a tray of drinks. He wasn't drunk, not even tipsy. Just so tired and so terribly empty inside.

'You guys mind?' he heard himself say as if from a distance, inclining his head in the direction of the piano.

'Knock yourself out, buddy,' the piano man said raising a glass in a toast. His accent betraying him as a Texan.

Sliding onto the stool he stared down at the keys, his fingers finding their way to familiar territory as if it had always been. It was a Steinway and for a moment he thought about that. Something a German had made, something beautiful and not destructive and part of him wondered what good old Germany, whatever remained of her, would be making in the future. Then, with a sigh, he banished his heavy heart and played Night and Day. It was a favourite song going all the way back to carefree days in a Boston he was probably never going to see again. Skipping the opening bars he moved into the refrain, softly mouthing the words as his fingers glided over the keys. All sounds faded from the room as the music took him way back and after a while he slid into I Get a Kick out of You, the piano soaring now as groups of people stopped their conversation to listen.

'What is that you're playing, li'l Buddy?' the Texan asked, suddenly interested. His partner on the saxophone had joined in, tentatively picking up the swing as Winter settled into the song, the piano now sounding like a carnival.

'Cole Porter,' Winter replied, his mind elsewhere as other songs started coming to him. It had been a long time since he had last played, a one time passion that had laid forgotten since... well, since that time in Boston.

'Never apologize for Cole Porter,' a quiet voice said standing behind him. Before he could react, she said, 'Would you play the song for me?'

'What song?' he said hoarsely as his hands dropped lamely to his side, his tongue suddenly as dry as the desert outside.

'You know what song,' Eva said as she touched him lightly on the arm, a touch that sent shockwaves through his body. She was not moving, her face hidden from view and yet its features as clear as that last day. The perfume was still the same and ... 'I... I vowed never to play it again.'

'Then I will sing it, to the people watching us now. I don't care, if I can stand it why can't you?'

'Eva, don't...' he said softly, slowly turning around to look at her. She was standing quite close now, the light behind her casting her face in shadow and yet it was unmistakeably her. There was moisture brimming on her cheeks, he could see that, and the hand on his shoulder was cool yet burning through the thinness of his shirt.

'I always knew one day we'd meet again,' she said. 'I knew life could not be that cruel not to bring us here tonight.'

Becoming vaguely aware of people staring at them, the saxophonist and trumpeter looking expectantly at him, other faces taking on shape as they emerged from the fog, he turned back to the keyboard and, after a second's composure, played I've got You under my Skin. Standing close to him now, she was softly miming the words.

Behind them people were dancing now, the women smiling as they whirled past and suddenly he couldn't do it any more, changing quickly to A Foggy Day in London Town before rising from the seat with a nod at the Texan who was shaking his head and saying to the trumpet player that he had heard of music turning the li'l ladies on but this guy was one smooth *hombre*'.

It was suddenly hot in the room, hot and claustrophobic and noisy. Winter needed time to think and found himself somehow walking with Eva on his arm and spotting glass fronted French doors leading to a small enclosed inner plaza, he steered her there. Sensing his urgency, not knowing why but aware of a new sensation, one of sudden extreme anxiety, Eva followed him without resistance. 'Alex, I... What is happening?'

'Come,' he said, he voice little more than a whisper as they left behind the lights of the lounge and bar to momentarily pause as he anxiously checked their surroundings

They were standing in the shadows of an open air section of the hotel, nothing but stars above their heads and the tinkling sounds of a fountain mingling with the muted music spilling through the open doors. The patio was used for weddings and such and surrounded on three sides by an overlooking balcony with wrought iron rails. Soft lights glowed from behind a large painted glass tiled wall off to one side and at the far end, visible between open glass doors, a fire was beckoning in a large decorated hearth. Lit by a few wall mounted lamps turned low the area was largely in darkness, the only sign of not being alone the intermittent glow of a cigarette at the far end of the plaza.

Drawing her close enough to feel her tremble he kissed her, raising a hand to softly caress her cheek and the side of her neck, acutely aware of all those old long buried emotions coming alive. Raising his head he drew in the smell of her hair, like dew of freshly reaped hay in the morning he always thought of it.

'You are in extreme danger, Eva. You must not be seen with me,' he managed hoarsely, the need in him now shallow and primeval. There was a bench and taking her by the hand they sat down.

'You are a spy,' she said simply, holding onto his hand and stroking it with the other. 'You are here to get something from The Hill.'

It was a statement and he saw little point in trying to deny it. 'Yes. Max is up there and I have to find him.'

She nodded, 'I know.'

'You *know?!* You've *seen* him?'

'I also work there, as a mathematician.' Seeing the questions in his eyes she went on, 'He's changed. Uses the name Berkowitz. I think he has had plastic surgery done but it didn't fool me. He pretends not to know me and I have been wracking my brain how to handle this.' She fixed him with a questioning gaze, eyes moving rapidly side to side as she searched for a clue in his eyes, his expression. 'Is this why you're here? The two of you, spies together?'

Forcing himself to stay calm Winter thought this over, finally shaking his head. 'No, Eva. I'm here to save him from himself. They, Hitler and the others, want him to carry out some mission that I don't have the details for. Somehow he won't and I was taken from the battlefield – I'm an army engineer – to rescue the mission.' As the words rolled over his lips he realised how utterly stupid the whole thing was. Here they were, a world away from the horror of a Europe in flames, a war all but over and instead of being with his men, trying to keep them alive, he was sitting on a bench with a woman he once loved and planning to see a brother that in so many ways was nothing but his evil mirror image.

They sat in silence for a while, Eva studying his hand as if seeing something there for the first time. Then, in a voice so soft he had to strain to hear, she told him a story. In a way it was a story he knew, something he had worked out for himself a long time ago, never had time to live it through with her.

'That time, when it happened. When we all went down to New York to see the ball game, you and me and Max and Karen in your car with Jake and Maddie in his. Remember that weekend?'

'I remember,' he said. How could he ever forget.

'It was the first time we spent a whole night together, making love I don't know how many times. Then, there was a commotion in the car park, someone breaking into cars I think and you went downstairs to see what it was.'

Part of him wanted her to stop, another part wanted her to tell the story. The lie that ruined his life. He said nothing, just sat there and stared at a glowing cigarette tip that seemed to draw nearer.

'You stayed away for a long time and I was asleep when you came back ---'

'The cops were there,' he said softly, 'I had to make a statement.'

'... we made love again...'

'I love you,' he said but she was opening her heart now, letting it all out and he wasn't sure she had heard him.

'Then, the next morning, on the way back when we stopped for lunch, I overheard Max tell Jake how you and he had planned the whole thing, how you always shared everything...' There was a sob in her voice now and as the memories flooded back Winter was aware of a sharp, very ancient, pain burning in his chest and threatening to choke him.

'How the two of you had swopped girls so Max could also ---' She broke off, momentarily overcome by emotion before, gathering herself with visible effort, going on. 'I remember them laughing and that bastard Jake making some comment about me and I... I just lost it! Ran off and found a cab and never wanted to see you again.'

Sitting quite still as the memories flooded back Winter shared her pain, the hand clasped in his warm and alive and very real. 'I tried to reach you,' he said at length, 'tried to explain how a jealous Max had lied as he always did. Tried to destroy my life once again.'

'I loved you so much, Alex. I just couldn't ---'

He wanted to say something but she put a finger to his lips, whispered about letting her finish, get it all out. 'I never read your letters, burned them all. Vowed never to speak to you again until, when my mind had cleared enough, I realised that it couldn't have been. That Max had lied all along.'

'The scar on the thigh,' Winter said dully, 'you always liked to run your fingers over it. Max's scar is on the opposite side.'

'Yes,' she said after a pause. 'By then it was too late. You had left for home and I, I stayed behind and tried to pick up the pieces of my life.'

'You got married,' he said. A statement more than a question.

'Yes. A good man. I even loved him, something I thought would never happen again.' Adding, after a moment, 'he died.'

'What happened?'

Eva shrugged and Winter put an arm around her shoulder and held her. 'It was the summer of forty four. Some hellhole in the Pacific.' He sensed more than saw the wry sad smile, heard it in her voice, 'I still remember the day the army car came to the house, the lieutenant checking out the numbers, making sure he had the right one.'

'I'm sorry,' he said, aware of how lame it sounded.

After a while she asked about his mother and then she asked what he was going to do before correcting herself, asking what *they* were going to do.

Thirty paces away, standing in the deep shade of a potted palm, the cigarette long extinguished, Burger heard enough to know their carefully laid plans were now in grave danger of being thwarted by this pathetic pair of lovebirds. Something would have to be done.

They sat in silence for a while, two people lost in their memories of a simpler time and discovering – no real surprise there – that, after all the years apart, all that had happened while trapped in the darkness a world gone mad had woven around them, they still loved one another.

Still harboured that burning flame of desire.

'I want to make love to you,' Winter said simply.

'I have a room,' she said, 'upstairs, room 213. I planned to come down for the weekend, do some sightseeing. Come.' She rose pulling him up next to her and melting in his arms, kissing him and savouring the rush of warmth coursing through her trembling body.

32

CHAPTER

I t was at that moment that he heard Jaeger's voice, calling out to him from the direction of the open patio doors, his silhouette outlined against the backlighting. 'Alex? Are you there?'

Moving quickly he drew Eva into the shadows, a finger to his lips motioning her to silence. 'It's the other German. I'll go and get rid of him. You must not be seen. Wait here for five minutes then go to your room. I'll meet you there!'

'Coming!' he called out, stepping out into the light. 'I was just enjoying a quiet cigarette out here.' Adding, 'what is it?'

'Where is Pickens?' Jaeger asked as they went inside, the SS man glancing at his watch.

'He passed out at the bar, about two hours ago. Met up with an old drinking friend and had, I don't know, a dozen beers plus, God knows how many tequila chasers. The friend offered to take him home.' Noticing the other man's agitated state he asked what was up.

'There's been a phone message, from Elektron. Something has happened and he wants to meet urgently, to-night.'

'What?!' Stunned he wanted to ask if Max was alright but then when had his nemesis brother not been?

'Twenty three hundred hours, at the bridge.'

'Christ!' Eleven o' clock, that was less than an hour away. He would have to warn Eva, let her know what was happening. There was no way he was going to lose her again through a senseless misunderstanding. The absurdity of their situation – of the whole damn thing – did not escape him. Once again his beloved brother, his evil twin, was threatening to destroy his world. Thinking quickly he patted his pockets, informing Jaeger that he had left his cigarettes outside, that he would be back in a minute.

Then, without waiting for a reply, he walked quickly back to the spot where he had left Eva.

She wasn't there! Glancing wildly around as panic gripped him he wondered if she had gone to the room, deciding no, he would have seen her come through the doors, the only way inside. A sudden movement at the far end of the plaza caught his eye, the swirl of a dress, a flash of light on sweeping auburn hair, instantly disappearing as the woman – his Eva – entered the small washroom facility he had noticed earlier leading off from the hallway across. As he made to follow he saw a shadow detach itself and quickly follow Eva, a flitting shadow as it crossed the dull glow from the fireplace.

No alternative, he would have to go over and speak to Eva *now*, before Jaeger came looking for him. With that he hastened across. Ten paces from the small alcove and open door where the light was streaming from he heard the cry, soft and quickly muffled. Eva! The other person, what the hell?! Instantly numb with shock he burst through the door.

The washroom was tiny, planned for use during those occasions, mainly in the warmer summer months, when private outdoor events were sometimes held in the enclosed garden plaza, it consisted of a single stall with a washbasin in the alcove. Eva was struggling in the grasp of a tall woman in a floral dress who had a hand clasped around her mouth from behind, a blade of a slim stiletto glinting in the other, poised to strike at the exposed throat.

As a scream burst from his lips the woman whirled around, gaunt deeply tanned features contorted in an animal-like snarl.

Momentarily letting go of a terrified Eva who collapsed against a wall, the woman – Winter had a fleeting glimpse of dark yet blazing eyes – lunged at him, a thrust he easily avoided, as the would-be killer bumped into him, trying to escape. Acting with blind instinct an off balance Alex swung at the looming face and felt his clenched fist strike solidly home against the side of the woman's face. There was a sickening wet crunch as her head hit the edge of the washbasin and then she was down and motionless, the stiletto skidding across the tiled floor to fetch up near a cowering Eva.

Forcing himself to move quickly he knelt next to Eva who, apart from shock, appeared unharmed. There was no time for words, Jaeger might come looking for him at any moment. Gently but firmly raising a now sobbing Eva to her feet he ushered her towards the exit, in the process stepping over the inert body where a pool of blood was slowly gathering. Pausing for a moment he knelt to feel for a pulse and found none. The dark eyes were sightless now, staring at something no living soul could see. Rising to meet the horror filled gaze of a still speechless Eva he shook his head. Dear God! Not only had he struck a woman, he had killed her!

Supporting a still too stunned to speak Eva as they exited into the mercifully deserted outside darkness his last glimpse of the dead woman was the leather knife sheath strapped to a thigh where the flimsy dress rode up. Right next to a small tattoo of something he had seen all too often; a Nazi swastika.

As her lifeless body cooled Heidi Burger knew nothing of this. Her war over, she was sleeping the sleep of the dead.

It was only much later, revisiting the scene in his mind's eye, that Winter realised the assassin could easily have killed him but tried to escape instead, realising that in even just wounding him she would have destroyed her mission. For he was, after all, the golden key that would unlock Korsika.

33

CHAPTER

fter making his phone call Berkowitz was hesitant as to what to do next. The words of Dr Esther Stern came back to him, "Just because you're paranoid, Maximilian, does not mean they aren't after you." Spoken in jest, perhaps, but surely what he was experiencing now was not just his overactive imagination?

As had become increasingly frequent during times of stress the old demons of his childhood started rising from the shadows of his subconscious once again, the words of the dreaded poem milling through his feverishly burning mind. The terrible image of the father on horseback, racing through the night, the dying child in his arms. Over his shoulder, visible only to the boy, the terrifying spectre of the Erlkönig coming to claim his soul.

"Mein Sohn, was birgst du so bang
Dein Gesicht? –
"Siehst, Vater, du den Erlkönig nicht?
Den Erlkönig mit Kron' und
Schweif?" –
"Mein Sohn, es ist ein Nebelstreif..."

Overcome by a sudden rush of nausea he collapsed on the bed, burying his face in the pillow. Ivan... Ivan... Where are you, Alex? Why have you abandoned me?! You always knew how to fend off the clasping hands of the monsters. You and Ivan, he who, tired and battle weary as he was, would take up his sword again and again; to be that lone warrior fighting for those too powerless and too afraid to defend themselves ---

After a while the images faded, to be replaced by the usual headache. Rising slowly he sat for a moment on the edge of the bed, waiting for the room to stop spinning. Staring down at his hands he saw they were shaking. Summoning all his will he concentrated and gradually the shaking stopped. With it came clarity of thought. He knew what he had to do.

Twenty minutes later he was back in his workshop, now the only person left in the Technical Block. If the guard at the gate had been surprised to see him at that hour he kept it to himself, checking the pass and waving him through with a "Good evening, Doctor."

Carefully drawing the blinds he switched on the lights then went straight to the row of lockers. Even from two paces away he could see his own had been tampered with, his keen eyesight picking up the scratches on the paintwork. More proof they were on to him. Striding past he stopped at the second locker from the end, the one that still bore the name of Rick Johnston, Technician. The young man who had died in a motorcycle accident on the Los Alamos road just three months earlier. Being in charge of the workshop Berkowitz was responsible for allocating the lockers. This one he had kept unused but locked. Sensitivities had prevented anyone from questioning the matter. Besides, there was enough locker space for everyone.

Working quickly now, his ears attuned to any outside noises, he unlocked the door and hauled out the large canvas backpack, carrying it across to the main workbench. Setting it down next to the disabled coffee urn he opened it to remove the explosives. Next he went to the bench where the lenses were assembled before being transported to the testing area. Carefully selecting twenty four of the hexagonal metal blocks he packed them with the pre-calculated mix of explosives. The Trinity Device would take thirty two lenses but these were smaller, initially built as a scale model for the ones now being used and, carefully fitted together, would fit snugly inside the cylinder casing.

It was precision work and the concentration raised a film of sweat on his brow, the ever lingering headache dismissed with a shake of the head. The next step was to bring over the urn and, with the use of a screwdriver and pliers remove the bottom section. Staring at the inside of the casing he nodded in grim satisfaction, the design was good. It *would* work! Carefully extracting a close fitting interlinked belt designed to hold the lenses he set about loading it.

It took twenty minutes of hard concentration and when he finally stepped back to survey his handiwork he was satisfied. All the planning, all those hours of surreptitiously working late at night when the others had left, carefully preparing the belt and casing was paying off. Turning his attention to the base plate he removed the original warming element and electronic segment and replaced them with the detonator and its timing apparatus. The last task was to connect the two wires to the socket that led to the individual lenses.

Stepping back he arched to ease the strain on his aching back and thought for a moment. All that was still needed was the core and the initiator and Magda as he had come to think of her, would be ready. "Magda." Was it strange that he had named it after his mother? Darling *Mutti?* He somehow did not think so, after all was this not an instrument of awesome destruction, a device with no other purpose but to intimidate and control? All in pursuit of some dark and terrible horizon?

His mother, she was always the one who ultimately held the power over all of them, even his father who only *thought* he was in charge. Oh how she had played them all in her madness! It was only in recent months, once he became aware of the awesome power and implications of this, this *thing* they were building, that the mist started lifting from his mind and he could see that she never loved them, her boys. They had only ever been tools to the greater cause! Did she not imply that the time the Führer came to the house, accompanied by Bormann and Himmler? Stating quite calmly while gazing at the boys who had been ushered in to meet the great men, that no sacrifice was too great, that a revolution devours its children. That she could not live in a world without National Socialism.

Even Hitler, normally friendly and surprisingly at ease around children, had looked embarrassed.

There were two plutonium cores on The Hill that night. Weapons grade plutonium 239 to form the explosive nucleus of the Device now being readied for final testing. One was locked away in a secure area which he did not have access to but the second core was at that moment still in the building where they had been conducting the Dragon's Tail experiments. Careless really but with cowboys like Louis Slotin and fellow boy scouts running wild, only to be expected.

To this building he did have a key.

Placing the now much heavier urn inside the backpack he slung it over his shoulder and headed for the door, switching off the lights as he went.

If the guard at the gate thought it strange that the scientist would leave with a large backpack it did not merit undue concern. These people were pretty eccentric at best and had he not seen this particular one carry that bag before. A cursory check confirmed what looked like a coffee urn, the man's explanation of taking the repaired appliance over to the kitchen of the single men's quarters a perfectly acceptable one.

He even helped Berkowitz load it into the back seat of the car parked in the shadow of the nearest hut.

It was at that moment that Rusty Miller, about to drive back down to his room at the La Fonda in Santa Fe, get a good night's sleep for a change, was halted by the voice of a young woman calling out to him from the entrance to the duty office. Pausing, car keys in hand, he waited for her to come closer. It was one of the WAC telephone operators, a pretty girl by the name of Penny Kerrigan whom he thought filled out her uniform rather nicely.

Slightly breathless she paused and smiled uncertainly, 'Excuse me, sir, but earlier today we were instructed to let you know of any phone calls or messages for Dr Berkowitz?'

'Yes?'

'He placed a phone call from his room at eighteen fifty eight. To what sounded like the receptionist at a Santa Fe hotel, asking for a Mr Feldman. Something about a meeting at twenty three hundred hours tonight.'

A sudden rush of adrenalin had Rusty fight down the impulse to shake the woman by the shoulders, 'Where? What hotel, dammit?!'

'I...I, well ---'

Instantly regretting his harsh tone Rusty forced himself to insert a note of calm into his tone. 'Sorry, you've done well. Do you know the name of the hotel?'

Straightening her hair, the WAC cap slightly askance after the sudden step back she had taken, she hesitated then added, 'The Wigwam Hotel, in Montezuma Avenue.'

'There's more,' she said in a voice that had just a hint of hurt.

'More?' *Jesus Christ, woman!!*

'Twenty five minutes later, at nineteen twenty three hours he received a phone call to his room, from a Dr Frank. I wrote the conversation down. Here.'

Thanking her with a forced smile, Rusty took the slip of paper and speed read it. Carefully worded it suggested someone who suspected their call might be monitored, most likely Berkowitz's contact man in town. Confirming the meeting but where? Another thought struck him, Berkowitz had made and received those calls not long after they had searched his room, meaning they had almost certainly been spotted, setting the ball rolling.

Fiorentino had gone off for the night but, with the action heading for town he would not have any jurisdiction there anyway. Weighing his options Miller decided there was nothing for it but to drive to the Wigwam in the hope of finding Berkowitz. Could

Berkowitz still be in his room? Quickly dismissing the thought as extremely unlikely he started the car and headed for the main gate.

On impulse he paused next to the guard at the Technical Area, motioning for the corporal to come over. 'Did you see Dr Berkowitz come in here earlier?' Holding out a photo of the man to jolt the soldier's memory.

'Sure did, sir,' he said, straightening up from where he had been squinting at the photo. 'He left a few minutes ago, in his car.' He pointed to the spot where the vehicle had been parked, adding, 'I helped him load his canvas pack.'

Sweet Jesus Christ!

'Did he say anything!? Did you see which way he went!?'

Tilting back his steel helmet, eyes suddenly wary, the soldier scratched his head. 'Well, I dunno. He headed thataway, towards the main area of the compound then I kinda lost sight of the car, in the dark.'

His mind racing, Rusty asked whether there was any other exit to The Hill except for the main gate. 'Heading for the main gate he would have to come past here, not so?'

The corporal nodded, 'I woulda spotted him if he was headin' for town, for sure. There is another gate, up over on the far side but that's closed at night. There'd be a guard posted there.'

Sitting still for a moment, thinking, Rusty switched off the engine and, brushing past the guard headed for Berkowitz's workshop at a run. Inside he paused, taking in the scene, his gaze finally settling on the end row locker door standing open at an angle. Three big steps took him there, only to confirm it was empty. That would be where the man had kept the bloody explosives. Jeez, in only he'd had access to an explosive sniffing dog he would have had the bastard by now!

Something else was missing, something that had been in open display, something so ordinary no-one would look at it twice.

The coffee urn was gone!

Suddenly cold to his core Rusty Miller rushed for the door bursting into the cooling night air with enough speed to almost collide with a startled technician walking down the path on his way home from one of the other bungalows.

'Hey, watch it buddy!' the man, alarmed, exclaimed as he bent to pick up a sheaf of spilled papers.

In his mad hurry Rusty was on the point of mumbling an apology and rush off when a sudden thought made him pause, grabbing the startled man by the arms to raise him to his feet. 'Do you know how to make an atom bomb?!'

'Whaaat?!!' Suddenly gripped by panic the technician lashed out in a desperate bid to get away from the madman.

Easily brushing off the flimsy blow Rusty shook his head, forcing the technician to look at him. 'No! I'm not mad. Someone has stolen explosives and is making an atomic device right here. I need to know if there's anything more needed to build this thing. Now!!'

'I..I'm just a metallurgy tech, I don't know this!!'

'Where have you just come from? Is there anyone here who *does* know?'

The man hesitated, clutching the papers to his bosom as he tried to extricate himself from Rusty's grip. Inclining his head in the direction of the one of the nearby huts he stammered, 'Oppy is here, over in the hut. He's been going over the latest figures.'

'Who? Speak up man?!'

'Professor Oppenheimer, the man in ---'

But Rusty was already gone, heading at a run for the hut where a light was showing. Seconds later he burst through the door to be confronted by a startled Oppenheimer who had been poring over several large sheets spread out on a trestle table.

'What the ---?'

Stopping short and holding up a hand to indicate an explanation was coming as soon as he could catch his breath, Rusty forced himself to be calm, speak in a slow measured tone. 'We have a big problem, Professor. Dr Berkowitz is a spy and has just left these premises with a large backpack I believe contains a mini-nuclear device. Explosives he has stolen was in a locker in his workplace and he took this together with a stainless steel coffee urn he was claiming to be fixing.'

'Coffee urn ---' Oppenheimer whispered, feeling for the edge of the table for support as he grappled with what he was hearing. 'A bomb?! I, it's unbelievable, I knew the man was under stress, we all are, but a *bomb?!*'

'Not just a bomb but I suspect, the kind of bomb you are working on here? Is that possible? I mean, something that small?'

Momentarily lost in thought, the scientist nodded absently, 'I suppose theoretically, yes. We have been working on a much bigger scale and nobody knows yet if the thing will work.' He shook his head as he struggled to come to terms with what he was hearing and, even in that moment of high anxiety Rusty could see the man was exhausted beyond human endurance, on the point of a nervous breakdown.

'Professor, you have to help me now! We know Berkowitz has the casing and the explosives, almost certainly a detonator as well, *what more does he need to build this thing?!!*'

'Well... there's no uranium missing so it cannot be a gun type, must be the implosion model. The core! He needs the core. And an initiator.' Drawing from an inner source Oppenheimer seemed to straighten up, the dull eyes of seconds earlier suddenly alive with a spark of intensity that suggested an inner source of energy others seldom have. 'The explosives compress the plutonium to reach critical mass leading to the explosion. The trick lies in ---'

'Where would he find this core?!'

Suddenly fully alert, Oppenheimer frowned, 'Feynman and Slotin was doing a criticality test with the core earlier to-day, at the guillotine shed down near V Block. By itself the core is not radioactive – it's an alpha emitter only – and can be handled just wearing gloves. It's kept under lock down there.'

'How big is it?'

'About three and a half inches in diameter, weighs about fourteen pounds. Heavier than lead.'

'This "guillotine shed," where is it?'

'Head straight up the main street, about five hundred yards on the left. It the tallest building, corrugated aluminium siding. You can't miss it.'

'I'll go, you'd better raise Captain Fiorentino or whoever is on duty, tell him to place The Hill in lockdown!' At the door he hesitated, 'How powerful would this bomb be, if it works?'

'The world has never seen anything like it. Powerful enough to destroy a city.'

'What, like Santa Fe?'

'Try New York,' Oppenheimer said softly, adding, 'some say it might even set the atmosphere on fire...'

But Rusty was already out the door.

34

C H A P T E R

Inside the guillotine shed Berkowitz worked at a feverish pace as he forced the dull headache and its ever present companion, nausea, to the back of his brain. The large brass padlock to the small wooden shed within a shed where the core was kept provided little resistance. Three days earlier he had bought an identical padlock at a Santa Fe hardware store and swapped it for the unlocked one hanging from the door jamb when no-one was looking. The key had been left in the padlock while the team was busy conducting the experiment in a far corner of the big shed and it was the easiest thing in the world to substitute the two locks, leaving the new key in place as before and pocketing the old padlock.

This left him with the duplicate key. An astonishing oversight of common sense security measures but, in the mad rush leading up to the looming Trinity Experiment, not that unusual.

The only setback would be if the core had been moved to another more secure site since he had last checked. It had not and it took only seconds to retrieve the small square wooden box from its resting place on a shelf. Once again he marvelled at how something this awe inspiring could be housed in a simple cobbled together box suspended from what looked like the carrying handle of a discarded suitcase and festooned with several round rubber stops screwed into the wood that looked like they had come off the bottom end of walking canes. The latter bit a puzzle as there was no obvious need to protect the solid metal square inside from any accidental drop or bump.

Carrying the surprisingly heavy box over to a working bench he donned a pair of rubber gloves before opening it and extracting the plutonium core. Nickel plated it was slightly warm to the touch but quite safe to handle. An alpha emitter only unless the escaping neutrons were reflected back into the core, the radiation was only dangerous if handled with bare hands or inhaled.

Removing the coffee urn's casing from the back pack he unscrewed the base plate. It would, if his measurements had been exact, take only seconds to ease the core into the prepared space between the lenses and insert the initiator which had also been stored in the shed.

Needing more workspace he moved a pile of the tungsten carbide bricks that were used in the Dragon Experiments to one side and, having upended the casing to prop it against the wall, prepared to carefully insert the primed core into its slot.

Which was the moment a familiar voice from somewhere near the doorway shouted at him to stop what he was doing and raise his hands or be shot. Stunned Berkowitz whirled around to face the threat dropping the core. The momentum from the wild move had the plutonium land amongst the pile of tungsten carbide blocks and instantly there was an intense blue flash of light and a wave of heat as the reflected neutrons sent the core supercritical, ionizing the air in the room and emitting a massive dose of radiation.

The shock sent Berkowitz crashing into the trestle table which sent the bricks flying and the core to roll away which immediately went back to its normal non lethal state.

Staggering back from the effect of the flash where he had been poised in the doorframe Miller missed the two steps leading up to the door and crashed onto the footpath knocking him out as his head hit the cement.

Slowly climbing back to his feet from where he had collapsed next to the bench Berkowitz took a moment to reflect on his new situation. Standing that close to the reaction there was little doubt he had received a lethal dose of irradiation, that he would be dead within days if not hours. It was a cold undeniable fact and with a sense of detachment that only vaguely surprised him, he accepted the sentence.

No time to lose now, he had to get out of here before others, having seen the flash, came running. He would have to assemble the device later. Retrieving the plutonium core he shoved it into the canvas backpack together with the casing and, hefting the now much heavier load, headed for the door. At the bottom of the stairs he paused to glance down at the sprawling form of Rusty Miller who was groaning softly but showing no signs of moving. Noticing the big automatic pistol that had seconds earlier been aimed at him he stooped to pick it up, shoving it into a jacket pocket before heading for his parked car at a fast walking pace.

Suddenly overcome with intense nausea he vomited violently, his body breaking out into a cold sweat as the world seemed to turn around him. It took all his will to fight the nausea down and he knew full well what was behind it, the first reaction to a lethal dose of irradiation.

Then he was in the car and heading for The Hill's West Gate with distant headlights visible in his rear view mirror and the faint sounds of a siren in his ears. Less than a minute later he was at the gate, closed at that hour with the lone guard coming over to remind the doctor, whose car he recognised, of the fact. Having planned a much more controlled exit from The Hill, via the Main Gate, Berkowitz had not anticipated this but there was no other way. With the alarm raised that escape route would be sealed.

'Good evening, Doctor,' the MP said with a smile, shining a torch into the driver's side. It was Joe Driscoll, a likeable Brooklyn Irishman who always greeted Berkowitz with a smile and often a happy toss away one-liner. 'A bit late to go into town now, isn't it, Doc? Anyways, this one's closed, you'll have to head on back to ---'

Which was as far as he got before Berkowitz fired, the impact of the heavy calibre .45 bullet spinning the man round like a top and dumping him in a heap ten feet away, the flashlight describing a lazy arc before crashing into nearby bushes.

It took only a matter of seconds to retrieve the keys to the padlocked gate from the dead man's pockets and swing open the heavy gates. Dragging the body into the cover of bushes he drove through before closing and locking the gates behind him, all the while aware of the constant ringing of a telephone in the guard hut.

Back in the car he headed down on a road that would, once he reached the valley, offer him several options of reaching the Otowi Crossing Bridge along seldom used dirt tracks. Using the main road was now out of the question as road blocks would be sure to be in place before long. Hopefully it would take them a little while to find poor Joe's body and conclude he had used that gate and was no longer on The Hill.

The thought of the look on Joe Driscoll's face in that split second when he had seen the raised gun, realised he was going to die, brought the strange sensation of a lump to the throat of Max Berkowitz. He had liked the man.

Shaking off the unfamiliar sensation of remorse he settled down to concentrate on his driving.

35

CHAPTER

By the time Oppenheimer, accompanied by Captain Fiorentino and two uniformed servicemen, arrived at V Site Rusty Miller was sitting up and gazing around, wearing a puzzled expression. 'My head! It's splitting!' he managed somewhat incoherently, holding a shaking hand to a temple.

As Fiorentino ran up the stairs to search the building Oppenheimer knelt by the fallen man's side and asked what had happened only to be met with a blank expression and a mumbling about a flash.

'Berkowitz!? You were chasing Berkowitz!?' an exasperated Oppenheimer shouted, shaking Miller by the shoulders in an attempt to bring him to his senses. This only seemed to exacerbate the man's headache leading to tightly screwed up eyes and a low keening sound.

'Professor? Professor! This man is concussed and, if that flash someone reported was what I think it was, he possibly received a dose of radiation. We have to get him up to the sick bay immediately.' It was one of the senior medics and, nodding wearily, Oppenheimer got back to his feet to allow two men to load Miller onto a stretcher.

Gazing wildly about Oppenheimer saw Fiorentino come out of the hut accompanied by one of the nuclear physicists who had emerged from the growing crowd. 'The core?' he asked hoarsely.

'Gone, I'm afraid,' the physicist said spreading his hands in a gesture of defeat. 'There has definitely been a critical incident, one of the Geiger counters had been switched on and the recording is off the scale.'

'And Berkowitz?'

'No sign,' Fiorentino said, 'but we'll find him, alright.'

Which was when a sergeant informed him that there was no reply from the West Gate post, that a team had been sent over to check.

'Roadblocks,' Oppenheimer said as he fumbled for a cigarette, a shaking hand leading to a dropped Zippo, a soldier stepping up with a light. 'We need roadblocks.' Displaying an iron sense of self discipline the chief scientist's voice had now returned to a tone of normalcy but the hand that held the cigarette shook, spilling ash.

'I don't have jurisdiction outside of the military area, Sir. With his head start he would have bypassed the limits of our area before I can have men in place. He wanted to ask whether Berkowitz's gadget – better to think of it as that and not a bomb – was a danger to his men but one look at Oppenheimer's tortured features had him hold back. 'I'll get onto it, he said, standing aside as the prone form of Miller was carried to an ambulance that had pulled up.

'I'll contact the Sheriff's Office in Santa Fe and ask them to be on the alert for the fugitive. There is also a FBI agent in town, a man called Meads.' He was about to head for a waiting jeep when Oppenheimer called him back.

'Miller told me earlier that he had intercepted a call to and from Berkowitz indicating a meeting set up in town, to-night I think. Do you know anything about it?'

Fiorentino shook his head, 'No, I haven't seen him since early evening, must have happened after I went off duty. Did he have a name for this meeting spot?'

'No.'

'I'll check on him in a while.' With that he was sprinting for the jeep, calling at the driver to get the guards at the Main Gate to sound a general alert. With dread certainty he realised this was out of his hands already, it was now a matter for the FBI and there would be hell to pay.

Watching the tail lights of the jeep bounce down the road Oppenheimer took a deep draw on his cigarette, the nicotine coursing through his bloodstream providing a welcoming sense of returning calm. What was he going to tell General Groves when the man arrived back at The Hill as scheduled the next morning? The mere thought sent a shiver of dread all the way down his spine.

At that moment County Sheriff Joe Don Earl was sitting at his desk morosely chewing on a cigar stogie that had long since departed for wherever dead smokes go. Sighing he stared at a tin mug of strong black coffee close within reach, decided it was probably cold and turned a jaded eye to the man occupying the visitor's chair.

'Special Agent, you say? Is that supposed to mean something to us country boys?'

Meads smiled, leaned back in the creaking chair that looked and sounded like it went back to the days of Billy the Kid and glanced around the office, taking in the framed photographs of lawmen dead and gone lining the walls. Each and every one sported the kind of moustache that said don't mess with me. Much like the one Sheriff Joe Don Earl was now twirling with tobacco stained fingers. 'If you'd like a break from writing parking tickets and tossing drunks,' Meads said, 'I think I have something for a man of your fibre.'

'The suspense,' Joe Don said wearily, 'is killing me.'

Deciding the pissing contest could wait until later, Meads came to the point. 'A few hours ago I witnessed something over at Mama Teresa's Bar. Three men, strangers, being spooked by a newcomer, someone I suspect might be a lawman and taking off in a car, followed by this man.'

'A car chase,' the Sheriff said, 'happens all the time. Probably a woman involved somewhere.'

Ignoring the lack of enthusiasm Meads pressed on. 'I checked the place's registry, two of the men, Jaeger and Winter, have been staying there since Wednesday. Visitors.'

'We get that a lot,' the Sheriff nodded, 'beats me why.'

'I checked the names against the federal list of those suspected for a murder down Mexico way, these two come up as persons of interest, evaded a road block near Albuquerque. I reckon they're armed and dangerous, I'd like some help in having a chat to them.' He decided not to mention the suspicion that the fugitives were likely German saboteurs, landed from a submarine on the Mexican Gulf as per the most recent APB from NY Head Office.

'You mean those parking tickets might have to wait?' Without waiting for a reply Joe Don turned to a man who had hitherto been hovering in the shadows, leaning against the wall, silently listening to the conversation. 'Want to tell Special Agent Meads what we've picked up so far to-night?'

Shifting the gum to a new slot in a fleshy jowl Deputy Art Baez shrugged, 'Jeez, boss, you mean that white guy found murdered in his car over at the old church or the li'l lady killed at La Fonda's?'

They both looked at Meads who held up his hands in a token of apology. 'I take it all back, sorry. This white guy, what's he look like?'

Pushing back his chair Sheriff Earl stood up and reached for his jacket. 'Morgue's at back, let's have a look.'

Heading down a corridor leading to the rear of the building they passed the holding cells where a full blooded American Indian, complete with a solitary feather in his tied back hair, was sitting on a stool reading the evening paper. He had on a pair of denim overalls over a cattleman's shirt. 'We'll be at back, Chief,' Joe Don said tossing the man a ring of jingling keys. 'Get old Charlie sobered up, I'll want to talk to him.'

The Indian nodded without bothering to look up from the sports pages. 'Will do, boss.'

'The doc still at back?'

'No sir, he left ten minutes ago, says he'll be back for a post mortem in the morning. Jacks is still back there.'

If the ancient morgue attendant was surprised at seeing them there at that hour he did not show it, ambling over to the large door of the ice room to push out a sheet covered gurney then going back for another. Seconds later they were staring down at the cold pale white features of Little Joe Kowalski. The very bright overhead lights shimmered off the polished steel of the gurney and there was the faint smell of formalin coming from a distant corner.

With the door to the refrigerator open it was chilling in the room and Meads decided that explained the shivers down his spine. 'This him?' the Sheriff asked. A fresh cigarillo clamped between his teeth he seemed oblivious to the ash falling on the body.

'Yes. It's him.'

Joe Don nodded, pointed to the bulging red flecked eyes and the bruises around Little Joe's fat neck. 'Strangled. See that fine cut line? It points to a steel wire of sorts.'

'He was found behind the wheel of his parked car in the parking lot of the old St Francis Basilica. Art here saw old Charlie Creek loitering around the car in the deserted parking lot and went to investigate, Charlie being one of our regulars and up to no good.'

'Plenty of them parking tickets,' the deputy affirmed with a wink at Meads.

'And that's when he spotted the dead man?'

'Yep. The killer had taken his wallet, so no ID but the car's registered to a Mr Joseph Kowalski from El Paso, Texas. A Border Police man. We'll be on to them first thing in the morning, find out why he was up here.'

'Did this Charlie character see anything?'

'Let's go find out,' the Sheriff said but first get a load of this.' He pulled back the sheet covering the face of the second body and Meads found himself staring down at Heidi Burger, the congealed mix of blood and brains bringing a pungent sickly sweet smell to his nostrils and with it a sudden urge to be sick. Forcibly ignoring the impulse he asked who she was. 'Don't know yet,' Joe Don said. 'She was found in the toilet at the back of the La Fonda. Looks like she was hit on the side of the head and then bashed her head against a washbasin. No witnesses so far. But look at this!'

Using his pen as a tool the sheriff lifted the hem of the dead woman's dress to expose a leather sheath strapped to the thigh and, immediately above it, the small tattoo of a swastika.

'Jesus!' Meads said softly. 'And here I've been looking for Russian spies!'

'No sign of the knife that goes with the sheath,' Earl said as he dropped the hem back into place and signalled to the morgue attendant to push the gurneys back into the ice room.

'Any sign of rape?' Meads asked, still trying to grapple with the new turn of events.

Sheriff Joe Don Earl looked at Meads with an expression of incredulity, 'Gee, you mean this tattoo business and the knife is all just a sidetrack?'

Meads shuffled his feet, the damn nausea was still there. 'I dunno, just a thought ---'

'You're a sick man, Meads,' Joe Don said ruefully as he led the way out. Following close on their heels Meads could hear the deputy chuckle.

Back in the Sheriff's office Baez went off to brew fresh coffee as the Indian jailer brought in the prisoner to unceremoniously dump him onto a hardback chair facing the desk. Charlie Creek was not called "Old Charlie" for nothing. Definitely not as a term of endearment if the body odour that sat around him like a fog on a swamp was anything to go by.

Meads guessed him at anywhere between a rock solid seventy and an even harder place eighty. No more than about five foot nothing and eighty pounds he looked like the slightest draught could blow him away. The weather beaten deeply lined face sported a scraggly white stubble of a beard under the high cheekbones of his Apache ancestry while small black eyes flickering from face to face seemingly missing nothing. The whole was topped off by a full head of grey hair and the remnants of a pony tail.

'Good evening, Mr Earl, Sir,' he said in a hoarse smoker's voice, 'sorry to be a nuisance, again.' A yellow gap toothed smile crowned an anxious grimace.

'Call me Sheriff,' Joe Don said evenly as he studied the little man with no outward sign of pleasure.

'Ah, yes, Sheriff Earl. And may I point out that old Charlie here voted for you the last time. Yessiree! Sure did!'

Ignoring the remark Joe Don asked him what had happened in the car park. Making a show of gathering his thoughts, a deep frown settling on his brow, Charlie recalled minding his own business, just out for an evening stroll when he saw this man asleep behind the wheel of his parked car. Thinking he'd mosey over and touch the man for a smoke, he was shocked to notice the man's eyes were wide open and fixed, the body slumped against the door. Being a concerned citizen he opened the car door to see if the man was OK which was when Deputy Baez – this with a nod of deference to Baez who had now returned with a pot of coffee – arrived. Hands raised in a gesture of helpless innocence suggested that was it.

'You didn't take anything from the car or the man?' Joe Don asked.

'No Sir!' The little man replied, his voice rising in indignation at the very idea that he, Charlie Creek, would ever stoop to such depths.

'I strip searched him, boss,' Baez affirmed as he produced a few tin mugs, started pouring the strong black coffee. 'Nothing, same goes for the car and the surrounding bushes.'

'Hmm,' Joe Don said, reaching for a mug, 'any of those cookies Ma Carter brought still left?'

'I'll go check,' Baez said, passing Meads a mug.

'Were there other people around?' Joe Don asked.

Charlie shook his head as he eyed the coffee Baez had put on the desk next to him. 'Nope. I saw two men in a brown sedan drive out of the parking lot a little while earlier, this was when the last of the tourists were just leaving, the others being a family with kids.'

Noticing the frown on Joe Don's face he hastened to explain, 'I was taking a little nap under a shady bush back there, on that old bench and ---'

'Describe the two men' Meads said, pulling his chair closer to sit face to face with the man while striving to control his rising impatience. 'Did you see their faces?'

'I dunno, I might have... Say,' he added glancing over at the sheriff, 'it's mighty hot in here sir, a man could die of thirst right here. There wouldn't perhaps be a little nip of something a bit stronger than ---'

'No,' Joe Don said firmly, 'answer the man.'

'Well, I'm not sure. It was kinda getting dark and ---'

'It was broad daylight,' Baez corrected him placing a plate of oatmeal cookies on the desk.

With a deep sigh Meads moved his chair closer until his knees almost touched those of a now apprehensive looking Charlie.

'Wha... what you doing?' Charlie managed, his gaze switching rapidly between the faces in the room that seemed to be watching with interest. Moving with unexpected speed for a big man Mead's arm shot out to grab Charlie Creek by the crotch in an iron grip so painful it cut the man's cry of pain off instantly.

'So God help me, you slippery son of a bitch. Talk to me or I'll rip your balls out right here!!'

'White! White men. One tall and thin with a --- Oh Jesus. Please, the pain!!'

Easing off his grip Meads indicated the man should go on, finally letting go to look over at Earl and Baez. 'It's the two men in the bar, alright.'

'What do you think, boss?' Baez asked, reaching for a cookie.

'I think Special Agent Meads might just have the makings of a real lawman under that fancy suit after all.' He reached for his hat and made to get up. 'Guess we'd better go and talk to these gents.

Charlie, go back to your cell. You know where it is. Get the Chief to find you something to eat.'

The desk phone rang.

Baez glanced at the sheriff who shrugged, 'Answer it,' he sighed, pulling on his jacket.

'It's for you,' Baez said, handing over the phone, 'a Captain Fiorentino, from up on The Hill. He says it's urgent.'

And as Fate played its hand it would be almost two hours before Special Agent Meads got around to making that call at Mother Teresa's Cocktail Bar and Lounge. As for the sheriff, in the end he never did make it.

$$37$$

CHAPTER

A tourist attraction during daylight hours the bridge over the Rio Grande at Otowi Crossing was deserted at that late hour. Driving down the Old Taos Highway on the northern outskirts of town, Feldman at the wheel, they had passed a few homes where people were reclining on their porches, sipping at their drinks and enjoying the welcoming coolness of the night. One old couple waved lazily as they slowly cruised past and from somewhere nearby came the sound of a guitar playing a song that was vaguely familiar. In that part of town there were few other cars about, what nightlife there was happening over at the main plaza several blocks away.

Jaeger was sitting in the passenger seat with a quietly agitated Winter in the back striving hard to bring his turmoil of thoughts under control. The Argentinean was strangely quiet, brushing off questioning from Jaeger as to what he thought was happening, simply stating that they would find out soon enough. In truth he was grappling with what he had found when he went to look for Burger shortly after Jaeger and Winter had entered the La Fonda's lobby to head for the parked car. Waving them on impatiently he had intoned that he was about to follow then turned on his heels to go and find Burger, tell her what was happening. Her instructions had been to keep an eye on Winter so logically she should be close by.

It was the moment he entered the main lounge that a woman came running in from the darkened terrace area hysterically sobbing about there being a dead woman out there in the washroom with lots of blood and a knife and --- It was enough. With instant cold clarity he knew who that woman would be, the discarded knife the clincher. But he had to be sure and brushing past the crowd that had instantly formed he rushed through the indoor plaza reaching the lit corridor at a run and, spotting the light spilling from the washroom, reached it in seconds.

Burger was dead. Catching sight of the discarded stiletto he pocketed it then, in a rare moment of tenderness, he knelt next to the body of Heidi Burger and pulled the hem of her dress down, covering the tattoo. There were urgent voices outside now and fast approaching. Encountering them as he left he shouted about going to fetch a doctor and headed back at a run.

It was when they were two blocks away and passing under the yellow pool cast by a streetlamp that Winter, who had been watching him intently, noticed the smear of blood on the cuff of the man's shirt. He kept it to himself, pretty much sure of whose blood it was and what that spelled for his own chances of long term survival in this increasingly complex game they were now playing.

'Are you quite sure this is the spot?' Jaeger asked as Feldman pulled up in the deep shade of a large ponderosa pine tree. Some fifty yards from the bridge and on a rising they had a good view of any approaching traffic or pedestrians.

'Yes,' Feldman said, dousing the headlights and opening his door. Glancing around to take in the surroundings he was satisfied that no-one else was about, the nearest house was several hundred yards to their rear and in darkness. Across the river, set well back from the road, he could vaguely discern the outlines of the old teahouse often frequented by visitors down from Los Alamos. To-night, save for a solitary porch light, it was doused in darkness. 'He will be driving and could come from any direction. We need to have a man on the other side as a lookout, should there be any signs of trouble.' He did not elaborate on the nature of this trouble and no-one asked.

'I'll go,' Jaeger said, producing an automatic and checking the magazine before slotting it down the back of his belt. 'Winter, you stay here with Feldman. Signal with the car's lights if Berkowitz arrives at your end, I'll take this.' He held up the flashlight he had taken from the glove box and seconds later disappeared into the gloom.

Leaning against the car, arms folded and studying Feldman with interest, Winter asked what exactly was to happen if and when this Berkowitz turned up. At the same time thinking how ironic it was that even he was now thinking of his brother as "Berkowitz."

'We won't have much time,' Feldman replied as he produced a cigarette from a silver case, running it under his nose before slowly, reluctantly, deciding not to risk a light, returning it to its case. 'It depends on what has alarmed him. If he can produce the object we – you – will activate the plan.'

'I see,' Winter said not really seeing at all. 'And what exactly *is* this plan again? Presumably it has changed from when Max was first inserted here under this ludicrous disguise, otherwise why the need for me?'

'Max?' Feldman asked arching a brow, what hinted at a sneer at the corner of his mouth.

'Yes, Max,' Winter said wearily. 'My brother, Max Winter.'

Feldman nodded, 'It is good, good, this brother thing. It means you will do the right thing, when the time comes.'

'When the time comes...' Winter echoed softly.

'Which I think is right now,' Feldman said, pushing away from the car and stepping out of the shadows as a sedan approached the bridge, driving much too fast and raising a cloud of dust in its wake.

Sliding to a halt with a screech of brakes just short of the bridge, the driver was clearly hesitant and presumably surveying the area. Leaning inside the open driver's side window Feldman flashed the headlights twice in quick succession and after a moment's hesitation, the sedan started rolling forwards to head their way. If the driver was alarmed by the man who had suddenly appeared on the passenger side running board of his car it did not show.

Then Berkowitz was there, stopping next to the parked car and dousing his lights before slowly, carefully, getting out. It was at that instant that Winter stepped forward to lay eyes on the brother he had long thought dead and, perhaps, was. 'Hello Max,' he said softly, working at keeping his voice even, the way their despot of a Teutonic father would no doubt have approved.

'Alex...' was all the other man could muster as his arms dropped lamely to his sides.

'A touching scene, no doubt,' Feldman's dry voice interceded as Jaeger came round to join them. 'Sadly we are at war and sentiment will have to wait. Have you got what we asked for?'

His gaze still fixed on his brother with a look akin to wonder, Berkowitz nodded, 'In the car.'

Jerking open the rear door Jaeger studied the backpack. 'it's quite heavy, fifty or sixty pounds at least.' Quickly unfastening the straps he stared down at the metal casing with a look of puzzlement. 'It doesn't look like a bomb to me.'

Nobody deigned to comment, Feldman stepping up closer to stare intently into Berkowitz's eyes. 'What happened up on The Hill, tonight?'

In a few sentences, speaking in seemingly listless monotone, the scientist told him.

'Do you think you have been followed?' Feldman asked with a growing sense of urgency, resisting the impulse to grab the damn man, shake him by the shoulders.

'Ich weiss nicht.' came the soft reply as Max Winter in a moment of deep despair reverted to their mother tongue, desperately searching the face of his brother, a terrible look in his eyes.

'Alex, ich ---'

'Enough!' Feldman snapped, 'we have to get out of here! Come!' Motioning Jaeger to get Berkowitz and himself into the car he told Winter to follow them in the other car, that they were going to

Mama Teresa's. A snap decision had him decide to for the moment keep the two brothers apart until they got to a more controllable situation. There was, of course, still the unanswered question of what exactly had happened over at the La Fonda, something he would have out with Mr Alex Winter when the time came, that a promise made to himself.

They drove in silence, Feldman keeping to a slow speed to minimize the risk of raising undue attention with Winter keeping a steady fifty yards back in his rear view mirror. Sitting in the passenger seat with Jaeger in the back and still staring at the backpack and its contents with a look of puzzlement, Berkowitz was quite motionless as he stared straight ahead, seemingly lost in thought. A fine film of sweat on his forehead glistened under the overhead light from the passing streetlamps and Feldman's keen eye did not miss the clenching and unclenching of white knuckled fists as the man struggled with unseen inner demons.

It was past the midnight hour when the two cars rolled up at Mama Teresa's and there were few cars about in the parking lot, Sam Pickens' old biplane now accepted by the regulars as part of the ambience of the place.

In the bar and lounge area the only sign of life apart from José the barman was two old timers, locals at a guess, propping up the far end of the counter and studying the newcomers with hazy disinterest in the bar mirror as they strolled in. Without looking up from where he was restocking the fridges José asked what their poison was. Nothing was further away from Feldman's mind at that point than a drink but, having decided on their way that the now deserted lounge was the best place for what had to happen, four men crammed into a small bedroom with razor thin walls too risky, he bowed to the inevitable. 'Tequila,' he said, 'bring a bottle over to the table over there in the corner, 'and four glasses.'

'Thees will be last round, *Señors*,' the man said apologetically as he placed the bottle on the table and proceeded to unload the shot glasses. 'The bar, she iss close now.'

'What about him?' Winter asked, inclining his head towards where he had just noticed Slippery Sam passed out in a club chair, hat down over his eyes and snoring softly, the corpses of half a dozen beer bottles marking his territory.

José shrugged expansively managing a sad expression. 'The Madam, she say leave him. He *too* much drunk,' the latter statement accentuated by an index finger drawing down the corner of an eyelid.

They watched as the two men at the bar slowly climbed off their barstools to head for the door, exchanging a farewell wave with the barman who had now produced a broom and was starting to sweep up.

Turning his gaze back to Berkowitz who was seated between Winter and Jaeger Feldman leaned closer, 'Korsika,' he said slowly, clearly. All eyes drifted to the small ivory domino piece that had appeared on the table seemingly from nowhere.

Double one. Snake eyes.

Spellbound all stared as the face of Max Winter, suddenly no longer Berkowitz, lost all expression. The bottle of tequila sat on the table, untouched.

'My God!' Jaeger said softly as Max Winter slowly raised his gaze to meet that of Jaeger, the previous dazed look now replaced by something new, something deeper, unfathomable.

'Ivan...' As the word rolled over his lips Max Winter looked at his brother and suddenly Jaeger knew what the look behind those troubled eyes were. It was a cry for help from a doomed man. 'Ivan...'

Alex Winter sat quite still, his face pale as a sheet. As his brother repeated the word, now rising with a hint of panic, he looked steadily at Feldman. 'Is this it? This all you got?!' This what you brought me all this way for, the ramblings of a sick man who needs urgent psychiatric help?'

Feldman said nothing. Then, without a word he pushed back his chair and walked over to the barman who was still sweeping, pretending not to notice the scene now unfolding. 'Lock the door,' he said and when the man made to protest he showed him the gun.

'Lock the door, then close the curtains and go and sit over there where I can see you. Do it now!'

Mutely the man nodded, under Feldman's menacing gaze locking up and drawing the curtains before sitting down at Pickens' table to study them with large fear filled eyes.

Resuming his seat Feldman took a slip of folded paper from an inside pocket and proceeded to carefully unfold it. Placing the gun on the table he smiled wolfishly and began to read. In the stillness of the room his voice was clear, his German with the faintest of an accent that, to Jaeger's ears, hinted at a Bavarian background.

'"Mein Sohn, was birgst du so bang
Dein Gesicht?" –
"Siehst, Vater, du den Erlkönig nicht?
Den Erlenkönig mit Kron' und
Schweif?"
"Mein Sohn, es ist ein Nebelstreif."

The dull ache in Winter's thigh that had been a constant presence now for weeks was growing in intensity as the words of Goethe's epic poem filled the room. A pain only matched by old long repressed memories of a childhood he had tried so desperately to ban to a subconscious netherworld never to be revisited. Without having to look at his brother he knew Max would feel it too. A shared pain that bound them together, forever. *'Please,'* he managed hoarsely but no-one seemed to notice his pain as Feldman's voice droned on.

'"Mein Vater, mein Vater, und hörest
du nich,
Was Erlenkönig mir leise
verspricht?" –
"Sei ruhig, bleibe ruhig, mein Kind;
In dürren Blättern säuselt der Wind."'
'Stop!' Winter shouted, the pain now unbearable. *'Please stop...'*

He was staring at his brother now, Max Winter seemingly unaware of the tears streaming down his cheeks as his lips wordlessly mouthed over and over, *Ivan...Ivan...*

Alex Winter wanted to reach out to his brother, wanted to take his hand, hug him and tell him it was only a dream, that it would soon be over. But he couldn't.

'What do you want from me?' he said dully, not looking at Feldman who was studying him with a strange light in his eyes.

'Ivan. The psychiatrist felt this was a blocking mechanism in his mind, something that goes back to when he was a child, when you were a child. Something only you hold the key to. I want you to unblock him, get him to obey what he was programmed for.'

Programmed for... like a robot, a Pavlovian experiment...

'I won't do it,' he said finally. 'I won't destroy my brother.'

Picking up the automatic, its matt black shape gleaming under the overhead light, Feldman pointed it at Jaeger who, if alarmed by the sudden turn of events, showed no outward sign of panic. 'I will count to ten, if you still have not complied I will shoot Herr Jaeger. One!'

There was a deathly silence in the room now, broken only by the faint sounds of traffic in the distance somewhere and, closer, the barely audible moaning of the bartender who was rocking to and fro in his chair and not looking at them. Slippery Sam was by all appearances still passed out but the snoring had stopped.

'Two!'

'Ivan...' Max pleaded, looking at his brother now.

'Three!'

Alex Winter's mind was racing. He had no doubt this madman would carry out his threat but what terrible thing would he unleash in this empty shell of a man that had once been his brother if he complied?

'Four!' The hand that held the gun was quite steady, the hammer cocked, finger on the trigger. His dark eyes hooded Jaeger seemed unperturbed, his steady gaze meeting that of his would be assassin with not the slightest sign of fear.

'What is Ivan!?' Feldman had picked up the slip of paper and was preparing to read more from the poem, the paper held far enough away so he could still cover the man sitting across the table from him.

'Five! *Mein Vater, mein Vater, und siehst...*'

'Ivanhoe,' Alex Winter said staring helplessly at his stricken brother, willing him to listen, to understand. 'Ivanhoe is coming to rescue us both. He is riding on his white horse and tired and wounded as he is, his shield is held high, his sword shiny and his eyes bright...'

'Ivanhoe,' Max Winter said nodding solemnly, the next word a mechanical 'Siegfried...' his voice now that of a different person. A boy, Jaeger thought in wonder, he has become a boy again!

They watched, spellbound, as Max Winter slowly stood up from the table. There was a faraway look in his eyes, his voice now a soulless monotone, much like his movements. 'Korsika, must go to Siegfried.'

'My God!' Jaeger exclaimed, saying it for all of them.

They watched as Max picked up the heavy canvas bag they had brought in with them and placed it on a table. Slowly he unpacked the items, the plutonium core last and almost innocent looking as it lay there for all to see. The overhead light glinted off its shiny surface which was when Alex Winter first noticed the blisters on his brother's hands. Lifting his gaze he saw the same blisters now breaking out on the man's neck and face, noticed the bloodshot eyes, took in the swelling of the lips and the slight slurring of the voice.

Ignoring Feldman who had motioned for him to remain seated he got up and went to his brother who was now in the process of inserting the metal ball into the shiny metal cylinder that looked suspiciously like a coffee urn. 'Max,' he began hesitantly, 'what happened to you, to-night?'

'Ivanhoe,' came the answer, the accompanying smile ghastly.

'Was it something to do with this, this thing?' A sudden thought had him ask about irradiation, whether there had been an exposure.

'It is all over,' Max Winter said mechanically and without looking at his brother. 'From the core, maybe 300 rad. Don't know how long...to live. Maybe days, maybe hours only.' Then, returning to an inside world of his own, he turned to the task of assembling the apparatus, expertly inserting the trigger mechanism and connecting up the wires before reaching for the base plate.

Incredibly he was softly whistling a tune. It took a minute for Alex Winter to recognise it. *Und das heist, Erika!'* Memories from a long ago family holiday in Austria, one of the few happy moments they had ever known.

'One more thing,' Feldman said producing a small object from a jacket pocket and placing it on the table. To Winter's expert eye it was a timing device consisting of a clock mechanism attached to a detonator, the two connected by twin wires, one red, one blue. 'Attach it. We'll set the timer later if need be.'

A protest died on Winter's lips as Feldman held up a hand stating it was simply a precaution, an extra level to the standoff should the Americans decide to call their bluff. 'They would need us to disarm it and that provides all kinds of possibilities,' he said in a voice that invited no contradiction.

Numbly and with a growing sense of impending doom Winter watched his brother, moving mechanically, attach the timing device before screwing home the base plate.

'Vertig' Max said dully as he stepped back to study his handiwork. 'It is ready...'

With a feeling of helplessness Winter watched his brother sink into a chair and drink noisily from an offered glass of water. After a short while Berkowitz declared himself feeling better and Jaeger helped him place the device in the backpack and then all looked at Feldman.

'What now?' Jaeger asked waving a hand at Feldman to put the gun away.

Stepping back from where he had been studying the outside scene through a crack in a curtain, Feldman seemed lost in thought for a moment. 'Tie up this lot,' he said, pointing to the barman and

Sam Pickens, the latter still showing no signs of conscious life. 'Use the ropes from the curtains. And use the barman's bandanna to stop him calling for help. I have to get a suitcase from the boot of my car and send a radio message, then we can be on the way to our destination.'

'That being?' Jaeger asked as he snapped a rope cord away from the nearest curtain.

'Lamy Station,' Feldman said, indicating Jaeger should shoulder the backpack with its deadly contents. 'We're going on a train trip.'

Taking the rope from Jaeger Winter went over to Slippery Sam and proceeded to tie the man's hands behind his back and to the chair. His face was close to that of the old timer when Sam lifted his head just enough for their eyes to meet while still hidden under the hat's wide brim. The wink was slow and deliberate, the whisper all but inaudible, 'Hi buddy, get us a li'l drink, will ya?'

Turning his back to the others in the room Winter returned the wink. 'Be careful,' he whispered before stepping away to inspect his handiwork.

The next ten minutes was spent as they watched Feldman set up the short wave radio taken from a battered looking brown leather suitcase. Jaeger was instructed to take the antenna over to the nearest window and minutes later Feldman's call was being answered from a distant operator with surprising clarity. He had produced a code book and was sending in what Winter thought was Morse Code.

'A clear signal,' Jaeger said, peering over the man's shoulder, 'Mexico?'

'The embassy is no more but our Bolivar network survives,' Feldman said. 'The network will relay to Germany.'

'Mind telling us what the message is?' Winter asked, his mind furtively at work at trying to decide what his next step should be, how to stop the madness that he now seemed inextricably part of. There was little doubt this crazy Argentinean Nazi would kill him without the bat of an eyelid at any sign of wanting to stop the mission. Quite possibly the only reason he was still alive was in the event of brother Max regressing at some vital moment and needing another little pep talk.

'*Götterdämmerung,*' Feldman said matter of factly, 'the Twilight of the Gods...'

'One more thing, Feldman,' Jaeger said softly as the other man packed his equipment into the suitcase, snapping the lid shut.

'Oh?'

'Next time you point a gun at me, smile. So I know we're still on the same side ---'

38

CHAPTER

'How is he?' Oppenheimer asked, the hand holding the cigarette trembling, the anguish in the man's face there for all to see. The medic shrugged as he fiddled with the intravenous infusion while studying the gauge on an oxygen cylinder and adjusting the flow.

'Just coming round, I think. The skull X ray shows no fracture and his neuro observations are OK.'

'What about the irradiation?'

'We think the event took place on the workbench about twenty feet away from the door where the patient had been standing. That is judging by where the tungsten carbide blocks were lying. With Doctor Berkowitz possibly shielding him at least partially and the rapidly distance related diminishing effect I reckon he'll be OK.' It was one of the nuclear physicists, Feynman, replying in a cold clinical tone.

Oppenheimer was about to say something when the man on the bed groaned and made to sit up. An orderly tried to restrain him but was waved away by the medic. 'He's coming round, move that bright light away from his eyes.'

Eyes wide open now Miller took in the scene surrounding his bed. A warning gesture from Oppenheimer had everyone quiet as they waited for Miller to speak. 'Water,' he said finally and at a nod an orderly stepped up and held a glass to the patient's lips. They watched him drink then watched as he raised a hand to gingerly examine the back of his scalp, his hand coming away sticky with congealed blood.

'How long have I been here?' Miller asked.

The medic glanced at his watch, 'About thirty eight minutes. Try not to speak now, you need rest.'

Ignoring him Miller said, 'Where is he?'

'He got away,' Oppenheimer said gently as he watched a nurse fluff up Miller's pillows.

'My head hurts.'

'You're concussed,' she said, handing him two tablets and watching as he swallowed them with water.

Moving slowly to minimise the pain of sudden movements Miller turned his focus back on Oppenheimer, 'The thing he was making, is it gone?'

'Yes. We have roadblocks out and Captain Fiorentino has contacted the Santa Fe police, he's gone there himself.'

'I must get up, help find him.'

'You're going nowhere,' the medic said firmly. 'Concussion is a dangerous thing.' He stood back a few paces as Miller, moving with visible effort, pushed back the blankets and swung his legs over the side of the bed. The sudden rise brought a rushing sound to his ears and with it the vague sensation of nausea. Giving it a moment to stop his head from spinning he managed to locate Oppenheimer who was in fact standing right in front of him.

'The General,' he said in a voice that sounded alien to his own ears, 'does he know?'

'I spoke to him on the telephone half an hour ago,' Oppenheimer replied, searching for an ashtray to stub out his cigarette. 'He's still at the Pentagon and will be flying in tomorrow morning. His main concern was whether the Device – our main official one – is safe and whether the project is on time. And it is.'

'What about the President?' He was referring to the Oval Office's new incumbent, not yet two weeks in office after President Roosevelt's untimely death.

Glancing nervously around Oppenheimer leaned closer and lowered his voice. 'General Groves has not yet informed President Truman of the exact nature of the Manhattan Project. He feels we are so close now and ---'

' --- we don't want the funds stopped.'

'Something like that,' Oppenheimer said softly.

A voice at the door had him turn, 'Professor? We need you over at the Technical Area, some concern about sabotage, we're not sure.'

Suppressing an expletive Oppenheimer made to follow, pausing to glance back at Miller with an order to stay put, he'd be back later with news.

Two minutes later Miller was dressed, an enterprise that took it out of him as his head was still spinning and the co-ordination not up to speed. Then, brushing by a protesting medic with a brusque "I'll be back," he was outside and heading for his parked car. If the action had shifted to the town that was where he would be.

CHAPTER 39

Winter was in the process of tying a gag around Sam's mouth and neck when he saw the man, now seemingly quite awake, staring steadily at something behind his shoulder. Still kneeling and out of view of the others he turned to see what Sam was seemingly indicating.

The doorhandle was slowly turning then released again! Someone was trying to enter from the reception area. Someone who now noiselessly made a retreat. But, at that hour, who could it be?

Sam was trying to say something and, easing the gag Winter put his ear closer. 'Stay here,' Sam whispered hoarsely, 'watch the door behind the bar ---'

At the other end of the lounge Feldman was unlocking the bar's front doors with a stooped Berkowitz next to him and leaning on a table as he seemed to struggle with his balance. Close behind was Jaeger who had the backpack slung onto his back. The door open they paused to look at Winter, Jaeger inclining his head to indicate they were waiting for him.

Which was the moment the door behind the bar counter swung open to reveal Mama Teresa standing there. It took her no more than a second to see what was going on and that was all she needed.

'Bastards!' she snarled and lifted the twelve bore shotgun that had magically appeared from under the counter. The first shot made matchsticks out of the deal table next to the party at the door, the second shattering the glass fronted doors where a micro second earlier the party had been frozen in time and space.

It was Jaeger's lightning fast reflexes that saved them, the battle seasoned soldier diving through the doors and sweeping the other two with him to land with a bone shuddering thud on the dirt of the parking lot.

Rolling like a cat Feldman was on his feet and reaching for his gun when Jaeger grabbed him by the arm to forcibly drag him towards the nearest car, Berkowitz stumbling blindly in their wake and breathing hard.

'Don't be a fool!' Jaeger hissed as he jerked open the car doors to push Berkowitz inside and with little visible effort tossing the backpack in on the back seat next to him. 'That's a twelve bore pump action gun! She'll ---' His next words were drowned in the boom of the shotgun as the car's windscreen shattered into a thousand shards of flying glass.

'Drive!!' Feldman shrieked as he dived into the passenger side with Jaeger already gunning the engine. Then they were away, spinning wheels raising a cloud of dust in the light spilling through the hotel's shattered doors.

As they passed Feldman's parked car – they were in Berkowitz's sedan and with the hotel empty there were no other cars parked – Feldman leaned out the passenger window and fired several shots at the tyres, the car instantly sagging to one side. Still swearing in a torrent of Spanish Mama Teresa fired one last shot into the night before lowering the smoking barrel and turning to go back inside.

'Bastards!' she said again, followed by a rapid torrent in Spanish that Winter could not follow but had Slippery Sam wince. He got up from where he had dived onto the floor, taking Sam with him and reached to pull the other man, still tied to the chair, upright.

'Look at this mess!' Teresa said as she came over and for a moment Winter was not sure if she was referring to the state

Slippery Sam was in or the general condition of their surroundings. Seemingly oblivious now of the shotgun still clutched in her hand Teresa whirled to take in the shambles of her barroom and in the process Winter felt obliged to gently push the barrel away to point in a less threatening direction, while he worked at untying Sam.

'Thieves!' Teresa spat, *'Bandidos!* I knew that thin one with the gigolo moustache was no good! But Jaeger, I liked him!' Shaking her head at the unpredictable vagaries of life she went across to a visibly agitated José, setting the shotgun aside to quickly untie the barman whom she promptly slapped into silence when he broke into hysterical chatter.

By now Sam had recovered to the point of enquiring whether there was any chance his thirst could be ---

'You want drink?' Teresa called from where she had been replacing the shotgun behind the bar.

'Yes, please!' Sam shouted back, his face lighting up at the prospect of this unexpected windfall.

'Here,' Teresa said coming over with a glass of water. Sam's face collapsed into a study of deep disappointment but he dutifully took the glass in a shaking hand and made a manly effort at downing the unfamiliar liquid.

Winter watched in silence as the lady pulled up a chair and indicated the two of them should join her. A few barked orders had a still mumbling Jose' start clearing up the debris of the table and broken glass. 'Now you tell me what is going on.'

And Winter was surprised at how easy it was to tell this woman, whom for some inexplicable reason he felt he could trust more than even his own mother, the story of two brothers and how it had all come to this.

And as the minutes ticked away she never interrupted him once and even Sam was showing signs of listening, nodding solemnly at parts he thought resembled wrong turns in his own life's adventure.

When he had finished they sat in silence for a while, each lost in their own thoughts. It was Teresa who spoke next, 'This bomb you say they have, they plan to kill people?'

'The plan was always to use it to strike a deal with the Americans, like a get out of jail free ticket. Now I think the plan has changed. Yes, I think they mean to kill people. Lots of people.'

'We must stop them,' she said, 'you say they are going for the train?'

'Maybe we call the sheriff?' Slippery Sam said which, Winter thought seeing as to the man's chequered personal experience with the law, was a brave thing to suggest. It also made him wonder why the long arm of the law had not yet shown up, seeing as to loud gunfire in the night, neighbours complaining, that kind of thing. He said so only to be told by Teresa that in the peaceful town of Santa Fe gunfire at night was not that uncommon and besides, unless there was blood and a body or two, they were not really that interested.

'We call the cops, no?' Jose' muttered as he surveyed the carnage of his bar, 'too much mess!'

'You don't think it is good idea?' Teresa said studying Winter's face and noticing the deepening frown.

'It runs the risk of them exploding the bomb when the police close in. People will die. No, *we* have to stop them.'

'I was afraid you were going to say that,' Sam Pickens said wearily. 'And here me with a headache and a thirst that could kill a camel.'

Ignoring him Teresa said, 'We get to train and you go inside and get bomb. No other way!' A thought made her hesitate, 'what about this lady you say you love? The one waiting for you at La Fonda, maybe she has car?'

'She is here,' a voice said from the direction of the front door as Eva stepped into the light.

'Eva!' Winter called out, jumping to his feet, 'I...I...How much did you hear?!'

'Enough,' she said as she strode over to pull up a chair. 'All the bits of the puzzle that were still missing.' She smiled and took his hand, caressing it with the other. 'I was worried about you, darling.

When you didn't return I had to come and find you.' There was a light in her eyes and it held a promise, never to lose him again.

'A real woman never let go of good man,' Teresa said enigmatically, gazing at a fidgety Sam with a look of softness Winter had not noticed before. 'Even when he *bad* man.'

A philosophical point no-one seemed inclined to debate.

Minutes before they had discussed the issue of finding a serviceable car and the arrival of Eva seemed to offer a solution. This was quickly quashed when it turned out she had cycled from her hotel.

'Cycled?!' Winter exclaimed, 'how? Why?!' he pleaded, as he sunk into the nearest chair.

'I took the night porter's bicycle,' she said matter of factly, 'He won't notice before morning, besides it's an emergency,' she said, indicating with a sweep of a hand the chaos of their surroundings.

Sensing more of an explanation was needed, she added, 'The keys to the pool car is with one of the other girls and at this late hour I could not get a cab. So I cycled, it's not that far and there's still quite a few people around nearer the centre of town.' Another thought had her frown, 'There's also police road blocks, I noticed two on my way over. They're stopping all cars and searching them. Also quite a few uniformed men from The Hill at these roadblocks.'

Up to that point Winter had been considering stealing a car but that now seemed out of the question. Also, with the head start the others had, if they got through the roadblocks, they would never catch up with them.

'There's an aeroplane parked outside,' Eva said the matter of fact tone of her voice hinting that after tonight nothing would ever surprise her again. 'Anybody here fly it?'

All looked at Sam who shifted uncomfortably in his seat and had difficulty making eye contact with Teresa. 'Well, I...'

'He be *drunk!*' Teresa said, not quite managing to hide the disgust in her voice. 'Like always!' Shrugging expansively she added with a sigh, 'But he be our only chance. Jose'!'

'Yes, Mama Teresa?'

'Bring some fresh coffee for Meester Sam. Make a lot, we want too.'

As the scowling bartender retreated to the kitchen while muttering under his breath Winter raised the issue of fuel, recalling that the plane had been all but empty.

'There's a drum full of kerosene in the shed at back,' Sam said, his head between his hands and rubbing his temples in a vague attempt at driving out whatever was hurting inside. 'I keep it there to refuel, it's cheaper than at the airport.'

'What time does the train leave?' Winter asked.

They watched as Teresa got up and went across to the bar, retrieving a small booklet from behind the counter. 'Eight twenty,' she said having located the timetable. 'She be standing at Albuquerque Station now.'

'Which gives us about two hours to sober up our pilot,' Winter said looking at Sam.

'Lamy Station,' Sam said with a deep sigh as they made space on the table for the coffee, 'Someone there once gave me a beer.'

40

CHAPTER

eichsführer SS Heinrich Himmler received the radio message at 14h45 on the morning of 22nd April 1945, two days after Hitler's birthday. Radio contact with the world outside the Führerbunker had been temporarily lost earlier and the message received at General Wenck's Army Group West Headquarters was delivered by a grime and blood smeared despatch rider that looked like he had passed through the gates of hell and probably had. How the man had managed to get through the encircling Russian vice grip that was by now in areas as close as a few hundred yards from the bunker, was nothing short of a miracle.

Snatching the folded message from the man without a word while ignoring the salute and avoiding contact with the feldwebel's bloodshot thousand yard stare, Himmler went inside his office and shut the door. It took him no more than few seconds to read through the hastily scribbled message: *Götterdämmerung* and, next to it, the date and time it was received by the Bolivar resistance group in Mexico City, more than eight hours earlier. A hint of a smile was gone in an instant as he carefully refolded the message, tucking it into an inside pocket of his tunic to head for the Führer's private quarters. It would be a perfect present for Hitler and perhaps put him in the right frame of mind to consider the proposition he and Göring were framing.

Götterdämmerung. The Twilight of the Gods! The atomic bomb was in the hands of Germany and about to give the Americans their own taste of the fiery hell that was Dresden! Hitler would be so pleased! As he weaved his way through the central corridor now lined with the slumped and squatting forms of several dozen battle weary and dazed soldiers who stared up at the man in the immaculate black uniform with dulled eyes and expressionless faces, he reflected wryly how providential it was that only days before, on 12th April, what remained of the Berlin Philharmonic Orchestra had performed Wagner's opera, one of Hitler's favourites.

In the common room of the afterbunker all pretence at discipline had by now broken down as the prospect of Armageddon loomed large. A few days earlier the near hysterical party atmosphere had usually only started once the Führer had retired behind closed doors, now the scenes of a drunken orgy was all around as the champagne flowed and secretaries, some half naked, danced on tables while drunken officers stumbled about shouting incoherent messages across the room as they sang and fumbled with the clothing of giggling equally drunk females amidst a stench of sweat, cheap perfume and vomit.

Totally ignored as he crossed the floor he was halted by a warning glance from Reichsmarschall Göring, looking ridiculous as ever in his white and gold fairy tale prince's uniform, who had just stepped from Hitler's study. Allowing himself to be taken aside by the visibly shaken Luftwaffe chief, the man's fat jowls shaking as he glanced uneasily around, Himmler was told that Hitler was in one of his now frequent demented rages and threatening to shoot whomever he suspected of the slightest disloyalty.

As if to illustrate the point the steel door to the room swung open to let out a grim faced trio of generals and they could hear the Führer's high pitched voice screaming *Verräters! Verräters!* Traitors, everyone.

'It is over,' Göring said with a quaver in his voice, 'he has gone quite mad now. I would not advise you to go in there.'

'What about Martin, can't he talk to him, try and ---'

'Pah! Bormann?!' The Reichsmarschall made a dismissive motion with a pudgy hand that still clutched the ornate field marshall's baton he was so fond of waving about. 'The only spirit left in Bormann is what comes from the inside of a bottle!'

Instinctively ducking as an artillery shell exploded on the concrete above their heads sending a shower of dust sifting down, Himmler waited for the rolling thunder of the explosion to die before informing the other man of the radio message. But Göring was not listening, having already made up his mind to leave the death trap of Berlin he donned his officer's cap and, with a farewell gesture headed for the exit closely followed by an aide.

Only hours before Göring and Himmler had been discussing the possibility of suggesting Hitler steps down and hand power over to them, enabling them to try for a ceasefire with the Americans and staging a scenario where the remnants of the Wehrmacht could side with the US Army to counter the advancing Russians and save Berlin.

This was now clearly no longer an option.

Casting one last wistful glance at the door from where torrents of abuse still issued, Himmler sighed and set off for his office. It was time to set in motion Plan B, a course of action he had not seriously considered until now but offered him a glimpse of a way out of the nightmare his life had suddenly become.

Unlocking a small strongbox housed in a bottom drawer of his steel desk, also kept locked, with a key taken from a chain worn around his neck, he selected a thick manila envelope from a stack of carefully indexed documents and quickly shoved it inside a brown leather briefcase. Then, without a backward glance to the surroundings which now seemed nothing other than a mausoleum to a failed cause, or a word of farewell to questioning looks from vaguely familiar faces, he headed at a fast pace for the underground parking garage where his car and driver would be waiting.

Fifteen minutes later the unmarked black Mercedes was weaving its way between the rubble that was now the streets of Berlin, keeping close behind the despatch rider who had earlier delivered Feldman's message. At Himmler's orders the exhausted man had been ordered to wait, the thought that as he had managed to navigate a way through the increasingly trapped city, he could lead them out.

It was late afternoon when they crossed one of the few remaining bridges spanning the Spree River and here they parted company, the feldwebel riding off in search of whatever remained of his unit while the big car turned north, heading for the Baltic. Progress was slow, the roads clogged with refugees and long columns of wearily trudging German troops now heading seemingly nowhere.

As he scanned the endless parade of what remained of the Reich's erstwhile juggernaut of military might it struck Himmler that there was not an officer in sight, that some of the brain dead ghosts now stumbling dully along seemed to have lost not only their steel helmets but even their rifles. Had the Reichsführer been a man possessed of even the slightest sense of irony he might have reflected how different this was from the glorious *Triumph des Willens* with its fiercely burning torches and Wagnerian grandeur of only a yesterday away.

He might even have noticed how terribly young the faces were, boys really with a vision of hell already burned into their collective psyche; a generation scarred forever. But such trivia was not for Heinrich Himmler, 'How much longer to Lübeck?' he demanded of the driver who, swerving violently to avoid a horse drawn cart that had just lost a wheel, replied that it would be less than an hour provided they did not have to seek cover from marauding enemy aircraft.

It was dusk when they finally rolled into the streets of the old sector of town and Himmler directed the driver to the Swedish Consulate where, after a short wait, he was ushered into the office of a senior official, the consul having left the building earlier. After a brief discussion – no refreshments were offered – a meeting was set up for the next day with a representative of the World Jewish Congress but an agitated Himmler insisted that the matter was urgent, that he had to speak to a high ranking officer of the American High Command immediately, about a matter that could save the lives of thousands of American citizens, perhaps even millions.

Fast tiring of the whining little man in the ridiculous puppet dictator uniform the aide relented and a short while later the Nazi found himself talking on the telephone to Count Folke Bernadotte, vice-president of the Swedish Red Cross and the country's chief diplomatic go-between. Bernadotte listened attentively, only interrupting in an attempt to obtain more detail regarding the doomsday weapon they were talking about.

Extracting from a reticent Himmler that deployment of the weapon was imminent and that he, Heinrich Himmler, Reichsführer SS and now de facto in command of all German forces, was the only man that could stop this.

And yes, there was a small matter of certain *quid pro quo,* so to speak, starting with immunity against persecution for himself regarding any alleged war crimes concocted by the lying Allies.

Suspecting the man might be crazy, weren't the Nazis all? Bernadotte nevertheless thought it prudent to tell Himmler he would make some calls, get back to him within the hour.

Uneasy about the possibility it might just be a Nazi bluff, a last ditch attempt at escaping the fate the world had in store for them, Bernadotte made a concerted effort to reach the headquarters of General Bradley's 12th Army Group, now less than fifty miles from Berlin and temporarily regrouping south of Magdeburg. Earlier attempts to get through to any senior brass on General Eisenhower's staff at SHAEF had been unsuccessful, the place a beehive of activity with the war entering its final phase and diplomacy of the lowest priority.

An initial instinct was to view the approach from Himmler as just another sign of a war criminal seeing the end coming and desperately trying to save his own skin, an elaborate bluff. But what if...?

Finally, after more than thirty minutes wait, he was put through to a Lieutenant Colonel Watterson who listened to him in silence interrupted by frequent static or crossed phone lines.

'And that's it?' the colonel asked at length, striving to keep the incredulity out of his voice, 'He's got this bomb and he's what, going to dump it on some US city?!'

Bernadotte had to admit that it did sound somewhat far fetched.

'Look,' Watterson said, trying to sound reasonable. He was after all talking to a senior Red Cross man and directives were already going out regarding diplomatic relations to come. 'The Nazis had a fledgling nuclear program which ground to a halt when we destroyed the heavy water project in Norway. Our boys recently liberated their uranium stocks and assembly plant and found, well, nothing suggesting any bomb had ever been put together. In a nutshell, Sir, the man's bluffing. Any chance of stringing him along, keep him hanging around 'till we get there? It shouldn't be more than a few days now. Then we'll take this bad boy off your hands, put him in the prison cell where he belongs?'

But Bernadotte wasn't listening any more, the line now so bad there seemed little point in holding on. With a sigh he replaced the receiver and went back to where Himmler was waiting.

'The message is being passed on to General Eisenhower himself,' Bernadotte said smoothly, 'they will look into it as a matter of urgency and, should such a weapon of mass destruction be found and countered, your own situation will no doubt be favourably influenced.'

A typical diplomat, Himmler thought, rising from his chair and reaching for his gloves and cap, even when the answer is go away they will try and dress it up in such a way you look forward to the journey. Well, New York or Chicago was lost and that might give pleasure to the Führer in his last moments but he, the loyal Heinrich as the man referred to him, needed a little more than mere *schadenfreude.*

Plan C: 'There is one other matter,' he said, pausing at the door. 'Yes?'

'The *Juden*. In the camps.'

'Ah, yes, the Jews,' Bernadotte said, his interest immediately pricked.

'I may be able to facilitate the immediate release of these people...'

'It would appear we have much to discuss,' the diplomat said, a frown creasing his brow. He looked at his watch, 'the hour is late. I will have to contact my people and no doubt you have arrangements to make. Let us arrange an urgent follow up meeting for to-morrow?'

In a small office in another section of the building Olav Magnusson gently cradled the telephone handset and leaned back in his chair, a small smile settling on his normally expressionless features. What he had just overheard was truly stunning news. A middle ranking staffer in the consulate he had immediately recognised the Reichsführer SS when the man in black first entered the building to ask for Count Bernadotte. Realising something momentous was happening Magnusson had guided the visitor to an office that was infrequently used and then only for the most sensitive of meetings.

The office that the consul, cognisant of the times, had earlier instructed to be fitted with facilities to record any conversation taking place. This included the option of listening in discreetly as had just happened.

Lighting a cigarette with a shaking hand as excitement gripped him Magnusson produced a small notebook from an inside pocket and, quickly finding the number, reached for the telephone once again.

Minutes later he was speaking to Jim Molan, a Time Magazine reporter embedded with General Bradley's command. 'Does our deal still stand?' he asked after a brief exchange of greetings.

'Of course. Cash on the nose for anything I don't know already.'

Magnusson's smile broadened to include a soft chuckle. 'How about, how you say, a scoop?'

There was a moment's silence on the line as it took a moment for the American to recall "scoop" was a term he had overheard his English colleagues use.

'You mean an exclusive? Breaking news?'

'You could say that. I hope you are sitting down for, my good friend, have I got something for you!'

41

CHAPTER

'What about Winter?' Jaeger asked as, nearing the centre of town, they slowed down there still being traffic about and people on the sidewalks.

'It is too risky to go back for him, we will have to manage without him but I think this one,' Feldman inclined his head in the direction of the slumped form of Berkowitz in the back seat, 'is programmed OK, now. No need for big brother, no?'

'He's sick,' Jaeger said, casting a glance at the man in the back who had just vomited, the sour smell filling the car and having Feldman open a window. The sudden blast of cold night air had Berkowitz lift his head and Jaeger was shocked to see blood oozing from his nostrils and also around the eyes.

'What is that?!' the Argentinean exclaimed suddenly as Jaeger instinctively stood on the brake and the car screeched to a halt.

Momentarily mute they stared at the scene down the far end of Cerillos, the main street leading west towards the distant railway station, where a police cruiser was parked, lights blazing with several men moving about.

'Roadblock,' Feldman said, motioning Jaeger to turn the car around. 'They're just setting up and have not seen us, I think.'

'It's a fair guess there will be more,' Jaeger said, 'most probably the alarm has gone out from The Hill and they're looking for Berkowitz.'

Paused in the lee of a downtown store, the engine softly idling, they considered their options. 'It was a mistake to mention Lamy Station back in that bar' Jaeger said wistfully, 'the police will find Winter and the others and will head to the station, perhaps already be there.'

'But the train is essential to the plan,' Feldman protested, 'how else do we reach Chicago?' Glancing over his shoulder at a slumped Berkowitz as if searching for inspiration there he motioned Jaeger to put his foot down, saying 'First we must get out of this town, before we are caught in the trap. Drive while I think, head the opposite way.'

But it was Jaeger who came up with the plan. Five years of combat in some of the harshest theatres of war had taught him to think on his feet, to find a way when there was no way. 'We still use the train,' he said softly, his mind racing, 'except we are not on the train. At least not until later.'

'Explain,' Feldman said indicating Jaeger should take a left turn at the next intersection, away from the town plaza.

'The train leaves Albuquerque at six in the morning, I checked earlier, then arrives at Lamy at eight twenty five. They will expect us to board there but what if we load the bomb in the goods wagon at Albuquerque, then take a plane and meet the train somewhere between Lamy and Chicago?'

'I like it,' Feldman nodded after a moment's thought, adding that they would still have to get past the road blocks first.

Driving down Rufina Road now, heading west and nearing the fringes of the town and approaching the airport road junction Jaeger, who had been quiet, suddenly said, 'We're driving Berkowitz's car, right?'

Frowning Feldman nodded, 'Yes, because of that damn woman with the gun!'

'And that would be a car they would be on the lookout for, if it is his known regular vehicle.'

A thoughtful Feldman, starting to glimpse where the German was going, nodded. 'Yes.'

'They don't know we have Berkowitz. So, if we stage a crash, set the car on fire with what appears to be the body of a man inside, it might just fool them. At least long enough for us to escape ---'

'But leave us without a car.'

'Teresa's car should still be at the La Fonda, where we picked up Winter. We could collect that, or steal another.'

Rounding a street corner on the edge of town with a sultry yellow moon etching the outlines of the old Rosario Chapel and casting long shadows in the lee of the gravestones Jaeger's searching gaze spotted the darkened silhouette of a car rolling up to park in the deep shade of an outbuilding and switching off its headlights. It was at least five hundred yards away but just before it was swallowed up by the darkness Jaeger's keen eyesight made out the roof mounted lights rack.

'Road block,' he swore under his breath, 'that's a police car down there, watching the airport road. They're covering all options.'

'The more I think about it, the more I like your plan,' Feldman said calmly as he lit a cigarette with the car's dashboard lighter. 'Let us head for the hotel.'

The streets near empty of traffic now as the town settled down for the night they encountered no other cars on the short trip back to the central plaza where it took only a minute for Jaeger to spot the old Dodge in the hotel's parking lot. The keys were under the driver side sun visor and a quick check confirmed a tank filled with gas.

'I'll bring the car,' Feldman said, coming back to where Jaeger was waiting and anxiously scanning their surroundings. 'We'll drive back to the bridge where we picked him up earlier,' he nodded in the direction of the slumped form on the back seat, 'and stage the accident there. I recall the woman telling Winter there's a can of kerosene in the trunk.'

Then there were away, Feldman in front with Jaeger following far enough back to dispel any notion they might be travelling in convoy. The trip back to Otowi took ten anxious minutes but at that late hour they encountered no other traffic and, to Jaeger's relief, no cruising police cars. Nearing the bridge they doused the headlights and crept forward slowly while on the lookout for another roadblock. Still their luck held with not a sign of life stirring under the soft yellow pool of light cast by the solitary streetlamp on the town's side of the bridge.

Parked in the shadows it took only a matter of minutes to carry Berkowitz over to the other car, the man protesting that he was in pain and nauseous and had there been better light his two companions might have noticed the fast growing blisters and bruises that now covered his whole body. The next step was to transfer the canvas pack with its vital contents, all the while working feverishly, acutely aware that they could be discovered at any moment.

Meanwhile Feldman had discovered a bulky piece of driftwood in the dry riverbed, managing to drag it up to the bridge with some effort. This, propped up with some rocks and whatever else they could find, would have to pass for the torso of a man behind the wheel of the burning car. By now Jaeger had pulled the car up at the far side of the bridge, the side a driver from Los Alamos would be expected to approach and with the help of the other man pushed it down the steep embankment to watch it crash into one of the pillars of the bridge below, the car's nose sinking deep in the mud of the Rio Grande's bank.

While Jaeger kept watch over Berkowitz Feldman poured kerosene over the crashed car's interior and carefully positioned the dummy human shape behind the steering wheel, as a last touch draping Berkowitz's jacket around the propped up shape. Satisfied that his handiwork was good, he stepped back and setting fire to a handkerchief serving as fuse to a glass bottle filled with fuel, tossed it into the car which immediately exploded with a loud whoosh and the crash of shattered glass.

Then, with a last look back, they were off and heading back into town. Lights were coming on in the nearest houses with a solitary pyjama clad old timer out on his porch and scratching his head when they rolled past. It was twenty three minutes past three on Jaeger's watch with no traffic about. 'This is not going to work,' he said, staring out the window. 'We might have temporarily covered the Berkowitz angle but there's still road blocks out there and we're bound to be stopped.'

'What are you thinking?' a grim faced Feldman asked.

'I'm thinking we join them. We become the police.'

42

CHAPTER

lex Winter had been scared many times in his life, mostly on the Eastern Front when men dropped silently next to him as the omnipresent Russian snipers took their toll. Or the heavy panzers rolled over the swinging pontoon bridge fifteen feet above his head as he and his men, chest deep in freezing water, battled to steady the failing links holding the floats together.

But never as scared as he was now. balanced on the lower wing of Miss Rosie. Crouched over and desperately hanging onto a wing strut, he was struggling to keep the flashlight aimed at the central white line markings on the street, all the while acutely aware of the lethally spinning propeller only feet away and unseen in the dark.

At least partially revived by the gallon of coffee a cursing Mama Teresa had poured down his throat Slippery Sam was keeping the plane on course, more or less, as they rumbled along heading for Boyd's Field while hoping to escape any encounter with an unseen object in the street or an overhanging branch. Out on the wing the noise of the engine compounded by the rush of the wind was deafening and if Eva, at back in the passenger seat, was shouting something as he thought she was, Winter could not hear it.

Even as he shivered in the cold the hand that held the torch was sweating, the temptation to highlight their peripheral surroundings almost as overwhelming as the grim foreboding that he was about to take flight in the middle of the night with a crazy drunk at the controls of an ageing biplane with questionable fuel reserves heading for an uncertain destination.

And, in the rear cockpit, his woman. The love of his life.

Stalingrad suddenly seemed almost sane in comparison.

Then they were there and taxiing over the uneven grass grown dirt strip towards the distant end of what served as a runway in the days before Santa Fe had a proper airport. Swinging the plane around Sam waited for Winter to get off the wing and into the rear cockpit with Eva who was now sitting on his lap, the seatbelt almost as tight around her waist as his encircling arms. 'A different time, a different place and this could be a romantic position,' he whispered in her ear.

'Keep it in your pocket 'till later, lover boy,' she laughed and there was the thrill of excitement in her voice.

'Tally ho! Albuquerque here we come!' Sam shouted as he positioned his flying goggles.

'Lamy Station!' Winter shouted back, *'Lamy Station!!'* urging Eva to tap the man on the back, grab his attention.

'What?!'

'Lamy Station! We're going to Lamy Station!'

'OK, OK!' Sam grumbled as he opened the throttle, 'I wish you people would make up your minds.'

With an ear splitting noise from the unmuffled exhaust the plane lurched forward and then they were in the air, the ancient airframe bending and creaking ominously as the wind speed built to a rush of buffeting and thundering noise.

Low over the town and flying by the light of the moon they banked steeply then, tapping the compass with a gloved finger, Slippery Sam set course for what Winter could only hope would be Lamy Station and a chance to avert disaster.

And as they climbed he was aware of the sloshing half jack of Wild Turkey Mama Teresa had secreted in his coat pocket before their departure. Together with the whispered instruction that this was to be administered to Meester Sam (him *bad* man) the moment they landed on the other side. On account of him going off in the absence of a fixer after a bender like the night before.

'Only give half bottle, OK? He *bad* man but he *my* man, OK?'

Closing his eyes against the buffeting wind he could still see her face, the expression a mix of worry and tenderness. 'You bring him back,' she said simply as she watched them roll off into the darkness.

43
CHAPTER

'The police car is parked where the road to Albuquerque leaves town? What if ---'

'He'll be armed and alert,' Jaeger said, we'll have to sneak up on him. Here's how we'll do it.' As the plan – slightly more elaborate than he was laying out to the Argentinean – crystallised in his mind it brought a sardonic smile to his lips. Memories of skirmishes with a formidable enemy fought and sometimes lost but with some experience gleaned along the way.

It had worked when he bluffed his way out of the *kessel* of Kursk and it might just work again.

Minutes later they were in position. Having dropped off Jaeger who was making his way stealthily towards the parked patrol car a short distance away, Feldman waited a full ten minutes as instructed before slowly starting to drive towards the road block.

Deputy Baez saw the car coming when it was still a hundred and fifty yards away. Lights dimmed it was driving slowly, the outline of a solitary figure behind the wheel as he switched on and angled his searchlight. 'Car approaching Route 25 checkpoint,' he reported over his radio, driver only by the look of it, over.'

After a moment's static Sheriff Joe Don Earle replied, his voice testy and the sounds of excited voices in the background. 'We've found the burning wreck of the missing man's car over at the Otowi

Crossing Bridge, looks like he's inside. Stay there and be careful. Get back to me in ten minutes.'

'Roger, boss,' Baez said, feeling himself relax at the thought of things winding down, perhaps catching some shuteye after all. Replacing the handset he turned his focus back on what was most likely an old timer heading to Albuquerque's market. Switching on the police car's flashing roof lights and unhitching the rawhide flap securing his holstered gun he stepped into the road holding up a hand.

As the car rolled to a halt he came up to the driver's side and carefully checked the vehicle's interior before settling on the man's face. Feldman had the window down and was making a show of blinking in the harsh light. 'Is there a problem, Officer?'

He made a show of keeping both hands on the wheel and clearly visible.

'No problem sir, just a routine check. Can I see your driver's licence please?'

'It's in my inside pocket.'

Basic training came back to Baez who, barely suppressing a sigh, asked Feldman to step out of the vehicle then take off his jacket and remove the item with his left hand.

Taking his time all the while keeping his hands in full view Feldman complied. Which was when Jaeger emerged from the shadows and, pressing a gun into Baez's back, said softly, 'This is a Colt .45, keep still and raise your hands.'

Without a word the deputy complied and, relieved of his own weapon, there seemed to be little option other than to strip off his uniform when so ordered next. Moments later, handcuffed and muzzled by his own necktie, he found himself trussed in the trunk of his own car.

While Feldman drove the Dodge towards a distant clump of bushes and set about covering it with broken off branches and shrubbery Jaeger put on the policeman's uniform. The jacket was a tight fit around the shoulders but left ample space around the gut. Struggling into the pants he found them several inches short but decided it would do. Lastly he strapped on the gun belt and, checking that the revolver was loaded, slid it into the holster.

This took longer than anticipated and during that time there was intermittent chatter coming over the police radio including the increasingly urgent request for Baez to call in. With no mention of a search for fugitives other than the body behind the wheel of the burning car Jaeger concentrated on his task while idly wondering why the roadblocks were still in place. Was it to do with the dead border control officer or perhaps the fracås at Teresa's? Shrugging off the thought he was about to toss his own gun on the cruiser's back seat when his attention was drawn by the sight of another car approaching from the direction of the town.

Standing next to the car, which he only realised now still had its revolving flashing roof lights on, he hid the Colt behind his back as the other car slowed down to pull up next to him in a cloud of dust. It was a police cruiser like his and the man who got out from it wore a wide brimmed cowboy hat and had a sheriff's badge that glinted in the light.

'What the hell, Art!' Joe Don snarled, didn't I tell you to get back to me in ten min ---' He halted in mid sentence as he saw the man in the uniform was not his deputy.

'What the hell?!' he exclaimed, his eyes suddenly wary. 'What did you do with Baez?'

'I presume you refer to the deputy,' Jaeger said, 'he's in the trunk. Alive.'

'Godammit!' Joe Don, now visibly angry, shouted. 'Why'd you have to do that?!' It was a rhetorical question requiring no answer.

Jaeger said nothing.

'Raise your hands!' the sheriff ordered as his hand dropped to his gun.

'Don't do it,' Jaeger said, bringing the Colt automatic into view, not pointing it.

'Can't do that,' Joe Don said, 'you know that.'

'I know,' Jaeger said softly as Joe Don drew his gun. A renowned shooter he was fast but never stood a chance. The big gun in Jaeger's hand boomed once and Joe Don froze, just stood there for a second or two, then slowly sank to his knees before reaching out a shaking hand and stretching his body onto the ground. Then, with a barely audible sigh, he rolled onto his back.

He was still alive when Jaeger reached him, kneeling next to the fallen man to gaze at him with a strange look of concern. He was hit in the right side of the abdomen, high up and Jaeger reckoned it for liver.

'Goddammit!' Joe Don said with feeling as his hand came away wet with blood. 'I'm going to die, aren't I?' His face was contorted with pain and, his hat having come off, Jaeger could see the grey roots of the old man's hair under the black, noting in a detached way that he dyed his hair.

'Yes,' he said simply. Staring into the faces of too many dying men he had never seen a liver shot live.

Joe Don nodded, 'Damn,' he said in a voice already growing weaker. 'Just when I was about to move into my new house, by the river.' A sudden thought had him rally, raising himself on his elbows with visible effort, a hand grabbing that of Jaeger. 'Don't you take my guns, you hear? They belonged to my pappy. Ma will put them into the ground.'

'I promise,' Jaeger said softly. Feldman was still not back and squatting there, next to a dying man, Jaeger suddenly felt totally and utterly alone. It was a feeling he had come to know over the years and he dreaded it more than fear itself. Becoming aware that the man on the ground was no longer breathing he leaned forward to gently close the dead man's eyelids.

Terrible to die like this he thought wryly, even more so when the man who puts you in your grave is the only face you see when you take that slow fading last view.

44
CHAPTER

The man in the darkened car sat for a full five minutes, not moving, just sitting there. And staring at the shattered front entrance to Mama Teresa's Lounge and Cocktail Bar.

Something happened here to-night, Special Agent Meads decided, the shattered door now held closed by several nailed planks, the lounge window, or what was left of it, lying amidst a heap of broken glass. The parked car with two flat tyres that might just mean something or maybe not.

Lights were on in the bar but no signs of life. Apart from the disabled car only two other vehicles in the parking lot, an old pickup that had not moved since his first visit and a small delivery van parked under a tree with the name of the establishment stencilled on its side panels.

No sign of the biplane.

With the sheriff rushing off on some undeclared errand and Captain Fiorentino and his men currently standing around staring at a furiously burning car, he wondered if anyone was still looking for his two suspects. The murders temporarily on the back burner, the Nazi angle a cute anecdote to be shared with the grandkids. So he had climbed into his car to do some chasing of his own, the place to start where he had first spotted the suspects.

Slowly driving up to Mama Teresa's he had doused his headlights when still a street block away and had parked far back, beyond the reach of the light spilling out from inside the place. Would they have returned here? Criminals did stupid things. Besides, would they even know they were being hunted?

Nothing for it but to get out and go inside. On reflection he decided not to call out, ring a doorbell if there was even such a thing. No, he'd pry loose a plank or two and go inside stealthy like, gun in hand just to be on the safe side. As anticipated the hasty repair job wasn't up to much that a strong man couldn't handle and seconds later he was inside and slowly scanning the surrounds.

There had been some action, alright, the swept up remains of a deal table and broken chairs witness to that, say nothing of the pock marks left on the wall and woodwork by what he reckoned was a twelve gauge shotgun. No sign of any person about, probably all sleeping by now, somewhere at back, he reckoned.

Perfect. Moving slowly, his soles crunching on broken glass, he crossed the floor heading for the open door leading to the passage and presumably the rooms at back. He got as far as the door then stopped and stood quite still. After a second he pushed back slightly, decided yeah, the object pressing into the back of his spine was probably compatible with a large bore shotgun. Not waiting for the command he dropped his Service .38 Special which hit the floor with a dull thud, then moving slowly raised his hands.

'Go sit at table over there,' Mama Teresa said, 'keep hands on top. No monkey business or I shoot!'

As Meads complied, a wry smile hovering, she recognised him, said as much. 'Why you here?' The gun never waivered.

'Please put that down, I'm a federal agent as you know. I'm looking for the two men I checked up on yesterday. Are they here?'

'They check out. No leave address.'

Meads nodded, 'I see.' Glancing around his smile widened, 'Looks like there's been some action here, is it always like this?'

Teresa shrugged, 'Sometimes, on weekends. Singing 'till eleven, fighting 'till twelve. Then I throw out! Some make too much trouble, need help leaving.'

'Did you call the cops?'

'Police?! Hah! They come too much late, want drink beer for free, do nothing. I take care business self!'

'Uh huh. How about the plane that was parked outside?'

'They leave too, Meester Sam, he ---'

'*They?* You said they, who are the others, the two men?'

Teresa shook her head, 'No other, *Inglisi* not too much good. Sam only. I think he go back to Los Lunas, he live there.'

'You're lying,' Meads said studying her closely.

'*No hoy derecho!*' she exclaimed hotly, raising the shotgun. 'You have no right! You go now!'

'I'm going,' Meads said, pushing back his chair while still keeping his hands up. 'I'll be back. With the sheriff.'

'Take your pistol,' Teresa said, picking up the fallen gun and deftly flipping out the cylinder to eject the bullets onto the floor before tossing it to him. All the while the shotgun never moving away from Mead's midsection.

Her face as impassive as ever she watched him leave, get into his car and drive off. Then, still standing in the doorway, she glanced down at the hand that held the gun which was shaking. Suddenly overcome with long suppressed emotion she blinked back the tears with an angry shake of her head. 'Damn you, Sam Pickens, damn your friends too,' she said softly and went back inside.

45

CHAPTER

By the time Meads arrived back at the bridge, where firemen had finally managed to douse the burning car turning it into a smouldering soot covered wreck, he found Captain Fiorentino in a heated discussion with the duty officer back on The Hill. He was on the radio of his jeep and clearly a very agitated man. Standing next to him, his face a mask of high anxiety, was a plainclothes detective by the name of Jake Bressler Meads knew from a previous meeting.

'Of course I'm bloody positive, Sergeant! It was a tree stump in the car camouflaged to look like a man! Berkowitz is gone and so is his goddamn toy! Hell alone knows where the sheriff is, he raced off somewhere an hour ago and is not answering his radio, neither is his deputy. What do I want you to do?! I want you to find Professor Oppenheimer and get back to me, at the double!'

Spotting Meads from the corner of his eye he motioned him to wait as he returned to the radio set. 'What? The General? NO!! Do not disturb the general now, he's on his way back here anyway. I'll speak to him myself when I know what the hell is going on. Over!' With that he tossed the handset back to the driver and took Meads aside.

'Nothing here. I reckon he was picked up at this spot by a contact and is on his way to God knows where. There's still a chance a road block might pick them up but Jake here,' he indicated the detective who had taken off his jacket and was fanning himself with a hat, 'says that even with the state troopers' help the town does not have enough personnel to man roadblocks at all exit roads. He's worried as hell about Sheriff Earl as well as Baez, the deputy, thinking of going off in search of them.'

'You reckon they've been ambushed?' he asked Bressler who shrugged, 'Sure looks like it,' he said glumly.

'Any leads on those men you went looking for?' Fiorentino asked.

Meads shook his head, 'Nope, they've disappeared. Most likely skipped town earlier. The old landlady isn't too co-operative neither, near as damn got my balls shot off.'

Realising he was thirsty he took a few deep pulls from a water bottle Fiorentino held out before handing it over. Thinking back on his visit to Mama Teresa's his eyes narrowed, 'There was one curious thing though, an old yellow biplane that had been parked in front of the place earlier, was gone. She denied any knowledge of its occupants or when exactly it had left.'

'That'll be ole Sam Pickens,' Bressler said, 'man's as mad as a prairie dog, parks there all the time, no matter how many times we've warned him off.'

They pondered this in silence for a while, then Meads looked at Fiorentino and said, 'Could be they're up there. How about scrambling one or two of those fighter planes I've seen parked out at the airport?'

It was a thought Fiorentino dismissed immediately. 'For that I'd need to alert the local USAF commander who, last I checked, was pretty huffed about not being in the loop of what's happening on The Hill. The area in the desert where we're planning to test the Trinity Device is inside an Air Force bombing range and I was there when the General broke the news, at the same time declining to tell them what exactly it was we'd be testing.' Seeing the renewed look of interest in the eyes of the two men he hastened to add, 'Forget I mentioned any of that. It's top secret.'

Suddenly looking utterly defeated and weary beyond words, he said dejectedly, 'Fighter planes in the sky, perhaps shooting down an innocent biplane, or worse causing a massive explosion?' He shook his head,' I don't think so. I think our bird has flown, Jake here is still planning a house to house search of the town as soon as he locates his fellow officers, but I reckon it's now up to you guys, the FBI, to span that wider net.'

The sound of a car fast approaching had them spot the set of headlights seconds before the sedan pulled up next to the gathering with a screech of brakes and a billowing cloud of dust. It was Miller, the man looking pale and wild eyed in the harsh light of torches pointed at him before the others relaxed and lowered their guns.

'What's the situation?' he asked anxiously, glancing from face to face in search of any news that might make the feeling of impending doom now building in his chest go away. Meads' expression of concern regarding his head injury was brushed away and it was Fiorentino who, worried that the man might faint, persuaded Miller to resume his seat behind the wheel of the car while he stood next to the open door and in a few brief sentences informed him of the state of affairs. The captain realising as he spoke of how desperate their situation was.

'So all routes of escape are being blocked?'

'Well, yes. At least as far as we can with the manpower we have. You see, we ...'

'What about planes flying out, trains?' Miller interrupted as he fumbled for a cigarette with a shaking hand, Fiorentino lighting it for him with a kitchen match.

'We have men covering the local airfield and trains?' He scratched his head and frowned, 'well, there's no local train station, the nearest is at Lamy, twenty miles away. The next train would only be at about eight or so. I suppose we could ---' He glanced uncertainly around as the realisation hit him that they simply did not have anyone available to cover that angle right now.

'Where does the train go to?' Miller asked as a sudden feeling of nausea had him discard the cigarette in a shower of sparks which Fiorentiono stomped out.

'The morning train heads to Chicago, the afternoon one to Albuquerque then Los Angeles.'

'Chicago?'

'Yes. Why?'

Chicago. America's second largest city. Millions of people! It had to be!! 'I'll cover it!' he said, swinging his legs back inside behind the wheel and slamming closed the door before roaring off leaving a worried looking Fiorentino helplessly glancing around and shaking his head.

'No point all of us hanging around here,' Meads said wearily as they watched Miller's fading taillights. 'I'll head back into town, see if I can rustle up some help.'

'What help?!' Fiorentino shouted at Mead's retreating back but the FBI man was already in his car and, with a mesh of gears, he was off too, leaving Fiorentino softly reciting his favourite list of curses between tightly clenched teeth.

Twenty minutes later, back in his hotel and three cups of strong black coffee later, Meads was wide awake. Steeling himself he picked up the phone and recited a number from memory to a sleepy telephonist. The emergency desk at the FBI's New York Station is manned around the clock and it was only minutes later when he was speaking to a lady operator who, after confirming his identity, called over a supervisor.

Keeping it succinct Meads described the situation unfolding on the ground at Santa Fe, the sheer urgency in his voice rendering the other man silent as he listened to the end before speaking. 'Code Black?' he asked, the excitement in his voice clear despite the static on the line.

'Yes, Code Black,' Meads said simply as he lit another Lucky Strike from the still glowing tip of its predecessor while searching vainly for an ashtray. 'I'll hold on,' he said, 'while you get the boss on the line,' knowing that by now all hell would already have broken loose at the Bureau.

'What the hell is going on, Meads?!' Brewster near as shouted when they finally got him on the line. A practical man always he listened in silence as Meads quickly ran through the events once more.

'Jaysuuus!! You mean this, this nutcase, has the fucking bomb or whatever it is they're playing with up there?!!'

'Yessir,' Meads said simply.

'Where the hell's Miller?'

'He rushed off more than an hour ago, Sir, to check the nearest railway station which is some miles away. I suspect it's acting on a hunch where Berkowitz might be heading.' He had already informed Brewster of the earlier incident leading to Miller's head injury.

'What do you need?' Brewster finally asked.

'Fifty men,' Meads said calmly, 'also two spotter planes.'

'Not asking for much, are you?' Brewster growled, 'OK, I'll muster them from California and Texas but it'll take the best part of a day to get them there.'

'Thank you, Sir.'

'And Meads, not a fucking word of this gets out, you hear?!'

'Yessir,' Meads said as the line went dead leaving him wondering how on earth the arrival, in convoy, of fifty business suited clean shaven college boys with bulges under their armpits, some carrying violin cases, was ever going to go unnoticed in the sleepy little town of Santa Fe.

46

C H A P T E R

'What are you thinking?' Feldman asked as he wound down his window to empty the overflowing ashtray into the rushing wind. 'You have said nothing for the last half hour.'

Jaeger, who was driving, maintained his silence for another minute then he said, 'I hated having to shoot the old man, the sheriff.'

Feldman shrugged, lighting another cigarette from the dashboard lighter, 'It bothers you, the killing? It had to be done.'

How many cigarettes does the man smoke Jaeger wondered. He had counted ten in the hour they had been on the road, the car beginning to stink of the foul Mexican brand the man favoured.

'In five years of war I have killed many men. Some dead inside the burning shell of a tank, some face to face in close fighting. Young faces, people I would have shared a beer and a joke with in a different world. But they were all soldiers, like me. We all knew what we were doing even if we did not always know why ---'

'You are wondering what the plan is with this bomb on the back seat, perhaps?'

'I was told the mission was to capture this powerful new weapon and Berlin would then use it as a threat, to get the Americans to join forces with us against the Russkies. Now I'm not so sure.'

'What makes you think that is not still the plan?' Feldman asked casually, blowing a thin stream of smoke Jaeger waved away impatiently.

'Time,' Jaeger said. 'The war will be over in a matter of days. There is no longer time for this, this *threat,* to work. Yet, here we are still going through the motions and killing people, innocent people, in the process.' For the first time the Argentinean noticed a hint of frustration in the other man's voice.

'What do you want to do?'

'I don't know,' Jaeger said with a sigh, 'I have to think. For the moment we carry on but there will be no more killing.'

To this Feldman had no reply.

They were driving the deputy's car with the owner still locked in the trunk, his protesting sobs just audible when they went over a bump in the highway. On the rear seat Berkowitz was asleep, his rattling breathing building and fading in an increasingly worrying way. Resting next to him an innocuous looking canvas backpack inside of which sat a weapon with a potential the world had never seen.

They had driven the sheriff's car into the shallow gully next to their own and covered it as best they could with broken off branches. At a cursory search it would be invisible from the road. The body of Sheriff Earl had been placed in the passenger seat and at Jaeger's insistence his guns had been left by his side.

What to do with the deputy was something that needed some thought. No more killing.

Nearing the outskirts of Albuquerque with the sky coloured a deep red hue and the morning's first rays glinting off the snow capped peaks of the distant Sangrĕ de Cristo Mountains, they stopped at a service station to ask directions to the train station. If the attendant, a young Indian, noticed the patrolman's ill fitting tunic he kept it to himself, directing them in heavily accented and broken English to their destination only a few blocks away.

The train was at the platform with people boarding and it took but a few minutes for Feldman to buy three passenger fares all the way to Chicago while Jaeger waited in the car with Berkowitz. At a signal from the man waving from the station building's entrance Jaeger got out of the car and hefted the heavy backpack. Berkowitz was still asleep and Jaeger banked on any passers by taking the man for a prisoner. Besides, the man was sick as a dog, even a policeman could tell you that.

Glancing down at his ill fitting uniform the thought brought a smile of irony, who said Germans had no sense of humour?

It took only minutes to load the canvas bag into the goods wagon, both men watching and memorising its exact location. The package secured Jaeger realised he was starving and after a moment's hesitation headed for the terminal's diner where he bought several sandwiches and two bottles of orange juice. The aroma of fresh roasted coffee overpowered his senses but he knew there was no time to down the no doubt scalding liquid and reluctantly had to forego it. Feldman, the ever present cigarette in hand, showed no interest in anything to eat, settling for a Coke.

Back in the car, now quickly warming up as the heat of the new day started building, they drove off towards the airport following street signs and the instructions obtained from a waitress.

While purchasing their train tickets Feldman had studied the route guide picking the small New Mexican frontier town of Las Vegas as a good spot to board the train. The first big stop after leaving Lamy it gave them ample time to get there by air before the train arrived.

Albuquerque Municipal Airport was situated three miles away at Bernalillo and there were plenty of charters operating. But first there was the little business of the man in the trunk.

Chewing on a sandwich and swigging from his drink Jaeger drove around the town's central business area until he found what he was looking for, a motel set far back from the street with rooms opening up to the back. several cars and pickups parked outside but at that early hour no sign of life. Driving up to the reception a sharp thump on a desk bell produced a sleepy eyed clerk from a back room.

Yes they had a vacancy and towels would be two dollars extra. Paying the man for one night Feldman opted for an early room service continental breakfast under the silently watchful eye of Jaeger who clearly did not trust him to do the right thing. Also, Jaeger added, they would appreciate Room Service bringing two cold beers up to the room at five that afternoon. At a nod a sulking Feldman paid for that as well.

'I still say a bullet behind the ear would be far simpler,' he growled as they got back to the car.

'There will be no more killing,' Jaeger said firmly.

Room 36 was round the back in a corner. While Feldman unlocked the door Jaeger, checking that no-one was about, hauled a wild eyed Baez from the trunk and quickly hustled him into the room, shutting the door. Explaining to the man that they were not about to hurt him he was allowed to go to the toilet under Jaeger's watchful eye before being offered a sandwich and a drink followed by being handcuffed to the bedstead. A second pair of cuffs – the sheriff's – secured his feet to the lower end leaving him stretched out with no way of removing the gag once again tied around his mouth.

'Room Service will be around by late afternoon. They'll set you free. I ordered two cold beers, should set you right for the long explanations to follow,' Jaeger said with a smile while stripping off the cop's uniform and donning his own clothes.

Leaving the door unlocked they drove off heading for the airport.

47

CHAPTER

Carmalita Charters, looked promising for their needs. A small operator judging by the solitary high wing single prop airplane parked outside the hangar that had "Sightseeing Trips and Fun Flips Available, Cheap rates, painted above the sliding doors in flaking faded red paint.

'Howdy gents, Chuck's the name, Chuck Mooney. What can I do you for?' the man who stepped into the sunlight was tall and thin with a gaunt weather beaten face highlighted by quick grey-green eyes. He was dressed in faded blue denim jeans and tired looking cowboy boots that had not seen polish in a long time, the whole topped off by an army issue brown top and flying jacket from which all insignia had been removed. Jaeger had him for about thirty.

As Mooney stepped forward to offer a handshake Jaeger noticed the limp. War injury was his guess.

'We're tourists, wishing to take a sightseeing trip. Follow the river inland, go as far as Santa Fe at least?'

'No problem,' Mooney said as he lit a Lucky Strike with a battered Zippo lighter. He blew a thin stream of smoke and studied his prospective customers through slitted eyes, the expression calculating. 'What's wrong with the old fella, he sick or something?'

'Our uncle,' Jaeger said, 'he got burned in an accident and is recently discharged from hospital.' He didn't elaborate, calculating the other man's need for a cash infusion would outweigh his curiosity.

'I check a bit of an accent?' Mooney said, 'Where you gents from?'

Feldman, who until then had said nothing, said, 'We're from New York, Brooklyn, home of the Yankees and we're Jewish. Is that a problem?' To Jaeger's credit he absorbed this startling announcement with no outward flicker of amusement.

Neither did Mooney, 'No problem at all. I charge thirty dollars an hour, minimum of one hour.' Adding, with a chuckle, 'cash. In God we trust, all the rest pay cash.'

Minutes later they were in the air, Mooney not bothering to notify the control tower of their destination. Apparently for these short fun flips there was no need to file a flight plan. As Albuquerque fell away below their port wing Jaeger, who was sitting in the rear seat with Berkowitz, leaned back and forced himself to relax. He had difficulty remembering when last he had slept and a sense of weary fatigue was setting in.

Glancing over at Feldman he marvelled at how the man seemed to be impervious to the steady stream of challenges coming their way, how he looked as fresh as twenty four hours earlier, the only giveaway of a rough passage the heavy two day five o' clock stubble that, if anything, made him look even more sinister than usual.

A cold fish, Jaeger decided, a dangerous man whom normally he would not turn his back on. But these were not normal times.

'That'll be the old river down there,' Mooney said, 'the Rio Grande. Glistening over there in the distance the Sangrě de Cristo Mountains.' He had banked slightly to give them a better view and now turned inland, the sound of the engine turning to a steady hum. Jaeger was about to doze off when his eye caught something that had him instantly awake. Mooney was sitting in the left hand seat and was fiddling for an object tucked down between his seat and the cabin door, a hidden object kept out of sight of his passengers.

A map perhaps, some kind of flight control? Somehow he did not think so, there was a degree of stealth about the man's movements. Something sneaky, something he did not want noticed. A clue was the way the man was watching him in a small console mounted rear view mirror although, behind the aviator shades, it was hard to tell.

Pretending to make himself more comfortable Jaeger slanted his torso to the left, at the same time reaching for a pillow to wedge under his head. From this new angle he could see what the pilot had been fiddling with, it was the butt of an automatic pistol inside a leather military style holster and the flap had been loosened.

The move, he decided, would come later, once they had landed. Snuggling into the pillow he said in what he hoped was a dreamy voice, 'I'm taking a nap, wake me when we're at Santa Fe.'

The steady drone of the engine and the gentle swaying of the plane soon had him drift off into an uneasy twilight zone where ghosts from the past seamlessly mixed with those of the present, the spectre that had been hovering at the back of his mind for so long taking shape. It was Elke. *His* Elke, or what had once been his wife. Elke, the mother of his boy. Elke who had coldly informed him barely two weeks ago in the letter nestling in his breast pocket, that she hated him and everything he stood for. That she never wanted to see him again. That Liev, their sixteen year old son, had been taken away with the rest of his schoolfriends to be forcibly mustered into a hastily formed Hitler Jügend volksturm unit and, with two days' basic training, thrust into the defence of Berlin.

That Liev had been killed on the first day facing the Russians.

Is this the dream you always spoke of? The promise of a glorious and triumphant new Germany, the Third Reich where the nation would finally ascend its rightful place as the herrenvolk, the masters of the human race? Those were the lines that hurt the most, he thought as he tossed restlessly, trying hard to escape the clutches of the nightmare and rejoin the only slightly less painful world of the mini cosmos in that cosy cockpit of a small plane.

I hate you... her lingering last words.

He woke with a supressed cry hovering on his lips when Feldman nudged him announcing they were five minutes away from Santa Fe and the pilot wanted to know what they wanted to do. Sitting up Jaeger made a show of studying the landscape over which they were drifting. 'Let's go on a bit further,' he said, rubbing the sleep out of his eyes. 'Let's follow that highway heading inland for a bit further, maybe as far as Las Vegas.' He had to raise his voice to be heard over the roar of the engine and Feldman repeated it for the benefit of the pilot who grunted but said nothing,

Still keeping up the pretence of sightseeing they were flying at low altitude and, not to raise undue suspicion, agreed to a few lazy circling loops over the town to take in the sights as Mooney pointed out the different landmarks.

'You sure you don't want us to land, have a bite, take in a few sights?' he asked hopefully and seemed resigned when his passengers declined.

Climbing again they were soon over Lamy Station and banking to follow the curve of the railway line as it headed towards a distant Dodge City and, ultimately, Chicago.

Rested after his brief nap, the images from minutes earlier forcibly thrust into the deepest recess of his mind where pain no longer registered, Jaeger asked Mooney if he had served as a pilot in the war.

'Yep,' came the terse reply, 'saw action in Italy, that's where I bought it in the leg, a Me 109, never saw it coming.' Adding, after a moment's reflection, 'bastard sneaked up from behind. I was lucky to bail out. Even luckier to be picked up by our boys and not the Nazis. You believe in luck, Mr Jaeger?'

'The more I practise the luckier I get,' Jaeger said with a shrug, 'I have never given it much thought.'

Fifteen minutes later they began the descent for the Las Vegas, New Mexico, Municipal Airport.

Chuck Mooney waited until all three passengers had climbed out of the plane, a now decidedly weak Berkowitz supported by Jaeger, when he produced the automatic, holding it waist high and covering them. Jaeger watched as Mooney pulled back the hammer, 'Now what?' he said.

'You're spies,' came the answer, Mooney motioning them to raise their hands, 'I'm taking you in.'

Exchanging glances no-one moved. 'How do you know?' Jaeger asked, striving to keep the sense of ennui out of his voice.

'Your wedding band, it's on the wrong hand. The way Germans do. The lie about being from Brooklyn, New York. I grew up in Brooklyn, any New Yorker knows the Yankee Ballpark is in the Bronx, not Brooklyn.'

'It seems your choice was an unfortunate one, my dear Feldman,' Jaeger sighed. He still did not raise his hands.

'Give me the gun,' Jaeger said, aware that there was someone moving about in a terminal building close by, others working on a military airplane a few hundred yards away. He stretched out a hand and took a step nearer.

'No! I warn you, I'll shoot!' Mooney said, raising the gun.

'Not without this you won't,' Jaeger held up the loaded magazine he had removed from the pilot's gun somewhere between Lamy and Las Vegas.

'I have a load in the breech!' Mooney shrieked as he took a step back, anxiously glancing around for help.

'Don't worry,' Jaeger said wearily, coming closer, 'we won't hurt you.' This more to Feldman. There would be no more killing.

With a barely audible sob Mooney pulled the trigger. Nothing happened and he stared down at it in disbelief.

'It's a Browning 9mm Parabellum,' Jaeger said with a sigh taking the gun from Mooney's unresisting grip. 'One of John Moses Browning's more curious designs, the only handgun that won't fire unless there's a magazine inserted.'

'Interesting,' Feldman said in a voice devoid of the slightest sign of interest, 'why would that be?'

'Designed for military use, the idea is if an enemy soldier grabs hold of your gun hand and tries to turn the gun on you, you drop the magazine and it doesn't fire.'

'Hmm,' Feldman nodded, as he studied his own weapon, produced from a hidden holster, with interest before shrugging and returning it to its holster.

Listening to the conversation with a mounting sense of incredulity Chuck Mooney was aware of a new sensation: overwhelming fear. He was at the mercy of professional killers.

Turning back to Mooney Jaeger pocketed the Browning and said, 'We're going to walk over to that building then head for the washroom. I will have a gun on you all the way. One word and I shoot.' Turning to Feldman he said, 'Bring along that first aid kit at back there, I'll take care of our guest and the pilot.'

Inside the pre-built hut that served as the small airfield's terminal building the air was hot and stifling. Furnishings consisted of a few tired looking lounge chairs, a kitchen table scattered with dog eared aviation magazines and a discarded copy of yesterday's Albuquerque Journal. A chipped enamel washbasin fitted with a solitary tap occupied a corner with several assorted coffee mugs upturned to the side next to a warm plate on which stood a metal can. The walls were covered with numerous pictures of aircraft, at least some taken from magazines.

There was no sign of a radio and presumably air traffic control was not big in Las Vegas, New Mexico.

The only sound was that of a lone blowfly buzzing against a window pane until there was a squeak of a screen door and an old man stepped inside from where he had been napping in a rocker on the porch.

'That'll be the Doc you be lookin' at, young sir,' he said in a rasping voice that ended in a rattling cough. A scrawny neck inclined in the direction of the wall mounted portrait Jaeger had been studying while Feldman, jostling the pilot along, had gone outside to look for any form of transport into town. Berkowitz was slumped in a chair and staring at them with reddened listless eyes.

'The Doc?' Jaeger asked, taking in the old timer who by all appearances dated back to a quieter less turbulent time, say the Civil War.

'Why Doc Holliday, of course,' chuckled the stranger, 'and that's Big Nose Kate right there next to him. They all came through here back in the day, Sheriff Earp, Jesse James, Handsome Harry Holland and of course the Big One.'

'The Big One,' Jaeger said mechanically, trying to see past the little man to what was happening outside.

'Billy the Kid!' the man, whose name tag pinned to the front of his brown denim overalls announced him as Zacharias Hawks, roared slapping his thighs in glee as if this was the funniest thing. 'Yessiree! They're all history in this here town!' adding, somewhat wistfully as an afterthought, 'Them were the days!'

Jaeger decided to keep his total ignorance of the characters mentioned to himself, instead enquired about the distance to town and more specifically, the railway depot.

'Five miles as the crow flies,' the old man said with a frown.

'And by road?' Jaeger asked, the bit about the flight of crows a mystery to a Teutonic mind.

'Five miles. I tole' you.'

'I see. I take it you are the janitor here?' Jaeger indicated the broom the other was leaning on.

Something about this statement was funny for Hawks burst into another bout of guffaws. 'Nooo! I just come once a week. Rest of the time I do council work, odd jobs, you know?'

Jaeger said he understood, asked about transport into town, pointing out that all he saw was a solitary pickup truck parked up front.

'That'll be mine. There's a telephone over there, ask Alice to connect you with ole' Pete, he done drive people.'

Alice proved to be the switchboard operator and it turned out Pete – Mr Armstrong – was not able to drive on account of having taken a turn and was in hospital. She could ask around but it might take some time? Thanking her Jaeger said there was no need and hung up. 'What about the men I saw working on a plane out there on the tarmac,' he asked. 'Where's their transport?'

'They be military. Air Force. Their jeep would be parked out there with them.'

Jaeger thought it over, decided tangling with the military would not be clever. 'You'll have to take us,' he said, turning to Zachariah Hawks. 'We have to catch the next train to Dodge City.'

Hawks' expression took on a calculating look, 'I dunno,' he said scratching his head, 'I still have some work here and...'

'Will ten dollars do it?' Jaeger asked, peeling a note off a wad taken from a hip pocket.

'I dunno, gasoline be mighty expensive now and ---'

'How about twenty?' Jaeger said, peeling off a second greenback.

'How about twenty five?' Hawks replied as a tongue darted over lips, his eyes fixed on the money.

'How about I snap your neck and take the truck anyway?' Jaeger said pleasantly. Twenty dollars was fine Hawks decided then frowned. 'How is all of us gonna fit into the truck?'

'The pilot isn't coming, he's flying back to Albuquerque. One of us will ride on the back.'

There was a swirl of dust in a ray of sunlight as Feldman came back into the room, pushing a sullen looking Mooney ahead of him. Jaeger explained to him in a few words what was happening as the old man went back to the porch to store away his cleaning gear.

'What about me?' A very scared Mooney asked in a plaintive voice as his eyes darted between the men. 'You're about to have a nice nap in that washroom over there,' Jaeger said, hustling the hapless pilot towards where a handwritten cardboard sign indicated a toilet facility.

Mooney was about to protest when Feldman struck him behind the ear with sickening force from the butt of his gun, the man collapsing in Jaeger's arms. It took only a matter of seconds to drag him into the small washroom and place him slumped forward on the toilet seat. Checking the man's breathing which was fast and laboured, the pulse slow and thready, Jaeger wished Feldman had applied less force but decided his own plan of shooting Mooney full of morphine taken from the first aid kit was probably even more life threatening.

Hopefully there was no internal bleeding and the man would be out cold for an hour, enough time for them to get away. Then again, Mooney, at least technically, was an enemy combatant and it was war. Or was it? Closing the door to the washroom behind him his eyes drifted over to the table where he had minutes before read the headlines. The shocking news in large bold letters. Feldman was there now, reading it and turned quickly away as Jaeger came back.

Avoiding Jaeger's questioning look he led the way outside to where Zacharias Hawks was fiddling with something under the raised hood of the truck. It proved to be a minor hitch with the starter motor and minutes later they were on their way, Feldman and the bag on the tray at back and Jaeger and Berkowitz crammed in the cab next to Hawks.

And as they drove through the flat featureless desert heartland of the old Wild West Jaeger felt a long suppressed weariness settle over his body and his soul. What was it all about? Why were they here? Why was this dying man sitting next to him here and not in a hospital? Inertia, he decided, the unseen force that keeps an object in space on a set path unless acted upon by an outside force, usually gravity. And with grim certainty gravity was coming for all of them.

On the outskirts of Las Vegas Berkowitz vomited bright red blood.

CHAPTER 48

usty Miller walked slowly down the aisle of the rocking train carriage, holding on to the high backed benches of the dining car for balance as he scrutinised the upturned faces of the diners. If they felt intimidated by the looming presence of this tall thin red haired man whose hat sat awkwardly atop a blood stained bandage and whose spindly fingers never seemed to stray far from something tucked on his belt and hidden under his jacket, they minded their own business.

Wisely too, for Agent Miller was in a foul mood. His head ached and there was a lingering blurring to his vision not to mention a hint of nausea.

Two hours earlier, on the outskirts of Santa Fe and with the promise of dawn a thin red sliver on the horizon, he had swerved for a coyote on the road, losing control and ending up in a shallow ditch with a savage jolt as the car buried its nose into a sand bank. The impact had been hard enough for him to bash his head against the side of the door opening up the wound which was once again bleeding freely.

Shaking off a feeling of dizziness he had jammed his hat down hard over the soaked bandage using it to control the blood loss. A quick inspection by the light of a torch had confirmed that the leading front tyre had a puncture and for once he was lucky, finding a spare in the boot.

Sweating profusely and mustering all of his reserves he had managed to jack up the car and change the wheel and as he straightened up from where he had been crouching the world suddenly spun and he collapsed in a dead faint.

It was the freezing cold that brought him around, that and the concerned voice of the stranger bending over him and wanting to know if he was alright. Painfully climbing into a sitting position with his back pressing against the side of the car he squinted at the face pressed close to his finally making out the features of an old man and, behind him, the shape of a battered looking pickup truck. The sun was well up now and in a sudden panic he checked the time to find he had been unconscious for almost two hours.

With the help of the old man he managed to climb to his feet and together they managed to get the car back on the road. After a moment's hesitation he had decided to take up the old timer – his name was Hernandez, a rancher – on his offer of a nip from his hip flask of whiskey. It might have been snake oil for all he knew but the searing liquid settling in his stomach had the desired effect of putting some semblance of energy back in his frame and minutes later he was heading for Lamy and praying to God he was in time to catch a train.

As it turned out he had been just in time to board at the small siding of a station where several passengers had minutes earlier disembarked while others presumably had climbed aboard. So far he had not come across the conductor who would know who had joined recently. As he scanned the faces, a mix of families, soldiers and locals, he realised he did not even know what he was looking for. Did not know who the others with Berkowitz were or looked like.

Did not know whether the train was where they would be.

Did not know for certain what day of the week it was.

But he had a pretty good idea what the item he was so desperately searching for looked like.

Pulling out of Lamy in a cloud of steam the train was already moving and he was lucky to reach the nearest coach before it picked up too much speed for him to make the jump. Running at full pace he was still able to take in the surrounds of the small stop with maybe a half dozen people, mostly soldiers, on the platform with all the signs of having just disembarked and waiting for their transport to arrive. No sign of Berkowitz or the item, the only odd sight a faded yellow biplane a short distance off, the pilot the only occupant and readying for takeoff.

The coach he initially found himself in was a sleeper with most of the sliding doors closed to the passage. Peering inside the few compartments left open he saw only the faces of strangers. Quick thinking had him decide that with the unlikely event the fugitives would have been able to plan well in advance and secure a booked sleeper they were more likely to be found in the open seating coach car.

He would check there first.

Seated three rows from the end and facing to the rear Eva saw him coming. In the window seat next to her Winter had nodded off, his hat covering his eyes. She had wrapped a scarf around her windblown hair and hidden behind sunglasses she was just another face in a crowd of excitedly chattering young people eager to get back to Chicago and the thrill of the big city.

The man slowly traversing the carriage and studying faces with a frown of intensity was clearly a lawman, FBI at a guess. Something about the way they walked, she thought. The John Wayne swagger they worked so hard at cultivating. Then again, the bandage around his head suggested an injury and perhaps he was just striving to keep his balance. There was something familiar about him but she could not quite place it. Could it be that he was from The Hill?

She wasn't sure and put it down to paranoia. Giving them a passing glance Miller was three rows past, heading for the front of the train, when Winter pushed back the brim of his hat and asked whether she knew him.

'No, but he might be from Los Alamos. I'm not sure. Do you think he's after your brother, and the bomb?'

'Maybe,' he said, wearily sitting upright. 'He jumped aboard at the last minute in a fluster and appears to be looking for someone. We've been through the train with no sign of Max and the others and somehow I don't think they're aboard.'

She wanted to ask why then were they still on the train but knew the answer to that one, fatigue. He was simply too tired to go on without at least a brief rest. And where would they even begin to search?

Minutes earlier, realising they were starving, they had bought some sandwiches and two steaming mugs of coffee from a passing steward and feeling slightly refreshed it was time to think of their next step. 'Where do you think your brother is now?' she asked, taking his hand and squeezing it.

'Close,' Winter said. 'He's close and he's dying.'

After a moment she asked how he could be so sure. Then, without waiting for an answer she ran a gentle finger over his thigh, the thick scar readily palpable through the thin material of his trousers. As he winced she took her hand away and clasped his again. 'The pain...' she said softly.

'Yes.'

'Was it always like this, that you could feel each other's pain?'

'Some years ago, at the time of the experiments, Professor Schmidt brought a young Doctor Josef Mengele to our home. This man was interested in identical twins, specifically any sign of telepathy between them. One day when I was distracted he did something to my brother's arm, an injection I think. Max did not cry out but I immediately felt the pain and whirled around, clutching my arm. I will never forget the look in Mengele's eyes when he saw this. It was a look of pure glee, a portal into a hell of depravity.'

'Yes,' he said, leaning over and kissing her tenderly, 'I feel my brother's pain.'

'What are we going to do?'

Alex Winter closed his eyes and when he opened them again there was a faraway look in his eyes. 'There were a lot of books by the great philosophers in our home, Eva. I read most of them, in fact could never understand how my parents, both intelligent educated people, so utterly failed to find enlightenment from these great works. Why they were so enslaved to this Nazi madness.'

Shaking his head at the memories he went on, 'As I searched for a meaning to all this *existence,* I concluded that if there really is a God then perhaps we mere mortals are placed in this world for no reason other than to, on a given day and at a given time, make a difference. Perhaps do or say that one thing vital to the grand order of things... that one vital thing no-one else was destined to do ---'

'Winter's Day,' Eva said softly, 'your moment of being there...'

49

CHAPTER

'What the hell?!' Zacharias Hawks exclaimed as he recoiled, the truck swaying violently and prompting a cursing Jaeger to lean over the heaving man in the middle and steady the steering wheel.

'Look at this mess! My truck!'

Jaeger, who thought the ancient Chevrolet was a mess to start off, said nothing as his mind raced ahead. Clearly Berkowitz was in serious trouble, the man now a deathly pale with sweat pouring down his blistered face and staining his shirt and jacket. The clever play would be to abandon him, dump him in the foyer of the local hospital, then make for the train with Feldman.

But even as he entertained the thought he knew he could never do it. Just like he could not leave behind his wounded men in the mud of the Russian steppe when the battlefield all around was an inferno of burning panzers and terrified men with the T34s prowling and shooting at whatever emerged from the smoke. Even when it had meant ignoring the order to retreat and going back for those men and --- Suddenly the faces of his men, blood and sweat stained from the fighting, were all around him. Eyes white against the soot and grime baked features and looking at him and saying you lead us, *Standartenführer*, show us where the iron crosses grow and we shall follow.

So many did. And died. *His son died!* Yet here he was, still alive, still fighting and suddenly not sure at all as to what for.

There was an urgent knocking at the truck's rear window, Feldman's distorted face mimicking what's going on? Ignoring him Jaeger said, 'Drive to the nearest hospital or doctor. Step on it!'

Mumbling all the way and not looking at the man slumped next to him Hawks pulled up at a large multi-winged brick building that came up a mile later on their right. 'There'll be a doctor in there,' he said, pointing at the sign above the entrance indicating a hospital. 'Just get him outta my truck, Jesuuus!!'

'Here's another tenner, get yourself another truck,' Jaeger said flinging a note on the seat as he half dragged an unresisting Berkowitz from the cabin. He did not ask a clearly outraged Hawks to wait as, having spotted an ambulance parked nearby, he had already come up with a better plan.

Not that the old man was planning to linger anyway, pulling away with an angry wave of a fist and a series of bangs from a smoke belching exhaust.

'What now?' Feldman said as he stared at Berkowitz's blood flecked front with a frown of distaste.

Jaeger glanced at his watch and calculated they had less than twenty minutes to reach the station if they wanted to make the train. Glancing around the building seemed strangely quiet with no-one about. Apart from the ambulance only a handful of parked cars and not a human being in sight. Not the usual scene he would expect at a hospital of that size. A closer study of the sign above the entrance offered an explanation; they were standing on the expansive front lawn of the New Mexico Hospital for the Insane.

How appropriate Jaeger thought, maybe they should all just check in right now. Turning to Feldman he said, 'You are adamant that we still need Berkowitz? He's not going to last much longer.'

'Yes. He still has to prime the gadget.'

Prime the gadget! What did that mean?!

Somehow the mission had changed but there was no time to discuss this now. Grabbing Berkowitz by the arm Jaeger herded him into the back of the ambulance and instructed Feldman to drive them to the railway depot. He would ride in the back with the sick man, see what he could do to revive him.

As was expected the keys were in the ignition and seconds later they were on their way, Feldman following the route Hawks had explained earlier. No-one came running and shouting in their wake and he reckoned its crew were busy somewhere in the bowels of the building. Hopefully it would buy them enough time to get away.

In the back of the swaying vehicle Jaeger had his patient lying on a stretcher and was deftly inserting a needle in a vein and attaching it to a glass bottle containing normal saline. It was something he had done many a time on the battlefield when a medic was not immediately available and it took him less than two minutes.

Berkowitz lay quite still with his eyes closed, his breathing coming in a series of rattling sobs with bubbles of blood flecked sputum around his lips. The grossly swollen hands and fingers were deathly cold and covered in weeping blisters.

Satisfied that his drip was running fast enough Jaeger set about bandaging the face and hands, leaving only the eyes, mouth and nose exposed. Then he took a white smock from a shelf and put this on the man back to front to cover the bloodstains, tying the strings around the back. Finally he donned a medic's white coat and as a final touch draped a stethoscope over his shoulders. A last act was to pack a bulky medical bag with two more bottles of saline and bandages.

If Feldman was surprised to see the transformation in the appearance of his travelling companions he did not show it, simply helped Feldman get Berkowitz seated in a fold up wheelchair found in the back of the ambulance before leading the way to the platform. He had parked the ambulance a short distance away wedged between a large canopied truck and the side of a building where it would hopefully not by readily spotted.

Ten minutes later the train from Albuquerque via Lamy pulled into the station and a helpful guard assisted Doctor Jaeger in getting his patient aboard together with the badly burnt man's very concerned brother. Lucky for them that they had bought tickets in Albuquerque, he declared, for all the sleeper cabins were now occupied, theirs being the last. Yes, he would send the steward around with some refreshments.

Sitting in the saloon car Winter and Eva watched them board, 'Is that your brother in the chair?' she asked, her soda instantly forgotten.

'Yes.'

She wanted to ask if he felt it in his side, checked herself. 'Is the bomb that small it can fit in the doctor's bag?'

'No. It'll be on board though.'

She asked who the other two were and he told her.

'What do we do now?' she asked as the guard blew his whistle and the train started moving.

'We wait for them to make their move,'

'And then?'

'I don't know,' Winter said as his thoughts drifted back to the tall red haired man on board. He was increasingly convinced he was FBI and what else was he after than Berkowitz and the stolen nuclear device? Jaeger and Feldman were on board, as was his heavily disguised brother. Which meant the bomb was on board. He had no way of knowing what their plan was, be it mindless revenge or possibly an extortion bid of sorts. Whatever it was, he had to stop them or thousands of innocent lives could be at risk. He also knew with grim certainty that his two erstwhile fellow agents would not be surrendering meekly, not when faced by him alone.

He would have to find a way to use the FBI man without compromising his own chances of a getaway, without putting Eva in danger.

The sleeper carriages were at the front section of the train and in cabin H7 Feldman was showing signs of visible agitation, a sight Jaeger had not witnessed until then leaving him with the sense of steadily increasing apprehension. Slumped on a bunk in the cramped compartment Berkowitz had just vomited blood again, this time the violent retching went on for longer and the blood was bright red with maroon clots. It left the stricken man heaving for breath and seemingly unable to muster the strength to lift his legs off from the floor.

There was no response when, kneeling next to him, Jaeger asked if he wanted some water. To his relief a rapid thready pulse was still there. 'He's dying!' Feldman exclaimed, a note of panic in his voice as Jaeger restrained him from shaking the man. 'We have to go right now, to the bomb!'

'Why?' Jaeger asked with a sigh, 'we have control of the thing. Why do we need Berkowitz?'

But the Argentinean was not listening to him. Roughly bringing Berkowitz into a sitting position he lifted him bodily to transfer him to the wheelchair with a show of strength that took Jaeger by surprise. 'Let's go,' Feldman snapped sliding open the compartment's door and pushing the wheelchair ahead. Snatching up the doctor's bag with spare infusion bottles Jaeger followed.

50

CHAPTER

Still seated in the lounge car in the mid section of the train Winter was hesitant as to what his next move should be when a he happened to catch a glimpse of a commotion at the front end of the carriage where a wheelchair seemed to have become wedged in a footplate crevice as a large lady insisted on squeezing past. Immediately there was a tinge of pain in his thigh and, acting instinctively, he grabbed a startled Eva by the arm and steered her towards the opposite, rear, exit of the car.

'What?!' she demanded as they reached the temporary sanctuary of the next carriage's passageway.

'They're coming this way,' Winter replied as he jostled her ahead of him. 'The bomb must be in the baggage wagon at the rear end of the train and they're coming for it.'

'Maybe they're just coming to the lounge or dining car? For a meal or something?'

'With a man in a wheelchair who has bloodstains all over his front? I don't think so. They're desperate, Eva, something's about to happen.'

His mind racing as a plan took shape Winter found what he was looking for, an unoccupied toilet and quickly bustled Eva inside, closing the door behind. 'What now?' she whispered as they stood close together in the cramped space, striving to dismiss a frivolous thought of what her dear mother would have said about the sight of little Evie shut in a train toilet with a man.

'There's two of them and they're armed. I'll have to alert the FBI man, it's our only chance.'

Easing herself into a more comfortable position she asked how, without compromising their own situation. Winter's situation.

'We'll hear them come past, the wheelchair has a squeaky wheel, once clear I'll follow and try to stall them. You go off in search of the red haired man, tell him there are men fighting outside the goods wagon at back. He'll come running.'

'But he might recognise me! From The Hill?'

'A chance we have to take, put on a fake accent or something. Hush, I think they're coming!'

They waited in silence as the party went past, Jaeger's voice clearly audible as he remonstrated with Feldman about what Winter could not be clear. Letting out his pent up breath in a long sigh Winter hugged Eva and tenderly kissed her on the lips. 'I love you,' he whispered then pushed open the door and ushered her out ahead of him. 'Go now!' he urged as he followed and if the elderly lady coming down the corridor was outraged at what she had just witnessed she managed to hide it well.

Tilting his hat as he brushed past Winter broke into a fast walk in pursuit of the others while Eva, with an anxious last look over her shoulder, headed off in the opposite direction.

As the trio rounded the corner at the end of the passage leading to the goods wagon their way was suddenly blocked by the guard who had just exited from his cubicle. It took him a second to recognise Jaeger and Feldman as the two men who had loaded the canvas bag in Albuquerque. Which was a second too slow as Feldman slammed a fist into his belly instantly doubling him over, followed by a vicious chop to the side of the neck which had him slump into Jaeger's outstretched arms.

Drag him back into his cubicle!' Feldman urged, digging the guard's pass key from a vest pocket. 'Tie him up while I go ahead and find the bag.'

Leaving a softly cursing Jaeger to find something to tie the dazed man up with, as well as gag him, Feldman reached the door to the goods wagon and, using the guard's master key, had it open in seconds. Wheeling Berkowitz ahead he found himself in a fairly spacious area with the baggage piled on high in the rear section. Deposited recently as opposed to most of the baggage that had been loaded back in California, the object of his feverish search was quickly located and dragged over to the centre of the open space.

Untethered at its rear end the goods wagon was rocking and careering alarmingly at times and he was forced to keep his centre of gravity low while struggling to locate the brake on the wheelchair. Light streamed in from a single elongated window up high on one side and on the opposite side was the large sliding loading door, secured by an iron rod shoved down through an eyelet ring.

After a moment's indecision he lifted an unresisting Berkowitz from the chair depositing him none too gently on the floor next to the canvas bag. The next step was to retrieve the heavy device from the bag and unscrew the base, a task that took him less than a minute.

Which was when Alex Winter stood in the doorway and said, 'Leave him alone, Feldman. My brother is dying.'

Rising to his feet, a fierce scowl darkening his features, Feldman's hand hovered near his holstered gun. 'Don't,' Winter said, pointing his own automatic, 'I won't hesitate to shoot.'

As Winter stepped forward to where his brother lay face down there was a sudden lurch as the rocketing train crossed a set of points and, lunging like a cornered wildcat, Feldman body slammed Winter sending him crashing into the sliding door with a sickening blow. The movement had knocked the other man off balance as well and as both men scrambled to their feet Winter yanked out the sliding door's steel rod and with a wild swing knocked away the gun that had appeared in Feldman's hand, the other man screaming in pain.

Pulling out the rod had however allowed the baggage door to slide open aided by the jarring forward motion of the train.

Without warning Winter found himself teetering on the edge of a gaping chasm as the outside world flashed by in a blur of motion. Desperately flailing out for anything to grab hold of his hands found the outside door handle and then he was swinging in space, the impact of his body against the side of the train all but knocking his breath out.

At that moment Jaeger entered having secured the trussed up guard and it took him a fraction of a second to assess the situation which was when Special Agent Miller came up behind him and shoved something against his spine and told him to put his hands where he could see them. Next to him Eva peered anxiously into the goods wagon and when she saw the wildly swinging form of Winter suspended from the open loading door she screamed and rushed forward pushing an off guard Miller roughly aside.

It was the chance Jaeger was waiting for and, twisting sharply he slammed an elbow into Miller's ribcage while grabbing for the man's gun hand and twisting it with force as the two men crashed into the side of the passageway.

CHAPTER 51

Kneeling next to Berkowitz, one eye on the struggle yards away, a desperate Feldman stared at his watch and after a quick mental calculation instructed the now barely conscious man to set the time switch on the detonator for what would be nine o' clock the next morning, Chicago time. The peak of rush hour. As the dying man struggled with the compact timer, seemingly going by touch more than direct vision, swollen fingers clumsy and fumbling, Feldman glanced anxiously towards the end of the carriage where Jaeger was still locked in a desperate struggle with a cursing Miller, the FBI man trying to bring his revolver to bear and the German knocking it out of his hand by slamming it against the carriage door with vicious force.

The train was crossing a series of points and the sudden violently rocking motion caused both men to lose their balance, the stronger Jaeger managing to twist his body to land on top of a furiously lashing out Miller who landed several blows with seemingly little effect as he was pinned down until an uppercut snapped back his head and for the second time that day Miller was out cold.

Rubbing his bruised hand while getting to his feet with some effort, the hard tumble had hurt his back, Jaeger stumbled over to where Berkowitz, having completed the task, glanced up at a hovering Feldman to indicate the atomic bomb was primed.

'*Der Teufel!!*' Jaeger exclaimed as he took in what had just happened. 'You've activated the thing?! This was not the plan! It is meant to be a bargaining device, for a better deal for Germany! Not to destroy a city!!' Reaching Berkowitz in two steps he grabbed the scientist by the shoulders, shaking him, forcing the near lifeless features to look at him, 'Disarm it! Do it now!'

'No,' A suddenly very calm Feldman said in a voice gone cold causing Jaeger to step back and face the other man with, for the first time in their long journey, a clear sense of understanding.

'I see it now. This was always your plan, wasn't it? To destroy an American city, kill thousands, perhaps millions, of its people ---'

'At the airport,' Feldman said in a conversational tone, 'when I saw you glancing at the newspaper headline announcing the treachery of Himmler and the imminent surrender of the Fatherland, you said nothing but I saw your face. I knew then that you were going to do nothing. Nothing to avenge the rape of a proud civilisation, the utter humiliation of the *herrenvolk*. The beautiful dream of National Socialism we have all sacrificed so much for. Nothing?!!'

He was speaking in German now, his voice having risen to a near scream and as Jaeger stared deep into the eyes of what was a stranger he saw the madness and went for his gun. The two shots reverberated as one, Jaeger's heavy .45 slug striking Feldman square in the centre of his body flinging him back to land in a crumpled heap against a piled high load of luggage that descended atop him, covering him in an instant. He was dead before he was down.

Jaeger was hit in the chest, near the apex of the lung, the smaller calibre bullet from Feldman's 9mm lodging against the scapula at the back with the pain excruciating to the point of bringing him sagging to his knees and fighting to clear his vision.

As his surroundings slowly came back into focus he became aware of a sobbing and a cry for help from somewhere close by and turning his head he saw Eva where she was half lying, half wedged against the side of the open baggage car's sliding door and desperately holding onto Winter's trouser belt as he dangled inches above the rail sleepers flashing by at speed. Legs flailing as he searched for some kind of purchase and not finding any Winter was grimly hanging on to the long handle of the sliding door which was slowly closing as gravity and buffeting wind speed took effect.

'Help me!' Eva, too exhausted to speak, mimicked with pleading eyes searching for those of the wounded Jaeger. 'Please! I can't hold on!'

Clenching his teeth against the pain that threatened to drown his senses and moving with agonising slowness Jaeger crawled over and, grasping hold of the side of the carriage, reached down to grasp Winter by the man's outstretched hand. Then, with superhuman effort and mustering the last vestiges of his fast ebbing strength, he slowly pulled Winter up and finally onto the wooden floor of the baggage car.

Then they were sitting side by side, backs against the wall as a softly sobbing Eva lay crumpled to the floor, her breaths coming in great shudders of sheer relief.

After a while Winter spoke, 'Why did you do it?' he said, 'Why bother to save me when, for a Nazi like you, all is lost?'

Staring over at the still form of Berkowitz and his device and beyond to where a motionless leg of Feldman's was just visible amongst a sea of baggage, Jaeger said in a voice now so faint Winter had to strain to hear. 'My dream for a better Germany was never this nightmare people like Feldman and Berkowitz were prepared to plunge us into. Germany is not dead, Winter. She lives on, her eyes fixed on a new horizon and it will be up to men like you to build that new dream. That is why I saved you.'

Winter did not have to look at the wound now pumping blood in rhythmic gushes of bright red to know that Jaeger was close to death. 'I don't even know your name ---' he said at length.

'Werner,' came the soft reply, ending in a rattling cough that brought blood running down a cheek and onto his shirt and jacket. Turning to face Winter with visible effort, his face a deathly pale, he managed a smile as he whispered, 'Funny, I always thought there would be the sound of bugles ---'

'Is he ---?' Eva asked after a while.

'Yes,' Winter said simply and then he reached inside the dead man's shirtfront to retrieve a small silver locket that had been suspended around his neck on a chain. 'I noticed this when we were back on the submarine, asked him about it.' He snapped open the locket and they stared at the photograph of a beautiful woman with tresses of wheat blonde hair smiling at the camera, the eyes radiant with the joy of life and possibly more.

'And?' she prompted, taking the locket from him to get a better view.

'He wouldn't say. But he did mention an address in Munich, made me promise to try and find her should I be the one to... live...'

And looking at the man she loved Eva knew it would be a debt of honour.

'He would have killed you earlier,' she pointed out, 'if it had come to that.'

Winter managed a grim smile, 'It wouldn't have mattered. We are still brothers in arms.'

Becoming aware of Eva's incredulous stare as he struggled to get to his feet, Winter leaned over and kissed her, gently. 'He who sheds his blood with me shall be my brother,' he said softly, 'Shakespeare, Henry V.'

Reaching the bomb, now out of its canvas bag with the base plate unscrewed to expose the timing device and its slowly revolving mechanism, Winter studied it with a sense of growing horror. Next to him Eva was speechless as the meaning of what they were looking at took hold.

'My God...' she finally managed as Winter touched the slumped form of his brother, gently turning him on his back. The horrible thing that now stared up at him bore no resemblance to a brother he once knew and loved, just a bloated blistered grotesquely swollen humanoid object that stared up at him with opaque eyes that seemed unable to focus as from somewhere beyond swollen lips came a voice of the past.

'Alex... is that you?'

'It is me, Max,' Winter, who realised his brother was now blinded from the radiation, replied softly. Adding, 'Eva is here too.'

'Eva... *Schöne Eva*... She was so beautiful, Alex. You have to forgive me... Always you... always...'

'Max, listen to me. You have to stop this bomb. Here, let me help you up.'

A sighing sound escaped from the dying man's lips and it took Winter a moment to realise what it was. A laugh, a soft mirthless laugh.

'*Erlkönig*. The *Erlkönig* is coming for me... I can ...'

'Ivanhoe! I am here and the *Erlkönig* cannot win!' Winter said urgently, resisting the impulse to shake the man by the shoulders. Changing tack he said, 'Max, listen, there are two wires connected to the timer detonator. A red one and a blue one. I'm an army engineer so I know one wire will deactivate the device but the other might just trigger it. You have to tell me, tell Ivanhoe, so he can save you from the *Erlkönig!*'

Berkowitz was very weak now, any effort to speak interspaced by lingering gasping bouts as fluid filled lungs battled for air. 'The blue wire,' he managed at last, 'cut the blue wire.'

Then as Winter and Eva stared at him he added with a ghastly attempt at a smile, 'Always together, my brother ---'

Eva watched as Winter leant over to gently close the dead man's eyelids. Giving him a moment of privacy to harness his emotions she went over to the canvas bag and came back with a small pouch of tools and, after a second's rummaging, a wire cutter which she held out to him.

Over in the corner Miller was beginning to stir as Winter became aware that the train was slowing. Glancing out the open sliding door he saw a few scattered buildings sliding by and guessed they were at a scheduled stop. Returning to the device he stared down at it, the two wires suddenly vivid and alive and taunting him to do it, grasp the nettle and cut one. Aware of Eva's eyes on him he sat there for what seemed a long time staring at his brother, a lifetime of memories flashing through his brain in a matter of seconds.

A lifetime of weakness and madness and selfish betrayal.

Then, moving too fast for Eva to stop him, he cut the red wire.

Numbed with shock they both sat like statues and it was Eva who finally broke the silence, 'My God!' she whispered in awe as they gazed down at the now motionless disabled timer. *He lied! How did you know?!'* she asked as tears streamed down her cheeks.

'I knew,' Winter said simply. 'I just knew.'

And even in that moment of madness Eva knew those last words were the saddest she had ever heard.

CHAPTER 52

'What do we do now?' Eva asked as she straightened her fallen hair, piling it on high and tucking it under her hat. Stubborn strands hovered at a cheek, softening the little laugh lines at the corner of her eye. Winter thought she looked more beautiful than ever.

'I don't know,' came the weary answer, 'I'll think of something.' He was standing in the open door of the carriage surveying the surrounding scenery as a station platform began appearing. Little more than a bulldozed embankment of earth there was a ramshackle shelter of sorts and two weather beaten wooden poles supporting a signboard that read Raton Pass in peeling black paint. Several buildings were coming into view now, mostly warehouses and, in the distance small adobe homes set against the base of rock strewn foothills.

Of more interest was the sight of a yellow biplane parked a short distance away and the lone figure of Slippery Sam Pickens standing on the platform, arms akimbo, watching the carriages roll by as he squinted against the sunlight reflecting off the windows.

'I don't believe it!' Eva shrieked as Sam spotted them and started waving excitedly, jogging next to the slowing train and waving an object clutched in his hand.

He was shouting something which was lost in the sound of the train's screeching brakes and it took several moments for them to realise it was Eva's handbag. Finally catching up with them as the train came to a stop he bent over, hands on knees as he fought for breath. Finally able to speak he held out the bag announcing in gasps that she had left it behind in Miss Rosie and he thought it might be important.

Jumping down onto the platform Winter resisted the impulse to hug the man, Eva harbouring no such restraint much to the embarrassment of Slippery Sam. Others were appearing on the platform now including a baffled station attendant who seemed unable to locate the train's guard. Leading Sam away from the open goods wagon door where a surfacing Miller might just be able to overhear, Winter brought Sam up to speed regarding the situation in a few terse sentences.

'So this weapon thing is now safe?' Sam asked, inclining his head in the direction of the carriage, 'in there?'

'Yes. With a government agent to take charge. We, Eva and I, need to get out of here fast, how's the fuel situation in your plane? Will we make it back to, say Albuquerque or better still, the Rio Grande, Mexico, the three of us?' As he spoke he was leading an unresisting Sam in the direction of the plane, Eva struggling to keep up as her high heels tripped over the uneven cobble strewn terrain.

'Well ---' Sam began, anxiously glancing over a shoulder to see if the aforementioned government man was not taking an undue interest in him or his machine, 'she's a mite low, I reckon, but she does glide a fair bit...'

Great, Winter mused, just great. 'Sounds OK to me,' he said as they reached the biplane. 'Let's get out of here!'

While Sam readied the plane for takeoff, switching on the ignition before going to the front to spin the propeller, Winter took his seat in the rear cockpit and waited for Eva to join him. Incredulously she had produced a small hand mirror from the retrieved purse and was applying lipstick with a critical self appraising look. And sitting there, fighting a bone weariness threatening to swamp him, the sun baking on his back with all hell breaking loose on a station platform not two hundred yards away, Alex Winter realised that he loved this woman more than life itself. Realised that the old ache in his thigh had given way to a much more urgent one in his groin.

'Contact!' Sam Pickens shouted as the engine sputtered then caught, thick belches of blue exhaust smoke filling the air with an acrid smell. Eva was on his lap now and securing the seat belt and putting his mouth close to her ear he whispered, 'I love you.'

Bringing a hand up to caress his cheek she said, 'I love you too. What do we do now?'

'You will return to Los Alamos with the story of being taken as a hostage by the fugitives at the start of the chase and as a last act forced to help in the escape of a desperado – me. Stick to the story and nothing will happen to you.'

'Los Alamos? I thought you said ---'

Her question was lost as Sam Pickens, now turning the machine and taxiing towards a dirt road which presumably was what he had used as a landing strip, angled his head to ask what exactly they were on the run from.

Nothing much, come to think of it, Winter thought; not if you discounted the shooting of several Mexicans, the theft of several official vehicles, resisting arrest and, of course, the little matter of stealing an atomic bomb...

'Nothing serious,' he shouted back, the increasing wind speed now making conversation difficult. 'I may be suspected of being a spy. But as the war is all but over I reckon a few weeks in Mexico might be a good thing, give some time for things to settle down a bit!'

As he opened the throttle Sam shouted back, 'Love Mexico! Know a little bar down Juarez way, great tequila and the ladies... Oh boy, Mama Teresa's gonna be pissed!!'

And as they lifted off Winter could still hear Slippery Sam shouting 'Yippee!' above the roar of wind and engine.

By the time they reached a thousand feet he was asleep.

By the time they crossed the Mexican border they were gliding.

53

CHAPTER

Ciudad Juárez, Chihuahua, Mexico. July 29 1945

It was a small bar in a less salubrious neighbourhood of the old city where she found him. It was the music that led her down the narrow alleys much like a moth to a flame and increasingly aware of the appraising eyes of the men loitering against the crooked walls of ancient buildings. It was past nine in the evening with the dying sun well below the horizon and only a vanilla sky a lingering memory of a long summer's day's testament of the evil men do. And, sometimes, the good.

She was tired. First the flight from New York, where she had spent a few days with her ageing mother. Then to Albuquerque via the City of Angels in a crammed to the hilt DC3 with a pilot that seemed to know where every air pocket was and how to have fun with it. Next the long dusty bone jarring bus trip to El Paso and, finally her destination. A long day's travelling into night.

Increasingly aware of the aromas of hot food coming from the many small restaurants all around she realised she had not eaten since an early breakfast but the thirst building inside her was for something more than just a tequila laced margarita. Stumbling over the uneven cobblestones she wished she had worn sensible shoes instead of the stilettos with their treacherously thin heels, perhaps dressed in something other than a white cotton dress which now probably bore the evidence of her journey.

Checking in at a small downtown hotel she had taken a shower after discovering the hot water service was not up to a nice luxuriant hot bath, something the hotel manager assured her would be fixed pronto. Carefully applying her makeup she studied her face in the mirror, decided she looked good. Beautiful even, no minor miracle considering the events of the past few weeks.

Declining the offer of a complimentary drink at the hotel's bar she set off on her quest. The evening was promising to be cool and breezy and after a moment's hesitation she decided to walk. People were out on the streets, young ones excitedly chattering and calling out to one another, workers hurrying home after the day's shift and families out for a stroll and perhaps an ice cream for the kids.

What traffic there was consisted mainly of older model cars, battered pickup trucks and exhaust smoke belching municipal buses on tired sagging suspension, often laden with baggage piled high on the roof. There was even the occasional horse drawn cart and what newer model cars were about invariably seemed to belong to rowdy American fun seekers.

Stopping at a small sidewalk kiosk to ask directions from the elderly attendant, she watched him pore over the scrap of paper Sam Pickens had given her earlier and felt a now familiar pang of anxiety. What if he wasn't there, maybe on the run from the police or even the FBI? Dismissing the thought with an angry shake of her head she listened attentively as the old man, in halting broken English, directed her towards a section of the town that he strongly advised her against exploring.

'Iss no good, señorita. *Muchos bad hombrě.*' He shook his head sadly, handing back the piece of paper.

Thanking him while assuring him she would take care, she set out quickening her step, suddenly aware of her own vulnerability in this alien frontier town. And all the while the lingering doubt, did Sam's message reach him? Was he expecting her?

More directions followed from a patrolling *federale*, more cautioning and more resolve to see the thing through. She simply had to see him, tonight.

If the directions had been correct she was close now and any doubts about being inside the red light district was quickly dispelled by scantily clad young women in garishly coloured dresses lounging against the doorways of establishments where music and laughter streamed through the open doors and windows. Striking provocative poses and smoking cigarettes and falling silent as she strode past aware of flashing hostile eyes on her back.

Turning into a narrow alley leading to a set of uneven stairs she became aware of footsteps close behind. Clutching her handbag tighter she was suddenly afraid and uncertain. Ahead were streetlights and the sounds of more music and laughter but here, in the alley there was no-one, just her and the footsteps.

'*Eh, puta!*' Whirling in panic she confronted a thin swarthy stranger whose leering smile exposed uneven yellowed teeth under a drooping moustache while small dark eyes glared at her mockingly. Grabbing her roughly by the arm he spun her round pressing her against the wall while fumbling with her dress, his hot breath burning down her neck and stinking of cheap liquor.

'Please! No!' she cried out, violently jerking free to stumble down the steps in mad flight. Cursing the man made to follow when a hand reached out from nowhere and touched him lightly on the shoulder. Spinning round he found himself staring at a lanky red haired man whose lazy smile betrayed piercing blue eyes totally devoid of any humour.

'*Basta, gringo!*' He muttered reflexively going for the knife strapped to a forearm. Which was when the tall American hit him in the gut with enough force to slam him against the wall, a punch to the side of the jaw sending him slumped in a barely conscious heap, retching and fighting for breath.

'That's the problem with you Mexicans,' the American said softly as he wiped his fist with a handkerchief, 'no class when it comes to the ladies.' Then, without a backwards glance, he proceeded to follow Eva, as before taking care not to be spotted.

Three minutes later, out of breath and still shaking from shock, Eva found herself entering the Casa de Caballero to be greeted by a concerned looking waiter who asked whether she was alright. When, in a hoarse voice, she indicated she was he found her a seat at the bar with the promise of a tequila coming right up.

It was a surprisingly roomy place with a high plastered ceiling where latticed wood fans slowly stirred the air and a long bar at one end and ablaze with the kaleidoscope of colour from dozens of bottles of whatever a man's drink of choice could possibly be. Dozens of small round tables filled the room and most were occupied. Lighting was from flickering oil lanterns on the tables and coach lamps scattered around the walls.

From a kitchen somewhere at back came the intermittent sounds of cutlery and crockery and quite a few of the customers seemed to be enjoying the house dish, a deliciously aromatic paella.

The first tequila settled her jarring nerves and by the time she was nursing its replacement she was ready to turn her back to the bar and study the room, her gaze quickly settling on the small stage in the far corner where a three piece combo was setting up while a man was at the piano, wistfully stroking the keys and doing it well enough for people to fall silent and just listen.

And, as the minutes went by, so did she. She listened in breathless silence as he played As Time Goes By, taking it light and easy and in D-flat major as it's supposed to be played and two couples slowly moving between the cramped tables as they swayed to the music's golden touch. Listening now, aware of that old feeling of an incredible sadness, a great loneliness she had known for so long, somewhere deep inside, she whispered the lyrics as the music filled the room.

You must remember this
A kiss is still a kiss
A sigh is just a sigh
The fundamental things apply

As time goes by...

As the last bars of the song trailed away there was clapping from the diners and shouts for more and with an acknowledging wave of a hand the pianist complied, sipping from a beer and picking up the beat with a fast rag that had feet tapping.

It was later, when working his way through the last bars of Art Tatum's Stormy Weather, the lingering melancholic notes drifting back as the smiling bartender softly whisper sang the words, that he knew she was there.

Not because he had seen her reflection in the ornately carved and painted bar mirror or in the gleaming shine of the trumpet player's instrument, not in a soft footfall and not even from a whispered hello.

He knew it was her because of a new sensation present in the room, the scent of a woman. A very special woman. Smiling now, something he had not done for a while, he moved into Cole Porter's Night and Day and if the three piece combo were taken by surprise they followed suit without missing a beat.

After a while she placed a hand on his shoulder and moved it to run a finger lightly down the side of his jaw, caressing the angle of his lips. 'You're a hard man to find,' she said softly when she could trust herself to speak.

'Sometimes hard men are good to find,' he said, smiling. She could do that to him.

Pushing his chair back, pressing her hand against his cheek then brushing his lips against it and drinking in the heady swirl of her perfume that instantly flooded him with memories, he said, 'You came. I always knew you would.'

Rising he took her in his arms and kissed her gently then held her at arm's length to drink in the face that could forever launch his ship. 'I love you' he said simply and too overcome to speak she nodded, her hand warm in his as he led the way to a back table in the crowded room.

On the small stage the combo had moved into a stylised version of Glen Miller's In the Mood and the Americans in the room, mainly servicemen down for a hot weekend of tequila and passionate ladies, made their appreciation shown by loudly shouting and clapping as the busy waitresses wove their way between the tables.

'So this is where you've hung out since we parted ways those few weeks ago? Wasn't the plan to go all the way down to Mexico City until things died down, it being an easier crowd to lose yourself in, so to speak?' She leaned back as a hovering waitress took her order, the dark eyed beauty apparently well acquainted with what the señor's preferences were, plonking down a beer with what could possibly have been an angry toss of long black hair.

'In the end it hardly seemed worth the effort,' Alex Winter said as he lit her cigarette with the flame from an old Zippo. 'I reckoned the whole affair would prove to be such an embarrassment to our American friends that they would not want me found. As for the Mexicans?' he shrugged, 'they've probably forgotten about the whole business on the beach already. Just another drug deal gone bad. Plenty of it in this town.'

'How is Sam,' he asked, 'and Mama Teresa?'

Eva smiled, 'Both are well and send their best wishes. It appears a vital part of his airplane's engine has mysteriously disappeared. It might take many weeks, months even, to fix. So he's stranded at Mama's place and, to his distinct displeasure, that hard woman – his words – has now placed him on prohibition, no more than half a dozen beers a day apparently.'

Winter shook his head, 'The cruelty of it.'

Suddenly serious he said, 'The war is over, Germany surrendered. Himmler, the architect of our own little foray into madness, is dead. Captured by the British he committed suicide,' adding with a note of bitterness, 'a hero to the end, the sick bastard!'

'So many dead,' Eva said, 'and for what?'

Winter thought of Jaeger and nodded, 'Yet, when a Nazi like Jaeger can, when all is lost, still have a vision of a new Germany. A vision strong enough that he wanted me to live for that, there is hope. In the end, I think, he wanted to give me a reason to go on.'

Lowering his voice he moved closer and asked how she had fared once back at Los Alamos, whether they had bought her story – their story.

'I arrived back at The Hill on the Monday and was immediately taken to see Captain Fiorentino and the FBI guy, Miller. I told him how I was taken hostage by the two men who later died as they made their escape. Then taken at gunpoint by another, someone who bears a striking resemblance to you, as insurance as he made his escape.' She shrugged, 'There are so many holes in the story but they seemed to accept it without too much reservation, almost as if they didn't want to know. A third, portly and older, man was sitting in the next room and they left the door open so he could hear. We were not introduced by I knew who he was nevertheless.'

'General Groves,' Winter said, 'head of the Manhattan Project.'

'Yes. I think he was there to gauge the overall security risk to his project.'

'So they let you back on the project?'

'Surprisingly, yes. I was moved to another section though, ended up working directly under Oppenheimer himself.'

An unseen signal from a grinning Winter had the waitress bring over fresh drinks and a menu which he handed to Eva while recommending the enchilada as a house specialty. They ordered and then he asked her about Berkowitz.

Reaching for his hand across the table and holding it in both hers she said, 'You do miss him, don't you? Your brother?'

'Yes,' he admitted and there was a faraway look in his eyes. 'He wasn't always like that you know, there was a time ---' As words failed him he made a dismissive motion with a hand as if to wave away all bad memories.

'The body was brought back to The Hill and placed in a special casket to quarantine it. An autopsy confirmed that he had died from massive radiation poisoning. The whole thing was hushed up to the point where nobody on The Hill spoke about it.'

'They, the others, must have known.'

'Of course,' she laughed bitterly, 'no secrets on The Hill! But Oppenheimer called us all together and made a short speech about the importance of the project and the crucial test coming up and once again stressed total secrecy.' She hesitated, then added, 'It's almost as if they were passing the whole thing off as an unfortunate industrial accident.'

Producing a packet of cigarettes Winter lit up for both of them as he mentioned that rumours of a new super bomb test in the Jornada del Muerto desert of New Mexico hinted at how it might put an end to the ongoing slaughter in the war against Japan.

'I was there, at Trinity,' she said at length, a note of awe in her voice as she relived the moment. 'Up until the last moment Oppy wasn't sure if it was going to work and then there was this unbelievable mushroom shaped cloud building where a moment earlier there had been just barren desert. Then the wind and the heat, even miles away where we were. I happened to glance over at Oppenheimer where he was standing next to Fermi and the others and his face was glowing, a look of awe and, yes, shock at what he had done.' She shook her head, 'He's a very religious man, something I never appreciated before. I guess that's why he called it Trinity. I distinctly recall hearing him say to an equally awestruck Fermi, *we have brought the sun to earth...*

It was then that the tall red haired American said, 'What a pleasant surprise to run into the two of you here, of all places. Allow me to introduce myself; the name's Miller, FBI Special Agent Rusty Miller.' Pulling out a chair he asked if he could sit down and with a shrug Winter told him to be their guest.

Smiling at Eva and Winter in turn Miiler said, 'Well, it's not really a surprise,' he admitted somewhat ruefully, 'I did tail you all the way here and, might I add, it has been nothing but a pleasure, keeping my eye on such an attractive lady.'

Turning to Winter he said, 'In the end it wasn't all that difficult to put it all together. You were the second man who came over from good old Nazi Germany to steal our atomic device ---'

'Not all Germans are Nazis,' Winter interrupted, a flicker of annoyance in his voice.

Miller shrugged, 'Of course not, some are just spies set on blowing up a major American city and its innocent people.'

Winter exchanged glances with an ashen faced Eva then sighed and said, 'Let my guess, you're here to arrest me?' Not waiting for a reply he raised a hand to wave at the bartender who smiled and waved back and, as Miller glanced over, lifted a cloth resting on the bar counter's polished zinc top just enough so Miller could make out the barrel of a large antique revolver. A big bore barrel that seemed to point in his general direction.

If anyone else had noticed it did not put a damper on the festivities, it was that kind of place. Grimacing Miller held up both hands in mock surrender then leaned forward and lowered his voice. 'As always you appear to have a talent for making friends in the strangest of places. First a certain elderly two bit pilot and now a grinning barbarian masquerading as a barkeep. In a perfect world we'd have been on the same side, maybe even friends.'

'Get to the point, Miller, are you going to arrest me?'

'On the contrary,' Miller said pleasantly, 'I'm here to make sure you go away. And stay away.'

Leaning back he waited for the waitress to place the steaming dishes on the table and, smiling up at her, said yes, he wouldn't mind another beer. American if they had one. He waited for her to dance away between the tables, deftly avoiding the clumsily groping hands of a bunch of middle aged Americans who were now considerably the worse for wear, before returning to his tale.

'I'm here with a message from my director. In the final analysis we feel a suitable conclusion would be that the two dead men found in that train carriage, were the same ones responsible for the Mexican killing and also the murder of Sheriff Earl. Nazi spies, they had help from the dead woman found at the La Fonda Hotel whose identity we are still trying to discover. Berkowitz, we now know, was an imposter who had taken over the identity of a Jewish scientist whom, we suspect, died in a Nazi concentration camp.'

Leaning back to take delivery of his beer Miller studied the label, grimaced, before taking a sip with a sigh of resignation.

'Who killed the woman at the La Fonda?' Winter asked between bites of the enchilada.

'I dunno. Why? Does it matter?'

Fighting to suppress a strange feeling of entering a surreal parallel universe Alex Winter shook his head, 'I suppose not.'

'So what happens now?' Eva asked, her food untouched, the hand bringing the glass to her lips shaking. Something Miller saw in her eyes made him soften his tone. Pushing away the bottle he shrugged and made to rise. 'I suppose that depends entirely on you, Mr Winter. With the war in Europe over you are technically no longer a spy. Nevertheless it would be wise to delay any planned trips to the United States for a while, say ten or so years?'

Reaching for his hat he placed some money on the table, at a glance enough to cover their combined tab. 'In a nutshell,' he said running a finger across his lips and fixing Miller with a suddenly intense look, 'keep 'em zipped.' Tipping his hat at Eva in a curiously old fashioned gesture he bid them farewell and was gone.

They sat in silence for a long time. The combo came back on stage, this time with a classic Spanish guitarist, the music taking on a Latin American flavour with more couples now moving to the languid rhythm. Another round of tequilas came and went and Eva asked what happens next.

The truth was his thoughts had increasingly turned to a warm bed and steamy lovemaking with his woman but then she knew that already, didn't she? Instead he reached in a pocket and produced a small silver locket on a chain. He held it up as they stared at it and Eva said in a whisper, 'The debt of honour. The lady whose name he never mentioned...'

'I think a trip to Munich is needed,' he said softly as he sat back, studying the soft lines of her face, the deep auburn halo of her hair framed in the glow of a lamp turned low. 'But first I have other, more urgent business that cannot wait.'

'Oh?' she said as he brought her gently to her feet then kissed her to cheers and jeers from the Americans' table.

'I have a room upstairs,' he whispered in her ear as he led her away, 'Follow me and I'll show you the way.'

A U T H O R ' S   N O T E

Shortly after the end of WW2, in the early days of the Cold War, the Los Alamos Scientific Laboratory designed a compact implosion tactical nuclear weapon designated the W54. Intended for deployment on the battlefield against enemy troops and armour, the Davy Crockett yielded between 10 to 20 tons TNT with later models 250 tons and up to 1 kiloton TNT for the Special Atomic Demolition Munition Device.

More than 2,000 were made for issue to mainly the US 82nd Airborne Division stationed in West Germany until the project's deactivation in 1967.

The core mechanism was 15.7 inches long and 10.75 inches wide. Weighing only 51 pounds it could fit into a backpack.

Or, a standard cafeteria coffee urn...